The
Indian's Daughter

A Thriller

Patti Dickinson

Bitterroot Mountain
PUBLISHING
P.O. Box 3508 Hayden, ID 83835

Bitterroot Mountain Publishing
P.O. Box 3508
Hayden, Idaho 83835

Visit our Website www.Bitterrootmountainllc.com

Printed in the United States of America

First Edition

10 9 8 7 6 5 4 3 2 1

ISBN: 978-0-9817874-7-3

Also by Patti Dickinson

Hollywood the Hard Way,
A Cowboy's Journey

Coach Tommy Thompson and
The Boys of Sequoyah

To my husband David

for his love, his integrity and unwavering faith

The Indian's Daughter

Political power swirls about in the air of Washington, D.C.,
fluid and shifting, altering lives and defining destinies.
There are some who view power as a means to do good
while others lose their moral compass blindly chasing after it.
Like a violent storm, political power's force is indiscriminate
in the people whose lives it saves
and the people it destroys.

Acknowledgements

Perhaps my life-long interest in the history, culture, and traditions of American Indians stems from stories I grew up hearing about my half-Cherokee grandfather. Whatever the reason, my interest has never waned. Fortunately over the years, my life has been enriched by getting to know wonderful men and women from various tribes, all of them I'm proud to call friends. My time spent listening to their stories and hearing their philosophies, have helped me appreciate my heritage and better understand what it means to be Indian. Precious lessons, my gratitude to all.

Sincere thanks to Sam Grubbs, former SWAT team commander and retired Captain with the Kootenai County Sheriff's Office in Coeur d'Alene Idaho. Sam's knowledge, experience, and expertise with weapons and raid procedures brought to life the peril and challenges law enforcement personnel face with every call. Sam is a guy I would always want on my team.

Many thanks also to Attorney Traci J. Whelan for her time and patience in answering my plethora of questions on legal issues and for enlightening me on the scope and duties of an Assistant U.S. Attorney.

A note of gratitude goes to Elizabeth Lyon, author, speaker, and mentor, for her sage advice and friendship.

Many thanks also to my editor Tracey Winikoff for her keen eye, her encouragement, and spot-on guidance and suggestions.

Lastly, enduring thanks to my wonderful husband, David, for keeping me sane with his humor and his steadfast support. You're the best!

—1—

K C Garrett exited her private office and crossed the dimly lit reception room, her Nikes silent on the worn Persian carpet. She looked forward to a good workout; it had been a long day but a good one for a change. KC reached for the doorknob but paused at hearing angry voices in the hallway. Half- past-seven on a Wednesday night, the halls of the Department of Justice were ordinarily quiet as a tomb.

Two men were obviously waiting for the elevator outside her fourth floor suite. "How in the hell could you let some pissant clerk get hold of those papers in the first place? Had your head up your ass, that's how." The man sounded like a southerner, and very angry.

"I already told you it was an accident. Besides, I took care of it." Clearly defensive, the second man spoke with a Boston accent. "The clerk is gone. I transferred her to a reservation in North Dakota. She's so far from civilization, she'd have to use smoke signals to communicate."

"I don't know what good that'll do with that damn Indian snoopin' around. Mark my words, Valerie pickin' Blackhawk to be Secretary of the Bureau of Indian Affairs is gonna blow up in our faces, you hear what I'm sayin'? Aubert should have kept her from doin' it."

Blackhawk? They're talking about Dad!

"Valerie doesn't know anything about the IIM funds. She picked Blackhawk because she believes he'll do a good job," Mr. Boston-accent said. *Who are these guys?* KC strained to hear. "Sweet Jesus, those Individual Indian Money accounts are our bread and butter. We can't afford that Indian figuring everything out," Mr. Southerner said. The muted whine of pulleys across the expansive hallway signaled the approach of an elevator. KC set her duffle bag on the floor and pulled open the door just enough to offer a glimpse.

Their backs to her, one man looked to be about six feet tall, the other shorter and beefier, both dressed in dark suits. KC's sliver of a view afforded no other details.

"Why don't we offer the Indian a piece of the action," Boston accent said. "It worked with…." The swoosh of elevator doors cut off his words as they entered. They turned and faced each other, but she couldn't open the door any wider for fear they would notice. "Yeah we could, but if it doesn't work, the jig is up, y'hear what I'm sayin'?" His words were clear. "Then we'd have no choice but to get rid of h–" The doors slid shut.

KC yanked the heavy door open and ran toward the stairs, her long, dark hair swinging wildly with each stride. Fragments of the conversation replayed in her head as she flew down the circular staircase three steps at a time. Reaching the lobby, she sprinted to the bank of elevators and pushed the *up* and *down* buttons. Off to her left, the guard's station stood empty; the Federal Protective Service agent was nowhere in sight.

KC waited in front of the far right set of doors. A bell sounded and she straightened in anticipation, her hands balled into fists. The far right doors remained closed and to her left the middle elevator doors slid open, revealing an empty silent car.

"Nooo!" her cry echoed in the cavernous space. The middle car had answered her call. The elevator carrying the men had descended uninterrupt-ed to the basement; she would never find them now. The Department of Justice had a mammoth underground, a city in itself with parking, a cafeteria, a gym, printing offices, and a labyrinth of cubicles. The realization they had gotten away registered like a body blow, but she stood motionless, stunned that there was nothing she could do.

The far right doors opened; the security guard exited. "Miss Garrett?"

"Oh good! Did you see two men in dark suits get off in the basement?"

Linebacker size, the former D.C. cop shook his head. "Didn't see any-body." He tapped his watch, and KC braced for his lecture which she knew by heart. "You're too young to be down here every evening. Your department will do just as well if you leave at five like everybody else. Would you like me to walk you to the Metro?"

"Thanks, but I left my briefcase in my office." KC replied, glancing at the stairs she had raced down. For all of her seven years as Special Prosecutor in the Environmental Crime Division, the five-story grand staircase had stood as the architectural embodiment of the might and power of the Justice Department. Now spiraling upward into shadowy darkness, it appeared more ominous than mighty.

Mystified at the sheer coincidence, had she left a minute sooner she would have exchanged superficial greetings with the men and right now would be at the karate studio working out, happy and unaware. Instead, either by fate or chance she found out her father had uncovered something dangerous, so dangerous it could get him killed.

* * *

The black Camaro crept through the Capitol's traffic, Sam Blackhawk's cell phone interrupting his profane thoughts on D.C. gridlock. He answered, "Blackhawk," and braked as the tail lights on the car in front of him lit up.

"Quick, where are you?" It was his daughter.

"On Eighteenth Street on my way home. You sound out of breath."

"Can you swing by the studio? It's important."

"What's up? Can't find anybody tough enough to spar with?" Sam chuckled, anticipating a flippant retort. None came. "I'm on my way."

Direct and forceful, no wonder she wins so many cases, he thought. Curious at what could be wrong, he concluded that whatever it was, she would want it resolved immediately. She was known professionally as KC Garrett, but he preferred her given name, Kaya, *beautiful bird* in the language of his tribe, and Calder in honor of her godmother, Sally Calder. His daughter had inherited his black hair and olive skin but little of his patience. How many times he had watched her in court, her eyes sparking fire at a hostile witness or arrogant opposing counsel. Her passionate respect for the law and no-nonsense courtroom style had earned her the mantle of an attorney not to be messed with.

He turned onto Maryland Avenue and pulled up in front of the studio. Karate's discipline and philosophy had helped forge a strong bond with his daughter. And as he hoped it would, it had also aided in redirecting Kaya's sorrow over her brother abandoning D.C. to live on the Lake Ponsiteau reservation. The thought of Takoda and his grandsons made him yearn for home. Despite living in the nation's capital for over forty years, the word *home* to Sam Blackhawk evoked images of forested mountains, blue skies, and the pristine lakes of the Idaho Panhandle.

* * *

KC positioned herself at a training bag in a mirrored alcove across from the studio entrance, the familiar odor of polished hardwood, sweat, and perfume somehow comforting. The men's threat had turned her shoulder muscles to stone and obliterated any satisfaction at finally being able to nail Scott Dunlap. Eighteen months of negligible advances and significant setbacks, painstakingly chronicled in the *Washington Post,* was about to end. She finally had the incontrovertible evidence she needed, a dozen photos, that proved Dunlap Plastics knowingly dumped toxic waste into Pine Creek Reservoir. Mega-wealthy Scott Dunlap, self-proclaimed pillar of the community, was about to get charged with perjury for lying to the grand jury. His squadron of attorneys would no doubt appeal the millions in damages she intended to seek, but the photos would reveal the truth about Dunlap and his company, her ultimate goal.

Steady breathing brought a measure of calm, as did the sight of Danny, her secretary's seventeen-year-old son instructing a class of teenagers. KC put on her gloves and began with short jabs to the four-foot bag hung by a chain from the ceiling. She added kicks, alternating fists and feet harder until she had a rhythm going, punishing the bag for letting the men get away. Did they meet in one of the high-powered attorney's office, on her floor? If so, some big shot in the Department of Justice knew that her father had found them out. Ten minutes of exertion and KC had an argument ready to convince her father to leave town. By the time she saw him enter the studio, she was jogging in place to cool down.

Sam paused to talk to Danny and his students, laughing and joking with kids he had taught at some point in their life. The concept that he could pose a threat to anyone seemed incomprehensible. She tried to view him objectively but decided he was exactly what he appeared, a dynamic Lake Ponsiteau Indian. Silver hair threaded his ponytail, but there was little else to reveal his sixty years. Funny, she thought as she watched him. *You and Takoda are Indian clear down to your soul, yet I don't feel any of that.* Regret seized her as it always did when she thought of her brother and her Indian family three-thousand miles away.

Sam said goodbye to the teenagers and walked toward her, a smile lighting his face when their eyes met. Why would anyone want to harm him? Didn't they know what kind of man he was, a decorated Vietnam veteran, a man whose only agenda was to help his people, who revered truth and straight talk and held strong to his beliefs? *Of course they know. That's why he's a threat.* Alone in the alcove, she motioned for him to step around the punching bag.

"Kaya, is something wrong?"

"I would say keeping an investigation into missing IIM funds from your attorney daughter qualifies."

"How could you possibly know about that?"

She leaned closer. "Not thirty minutes ago I overheard two men outside my office say they are going to offer you a bribe to back off your investigation." KC had to force herself to tell him the rest. "And one of them said if you don't take it they would have you killed."

"Are you sure they were talking about me?" He looked more puzzled than alarmed.

"Yes, they called you by name, and one of them said that Valerie has picked you to be the new Secretary of BIA. Dad, I'm scared for you. Shall I follow you home so we can talk?"

He frowned. "No, this kind of nonsense upsets your mother."

"What do you mean *this kind of nonsense*?" Her words came out louder than she intended. "You make it sound like threats are an everyday occurrence."

"You know this city, Kaya. The higher you go, the more enemies you make. I have made my share." He sounded tired, his stick-straight military bearing dissolving before her eyes.

Her panic returned at his reaction. "Dad, you've got to tell me what's going on."

He glanced at his watch. "I will, but not here and not tonight. Walk with me, okay?"

KC followed him outside, the damp November air making her sweat-soaked lycra shorts and top feel ice cold. Across Maryland Avenue, the street lights glistened off frost-dusted cars. Sam climbed into his Camaro. KC scanned the street and then crouched down beside the door. "Do you have any idea who the men could be? Or the name Aubert, it sounds familiar."

"Jules Aubert, Valerie Beckman's campaign manager in charge of her run for the presidency. I have no idea who the men could be." Sam slammed his palm against the steering wheel. "Three years of covert CIA work in Nam without blowing my cover, I must be getting old." He looked at her. "I'm too close to quit my investigation."

"I'm not asking you to quit, but you can conduct it incognito from out of town. Staying here is dangerous. Let's find you a safe location, and I'll help you from here." The grim set of his mouth and his white-knuckle grip on the steering wheel told her he had no intention of leaving. She decided to change tactics. "Okay, could we talk about this over breakfast, Joe's Café on Lincoln, tomorrow morning?"

His expression softened. "I can do that." He opened his daytimer on the seat beside him. "Is six-thirty okay? I'm hosting a conference this Friday. You remember my friend Charlie Dawson? He's arriving tomorrow. I can leave after our breakfast to pick him at the airport."

"Six-thirty, I'll be there. Speaking of flying, have you heard the weather forecast? There's a huge storm due Friday or Saturday. I hope it won't affect your conference." The cold had penetrated now. KC rose and rubbed her arms. "See you in the morning. Be careful, okay?"

"Like the coyote." He tapped his cheek with his forefinger. "One for the old warrior." KC kissed his cheek, which brought a smile. "My notes on the investigation are in the safe. I'll stop by my office first and bring a copy to breakfast."

KC let herself into her apartment just as the mantle clock chimed nine o'clock. Ivan, her Russian Blue cat, rose from the couch when she turned on the lights. He jumped down, followed her into the kitchen, and went to his feeding spot beside the fridge. Ivan looked up at her expectantly. "Hello, you comfort-loving creature." She bent down and pet him, then served up his favorite meal, tuna mixed with kibble. In the six years since her father had shown up with the abandoned tiny kitten he found, Ivan had grown to a magnificent seventeen pounds. "Dad's in trouble, Ivan. I'm afraid for him." His ears flicked back and forth, a signal that he was listening. He finished his food and began his bath ritual, first cleaning his face, a sight that always made her smile. "Do you have any idea how good you have it? You get fed on demand, sleep when and wherever you want, and don't have a worry in the world."

She dished up the hot broccoli beef she picked up from Peking Palace on the way home. The smell of ginger and garlic made her mouth water, and she managed to eat half of the food before fear put an end to her appetite. Her father had to leave town, and she needed to come up with an argument to get him to do it. But how? She paced in a circle around her living room, with each turn her fear ratcheting higher. The man's threat still echoed. KC shivered at how matter of fact he'd said it, with no trace of anger or fear. With no trace of feeling at all.

* * *

From his dark Buick, Elliott Wolf watched Garrett climb the outside staircase of her apartment. Juggling a briefcase, a duffel bag, and a brown paper sack, she shifted them around until she managed to unlock the door. He got a good glimpse of her before she shut the door with her foot. "Nice body," he said.

I'd better let Aubert know, Wolf thought, feeling the need to justify deviating from his orders to tail Sam Blackhawk. Donning his reading glasses, he retrieved his cell phone. Aubert answered after four rings. "Just wanted you to know the subject didn't go straight home. He stopped by a karate studio for about ten minutes and came out with the same woman he had lunch with last week. Good looking, maybe thirty."

"I wonder what that's all about." Aubert sounded pleased. "Where are you?"

"Outside her apartment. It's above the garage of one of those old Georgetown estates. Funny, she took her time climbing the stairs and didn't seem afraid which makes me wonder if she teaches karate rather than takes lessons." Wolf watched as lights went on in her apartment.

"Find out everything you can about her and get me some pictures," Aubert said.

"Hold it a damned minute. I'm not some two-bit detective you can order around. Forty years with the Bureau isn't just a day job. I suggest you hire somebody."

"C'mon, Wolf, Valerie considers you family and the stakes are as big as they get—her shot at the presidency. Find out what you can about the woman, and I'll make it right by you." Wolf heard a telephone ring in the background. "Call me, okay?" The phone went dead.

Wolf lit a cigarette. "What a jerk. You say it's for Mrs. B and think you can get me to do any damn thing you want." He had to admit Jules Aubert did have powerful friends, and he didn't hesitate to use them. He'd had enough clout with FBI Director Alonzo Volking to obtain special assignment duty for Wolf to provide security for Secretary of Interior Valerie Beckman, "Mrs. B" to Wolf. Aubert was also right about her treating him like family, a fact that he did not take for granted.

Wolf got out of his car, wincing as pain shot through his knees. "Weatherman's right about the storm." A dedicated runner since joining the Bureau decades ago, his knees had proved as accurate as any meteorologist's prediction. He walked around the two-story brick structure, taking note of the electrical and phone boxes. A deck had been added in back on the second floor, French doors probably exiting from a bedroom.

He started back toward the front of the house but halted when he spotted headlights on the street. A security patrol car crept forward, a spotlight on the driver's side sweeping the grounds in front of Garrett's apartment. Pressing his body into the thick ivy, Wolf waited until the spotlight moved on, dancing over the cars parked at the curb. Assuming the patrolman had a list of residents' cars, he wasn't surprised to see the patrol car stop beside his Buick. The patrolman got out and shined a flashlight through the window.

Reacting automatically, Wolf kept in the shadows as he walked to the front of the building. Near the bottom of the stairs, he turned and strode to the curb and walked briskly to his car. "Good evening, officer." A flashlight beam traveled up to his face. "I have ID, sir."

"Let's have a look then," the officer said and lowered the light. "I didn't see what house you came from."

Wolf gestured at the garage apartment. "The one with the outside stairs." He held out his wallet, his driver's license in plain view.

The guard scanned the license with his flashlight "Thank you, Mr. Wolf. Visiting Miss Garrett were ya?" He sounded Irish.

"Yes, but she just got home from karate. She was tired, so I didn't stay long."

The officer's stance relaxed. "Oh to be sure. Hard to believe that wisp of a girl has a black belt in karate." He nodded toward the dark mansion across a courtyard from the apartment. "The caretaker and his wife tell me she's won many an award."

"Living and working in this city, that's an excellent thing for a young woman to know," Wolf said. "Thank you for watching out for her. I appreciate it."

"You're quite welcome, Mr. Wolf. Good evening to ya."

Wolf climbed into his car and lit a cigarette, waiting as the security car moved on. He exited the neighborhood and pulled into a Zip n' Go parking lot two blocks away. Retrieving his notebook, he recorded the name Garrett, her address, the license number of her Honda, and the date and time of her meeting with the subject.

Wolf headed for home, curious what the connection could be between Blackhawk and Garrett. His route took him through a mixed neighborhood of old Victorian houses built next to stucco apartments, their dissimilar windows providing glimpses of families sitting around a dinner table or watching television. He couldn't count the number of times he'd driven this same route over the years, the vignettes a reminder that Elliott Wolf had no life outside the FBI. He'd never been in love, not even remotely close. Dutifully following his father into the Bureau, it seemed the years had just slipped away. His father didn't have as many years with the Bureau before he died in the line of duty, but he at least had left behind a wife and family.

I'm grateful to have Mrs. B and Phoebe in my life. A fortunate assignment to provide security for her ten years ago led to their meeting; he drove the newly appointed congresswoman home one evening from a political function. Sneaking a glance at her in the rear view mirror, she didn't fit the stereotype of an aloof politician. Valerie Beckman looked like a grieving widow trying like hell to be strong. He soon learned that her husband, Congressman Randy Beckman, and their son had died in an automobile accident. And though she didn't seek a political career, a senator from her state of Georgia convinced her to accept the appointment to fill her husband's congressional seat. Now, a decade later, she was Secretary of Interior and very possibly the next President of the United States.

Still, Mrs. B called him Elliot and invited him to family dinners and remembered his birthday with a call and a gift. Witnessing her struggle with her grief and then take on the responsibility of adopting little Phoebe, he came to realize the two of them were as close to family as he would ever get. Wolf glanced at his watch. *Too late to call and see how they are.* Just thinking about them brought a surge of loyalty and a fierce protective feeling. "Maybe that's all there is to love."

The word *love* prompted the question where Jules Aubert fit into Mrs. B's life. Admittedly, he had upgraded her career from coach to first class, but did he love her, or was his goal to ride her coattails into the White House?

Aubert seemed friendly enough at the family party last month to celebrate Phoebe's tenth birthday, but coincidentally, the next morning, he called saying he had a favor to ask. Aubert's favor sounded more like a command.

"Elliott, I want you to tail a man named Sam Blackhawk." He gave Blackhawk's home address and where he worked. Pressed for a reason, Aubert gave a politician's answer—wordy and ambiguous with no real substance. Wolf remembered him throwing in the word *security* and mentioning Mrs. B's campaign.

I don't believe security has anything to do with it. That doubt produced an unsettled feeling, but nothing Wolf could easily identify. It did, however, make him think. *If I don't deal with him right away, I wonder just how far Aubert will try to drag me into his plans—whatever they are.*

–2–

Thursday morning, the bright lights of Joe's Café lit up the pre-dawn mist. KC spotted her father through the fogged-up glass, coffee mug in his hand and a newspaper spread on the table in front of him. Sharing morning coffee and *The Post* had been their ritual through her three years of law school at George Washington University, a good memory. She pushed open the door and was greeted by the delicious aroma of fresh coffee, cinnamon, and yeast.

Sam smiled as she slid into the booth across from him. "It smells good in here." Groggy, with a lingering headache, she couldn't help but notice that her father looked as though he hadn't slept well either. Her fear sat like a rock in the pit of her stomach.

The waitress approached with coffee pot in hand. "What can I get you folks?"

"Coffee and a cinnamon roll for me," KC said. Her father nodded. The waitress filled their cups. "They'll be right up," she said and walked toward the kitchen.

Sam stirred cream into his coffee. "You look like I feel, only prettier." He stared at KC with a half-hearted grin. "Promise you won't repeat a word of what I tell you to your mother."

"Dad, I can't do. . ." KC stopped mid-protest, struck by his grave expression. *Lighten up,* she thought. "I don't see any notes. I could have you thrown in jail for breach of promise."

He chuckled. "Have I told you what a hard-ass you are?"

"You have. But with an army sergeant for a father, an Irish mother bent on saving every disadvantaged group in the country, and a militant Navajo godmother, what would you expect?"

"Good point, not your fault. My notes are in the car, but I still have to get a few names and phone numbers. I will call you with those. Can you join us for dinner Saturday night?"

"To celebrate your nomination? Of course." She reached across the table and squeezed her father's hand. "Do you have any idea how proud I am of you?"

He covered her hand with his. "I hope as proud as I am of you."

She asked about last night's dinner party with Gray and Claudia Rossiter. "Nice, under the circumstances. Your mother told them my news over champagne and then I announced that I plan to retire when I reach sixty-five. That gives me five years to straighten out BIA. After that, Kathryn and I are going to spend summers in Idaho and winters in Arizona. We'll have Takoda, Rayleen, and their kids come for Christmas and, providing my daughter ever gets married and gives me *more* grandchildren, I will let her come, too."

"And you call me a hard-ass." KC grinned. "Between nailing bad guys ruining the environment for the almighty dollar, I will make it a point to work in marriage and children before you retire. So that gives *me* five years." She took a deep breath, no longer able to maintain the facade. "Dad, I am sick with worry. Please, tell me what's going on."

"It's so ugly, Kaya, I'm not sure where to begin. Over the last fifteen months someone has been transferring $3 million dollars a month of IIM funds out of our office. Electronic withdrawals with no security code, no authorization number, no trace of a destination. It has to be an inside job."

"One of the men I overheard said they had millions at stake. That must be what they were talking about. Is IIM trust money?"

He nodded. "Individual Indian Money from timber sales, fishing, farming, oil, leasing land for grazing, any funds generated from reservation trust land. Like my friend Charlie Dawson's wheat income from his hundred-sixty acres. It doesn't go to him. It goes into his IIM account." Sam frowned. "Imagine how much income four hundred tribes and villages produce. Three million a month is peanuts. The big picture may involve a billion—maybe two."

"My god, Dad, I'm almost afraid to ask what constitutes the big picture."

The waitress approached with two plates and refilled their coffee cups. "Be careful, these just came out of the oven." Sitting right under her nose, the sweet aroma made KC's mouth water. She took a cautious bite. The roll melted in her mouth and, for the next few minutes, they both ate in silence. When she glanced up, her father's expression signaled more bad news.

He pushed his empty plate away. "For the last two years, a group of Indian attorneys has been gathering evidence and plaintiffs for a class action suit against the Department of Interior for mismanagement of trust money and breach of fiduciary duty. My contact is an Apache lawyer named Donyell Crawford. He says they have 350,000 plaintiffs, IIM account holders from every tribe in the country. It will be the biggest lawsuit ever filed against an agency of the Federal government. Can you imagine the political fallout when it hits?"

His question struck like a lightning bolt; KC felt the blood drain from her face. She started to rise. "We have to go to the U.S. Attorney's office—right now."

"Kaya, wait." He held up his hand. "Please, this is important." She reluctantly sat back down. "When I came back from Vietnam, I had a decision to make—either go home to the reservation and my family, or stay in D.C. and try to make a difference." His voice faltered, husky with emotion. "I wanted to go home, but I couldn't forget what I'd seen in Vietnam, desperate people barely surviving. Different faces, different language, but like my people, an entire culture dying by degrees. It made me want to do something to help our tribes get the same chance for a decent life as non-Indians. Gray Rossiter knew how I felt, and he convinced me I could do more from here than from the reservation. So I went to work for BIA, almost forty years ago. And tomorrow I get my chance."

Seeing her father break down, caused KC's whole body to hurt. Not the sharp pain of an injury, but a deep, soulful ache for an anguished man wanting desperately to do the right thing. "I paid a price for that decision, your brother deciding he wanted to live on the Rez rather than in D.C. Forty years of being three thousand miles from home and my family, can you appreciate all that tomorrow represents? Cross my heart we'll go to the authorities as soon as I put Charlie Dawson on the plane Monday morning."

She stared at her father, the rational side of her brain warring with the emotional side. *You can't let him ignore the danger, which is exactly what he's doing. His decision isn't rational. Talk some sense into him. But wait a minute, he's worked his whole life for this. How can you even think of depriving your father of his opportunity to make a difference?*

"You make this so tough," she said. "Of course I can appreciate all that tomorrow represents." She shrugged, physically admitting she couldn't deny him. "Okay, but I want your word we will go to the U.S. Attorney first thing Monday morning."

"Cross my heart." A smile emerged, a mixture of gratitude and relief. Sam straightened up. "Wait here. I'll get my notes from the car." He paid the bill on the way out and returned with a large manila envelope. "As promised," he said. Sam kissed her cheek. "Thank you for understanding. Call your mother for details about tomorrow's ceremony and the dinner."

KC hailed a cab to her office, the first part of the ride chastising herself for not taking him straight to the U.S. Attorney, the last part justifying why she gave in. She entered her suite and mouthed "hello" to her secretary on the phone. Agnes Richardson held out a pink message in with a stack of messages. "You look upset."

KC nodded. "But I don't have time right now to talk about it, okay?"

"Okay, but you have to tell me later." KC had tremendous respect for Agnes, a woman who accepted life's ups and downs with a built-in reservoir of humor. Plump, with brown hair tucked behind each ear, she gave little attention to makeup or fashion, most likely because she had no time. After fifteen years teaching college level computer analysis, Agnes was about to complete her final year of law school while working full- time and raising her son, Danny.

"Here's your daily dose of fun appointments." Agnes dealt the messages out like playing cards: "This one confirms your 10:30 a.m. deposition at the Department of Energy." She smacked down the next note with a flourish. "I am so proud of you. Dunlap's lead attorney called, whining like a worn out tire about the way you cross-examined his client. Next, here's a reminder to be in Judge Green's court at 3:00 p.m. He's sentencing those crazies that tried to blow up the chemical lab, bless their little radical hearts." She nodded at the note in KC's hand. "I promised your Mom you'd call her first. She is so happy about your dad's nomination."

At the reminder of last evening, KC changed the subject. "Have you found out for sure if you're going to graduate next month?"

"I did." Agnes flashed a grin. "Five weeks from now, yours truly will receive my Juris Doctor degree, and Danny graduates from St. Luke's High School. How about that for a fantastic Christmas? Since you helped us put our lives back together, I hope you will celebrate with us."

"Are you kidding? I'll treat. You and Danny get to pick the restaurant."

Agnes crossed herself at the mention of her son. After his father announced he'd found his soul mate and moved in with his aerobics instructor, Danny reacted with anger and then apathy. Years ago, KC had gotten him involved in karate shortly after Agnes came to work for her. Two weeks after his dad left and Danny refused to go to school at all, KC asked the owner of the studio if he would give him a job teaching a karate class to teenagers. The class was a success for the studio and for Danny; earning money and the respect of his students did wonders. He would be graduating only one semester behind his classmates.

"Tell Danny this calls for a major celebration," KC said. "Pizza is not an option."

"You got it." Agnes exited, humming as she closed the door.

KC's thoughts turned to her father on his way to the airport for a reunion with his boyhood friend. *That appointment represents a lifetime of dedication on dad's part. Come on, pull yourself together so you can help him.* KC took a deep breath and called her mother. "Good morning, I just came from breakfast with Dad."

"Then he told you his news, isn't it wonderful?" Kathryn Garrett Blackhawk sounded excited and happy. KC agreed and tried to keep any hint of worry from her voice. "After all the champagne we drank with Gray and Claudia last night, I was surprised he hardly slept. But he's excited about

Charlie Dawson's visit. It's been almost a year since they've seen each other."

I know why he didn't sleep, the same reason I couldn't. KC thought about sharing her news about the Dunlap case, but it didn't seem relevant now. Instead she settled back and listened, her mother's voice full of warmth and compassion, a reflection of the woman herself. She was as comfortable in the company of prime ministers and presidents as she was with members of her various fund-raising groups. KC wondered if her mother had ever wrestled with the issue of career versus marriage. Just out of college, becoming an administrative aide to Matthew Rossiter, President Lyndon Johnson's Director of Office of Economic Opportunity, Kathryn had helped rescue whole areas of the country, contributing to society in a way that KC could only dream. A summa cum laude graduate of Brown University in economics, what heights would she have reached had she not left her job to marry a handsome young Indian and raise a family. Did she ever regret walking away from a position only a few women of her generation had achieved?

"You are coming to the conference tomorrow, aren't you?" her mother asked.

"I wouldn't miss it," KC said, an idea forming. "You know, Dad seemed a bit distracted this morning. And emotional, have you noticed?" Silence followed. KC pictured her mother staring out the kitchen window as she pondered the question.

"Now that you mention it, he hasn't really been himself for quite a while. I just assumed it is the daunting responsibility he's facing. We talked about that last night with Gray and Claudia." Kathryn recounted the discussion. As she listened, KC rose and walked over to her wall of framed pictures, eyeing the photo of her father standing between his commander Jonathan Champion and Gray Rossiter, son of Kathryn's former boss, Matthew Rossiter. All three in combat gear, they stood posed against a backdrop of dense jungle. Sam had a crew cut and a big grin on his face. Forty years ago, he looked so young; they all did. *President* Champion and *Congressman* Rossiter now.

KC returned to her desk. "Maybe Dad needs a vacation before he starts the new job." KC glanced at her calendar, shocked to realize Thanksgiving was only a week away. "He said Charlie Dawson is flying back to Idaho on Monday. Why don't the two of you go with him?" The idea filled her with hope; the reservation was the one place her father might agree to go.

"If anyone can convince your father to take a vacation, it's you. That sounds lovely." "Good. I'll check for reservations. I'd like to surprise Dad with this, okay?" KC asked for details then her mother ended their conversation as she always did. "Consider yourself hugged, darling."

No sooner had she hung up than Agnes buzzed on the intercom. "Tyler Jackson just called to ask if you had anybody in your office. I can't lie to our boss, so he's on his way down."

Uh-oh, Dunlap's attorney must have called him too. "Thanks for the heads up." KC slipped her dad's envelope into a drawer and rifled through her purse for a mirror and lipstick. She checked her reflection. "I look awful." She quickly ran a comb through her hair and applied lipstick, finishing just seconds before Tyler Jackson tapped on the door and entered.

KC rose, relieved to see a smile. "Tyler, welcome to the trenches."

He glanced around. "Nice trenches." He stopped to look at the picture of her receiving her black belt, flanked by Sam and her karate instructor. "I'll be damned, you did it. Now I know who to hire when I need a bodyguard with an attitude." *You keep collecting angry ex-wives, you'll need one.* Tyler's third marriage had recently "bit the dust," as he put it. He tossed a file on her desk and plopped down in one of her chairs, appearing more like a good-looking ski instructor than a forty year-old crackerjack environmental lawyer whose job she coveted.

KC opened the file and read the top page, the synopsis of a mine contamination case in Arizona. Politicians in the area's largest town, located on the opposite side of a six-thousand-foot mountain from the mine, were working to develop a tourist industry. They wanted no part of the adverse publicity a major EPA clean-up suit would bring. The corporation that owned the mine claimed they followed acceptable standards. The third party, EPA, was charging that the mine had ignored repeated warnings to clean up soil and riverbeds replete with contaminates. A huge case with national implications, the caliber she'd dreamed about since joining the Department of Justice. "How many boxes of evidentiary material do you have?"

"A bunch. And FYI, the mine is a major employer in the area so it's a sensitive issue. Of course, you realize that KC Garrett was my last choice."

"What?" She glanced up and noted his mischievous grin. "I can be sensitive if I have to, and if you don't ask more than once a decade."

"Sure, and I can grow hair anytime I want." Tyler grinned and rubbed his tanned balding head. "That reminds me, I had a call from Scott Dunlap's attorney this morning. He said you verbally KO'd his client. He thinks you're scary. I told him that gracious cross-examination is not your long suit, and to be grateful you weren't in a bad mood."

"Thanks for backing me up–I think." She smiled, this was like old times. "That reminds me, you've got to see this." KC retrieved a picture from her desk and handed it to Tyler. "If he thinks I was tough, then wait until he gets a load of this." The picture showed Dunlap standing at the water's edge as two employees dumped the contents of barrels marked with a large, yellow X into the reservoir. "My incontrovertible proof in glorious color, what do you think?"

"Wow, where and how did you get this?"

"At Pine Creek Reservoir near Dunlap's plant. You've met Tim Carrell, the George Washington University student intern who's a big Redskin fan? I hired him because he was the only intern willing to give up his Sunday. He took all these photos." KC handed Tyler the rest of them. "I've prepared the paperwork laying the foundation for submission, and I have Tim's affidavit on the date and time the photos were taken. I am the witness. Dunlap is a bad guy, Tyler. This time, he can't buy his way out of this with his squadron of attorneys."

"Nobody can accuse you of not going the extra mile. Congratulations, and let me know as soon as you get a court date. I want to be there when you toast Dunlap." Tyler glanced at his watch and rose. "I can't believe the holidays are here already. EPA is chomping at the bit so I hope you can get to

Arizona in early January. You may be in for a fight from all sides, but don't go karate-chopping anybody because they tick you off. You behave."

"I'll try not to, but if I get thrown in the clink, you'll be the one I call for bail." She came from behind her desk. "Thank you for trusting me with this." KC walked him to the door.

"You don't need to thank me. You've paid your dues. You are the perfect attorney for this case. I'll have the boxes brought down." His look was openly inviting, his aftershave familiar and seductive. "I miss you, KC. What I miss is *us* and the fun times we used to have. Not one of my ex-wives likes football or basketball or skiing like you do. I had more fun with you than all my exes put together. Hey, speaking of football, how about I bring pizza for Monday night's game. How many people?"

"Ten, counting my parents," KC said, noting he hadn't given her the option to say no.

She closed the door, a little surprised at her ambivalence about the case. Huge with far-reaching environmental implications, it spoke volumes how she was viewed as an environmental attorney. Coupled with her imminent victory over Dunlap, this should be a milestone worthy of a celebration, but that wouldn't happen until her father was safely out of town. Tyler's comments about their past told her she needed to level with him that she had no interest in becoming wife number four.

That thought popped Tony DeMarco's image into her mind like the circled thought in a cartoon strip. *He's probably married by now with a couple of kids.* Before the image could lodge itself, she deflected the on-off thought that she may have made a mistake in breaking up with him. But two years ago, stepping away from her career to marry and have a family without having reached any of her goals seemed unthinkable. The irony did not escape her that this Arizona case represented one of those goals that played a part in her fateful decision.

KC returned to her desk and opened her father's envelope. There were three computer-generated sheets printed in the distinctive font Sam used. The first page, *Missing IIM Funds,* was a photocopy of a ledger showing a series of $3 million transfers in the credit column. Her father was right about there being no security code or authorization number. The transfers went back fifteen months, the initials RIC beside one transaction being the only clue to a destination. "I bet Agnes can figure out where they're going."

On the second sheet, *Mine Income,* Sam had written *audits of mine leases required by law not being done. Tribes repeatedly requested, no response, L.P. Camas Mine incl.* "L.P. Lake Ponsiteau—that's Dad's tribe," KC said. "Theoretically mine, too." Three leases had been audited independently, yet only one had met industry standards. In the margin, her father had written the name *Victor Ludlow* with a question mark.

The third page outlined the impending class action lawsuit. KC read through Donyell Crawford's summary. It claimed the Department of Interior routinely failed to charge or collect income from Indian-owned land held in trust. And the rare times when they did establish prices for products and rent, they set them so far below market value as to constitute largesse, reward to influential donors who contributed to members of Congress responsible for Indian legislation.

"Payoff on a grand scale and perfectly legal." Anger replaced her fear. Sam's lifelong goal to help his people now appeared to be naive in light of the scale of corruption. Over the last thirty years, BIA had lost track of $3 billion of Individual Indian Money. *Defendants: Valerie Beckman, Secretary of Interior, Carson Marsh, Manager Secretary of Indian Affairs, Hayden Culpepper, Chairman, Senate Select Committee on Indian Affairs, each charged with Federal mismanagement of trust money and breach of fiduciary duty.*

"Oh, Dad, life-long goal or not, I wish you hadn't gotten the nomination."

KC scanned her father's notes and saved them on her computer hard drive, then made two back-up CDs. One went in her briefcase with the hard copies, the other into her locked file cabinet. She grabbed her coat and briefcase and started for the door, then remembered the airline reservations. She retraced her steps and called American Airlines, no flights available to Sherman Falls, Washington, the nearest airport to Lake Ponsiteau, Idaho. She tried Northwest and Delta with the same results, then finally United Airlines.

As KC progressed through the airline's recorded options, potential implications sprouted like weeds. Billions unaccounted for, the biggest class action lawsuit to be filed against an agency of the Federal government, charges and counter-charges, careers down the drain–powerful, important people's careers.

Finally, a real person. "You are my last hope," KC said. "I need two seats from Washington, D.C. to Sherman Falls, Washington for Monday, November 19th. I'll take any two you've got, coach or first class, even if they're not together. And any time of the day or night." She waited, her hope fading as the minutes ticked by.

"Nothing so far but I'm still searching," the agent said. KC drummed her fingers on the desk as she waited. She was about to give up when the agent spoke. "I can't believe it. I found two seats on the nineteenth. They're not together, and the tickets are pricey. Does that matter?"

"No, I'm just grateful to get them." KC gave her credit card information and her parents' names and asked the agent to email the confirmation to her office computer.

With his laptop and an anonymous long distance calling card, Sam could disappear on the reservation long enough for the authorities to identify the men who threatened him. KC left for court relieved and hopeful. *With any luck, Mom and Dad will be watching Monday night's game three-thousand miles away at Takoda's house.*

She called her father's office on her cell as she waited for the elevator. "Dad, I read your notes and I have a plan. See you tomorrow. Until then, please watch your back."

—3—

Valerie Beckman shouted encouragement to Phoebe as her daughter advanced the soccer ball with short kicks. A picture of ten-year old concentration, Phoebe seemed not to hear. Despite the crisp November air, beads of perspiration covered her forehead, and crimson splotched her freckled cheeks. *Oh, that she would attack her studies that hard.*

The coach came up beside Valerie. Hands cupped, he yelled, "Phoebe, pass to your forward." She responded with a kick that scooted the ball to a tall girl running down the middle of the field. All around her Valerie heard parents shouting. "Kick it, Kristin, kick it." Phoebe raced ahead and took up position alongside Kristin. The forward aimed for the ball with the inside of her foot but missed a square hit and the ball spun lethargically in front of the girls.

Arms aloft like a bird about to take flight, Phoebe took a stutter step then slammed the ball straight toward the net. Surrounded by parents who rushed to the sidelines, Valerie held her breath as the opponent's goalie dived for a save—a second too late. The referee blew her whistle and raised both hands, signifying a goal and the end of the game.

Phoebe and her teammates erupted into a mass of squealing, pony-tailed pogo sticks, bobbing up and down in unison. The exuberant girl on the field in no way resembled the withdrawn child Valerie first encountered. *The two of us have come such a long way.* A soccer mom enjoying a Saturday afternoon game felt so much better than photo ops and speeches. Valerie glanced over her shoulder at the security guard, a stoic young man, extremely serious about his job of protecting her. As Secretary of Interior, ever since September 11, she no longer had the option to refuse security for any public event—even a Saturday soccer game involving her daughter. She had no intention of giving up doing things on her own and with Phoebe, so security had become a part of their lives. *Too bad Elliott isn't here. He would have loved to see her score that goal.*

Phoebe raced towards the sidelines, breathing hard and sporting a triumphant grin. Curly brown hair framed a freckled, intelligent face, her hazel eyes leaving no doubt what she was thinking or feeling. She glanced around. "Elliott didn't come?"

Valerie shook her head. "He must be on another assignment."

Phoebe's disappointment passed quickly as she helped distribute after-game snacks and juice. As soon as they were consumed, she said she was tired and ready to go home. They walked toward the car, Phoebe hopscotching along in sidewalk squares. Therapy had helped erase her nightmares of a house exploding, her father and another man inside manufacturing methamphetamines. According to the police report, three year-old Phoebe had been asleep in the backseat of an old car parked too close to the house. The blast threw her against the door handle with such force it broke her rib and right arm. Overnight, she became a ward of the court, and for the next two years was shuffled from one foster home to another.

Valerie and Phoebe's paths happened to cross when Valerie visited an interim foster care facility to deliver a speech for increased funding. Reporters asked if they could get a picture of her with one of the youngsters. Valerie spied a little girl standing away from everyone, a tiny tree of a girl, fragile and alone. The director said her name was Phoebe and she had just turned five. Photographers snapped away as Valerie walked over and knelt down beside her, their faces close. Valerie turned to Phoebe with a smile. Then, caught on video and still shots, she stared into eyes so filled with quiet despair that it took her breath away. Forgetting the photo op and speech she had come to give, Valerie gathered the little girl in her arms and held her. They clung to each other, seemingly unaware of the stunned audience watching. Valerie kissed Phoebe's cheek and whispered something to her. The little girl blinked back tears.

Valerie rose. "Why is Phoebe here?" she asked the director. "Have you not been able to find her a good foster home?" Voice barely audible and with tears threatening to escape, the Secretary stood stiffly fighting for control.

"Yes ma'am, but. . . ." The director darted a glance at the camera. "We rescued her the minute we discovered the. . .the situation."

Valerie's arm encircled Phoebe, an involuntary response. A lone camera flashed. "Well you needn't look any further. If Phoebe would like a permanent home, she has one with me." The little girl stared up at her as though questioning what she had just heard. A murmur traveled around the room as video cameras hummed and digital cameras captured their image.

Raw emotion, woman and child caught in a moment that needed no explanation.

A video of Valerie and Phoebe appeared on the evening news. The next day, their emotional embrace made the front page of every major newspaper. The following month, it appeared on the cover of *Time Magazine,* a chance encounter that touched a nation and unwittingly catapulted the widowed Secretary of Interior to political stardom.

Funny, thought Valerie as she unlocked the car. *You were so small, but you saved my life as much as I saved yours.* Phoebe had only vague memories of the mother who had given her life, then disappeared into the drug world. Only once during her five years of therapy did Phoebe ask about her. Thankfully, Valerie acknowledged that the bad times and her scars seemed healed. She drove toward home in the waning light, the security guard following in a nondescript car.

"Momma, are we going to live in the White House?"

Valerie glanced over at Phoebe. "Who told you that?"

"Jules," Phoebe said, peering around her seat at the security car. "That guard is no fun. I wish Elliott could have seen me win the game."

"You can call and tell him about it." Valerie cast a side-glance at her. "Too bad Jules couldn't have been there," she ventured.

Phoebe shrugged. "All he ever talks about is the campaign and you being president." She reached down and pulled up her sagging socks. "Are you going to marry him?"

Valerie paused, not sure how to answer. "We haven't actually talked about it, but how would you feel about that?"

Phoebe wiggled in her seat. "Okay, I guess."

Not exactly an enthusiastic endorsement. Valerie pulled into the garage; the security guard flashed his headlights and drove away. Phoebe jumped out and ran to the back door. "I'm going to take a shower, then can we eat?"

"Of course." Valerie followed her into the house, perplexed at Phoebe's response. After Marguerite served them dinner, Valerie tucked Phoebe into bed. "Too tired for a story?"

Phoebe nodded, hers eyes closing. "Don't worry 'bout me. If you like Jules, I can too."

Out of the mouths of babes, Valerie thought as she closed the door and descended the stairs, the image of her son crowding into her thoughts. *He would be twenty now. What would he look like? What kind of a young man would he be?* She shuddered, remembering the funeral. Stay in the present, she reminded herself as she entered the library.

Jules was waiting for her. Handsome and sophisticated, with a self-assurance born of wealth and an Ivy League education, Jules had been the bachelor du' jour of Washington's glamorous women before Valerie met him at a White House function. Their relationship developed slowly because of busy schedules and the lingering pain of losing her husband and son in a terrible accident. Though it seemed to be moving in that direction, any possibility of a romantic relationship disappeared when the *Time Magazine* hit the newsstands.

Valerie and Phoebe's picture and story ignited the public's infatuation with an empathetic congresswoman thrust into national politics by tragedy. The *Times* article revealed a sincere widow determined to carry on the work so important to her husband. The story opened the door to opportunities for Valerie Beckman, who seemed to have a knack for solving partisan issues and overcoming challenges. Ecstatic at the possibilities, Jules claimed in a candid moment on a Sunday morning TV interview that Valerie Beckman would be the perfect choice to be the first woman president. When President Champion obliquely endorsed the idea, there was no stopping the runaway train. Their budding relationship relegated to the back burner, Jules and Valerie's focus became the campaign.

Jules patted the ottoman in front of him. "Come and sit, I haven't seen you all day." His somber expression made him appear as tired as she felt. "Phoebe didn't want a story?"

Valerie nodded. "She was tired. I think she may be coming down with a cold." She poured two glasses of sherry and handed one to Jules. "You look exhausted too. I started this morning dishing up breakfast at a homeless shelter then rushed to a photo shoot at the Veteran's Memorial Hospital. I want to do that again and, this time, spend more time with the soldiers. I made it to Phoebe's soccer game in time for the kickoff, but could you ask your staff to ease up on my commitments until after Christmas? I need to shop." Valerie glanced at Jules.

Staring at the fire; he hadn't heard a word she'd said. Jules rose abruptly and walked to the fireplace. "I need to tell you something, Valerie, and I would appreciate it if you would hear me out before you react."

"That sounds ominous. React to what?"

"Valerie, if our situation holds, I am convinced the White House is yours. Today's online polls report you significantly ahead. Two pollsters went so far as to predict nobody can catch you. The first woman president, it's almost a *fait accompli.*"

She rose and faced him. "Skip the campaign speech, Jules. What's the problem?"

"Money, of course," he sighed. "What else? We anticipated an increase in campaign costs, but didn't expect them to skyrocket. With so many candidates staying in the race, contributions are spread thin."

"What about all of our fundraisers?" Heat rushed to her face. "And you said contributions were pouring in. That's a quote."

He nodded. "You've done a stellar job fund raising and, yes, contributions are still coming in. Unfortunately, not enough to cover the caliber of campaign we're conducting. Compared to the others our campaign is a Rolls Royce versus a Buick. Bottom line, our expenditures are greater than our income."

"How much greater?" Valerie wanted to know.

Jules withdrew two folded papers from his jacket and handed them to her. Computer generated figures filled the credit column on one page and continued onto a second that also had hand-written numbers in red ink scattered about randomly. At the bottom of the credit column in Jules' handwriting she saw $45,000,000.

"Forty-five million?" Valerie slumped down on the ottoman.

"That is not difficult to justify, Valerie. Please remember the dozen or more trips to England and the Continent, not to mention Mexico, South America, and the Mideast. We have twice the number of TV ads of any other candidate, and the receptions we hosted here and abroad were first class. It's unfortunate but the figure is not unreasonable."

"Of course, I remember, but I assumed we had the money to pay for everything." Anger took hold, as much at herself as at Jules. She had broken her cardinal rule: *never assume, always ask. I trusted Jules to make decisions that I should have made.* A blur of five-star hotels, lavish receptions, elegant dinners for Forbes CEOs and top-drawer political luminaries paraded through her mind. Her frustration mounting, Valerie held up the crumpled papers. "You're telling me you spent $45 million dollars we didn't have on a Rolls Royce campaign, on five-star treatment for heaven knows how many people—including the press? I can't believe you would do that."

"Press people who believe in you and support you, Valerie. Who daily keep you on the front page of every newspaper and not just in the states." He looked exasperated. "We don't *owe* anything. Everything is paid for."

"Then what are you saying? And it better be the truth." She stared at him, her heart hammering. "I suggest you do it now."

"We used IIM funds." He spoke in a half-whisper.

"You did what!" She tried to catch her breath. "You stole Indian trust money?"

"I did not steal, Valerie. I borrowed."

There it was, parsing words instead of the truth. "How dare you. How *could* you?" The sherry glass went flying in his direction. Jules jerked back, the left side of his face catching the amber liquid. The snifter shattered against the fireplace.

"Valerie, for god's sake, you almost blinded me." He strode to the bar and wiped his face with a towel. "Listen for a minute," he said, his blue eyes shooting sparks. "The IIM accounts have been an indecipherable mess for over seventy years. The money won't be missed. Besides, I plan to put it back."

"Don't give me that bull." Pulse pounded Valerie's temples. "Taking millions from innocent people, I call that betrayal pure and simple."

"I would never betray you! Who do you think put you ahead of all the other candidates? And how many of them have been seen on TV conferring with every major world leader and treated as though they are already president? Only you!" He threw up his hands. "You obviously have no clue how much planning or the people it takes to pull off what we've accomplished. Or how much it costs."

Valerie could not tell who was the angriest. Every nerve in her body felt on fire. Jules' normally handsome face was flushed and contorted. "You obviously don't understand that the reason voters love you is because I delivered you to their backyard so they could meet you and tell you their concerns. You are their candidate because they connected with you, and the press loves you for the same reason. Prime ministers and presidents support you because you sat down and talked with them. They got to know you, and they saw a woman capable of being a world leader. All of that is proof my campaign is working. So what if it cost more than I thought? That train already left the station. Bottom line, we didn't have the money, so I appropriated it."

"Someone had to help you steal the money. Who was it, Jules?"

His glare was her answer. She whirled, ready to leave. "Valerie, wait," Jules' angry demeanor evaporated. "Please, listen! From the minute you assumed Randy's congressional seat, everything you touched, everything you said and did turned to political gold. Whether you like it or not, or whether you even recognize it, fate has given you the greatest opportunity a person can get. You think I'm doing this for the fun of it? If I didn't believe you could win it all, I wouldn't be working sixteen-hour days planning every detail of your campaign. You've told me a hundred times you want to honor

Randy's dream. Well, correct me if I'm wrong, but I believe there's no bigger honor you could pay him than to win the presidency."

The mention of Randy brought the instant image of the 4:00 a.m. ringing of her doorbell. A social worker and two officers from the Maryland Highway Patrol, hats in hand, entered. They said they had news of her husband and son—who should have already been home from their father-son ski trip. *Please sit down, ma'am. There's been an accident. The roads were icy, ma'am. We are very sorry for your loss.*

"Valerie, I am sorry, but believe me all I wanted was to give you this opportunity."

Her fire and fury drained away, leaving leaden limbs and exhaustion threatening to overwhelm. "I believe you, Jules, but I'll never understand how you could do what you did."

He took her hands. "Try to see this from my perspective. If ever the end justified the means, this is it. You are about to make history or cast aside the opportunity of a lifetime. Focus on the things you want to accomplish. I *swear* I will make every effort to replace the money."

Valerie withdrew her hands. "I am not naïve, Jules. And I know right from wrong. Regardless of your intentions, what you've done is wrong." She closed her eyes, absorbing the implications. "And I don't understand, why now? After fifteen months, why tell me at all?"

"Why? Because you are intelligent. Because you've received monthly reports from the start. And because our campaign is such a cut above the others. I was sure you would figure it out." Jules led her back to the chair and knelt beside her. "We are there, Valerie, we're at the door of the White House. I tried like hell to find a solution but when I couldn't, it was either borrow the money or you miss the brass ring. I couldn't let that happen to someone I love."

"Get me a real drink, will you?" Valerie watched him at the bar and wondered how well she really knew Jules Aubert. He returned with two snifters of Chivas Regal, the word *love* suspended in the air, alive with electricity like seconds before a storm. "I've dreamed that one day I would hear you tell me you love me, Jules, but I never expected to hear it in defense of grand larceny. Did it ever occur to you someone else might discover what you've done?"

"Of course, I am extremely careful. And, Valerie, I'm sorry if I haven't verbalized how I feel, but you have to know I love you. Why else would I try with every fiber of my being, to give you this opportunity?" He looked and sounded sincere.

She stared into the fire, tears blurring images of endless miles of farmland from the air, countless airports with people lined up ready to shake her hand. School auditoriums and posh hotel ballrooms melded into a patchwork of memories of farmers, housewives, titans of business and industry, teachers and secretaries, all urging her to run, resting their hope and their future squarely on her shoulders.

Valerie glanced at the papers still clenched in her hand. "I listened to your perspective. Now hear mine. I have given my word to God only knows how many thousands of people that I would fight for them, that I stand for integrity. Now you've put me in the position of condoning embezzlement." Valerie stood up, her chin raised defiantly. "Understand this, Jules. Do not *borrow*–and I use that term advisedly–one penny more from IIM accounts. And replace the money, is that clear?" Her eyes bore into his, sending a message she felt down to her toes.

"Very clear, you have my word," he whispered.

"I hope so, because if your colossal error in judgment undoes everything I stand for and everything I've worked for, you will find out just how tough I can be."

—4—

S am Blackhawk took note of the darkening skies as he and Charlie
  Dawson arrived at the Bureau of Indian Affairs Friday morning. They
entered BIA's largest conference room and, immediately Charlie spotted a
friend. "I'll be darned, there's Steve Otakay. I haven't seen him since the
Sioux powwow three years ago. Thanks for doing this, Sam. It's a great
idea."

Sam smiled. "Go ahead and circulate, Charlie. I want to make sure things
are ready." He walked to the front of the room and checked each table for
conference materials. Satisfied they were in order, he worked his way
through the throng gathered in front of three banquet tables against the back
wall. Sam helped himself to a cup of coffee and mingled with delegates
holding plates loaded with selections from the continental breakfast. He
greeted representatives from the Cherokee, Navajo, Oglala Sioux, Seminole,
Creek, Seneca, Choctaw and Chickasaw tribes.

The Nez Perce, along with the Kootenai, Coeur d' Alene, Lemhi, Ban-
nock, and Shoshoni delegates from Idaho, made it a point to seek him out
and shake his hand. Charlie was the official representative of the Lake
Ponsiteau tribe. Of the country's more than four-hundred recognized tribes,
only half operated a gaming facility, though nearly every tribe had sent
delegates. Those that did not have casinos had come seeking information and
guidance on how to build a facility or get ideas on how to diversify their
economy. *Whatever brought them, we will help each other.*

At 8:00 a.m. sharp, Sam made his way to the raised stage while delegates
found their tables. "Welcome, ladies and gentlemen, to BIA's first annual
conference on economic diversity. We are here to help each other, and I want
to get right down to business. Charlie Dawson from the Lake Ponsiteau tribe

is our first speaker. He has operated the very successful Crystal Waters Casino for ten years. He is the one who made it all happen, and Charlie is here to tell you how."

Sam stood at the edge of the room listening and observing the delegates' reactions. He saw younger delegates taking notes, nodding at what they heard. Elders listened with impassive faces as Charlie recited facts and figures, but they perked up when he talked about his son returning from the army and, together, how they worked to make Crystal Waters a very profitable enterprise. The second speaker did an equally good job.

At 10:00 a.m., Secretary of Interior Valerie Beckman entered the conference room, followed by an aide. Kaya's godmother and longtime BIA employee, Sally Calder, came in with Pansy Wahiptu, Sam's secretary. Gray Rossiter's wife, Claudia, entered with Kaya and her mother. The sight of his wife and daughter filled Sam with pride.

* * *

KC was surprised when Valerie Beckman motioned for her to take the chair next to hers at the table. Friendly and surprisingly down-to-earth, Mrs. Beckman was either a genuinely nice person or a very good actress. KC turned her attention to the stage and her father. If he felt fearful or worried, he hid it well. Smiling, with his military posture returned, he looked strong and confident. Regardless, KC wished she could spirit him away to a safe place, preferably on the other side of the continent.

He nodded toward their table. "Madam Secretary, honored guests, and delegates. In 1988, President Ronald Reagan signed the Indian Gaming Regulatory Act into law. At that time, our people were the most impoverished minority group in America with the highest unemployment rate and the lowest life expectancy. In the decades since, reservation gaming is now a $300 billion dollar industry that creates hundreds of thousands of jobs on reservations across our nation. More than a century ago, we depended on buffalo for our existence. Today, gaming is our *new* buffalo, helping our people establish credit, buy homes and cars, and send our kids to college.

That's called hope, my friends." Sam slapped the lectern with his palm. "And hope is what this conference is all about."

KC studied Valerie Beckman's reaction to her father. Attentive, she nodded at times, and at other times raised her brows in surprise, totally involved in what Sam was saying. KC joined in the audience's enthusiastic applause as Sam nodded at the Secretary. "We are fortunate to have a good friend of the First People here this morning. I am pleased to present the honorable Secretary of Interior, Valerie Beckman."

Valerie made her way to the stage and smiled as she gazed at the audience. "A warm welcome to all delegates. It is inspiring to see so many leaders coming together to address the issue of economic diversity for your tribes." Valerie spoke of the importance of Indian sovereignty and pledged the administration's support in addressing the unique concerns of American Indians. Valerie Beckman looked and sounded sincere, making it difficult for KC to believe she could be involved with the men she'd overheard outside her office.

In her fifth year as Secretary of Interior, Valerie was the undisputed star of the female members in President Champion's Cabinet. It was a given that she had accomplished the impossible, captured the confidence of millions regardless of party. She motioned for Sam to join her at the lectern. "This is an exciting day for us at BIA, which is why I chose this gathering of tribal leaders to make this announcement. Today, November 16th, at the instruction of the President of the United States, I hereby place Sam Blackhawk's name in nomination to be the Assistant Secretary of the Bureau of Indian Affairs." She smiled. "Congratulations, Sam."

KC's heart skipped a beat as flashbulbs popped and television cameras captured the Secretary shaking Sam's hand. War whoops and whistles issued from around the room, and KC rose along with the rest of the crowd, in a standing ovation. KC watched as her father's lifetime of work, dedication, and sacrifice, culminated in one glorious moment. Overcome with pride, she stamped his joyous look into her memory. When the applause died down, the Secretary spoke about the many highlights of Sam's distinguished career at

BIA and, with a nod toward Kathryn and KC, assured the audience his confirmation would be a formality.

* * *

As he listened to Valerie, Sam caught a glimpse of movement at the far door. It opened and a Secret Service agent entered, then stepped to one side and spoke into a mike on the lapel of his jacket. A second agent joined him, and together they surveyed the room. They held the door open for a young woman who walked to the stage and whispered something to the Secretary. Valerie raised her hand. "Ladies and gentleman, a wonderful surprise. We are indeed honored to have a very special visitor. May I present Jonathan Champion, President of the United States!"

A hush swept over the room. Dumbstruck, Sam could only stare as the President strode through the door. At the sight of his former commander, Sam snapped to attention. Tall, slender, and fit, the President's silver hair crowned a rugged face that had aged, but his smile hadn't changed. Cheers and applause exploded when he shook Sam's hand and embraced him.

When the President released him, Sam found himself staring into clear blue eyes he'd known in another lifetime, on another side of the world. "You look surprised, Sam. There is no way I would have missed your crowning moment. Congratulations, my friend."

Unable to speak, Sam wiped away a tear. Network video cameras rolled; digital cameras flashed. Photographers asked for several poses: Sam with the President, Sam with the Secretary and the President. They complied quickly, directed by the cadre of technicians accustomed to the President's pace. When the main cameramen signaled they had finished, the President stepped to the lectern, his hands loosely gripping the edges.

His heart hammering, Sam watched President Champion look over the audience and smile, the mantle of world leader resting easy on his shoulders. Video cameras rolled when he began to speak, his voice pure authority but deeper and more resonant than Sam remembered. "I have known Sam Blackhawk for forty years. When I first met him in Vietnam, he was a kid, a private in the army. I had just been promoted to major and given the biggest assignment of my career. Even then, I recognized there was something special about this young soldier, and there was no doubt in my mind that Sam Blackhawk would distinguish himself." He glanced at Sam and smiled. "And he has done just that."

Sam listened as the President of the United States talked about their time in Vietnam, about his part in covert missions and how he earned a Bronze Star for saving the lives of two team members. President Champion praised his work on behalf of American Indians over the years and pledged his administration's support in his new endeavor. Sam's anger at centuries of injustice and inequity, his frustration at the suffering his people endured at the hands of the government, for the moment were swept away. Pride and humility engulfed him. His throat went cotton-dry. Champion motioned for Sam to stand next to him. The President shook his hand as flashbulbs popped like the 4th of July. "I know you join me in honoring this patriotic American and offering him heartfelt best wishes in his new role." Champion pulled Sam close. "You and Kathryn have to come to Camp David so we can catch up. That's an order, soldier."

"Yes, sir!" Sam saluted his Commander-in-Chief. Cameras recorded the moment, and continued to film, as Champion accompanied the Secretary from the stage. He stopped at the front table, and Charlie Dawson sprang to his feet, a photographer capturing the two of them shaking hands. The Secretary followed the President's lead, shaking hands and posing with delegates as they moved in opposite directions around the room. A Secret Service agent caught the President's attention and pointed to his watch. Champion waved to Sam, raised both arms to the crowd, and then exited with Secretary Beckman right behind him.

Suddenly, Sam stood alone at the podium, his hand still raised in a salute. He downed half the glass of water and leaned toward the microphone. Smiling, he shook his head. "Talk about a hard act to follow!" Still standing, the delegates laughed and clapped and whistled, caught up in the power they had just witnessed, spellbound by the good fortune of one of their own. Sam tapped the microphone. "I suggest we break for a few minutes." After a brief intermission, several more speakers addressed the crowd, and then lunch was served.

Afterwards, the delegates broke into discussion groups with notched-up energy. Sam strolled around the room, stopping to listen, interjecting comments and suggestions to spark debate. Every group was discussing community centers and health clinics, classrooms, and computer labs for tribal schools. A dream come true, Sam thought, as a young intern approached with a cell phone in his hand. "You have a call, Mr. Blackhawk. The man says it's urgent."

"Sam, this is Donyell Crawford in Albuquerque—the attorney who wrote you. I wanted to come to the conference but had to wait for a critical piece of evidence. I have it now, and if you could give me an hour tomorrow, I will catch a flight to Washington."

"Absolutely, but I am booked through tomorrow evening. I know it's late, but could we meet around 10:00 p.m.? I am glad you called, I understand the information you have is—"

"Going to blow this thing wide open," Crawford said.

—5—

As soon as KC donned her coat and switched on her bedroom TV, Ivan jumped up on the bed and stretched out. The television weatherman was issuing a warning, pointing to moving patches of green and orange. "Unless you have to go out this evening, I suggest staying home," he said. "We're in for heavy snow and high winds, with gusts up to fifty or sixty miles per hour." KC stroked Ivan, his attention on the screen, just like he did when she watched a basketball game.

"A cat who likes to watch TV, I would hate to explain you to a non-cat person, Ivan. Be grateful you don't have to go out in this weather."

The strong winds had arrived, but not the snow as KC pulled up in front of le Gaulois restaurant and surrendered her car to the valet. The Saturday-night crowd consisted of elegantly dressed political luminaries, and a few tables of mid-level professionals, perhaps celebrating a special occasion or wanting to rub elbows with the power crowd.

The *maître d'* led her to the table. Congressman Gray Rossiter, Sam's lifelong friend and former unit commander in Vietnam, rose, and with mock sternness, ordered Sam and Charlie Dawson to attention. KC chuckled. "At ease, men." She kissed her father on the cheek and took the empty chair between Gray's wife and her father's friend. "Good to see you, Charlie. It's been a long time." Charlie asked about her work at the Department of Justice, and how she liked living in Washington, D.C.

KC visited with Charlie until she felt a nudge, then turned to see Gray Rossiter staring at Charlie. "You've monopolized my favorite attorney long enough, Charlie. I need to talk to her."

Charlie laughed. "Okay, I get it that everything in D.C. has a price." He turned to KC. "Gray's taking Sam and me to lunch tomorrow. Go ahead, Congressman, it's your turn."

"You are very astute, Charlie," Gray said. "I need you to plead my case, counselor. Your father's been ragging on me because I missed his big day yesterday. My defense? I was fulfilling my congressional duty casting my vote on a critical bill. So help me out here, would you?"

Smiling at the exchange, Sam was thoroughly enjoying himself. "Kaya is a great lawyer, Rossiter, but she's not going to win this one. I'm not letting you off the hook." Their teasing had been going on as long as KC could remember. Like Sally Calder, KC's Navajo godmother, Gray and her father were family, not brothers by blood, but by a deep and abiding friendship.

KC rose and approached her father. "Do you have those names and phone numbers you promised me?" she whispered in his ear.

He shook his head. "I didn't bring them. Tonight is for celebrating, Kaya. Come to the house for breakfast in the morning. I'll give them to you then."

"Is she pleading my case, Sam?" Now in his eighth congressional term representing the State of Virginia, at the moment Congressman Rossiter looked mischievous. "Okay, I bow to Sam's good looks, his smarts, and all his other qualities, ad nauseam. Let's have a speech!"

Her father rose. "I do want to say something. This is a wonderful moment that I wasn't sure I would ever reach. But whenever I doubted myself, one or another of you stepped forward and would not let me give up." He put his hand on Kathryn's shoulder. "I owe a special tribute to Kathryn, an incredible woman who believed in me from the beginning, and who bridged cultural gaps with dignity and grace. I thank her and each one of you for sharing this moment with me."

KC couldn't believe it when her father called for the bill and signed the tag. "Charlie and I have an errand, so I thank you again, dear friends. And you, too, Ranger." Sam laughed and offered his hand. Gray pulled Sam to him in an affectionate embrace. "Tonto and Ranger, we were a helluva team, weren't we? What can I do to make things right?" Gray said.

"We sure were." Sam pumped his hand. "Just make sure you show up at my swearing-in ceremony. I want a picture of us with the President."

* * *

Wolf gave up trying to see inside le Gaulois. The snowstorm had arrived with predicted fury, reducing visibility to zero. The envelope with Sam Blackhawk's notes that he stole from Garrett's apartment, sat on the seat beside him. A cursory read-through made frighteningly clear the impact that Aubert's theft of IIM funds would have on Mrs. B. *It will destroy her and everything she's worked for. Damn Aubert. What the hell do I do?*

The dash clock glowed 8:45 p.m. A decision had to be made. Wolf autodialed Aubert's cell phone. He answered amidst the sound of music and conversation in the background. "Find someplace private where you can talk, Aubert. We have an emergency."

Aubert put him on hold and came back a minute later. "This better be good. We're in the middle of a fundraiser."

"Right now, Garrett and Blackhawk are partying with a bunch of people inside a restaurant in Alexandria. But in about an hour, Blackhawk has an appointment to meet a lawyer from Albuquerque who says he's bringing evidence that's going to blow things wide open. I don't know what to do. I'm hoping you have a plan."

"What lawyer? What are you talking about?" Aubert no longer sounded cocky.

"I'm talking about the $45 million of IIM funds you stole and transferred to Bermuda."

Aubert yelled a string of expletives. "How the hell do you know about that?"

"Didn't you get the message I left on your private line a few minutes ago? I said it was urgent." Dead silence. "I told you Blackhawk and Garrett had breakfast yesterday. He gave her an envelope which I just nabbed from her apartment. It's all in there—how much you stole, and that Mrs. B is named in a class action lawsuit. You're not as smart as you thought."

Complete silence. Wolf waited and then ventured "Are you there? What about Mrs. B?"

"Give me a minute. You just dropped this bomb on me."

"Don't tempt me," Wolf said. He lit a cigarette and waited. "C'mon, Aubert, you're wasting time we don't have."

Aubert's answer came back steely-hard. "Eliminate the source of the problem."

"That's your plan? Look, I'm not some lowlife hit man you can hire to—"

"I know that. But you are either Valerie's friend or you're not. You can't have it both ways. If you stop Blackhawk, Valerie will be President. If you don't, she will lose everything."

Wolf's cloud of doubt about the lies and secrets gathering force ever since Aubert took charge of Mrs. B's campaign, let loose with a force that matched the storm outside. His heart, his blood pressure, his pulse felt ready to explode as the full impact of Aubert's words sunk in.

"You wanted to know what to do? I just told you." Aubert's public persona kicked back in. "I realize what I'm asking, Wolf. Do it, and I will make it up to you in spades. Call me."

A click and then silence, Wolf had his answer. Mrs. B was no doubt at the fundraiser, unaware that Aubert had just dumped her career and her future in his lap. Mind reeling, Wolf broke into a sweat as he shivered from the cold. "What do I do—sit by and let her be destroyed? Remove the threat?" Verbalizing his only choices made the decision. Wolf turned on the wipers and breathed in cadence with their rhythm, trying to calm his runaway heart. It didn't help. The dash clock glowed straight up 9:00 p.m. He had to do something. The storm itself offered the answer. *Accidents happen on a night like this.*

* * *

KC followed her father and the others out of the restaurant, into a blizzard. Minutes after Sam and Charlie disappeared in the Camaro, the valet appeared with her car. Just ahead of her, the taillights of Sally's cab and Gray's car vanished behind a curtain of snow. KC drove the short distance to her Georgetown apartment cautiously, still wrapped in the warmth of the evening. *They were so happy. Every child of wonderful parents should have a night like this.* For a moment, KC couldn't remember whether or not her father had given her his additional notes. "I must have drunk more than I thought," she said as she pulled into her driveway.

Light from her living room window glowed like a beacon in the swirling snow. Separated from the main house by a walled courtyard, the brick garage with her apartment above, with its ivy-draped walls and moss-covered roof stood in stark contrast to the concrete and steel chaos most government workers called home. Jesse and Rose, the estate's houseman and cook were like surrogate parents, bringing over chicken soup when she was sick and looking after Ivan when she went out of town. As she unlocked her door, KC glanced over at the main house, dark now, but a reminder that Thanksgiving was only five days away. Breakfast with Jesse and Rose on Thanksgiving had become a tradition.

Inside, she was surprised at how cold it was. She could see her breath despite the gas wall furnace going full blast. A fire in the stone fireplace would feel good, she thought, but it was midnight, too late. What she needed was sleep. KC hung up her coat and peered down the dark hallway. "Ivan," she called out over the noise of the hall furnace. She turned on the bedroom light but found no Russian Blue cat asleep on her bed. An uneasy feeling gripped her. *He always comes when I call.* The bedroom felt like a deep freeze. The TV was still on, the late-night host at his desk talking with someone.

The drapes over the French doors were closed. KC pulled them open, an accompanying rush of adrenaline extinguishing her languid mood. The deck had been shoveled clean, and there was a fresh carpet of snow unmarred by footprints. Someone had been in her apartment, and not very long ago. The intruder must have scared Ivan, who dashed out the French doors. Knowing the cat's absence would give notice, the thief left the French doors open while he tried to coax Ivan back in. It suddenly dawned that, with no stairs down from the deck, the intruder must have lowered himself to the ground. *Why would a thief go to that trouble?*

"Oh no!" KC dashed to her office, her briefcase exactly where she'd left it on the floor next to her desk. She knelt and opened it. Gone were the manila envelope with her father's notes, and the back-up CD. She looked around, but the room looked as orderly as she'd left it. She placed her hand on the computer–cool, but not ice-cold like the file cabinet. *I remember turning it off.* KC turned on her computer and shivered as it booted up. She scrolled through dozens of files and opened *Recipes,* the file she created for her father's notes—empty! A check of her hard drive told her someone had spent thirty minutes on her computer. She opened dozens more files; *Recipes* was the only one with nothing in it.

Pushed to the back of her mind by the festive evening, fear for her father swamped her like a rogue wave. Hands shaking, she dialed her parents' number. "Please, Dad, answer." Kathryn's sleepy voice greeted her after the third ring. "No, he's not home yet." The static on the line made it difficult to hear her mother. "He said he and Charlie had an errand to run." A pain shot through KC's temples. "Gray and Claudia brought me home. What time is it?"

"It's 12:23, did Dad say what errand, or where they were going?"

Kathryn now sounded awake. "No, I assumed they would be right home. I must have dozed off." Her voice filled with alarm. "That was over two hours ago. Where could they be?"

"I don't know, Mom. I'll call Dad's cell phone again. If he doesn't answer, I'll call Gray. Maybe Dad told him where they were going." Her mother said something that KC didn't catch. "What? I can't hear you."

"I said Gray and Claudia are here. The storm was so bad they decided to spend the night. I'll go wake Gray and have him call you."

"No, I want to try Dad's cell phone. I'll call back in a few minutes." She autodialed her father's cell. "Come on, Dad, answer!" When he didn't answer, and when a worried Gray said he had no inkling where or on what errand Sam had gone, KC's panic exploded full-force. She opened her address book to the Ds and dialed the first number on the page. The phone rang several times. Tony DeMarco answered, sounding as if he'd been roused from a deep sleep.

"Tony, this is KC. Can you hear me? I'm sorry to call at this hour, but I didn't know who else to turn to." Her words tumbled out. "I'm afraid something terrible has happened to my dad. Could I come over?" It suddenly dawned that he might not be alone in that king-sized bed with the soft down pillows.

"I can barely hear you. Sure, you can come, but it's dangerous out there. If you need me, I'll come to your place. Do you still live on Willow?"

If you need me? KC closed her eyes and tried to stop the images his words delivered. *Tony and KC, the perfect couple.* "Yes, on Willow. Thanks, I–" Her throat constricted, squeezing off the rest of her words. She replaced the receiver, briefly distracted by the thought that she may have just made a mistake calling Tony. They had a past, and he had no doubt gotten on with his life, but KC dismissed the thought. He was a top FBI agent with the expertise and resources to help her. She tried her father's phone again. No answer. Carrying her cell and periodically hitting redial, she slipped on jeans and a sweatshirt, and grabbed a hooded jacket. KC opened a can of cat food, found a flashlight, and felt her way down the slippery stairs. *Don't jump to conclusions. Dad and Charlie are probably sitting in a bar drinking, talking over old times. And Tony is happily married, just being nice to an old girlfriend.*

A search of the bushes around the apartment turned up no sign of Ivan. She opened the heavy wooden gate and crossed the courtyard to the main house, calling for Ivan as she sluffed through calf-high snow. She found the big cat curled up on a pile of canvas lounge cushions under the covered patio of the main house. His sleepy meow greeted her. "I should have known you would find someplace comfy." When she held out the can, Ivan jumped down, purring. With his tail straight up, he followed her footsteps in the snow, hot on the trail of his favorite food.

The cold cleared her head, and she tried to view the situation rationally. The missing envelope and disk meant not only that Sam was being followed, so was she. But a second CD was safe at her office, and her mother was probably going to call any minute to say that Sam and Charlie were home. *When Tony arrives I'll just apologize for getting him out in this storm.*

"Come on, Ivan. Someday, I'm going to look back on this as a bad scare to an otherwise great evening." Ivan dashed up the stairs and into the apartment ahead of her. Already warmer, the apartment's rustic architecture buoyed her spirits. The huge stone fireplace, the soaring ceiling and walls of diagonal cedar gave the feeling of a hunting lodge. The only change she had made was to convert a storage room off the kitchen into her office. KC could not imagine living anywhere else and, up to now, had never given a thought to needing a burglar alarm.

KC led Ivan to the kitchen, retrieved his special bowl, and dished up half the can. "I wish you could tell me who was here." While Ivan ate, she autodialed her father's cell again. Still no answer, so she called Kathryn again. Her mother answered on the first ring and, though broken by static, there was no mistaking the panic in her voice.

KC grabbed a penlight and screwdriver and went outside again. She located the telephone and main electrical box, covered by bushes at the back of the building. Clamping the penlight between her teeth, she pulled branches aside and checked the telephone box. Its cover was so loose she removed the screws with her fingers. There was snow inside but no listening device. She screwed the cover back tight as she heard a car pull up in front.

KC walked around the building in time to see Tony get out of a slick-looking sports car. He was dressed in black sweats, with an FBI baseball cap covering his tousled hair. "What are you doing out here?" he said.

"Checking to see if somebody bugged my phone. All I found was snow inside the box."

"What's going on? You piss somebody off because you wouldn't let him pollute?"

"I wish it were that. Someone broke into my apartment tonight. They stole some notes my dad gave me, and hung around long enough to delete a file from my computer. I'm thinking my apartment might be bugged."

"I can check that for you." Tony retrieved a duffel bag from his car.

"What happened to your Bronco?" KC said, immediately sorry she asked.

"It died," he said and led the way up the stairs. "I'll do a preliminary sweep. As I recall, this place isn't *that* big." Once inside, he put a forefinger to his lips, and she couldn't help but notice he wasn't wearing a wedding ring. Activating a device twice the size of a package of cigarettes, he ran it lightly along the lower wall around the perimeter of the room. When they came to the kitchen, she pointed at the coffee pot, and he nodded. While he finished checking the apartment, she brewed coffee, filled two cups, hers black and his with one sugar. She caught up with him in the hall, and he mouthed "almost done." A few minutes later, he entered the living room and took the mug from her outstretched hand. "No bugs." Tony took a sip from the steaming mug. "One sugar, no cream–good memory." He sat down on the couch, his expression puzzled. "Okay, talk to me."

"I'm terrified for my dad." KC wrapped her fingers around her cup. "I overheard two men talking outside my office last Wednesday night." She relayed the conversation.

"You couldn't identify them?"

"No. If I had, this probably wouldn't be happening." When Tony asked what she meant, she summarized Sam's investigation and the men's threat. "We celebrated Dad's nomination tonight at le Gaulois. All of a sudden, Dad and his friend, Charlie Dawson, left the party. Dad said they had an errand, but he never said a word to any of us. They're not home and he doesn't answer his cell. I believe the errand has something to do with his investigation."

"Come on, Tiger. It's possible he's been delayed by this storm."

Tiger. More memories. Referring to her passion for the law, Tony had nicknamed her Tiger when they first met. "I hope to God you're right," KC said.

His voice turned professional. "Could you get me something to write on?"

KC retrieved a pen and legal pad from her office, then went to the kitchen and refilled their mugs. Tony was on the phone when she returned.

"Hi, D.C. Central. This is Special Agent Tony DeMarco, FBI." He gave his badge number. "I'd consider it a personal favor if you would put out an APB on this vehicle, license number….." He glanced at her and KC responded with a description of the Camaro and the personalized plates: *Blkhawk*. Tony repeated the information, gave his cell number, and then called the Alexandria police with the same request. He finished his coffee. "You always did make great coffee," he said as he scrolled through the call list on his cell. "I'm calling Joe Rogers, a buddy at the Bureau, our crime scene analyst. I'd like him to check your apartment for fingerprints. Or for anything that might identify who did this. Okay with you?" KC nodded, his remark about her coffee catching her off guard.

"Joe, I need you to do a crime-scene check for me. Yes, tonight." He rolled his eyes. "I know there's a storm. How do you think I got here? Yes, it's important or I wouldn't ask." He gave Joe the street address and directions. "Bring Jared with you, it'll be good experience." Tony listened, nodding. "Understood, buddy, I owe you."

—6—

S am drove back across the Potomac toward the Jefferson Hotel, his friend, Charlie, wanting to know what this errand was all about. "I'm meeting with an attorney about the IIM trust fund mess," Sam told him. "I'll do this as fast as I can. The weatherman called this a bad storm." He found a parking place and led the way through the Jefferson's entrance and U-shaped court to the bar. Dark-skinned and big enough to play center for any NFL team, Donyell Crawford was easy to spot. He rose as Sam and Charlie approached.

Sam extended his hand. "Sam Blackhawk. This is Charlie Dawson, from the Lake Ponsiteau tribe in Idaho. Thanks for agreeing to meet so late."

"Donyell Crawford, Mescalero Apache, from Albuquerque. I'm just sorry I couldn't make it to the conference. I appreciate you meeting me."

As soon as they were seated, a waitress approached and took their drink order. Sam glanced at the envelope in Crawford's lap. "Is that the evidence you were waiting for?"

Crawford nodded. "Proof that BIA breached its fiduciary duties, direct from the Office of Management and Budget, so it's got teeth. There's also a draft of the class action lawsuit. What's in this envelope represents two years of investigative work. The totality is damning. I'm glad to get all of it into your hands, just in case."

"In case of what?" Sam wanted to know.

"In case the guy that tailed me from the airport decides to do more than just follow. Our group heard about your investigation through the moccasin telegraph. Remember, Sam, there's no such thing as secrets in Indian country. Somebody is onto you and onto us. He tailed me to the Allen Lee Hotel near the White House, but I lost him and took the Metro here."

"Living in D.C., I forget about the moccasin telegraph—word of mouth—that's been around a lot longer than the Internet," Sam said. "Somebody tailing you ups the ante."

The cocktail waitress arrived with their drinks. Each man raised his glass. "Here's to you and the others in your group," Charlie said. "How did you guys get together in the first place?"

"We formed about two years ago with the idea to file a class action lawsuit. All of us are Indian and all lawyers. We work pro-bono and underground, not only to protect ourselves, but because this is so big nobody could do the investigative work and keep their practice going. My field is wills, trusts, and estates." Crawford looked disgusted. "In the private domain, trustees with BIA's record of incompetence would be doing time in Leavenworth. It is ludicrous."

"So we've scared our enemies," Sam said. "Is Secretary Beckman one of them?"

"No indication at this point, but she's named in the suit because it's still happening on her watch. Carson Marsh and Hayden Culpepper are definitely in on it, and the $45 million you found is just the tip of the iceberg. It's all in here." Crawford patted the envelope. "We're trying to fix a broken system, and our enemies have motive to stop anybody who gets in the way."

"So what is it you want me to do?" Sam asked.

"Call a press conference. You don't have to wait to be sworn in to do that. As President Champion's nominee, you have the authority. Demand an independent audit of all trust accounts. Provide full access to BIA's accounting records. The National Congress of American Indians and the Native American Rights Fund members are waiting to jump on the bandwagon. We're ready to rally a full-fledged assault to bring public pressure. Once this is out in the open, they can't touch us. We'll file the class action suit after your news conference."

Sam downed the last of his drink. "When do you want me to do this?"

"Monday, noon, on the steps of BIA. Our group is notifying the media. Everything you need is in this envelope—the legal wording, the exact records to ask for. I'll be at your side. I wouldn't miss this pony show for anything."

Sam shook Crawford's hand. "Thank you, and pass along my thanks to the others."

Crawford nodded. "See you Monday, noon." He reached into his coat pocket and withdrew a CD in a plastic case. "I almost forgot. Everything is on this. Call it insurance."

Sam glanced at his watch as he watched Crawford walk away. "Midnight, let's go home." He led the way to the lobby. "Hang on, Charlie." Sam approached the desk and asked the clerk if he had a CD mailer. "Yessir," the clerk said and placed a padded brown envelope on the counter. Sam addressed the mailer, slipped the CD inside, and sealed it. "Would you mail this for me? It's very important, so I need your word you will personally be responsible." He took a twenty from his wallet and handed it to the young man. "This should cover it."

"More than cover it, sir. My name is Doug. There's no mail pickup tomorrow, so I will put it in the safe tonight. And I give you my word I will personally put it in the mail Monday morning. Consider it done."

"My gut tells me insurance is a good idea," Sam said as they exited into the storm.

* * *

Jules Aubert's private cell rang, reaching sleepy depths, demanding consciousness. He fumbled for the lamp. "Yes," he answered, trying to focus on the clock, 4:00 a.m. Wolf's voice, he was across the street. Adrenaline delivered instant clarity. "I'll buzz you in." Aubert put on his robe and slippers, then switched on the gas fireplace on his way through the living room.

Five minutes later, Wolf tapped on the door. One look at his ghost-white face and Aubert went directly to the bar. "I'll get you a scotch." *He looks crazy!*

Wolf took off his damp coat, dropped it on the entry marble floor, and collapsed into a chair. He immediately covered his face with his hands. "My God, what have I done?" He mumbled, rocking back and forth.

"Drink this," Aubert handed Wolf the glass, hoping the liquor would halt his emotional slide. He drained the glass and handed it back to Aubert. "Forty years with the Bureau, I only killed one man. And that was because he was shooting at me." He stared absently at the fire. "I disabled the brakes on Blackhawk's car and pushed it into the Potomac. Tonight makes three."

Aubert started to say he didn't understand, but hesitated, afraid to question an unstable man on the edge. He refilled Wolf's glass; he grasped it with shaking hands. "There was a man in the car with Blackhawk. Whoever he was, he makes number three." The anguish in his voice matched Wolf's inconsolable demeanor. "I should've just shot Blackhawk. It would have been quicker. Even the Park Service deputy said, 'what a terrible way to die.'"

"U.S. Park Service?" Aubert repeated. Wolf was rambling, talking in disjointed sentences. Aubert *had* to ask. "I don't understand, what about the Park Service?"

"The Basin's their jurisdiction." Wolf downed his second drink and gritted his teeth as tears began to well. "I stole a tow truck off Sunset's lot and showed up at the scene a couple minutes after the deputy. I told him I just happened to be in the area and he bought it, I guess because he recognized the Sunset truck and probably because of the storm." Wolf shuddered as though trying to erase the memory.

"Get hold of yourself, Elliott. You saved Valerie. You've given her back the chance to be president." Aubert tried to keep his voice calm and reassuring, neither of which he felt.

Wolf struggled up from the chair. He removed two brown envelopes from his damp coat and dropped them on the glass coffee table. "I stole the dry one from Garrett's apartment. The wet one was lodged under the back seat of Blackhawk's car—the cops never saw it. The lawyer he met at the Jefferson must have given it to him. "

Aubert rose, ready to reassure Wolf, but his gaze stopped him. "I didn't do this for you, I did it for Mrs. B. That doesn't make it any easier. I'm not sure I can live with myself." Wolf let himself out. The minute the door clicked shut Aubert headed for the bar and poured himself a double scotch. The mere thought of what the envelopes contained flooded him with panic.

He drained half the glass; he had to know. Aubert opened the wet envelope first and gingerly removed the damp pages, the top page the script for a news conference. *Monday, November 19, noon, front steps of BIA.* The last line took his breath away, until he remembered thanks to Wolf, Blackhawk couldn't call a news conference on Monday, or any other day.

Aubert finished the drink and poured himself another one, then carefully examined one damp page and then the next until he came to the class action lawsuit. He stared at the names, his panic returning full-force. *United States District Court for the District of Columbia. Margaret Red Hawk, et al, Plaintiffs, versus Valerie Beckman, Secretary of Interior, Hayden Culpepper, Chairman Senate Select Committee for Indian Affairs, Carson Marsh, former Manager Secretary of Bureau of Indian Affairs, Defendants.*

He dropped the papers as if they were hot. In legalese, they claimed dereliction of duty by the Department of Interior and negligent accounting of IIM funds, followed by lengthy list of plaintiff tribes. Turning to the last page, he wondered which Washington D.C. judge had, in effect, signed Valerie's political demise. But there was no judge's signature, no notary seal, only a blank line with the notation underneath: *signature of United States District Judge.*

"It's just a draft. It hasn't been filed!" Giddy with relief, Aubert's euphoria lasted only a millisecond. *When the Indian lawyer hears Blackhawk is dead, he'll call the news conference himself—and the police!* "What do I do?" Aubert kept repeating, his lament echoing in the quiet. He crossed the room to his leather chair in front of the floor-to-ceiling windows. "There has to be a way out of this," he said to the city's lights. This view, twenty floors up from the mundane world, had never failed to offer a new perspective or a creative solution to whatever problem he encountered. And up to now, he hadn't lost one round in D.C.'s game of political roulette.

Except this was different. It wasn't about winning a congressional or senate seat for a client, or landing a committee chairmanship through persuasion or connections. This was a shot at grabbing the gold ring. Every newspaper and opinion poll had named Valerie Beckman the frontrunner for the highest office in the land. "I won't get this opportunity again in my lifetime."

Aubert swiveled his chair and surveyed his condo, a tangible measure of just how far he had come. Four thousand square feet of architectural excellence filled with exquisite furniture and art at the best address in Silver Spring. By any standards, it proved he had conquered a city that chewed up the timid and spit out the righteous. All of it paid for with years of shaping, guiding, transforming ordinary men and women into distinguished congressmen and senators.

Except Valerie isn't ordinary. Never before had he come across a client like her, someone who possessed an almost magical combination of intelligence, looks, and charisma, and who had that indefinable something that draws people to them. "Never, until you." He pictured Valerie. "I can take you all the way to the White House." The full impact of his covenant sank in: the planning, the timing, the lucky breaks and sacrifices, the courage and unerring commitment required to win the ultimate office. Clarity flowed into his consciousness, slowly at first and then faster. Potential scenarios and problems paraded through his mind like chess moves; issues to avoid, opportunities to grab, obstacles to eliminate; barriers that could derail the train. *Like the Indian lawyer.*

Aubert jumped up, awareness expanding like ripples across still water. *The odds of somebody with my knowledge and experience connecting at the optimum moment with that one-of-a-kind candidate who inspires by simply being who they are—are a million to one. No—more like ten million to one.* Fate, destiny, karma. . . he couldn't define it, but whatever it was shimmered in front of him, too seductive and irresistible to ignore. Valerie had it. She was a walking, talking set of perfect attributes that came along once in a lifetime, a history-maker.

Aubert felt the decision in his gut before it crystallized in his consciousness, locking in place like a bullet entering the chamber. The Indian lawyer
from Albuquerque was an obstacle, every bit as serious as Blackhawk. "Can't
ask Wolf," he said as he went to his desk. He flipped through his business
cards to *Ventresca Security Service,* Nick Ventresca a former classmate at
Princeton, who he had used many times. In twenty years of political
consulting, security had grown to such an issue that Aubert & Associates had
made it part of their package.

Ventresca had gained entry to Princeton via a football scholarship, but
upon graduating was recruited by the CIA. And rumor had it that the reason
he chose to end his five-year tenure as a CIA operative, was he feared
discovery that he walked on both sides of law. After forming his own security
business, Ventresca proved to be astute about politics and politicians. He
acted as go-to guy for Aubert's clients who had to campaign in questionable
neighborhoods. Aubert left a message on Nick's pager and then paced as he
went over different ways how to broach the subject. *He has to take the job. If
not, all is lost.* Ventresca's call came twenty minutes later.

"Thank you for calling back so quickly, Nick, I have a problem, a very
serious problem that calls for professional handling. I'm hoping you are the
man who can take care of it." They chatted long enough and obliquely
enough to confirm that his request did not shock Ventresca. Nor did he ask
for a reason. In obscure language, Aubert learned that the going price of
obstacle removal that appeared to be, say a drug overdose, was $50K wired
to a Swiss account. If the removal needed to be done in the next twenty-four
hours, the price doubled, but considering their business relationship,
Ventresca agreed to the job without any upfront money.

"I can't tell you how much I appreciate this, Nick, but time is indeed
critical." Aubert gave him Donyell Crawford's name, the Jefferson Hotel's
address, and mentioned that Crawford would likely be checking out Tuesday
morning. "Let me know when the problem is resolved and we will meet.
Again, I appreciate it."

Aubert replaced the receiver and searched his feelings for warning signs. Remorse? Fear? Doubt? *Yes, some of each. More than I like.* Waver in commitment? *None.*

He rose and gazed in the direction of the White House. Though he couldn't see it from this distance, it didn't matter. Its vision held crystal clear in his mind.

—7—

KC sat in a straight back chair in the living room of her parents' home. She glanced at her watch for the fiftieth time; 3:00 a.m. and still no word. Breathing was difficult, her mind rocketing between knowing something unspeakable had happened, to envisioning sitting in the sun with her parents by a pool at an Arizona condo. Unable to focus, she wondered if this was what it was like to lose one's mind. The frantic hours since leaving the restaurant jumbled together with Friday's excitement in a collage of euphoria and catastrophe. After Joe did the crime check at her apartment, Tony drove them to her office. Her file cabinet was still locked and her office undisturbed, yet the two CDs and the computer file containing her father's notes were missing, just like at home. The date and time on her computer told her that fourteen hours after her father gave her the notes, someone took them. Who? Who spied on them having breakfast and saw him give her the envelope? Who knew where she worked, where she lived? Who was clever enough to find where she hid her father's notes in her computer? Who could be that good? Or as Tony said, who was that well-connected?

KC glanced at her mother and Sally, huddled side-by-side on the couch, gripping each other's hands. She wanted to say something reassuring, but chaotic thoughts immobilized her. It didn't matter now. Nothing mattered except seeing her father and Charlie. Gray, pacing around the perimeter of the room caught KC's attention. Every few minutes, he walked to the window to look out at the street. She wondered why she didn't hear his footsteps on the hardwood floor. Was he in his stocking feet? Claudia must have noticed his pacing too; she held up her hand in a silent plea for him to stop. Gray collapsed his six-foot, four-inch frame down into a chair, elbows on his knees, his head buried in his hands.

Tony moved around the room, touching a shoulder, kneeling beside Kathryn and Sally asking if they needed anything. He stopped by KC's chair and gave her hand a squeeze; she nodded a silent thanks and he moved on. She jumped when a cell phone rang piercing the silence. Tony walked into the foyer and answered; his voice was quiet and calm. "Special Agent DeMarco." He said nothing for what seemed like an eternity and then cleared his throat. "Thank you, Captain." KC watched him draw himself up, then walk back into the living room, visibly shaken. "The U.S. Park Service has found the Camaro. Captain Appling is on his way over."

KC awoke hours later, on the couch and still dressed in jeans and a sweatshirt. Bolting upright, it all came back—the waiting, the fear, their despair when Captain Appling broke the news. KC could not remember the hours after Appling left; they blurred into a fragmented collage of nightmare and reality. She listened for signs of her mother or Sally, but the house was silent. Sally was in one of the guestrooms upstairs, the Rossiters in the other. For a moment, KC wondered if Tony was asleep somewhere in the house then remembered she had given him the key to her apartment. He promised to go by and feed Ivan this morning and let him out if the storm was over.

Trying to get her bearings, KC got up and followed a bright shaft of sun to the large east window and squinted at huge mounds of snow. The storm must have set a record. Across the street, a neighbor busied himself digging out his buried car, his children with the beginnings of a good-sized snowman. Padding to the kitchen in her stocking feet, KC splashed cold water on her face at the sink. Her eyes felt swollen. "God, help me get through the rest of this day." The clock on the soffit above the sink signaled 11:30 a.m. *The Dawsons need to be notified. So does Takoda.* "First, caffeine." She found the filters and coffee beans and went through the ritual she had done a thousand times. *I don't remember, did I thank Tony?* KC stood watching coffee flow into the pot. *I should have married him. We would have two kids by now. Dad would love that.* She cut that thought off somewhere between her brain and heart, instead concentrating on how good the coffee smelled.

Behind her, the wall phone hung above her mother's built-in desk. Next to the phone, a bulletin board held club-meeting notices and lunch reminders, mostly her mother's. An elaborately printed invitation on White House stationery stood out: *You are cordially invited to join Jonathan and Lila Champion, Sunday, November 18 at 7:00 p.m., to help celebrate their fortieth anniversary. No gifts.*

"That's tonight." Tears sprang involuntarily. And try as she might, KC could not stop the yawning emptiness that swamped her. She grabbed the counter and hung on. *He's never coming back.* Deep breathing helped it subside. She poured herself a mug of coffee and sat down at the desk. Opening the address book, she noted that most of the entries were in Kathryn's flowing script, only a few in her father's bold print. She looked up Takoda Blackhawk and found home and work numbers. She tried the casino. "This is KC Garrett calling from Washington, D.C. Is Takoda Blackhawk in?" The operator checked; he was not in. KC asked for Santana Dawson.

"KC Garrett?" Santana answered, sounding amused. "Are you calling to find out if you're an aunt again? Takoda and Raylene are at the hospital. He's supposed to let me—"

"Hospital? Raylene and Takoda are having a baby?" More tears. The White House invitation swam eye-level in front of her.

"KC, are you okay?" Santana's voice no longer sounded amused.

"No. Give me a second. I'll call you back."

She threw on a jacket and slipped out the back door, cell phone in hand. Looking skyward, she whispered, "How in the world do I tell him something so awful." When no idea came, she resolutely called the casino and concentrated on how good the sun felt on her face. Her mother's rhododendrons, white mounds of varying sizes, encircled the brick patio, reminding her of snowmen parts waiting to be assembled. The bare limbs and crevices of the old maple that had shaded so many summer parties were filled with snow. This scene hadn't changed since she was old enough to remember. But it wasn't the same. Nothing would ever be the same.

KC fought for control when Santana answered. "I'm afraid I have terrible news, Santana." She could not hold back a sob. "This is so hard. I don't know where to begin."

"My God, what is it?"

"We had a terrible storm last night. Dad and Charlie were on the way home from our celebration party. At the height of the storm, Dad's car went in the river." Tears flowed unchecked and, for a moment, she couldn't speak. "They didn't get out," she forced out the words, her throat so constricted it hurt to speak. A long silence followed. "The police are saying the storm caused the accident, but I don't think so."

"I don't understand. If it wasn't the storm, what do you th—"

"It wasn't an accident, Santana. It was murder."

* * *

KC paced the length of the main floor at National Ronald Reagan Airport, afraid that if she sat down, she would fall asleep. Dark outside, the windows mirrored a reflection she barely recognized, a gaunt face devoid of makeup, hair last combed she couldn't remember when, maybe this morning. Dressed in jeans and a faded Disney World sweatshirt, she didn't know what feeling to fight, fear or fatigue.

She didn't try to fight the overwhelming sorrow that shadowed her. Breaking the news to Santana and her brother had only intensified it. Surprised by her call, Takoda assumed she was calling about the new baby. She listened to his news, and then before she lost her nerve, she told him. His sobs undid her resolve; she wept with him. When they gained composure, he asked about their mother. "She's surprisingly calm," KC answered.

A long silence followed. "Bring Dad home, okay?" Takoda said. "He loved the reservation. It's where he would want to be buried." KC assured him she would, and asked if he could take care of funeral arrangements. Takoda agreed, then as she started to hang up, the words just slipped out. "I love you," KC said to the brother she thought had forgotten her. His "I love you, too," brought new tears.

KC pushed the memory of the call aside and scanned faces, looking for anyone that might be following her. She wondered if the businessman playing solitaire on his laptop had broken into her apartment. She studied the burly, bald man waiting in line to check his luggage at the United counter, then scowled at the graying Hispanic priest who glanced at her as he walked past. *I'm losing it,* she thought. A loud speaker announced United flight 2312 had been delayed twenty minutes due to heavy holiday traffic. *Holiday—that's right, Thanksgiving.* Her mother had scheduled the funeral for tomorrow, the Tuesday before Thanksgiving so people coming from out of town could get back home to be with their family by Thursday. KC paced to the end of the concourse then turned around and started back, aware of a mounting dread. *Santana will be here any minute.* She cringed at the thought. Would he blame Sam or the BIA? He would surely want to blame somebody, or was she projecting her own feelings? Santana had briefly broken down on the phone, then said it was very important to him to accompany his father's body home.

Just outside United's security area, KC watched as the crowd surged forward; the flight had arrived. She held back, peering over and around expectant relatives and friends. A dozen passengers exited through the security gate before Santana emerged and glanced around. He looked nothing like his short, stocky father. Short black hair framed a handsome face, his high cheekbones a mark of his Lake Ponsiteau heritage. Six feet tall and slender, he was dressed in jeans and cowboy boots, and a tan sport coat adorned with geometric Indian designs on the shoulders. Women were staring at him admiringly. Santana Dawson could be the poster model for Mr. Native America. KC approached and held out her hand. "You must be Santana."

"I am," he said with a slight smile. He shook her hand. "Thank you for picking me up. How are you doing?"

"It varies from moment to moment," she answered truthfully.

He glanced at her Disney World sweatshirt. "You don't look much older than you did when you visited the reservation. What were you then, fourteen or fifteen? I remember we played basketball and you beat me pretty bad." Another slight smile. Santana glanced toward the exits. "Would it be possible to see my father tonight?"

"Of course." KC led the way out of the airport, her thoughts too erratic to make conversation. *What is today? Monday. We should be watching the football game. Did I tell Tyler not to bring pizza? I don't remember.* KC glanced over her shoulder; Santana appeared lost in his own thoughts. She phoned the mortuary on the way. A night clerk unlocked the door and escorted them to a small chapel, in a kind voice telling them they could stay as long as they wished. Dimly lit, eerily quiet, and filled with so many flowers their overpowering fragrance made it hard to breathe. Straight in front of them two bronze caskets sat side-by-side in front of an altar table.

"I'm not sure I can do this," she whispered, fighting to keep from hyperventilating.

"Hold on, I have something that may help." Santana set down his suitcase and withdrew a long thin box. "Sacred eagle feathers," Santana said. Puzzled, KC stood aside as he placed one of the feathers on Charlie's chest. Covering it with his hand, Santana leaned forward and spoke to his father in Salish, softly, in words KC did not understand. When he finished, Santana kissed his father's forehead and straightened up, tears glistening in his eyes. He looked stricken, but calm and in control, not at all like she felt.

Tears flowed unchecked down KC's face, her breathing erratic. "Here." Santana handed her a feather and nodded at Sam's casket. "To assure your father will have a safe journey and a good life." He guided her hand and placed the feather on Sam's chest. "Would you like to say goodbye and wish your father a good journey? Maybe you will feel better."

Say goodbye? I'm not ready to say goodbye. KC desperately wanted to tell him that, but his stricken look stopped her. Santana turned away to afford her privacy. Her hand still on the eagle feather, KC tried haltingly to say goodbye but words wouldn't come. She wiped her wet face with the sleeve of her sweatshirt and tried again. "This is so hard. I love you, Dad. I am proud to be your daughter and I will always remember the things you taught me." She wiped her face again. "I do wish you a safe journey and a good life." She pressed her lips to his forehead and started to straighten up, then remembered something. She leaned close again. "I know what happened wasn't an accident. No matter what it takes or how long, I will find whoever did this to you and Charlie and I will make them pay. That's a promise." KC straightened up and glanced at Santana. "You're right. I feel better."

Tuesday morning, clouds hovered over the city and a steady rain began to dissolve the great mounds of snow. When KC arrived at her parents' house, she found Santana in the kitchen making coffee. "The sun *has* to come out today if I am to get through this day," she told him.

Santana handed her a mug of coffee. "I'll see what I can do." He sounded serious.

At half-past noon, their limousine pulled up to the Church of the Sacred Heart near the Meridian Hill district of D.C. Santana alighted and offered his hand to Kathryn and Sally. KC followed, exiting into dazzling sunshine. She shot a questioning glance at Santana. He responded by mouthing a silent *you're welcome.* The sun flooded the courtyard, glistening off moisture-laden shrubs in a kaleidoscope of color. Taking note of every detail as they entered the church, KC promised herself to remember everything she could about this day, a last tribute to her father.

His casket, draped with a flag and adorned with white roses, sat on a stand at the front of the church. Someone had placed Sam's Army dress cap on top.

Following a ceremony by the Bishop, Gray Rossiter gave a moving eulogy, saying that he spoke as Sam's friend and on behalf of the Blackhawk family. He ended his tribute by saying, "Sam Blackhawk was a patriot. He left a legacy of honor and service that will never be forgotten." Secretary Beckman spoke next, lauding Sam's accomplishments over his lengthy career and expressing grief over the loss of a great American. She concluded her remarks by pledging to keep Sam's dream alive at BIA. Valerie then introduced President Champion. KC couldn't help but notice that he looked older; not nearly as dynamic as he did on Friday.

Genuinely saddened, it showed in his eyes and the timbre of his voice. He spoke briefly of their time in Vietnam and their long friendship. "Sam was brave when courage was called for and kind when compassion was needed. His family has lost a husband and father. Native Americans have lost a brother, a leader, and an advocate. We have all lost a good and valued friend." KC sat straight, eyes glistening but shedding no tears. When the President glanced at her at the end of his eulogy, she mouthed "thank you."

As everyone rose to leave, President Champion and his wife approached, the President insisting they use a State Department plane to take Sam's body home to Idaho. After the funeral, more than a hundred mourners signed the guest book at Gray and Claudia Rossiter's stately home in Langley, Virginia. Nearing the end of the reception, Agnes Richardson caught KC's attention. "I'm sorry to interrupt, but I need to speak to you in private."

Puzzled, KC led her into Gray's study and closed the door. Agnes removed a brown envelope from her purse. "This arrived in the morning's mail. The printing looks like your father's." KC stared open-mouthed at her name and address in her father's bold print. Postmarked Monday, November 19, the return address had been stamped: *Jefferson Hotel, 1200 16th Street NW.* "Mailed yesterday? How? Why would he—" She stopped mid-sentence, her worst fear tumbling out. "Oh God, did he mail this because he suspected he was going to die?"

Agnes touched her arm. "What are you talking about? KC, you're white as a sheet."

KC clutched the envelope to her chest. "I can't explain right now, Agnes. I'm sorry."

Agnes looked confused but resigned. "Okay, just know I'll take care of your calendar." Agnes opened her arms and the two embraced. "I am so worried about you."

KC stepped back, still holding onto her hands. "Listen to me, Agnes. Pay attention to strangers. Don't let anyone, delivery people, carpet cleaners, telephone or computer repairmen, in our office to fix anything. Don't give out information on where I am or when I'll be back. Leave at five o'clock with everyone else. I know I sound crazy, but I'm not." Promising to explain when she returned, KC put the envelope in her pocket and the two exited the study. She slipped on her coat, thanked Gray and Claudia, and said goodbye to the few remaining guests. Tony kissed her cheek and asked her to call when she reached Idaho. KC nodded. "You're probably in danger now, too, Tony. Promise me you'll be careful."

* * *

Pressed back against the leather chair, KC felt the Gulfstream V's power lift them off the runway of Andrews Air Force Base. She caught a glimpse of the

White House off to the right before clouds obscured the view, but not quickly enough to miss a view of the Potomac. KC glanced at her mother, hoping she didn't see it. *The city looks beautiful from up here, but it isn't. It is too cruel to be beautiful.* KC turned away from the window. Santana sat across the plane's salon looking sad and lost, exactly like she felt. She knew nothing about him except that he had been in the army and now helped his father manage the casino. As soon as the G-V leveled off, a steward delivered a tray of juice, coffee, and sweet rolls then discreetly disappeared. Kathryn begged off and stretched out on one of the couches. KC spread a blanket over her and returned to her chair, the CD still safely in her pocket. She closed her eyes and pictured her father and his friend, Charlie, on their journey, guided by the sacred Eagle's spirit. KC dozed off, experiencing a feeling of calm.

When air turbulence awakened her, she glanced over at Santana, an untouched glass of juice and a half-eaten roll in front of him. Nice guy, she thought, but difficult to figure out. Santana must have felt her stare. He nodded at the chair across from him. KC joined him. "A kind gesture by the president," he said, indicating the plane. "He really meant it when he called your dad a valued friend." Santana leaned forward, arms folded on the table between them. "We haven't had a chance to talk." He spoke quietly with a side glance at Kathryn. "Have any idea who would want Sam dead, or why?"

"I don't know who, but I have an idea why." She told him about Sam's investigation into the IIM funds, and the two men's conversation she overheard. "I'm sure they're involved. When Dad and I had breakfast last Thursday, he told me about a group of Indian attorneys in New Mexico. They were about to file a class action lawsuit against the Department of Interior, which could bring all this to light." KC produced the envelope with the CD. "This arrived at my office yesterday. The Jefferson Hotel must have been the errand Dad and Charlie had Saturday night."

"Your brother is our computer expert. He'll be able to tell us what's on the CD," Santana said. "By the way, I notice you're now using your brother's Indian name rather than Brendan. If you don't mind my asking, how and when did that happen?" Involuntary tears filled KC's eyes. Santana reached for her hand. "I'm sorry, the last thing I want to do is upset you."

"Fair question—complicated answer. Brendan is a Garrett family name that my mom wanted. Dad said fine, but *he* wanted his son, and later me, to have an Indian name. Takoda means *friend to everyone.* Kaya means *beautiful bird.* I grew up calling my brother Brendan until Dad finally told me that he changed to Takoda when he moved to the reservation. It shows just how far we've drifted apart. I'm ashamed I allowed that to happen."

"Don't take all the blame. That's a two-way street."

"I know, but it's just one more issue Takoda and I need to sort out. But first, I need to tell him the truth. All he knows is that Dad and Charlie died in an automobile accident. That night at the mortuary, I made a promise to my dad, but I meant it for your dad, too, Santana. I will find out who did this and I will make them pay."

Santana nodded. "You can count me in on that promise. There is no place on this earth they can hide."

K C exited the Gulfstream onto the tarmac at the Sherman Falls airport. She paused on the top step and glanced at the brother she hadn't seen in how many years? A younger, heavier version of their father, he waited at the bottom of the stairs. Any DNA Takoda received from the Garrett side of the family had gotten lost. He gathered their mother in his arms, making no effort to hide his tears from her or from Santana when the two of them embraced.

The name Takoda fits. Her brother looked up at her and smiled. "Takoda!" she said, and descended the stairs. To her relief, he greeted her with a warm embrace. His greeting was interrupted only when two Lincoln hearses pulled up near the State Department plane. The four of them stood watching as the caskets were transferred into the hearses. Takoda then directed KC, Kathryn, and Santana to a limousine, its Idaho license plate *Casino* 1. He drove, leading the three-vehicle motorcade east into Idaho and the reservation.

The Lake Ponsiteau Catholic church was old and inviting, its stained glass windows reflecting the bright sun's rays into a rainbow of colors. Stoic faces turned her way as KC followed her mother up the central aisle to a front pew. To her left, a table of slender prayer candles glowed, their flames sending wisps of smoke spiraling upward. Santana waited until the Blackhawks were seated and then escorted his mother and members of the Dawson family to the front pew on the opposite side of the aisle. There were no empty seats; the overflow of mourners stood shoulder-to-shoulder along both walls of the church. The priest recited prayers in English, the same prayers spoken in the Washington service, followed by the congregation joining in more prayers in the Lake Ponsiteau language. KC listened intently to words that had no meaning yet they brought a sense of calm. She felt instinctively that the words had at one time comforted her father and Charlie. Stealing a side glance at her grandmother, she was surprised to see Angeni Blackhawk and Kathryn holding hands. Next to them, KC recognized Takoda's wife, Rayleen, who held their new baby, and beside her, their two boys.

After the service, the two families exchanged condolences. Santana bade KC goodbye promising to see her later at the casino. The two hearses departed in opposite directions, the Blackhawks to the family cemetery, a pristine site ringed by ancient pines and firs laden with snow. Sam's grave had been dug beside his father's. On the other side, KC saw headstones for Sam's grandfather, grandmother, and his great-grandparents. After the priest's prayer, she took her turn kneeling by the coffin and said her final goodbye, then rose and escaped to a promontory away from the knot of mourners surrounding her mother and grandmother.

She fought back tears, overwhelmed by sorrow, regret, and anger. Her father would have loved to hold his new granddaughter and play with his grandsons. His decades at BIA should have earned him the right to retire feeling that he had helped his people. At the funeral in D.C. friends and colleagues offered words that were intended to comfort, but the glaring truth was there were no words that could placate murder.

Awareness of her surroundings began to filter in, a panorama that caught KC off guard. A green-carpeted mountain range filled the horizon, dizzying in its vastness and majesty. Stretched along its base, the waters of Lake Ponsiteau glistened in the afternoon sun. Was it the beauty of this land that drew her father to the reservation, or the generations of Blackhawks whose history went back hundreds of years? Footsteps crunching on snow intruded into her consciousness. "Everybody went back to the church for the reception. They thought we might like to talk," Takoda said, his shoulders hunched against the cold. "Losing Dad is hard enough, but seeing you, I realize how much we've missed. How did we ever let that happen?"

"I have no idea, but I don't want it to stay that way. I am ashamed to admit I didn't know you started going by Takoda when you first moved here." She pulled her jacket tighter against the breeze. "It fits you, though. You are not the same brother I remember. Is it Rayleen and the kids? Is it this place? I need to know because right now, I am lost."

He nodded. "Maybe both, but you're right. I'm not the angry guy who left D.C. I'd like to think it's because I finally discovered who I am and where I fit into all this." He gestured at the vista, the sincerity and force of his admission taking her by surprise.

"Wow, Takoda, if you've figured *that* out, please tell me," KC said.

His exhale floated upward in the frigid air. "The summer I spent here after I graduated from high school is when everything came together for me. I realized this was where I was meant to live, and I still feel that way. If I could make a hundred times more money somewhere else, I wouldn't leave. I am as much connected to this land as those trees." He indicated the pines. "You don't leave *this* for money or because some place else is warmer in the winter so you can play golf, or the restaurants and shopping are better. The *home* I'm talking about is in here." He tapped his chest. "It's waking every morning with a feeling of peace. It's teaching your children to fish in waters your father and grandfather and generations before them fished. It was their home, and now it's mine. It is a gift." KC closed her eyes and listened to his voice, so much like their father's. "When you understand that, Kaya, you cannot help being changed. Being Indian means more than just not being white. It is feeling a connection to the land, to each other, and to Spirit. Does any of this make sense? Because it is important to me that it does."

KC nodded, suddenly realizing she was holding her breath as fragments of conversations with her father flashed, talks begun that took a turn and somehow were never finished. Breakfast and lunch hours filled with banter about news of the day, office cases, and karate routines. Nothing memorable, nothing she could hang onto now. *How many times did Dad want to share all this with me?* Eyes closed, she pictured him shaking his head and smiling skyward as if pleading for Divine intervention for her to understand. Opportunities lost, special moments she could have had with her father that she would never have. "How disappointed Dad must have been that I showed no interest in the very essence that defined him."

Takoda put his arm around her. "Dad was proud of you and what you do. He called about a week ago and said that after the baby came he was going to ask you to come with him and Mom to see the family and the changes in the reservation. You brought him home, Kaya. You're here now, that's what counts. Let's go be with our family."

The following morning, her brother had a pot of coffee waiting. Noting how light it was outside, KC asked, "What time is it?"

"Ten. I'm amazed you slept through Rayleen getting the kids up and dressed. She and Mom took them to a Thanksgiving program."

"That's right, today is Thanksgiving." KC poured herself a cup of coffee, dreading to tell him the truth. She sat down and faced Takoda, knees to knees, and then told him about the men she overheard, and why she believed their father was murdered. A parade of pain and disbelief crossed his face, followed by tears. "I don't understand why *anybody* would want him dead." They remained sitting together until both regained composure, and then KC told him about the CD and asked if they could meet Santana at the casino to find out what was on it. Takoda was in the car with the motor running by the time she retrieved her purse and grabbed her jacket. He called Santana on his cell and told him they were on their way. Fifteen minutes later, they pulled up in front of the Crystal Waters Casino.

Donald Trump's Taj Mahal was the last casino KC had been in, and that was years ago on a brief vacation to Atlantic City. Upon entering Crystal Waters Casino, it occurred to her that if the Taj Mahal represented the Rolls Royce of gaming establishments, this one in the mountains of Idaho represented a top-of-the-line Cadillac. The foyer was a mammoth half-circle of black marble with an impressive inlay of a shield and feathered spear, the tribe's logo. From the foyer, she looked over a sea of showy slot machines grouped into segregated sections. The ceiling of dark mirrors reflected colorful, dazzling lights from the hundreds of slots. Above each section, a revolving neon sign displayed its name; one read *Dreamcatcher,* another *Megamoney.* As she followed her brother through the casino, KC counted at least six more sections.

Takoda went directly to his desk. "Give me a minute."

Santana motioned for KC to follow him across the hall. "Dad's office," he said, turning on the computer. "On the way to the airport, Dad mentioned a problem with Camas Mine's income. He said he was going to talk to Sam about it then we got off on another subject and forgot about it." Santana handed KC a folder. "The last BIA statement on the mine is on top."

KC looked over the September 30 statement. The two month old figures showed the tonnage crushed, the ounces of silver produced, and the tribe's royalty for the ore extracted. Charlie's orange post-it read: *no variation in tonnage last six years*. The signature at the bottom of the report: Victor Ludlow, Operations Officer, Bureau of Indian Affairs.

"Victor Ludlow, that's the same name my dad wrote in his notes," KC said.

"You'll want to see this," Takoda called out. KC and Santana crossed the hall and stood behind him. Names and dates appeared on the monitor. KC recognized the name Donyell Crawford, the Apache attorney working on the class action lawsuit. Takoda scrolled through pages of information and stopped on the first page of the lawsuit. *Margaret Red Hawk et al, Plaintiffs, vs Valerie Beckman, Secretary of Interior, Carson Marsh, Manager Secretary of the Bureau of Indian Affairs, Retired, and Senator Hayden Culpepper, Chairman of Senate Select Committee of Indian Affairs, Defendants."* On the last page of the document was a brief, chilling paragraph: *Sam Blackhawk to call a news conference, Monday, November 19 at noon on the steps at BIA to announce a full investigation and audit of IIM trust accounts.* "Somebody didn't want him to hold that news conference," Takoda said, his voice breaking.

KC pressed her check to his. "Read me Crawford's phone number. Maybe he can help us." KC dialed the New Mexico number and listened to a recorded message that the office would be closed for Thanksgiving until the following Tuesday. "I keep forgetting this is Thanksgiving." KC made herself a note to call again when she returned home.

Takoda rose. "It's 12:30. I hate to quit on this but I promised that we'd be at Rayleen's folks at 1:00 for Thanksgiving dinner. But first, I want to show you some of the rez." KC told Santana goodbye along with a promise to keep in touch, and then followed her brother out of the casino. On the drive to his in-laws, Takoda pointed out the tribe's medical clinic and new wellness center, which he said had weight rooms and an Olympic-sized lap pool. He seemed most proud of the tribe's school. "Great teachers and curriculum. We have a computer lab with the Lake Ponsiteau language program on every machine. It used to be that only a few tribal elders, like grandmother, spoke our language. Now kids are speaking it, and we even have a choir that sings in Lake Ponsiteau."

Takoda said there was one other place he wanted her to see. They pulled up before a massive log structure adorned with Indian art and figures. When they got out of the car, KC could see acres of a lush green golf course stretching into the distance, snow blanketing parts of it. "Howling Wolf Golf Course was Santana's doing from idea to completion. It's rated in the top one hundred golf courses in the country. Big-name golfers fly up here to play." The look on her brother's face spoke volumes about how he felt about the reservation.

At Rayleen's parents' house, KC sat next to her mother at the Thanksgiving table. Surrounded by a half-dozen curious youngsters vying for her attention, KC's grief temporarily disappeared as the feeling of family began to take hold. At the end of the dinner when Takoda rose to leave for work at the casino, he whispered to KC that she was expected to pay a call on their grandmother to show her respect. Rayleen wouldn't let her help with the dishes, but did offer her car and give KC directions to Angeni Blackhawk's house. KC located the house on a gravel street in a neighborhood of small HUD homes on the reservation.

Angeni lived alone, widowed ten years ago. She led KC to the kitchen and motioned for her to sit at the chrome-legged table with a blue Formica top. "It has been a long time."

"Yes, too long. I am sorry about that, Grandmother."

"Your brother calls me Ya-Ya. You can, too, if you wish." She asked about the funeral service in Washington, and her expression revealed surprise when KC told her that President and Mrs. Champion had attended. Silver wisps of hair loosened from a long single braid framed her sun-browned face.

Thin straight lips turned up abruptly at the corners where they encountered deep creases that became even deeper when she smiled. KC remembered her father saying that Angeni's passions were preserving the Lake Ponsiteau language and the health of Mother Earth.

KC learned Ageni spent three days a week teaching language at the tribe's school. "I teach the children by telling them stories. At first I had to tell them in Lake Ponsiteau and then in English, but not anymore. They do not speak English in class now." Angeni spoke softly, her words unhurried, almost rhythmic. On alternate days from teaching, if the weather kept her from gardening, she told KC she drove to the casino and played bingo with her friends.

Angeni went to the refrigerator and returned with a bottle of grape soda. She filled two glasses and handed one to KC. "You need at least one vice." An impish smile activated her wrinkles as she raised her glass in a toast in Lake Ponsiteau. "You do not speak our language?"

"I don't, Ya-ya. Dad never spoke it at home and I never studied it."

"It seems you have lost your connection with your tribe, Kaya. It is easy to do, living only in the white man's world." The comment was said softly with no hint of malice, but in it, KC detected her grandmother's regret over their years of separation.

"I am beginning to understand why Dad loved this place so much. And I see what I've missed." Angeni covered KC's hand with hers. "I see it saddens you."

"What saddens me most is how much Dad wanted to share all this with me, and I was too busy with my job to listen. I can't put into words how much I regret that."

"Kaya, you should know, your father spoke of you with such pride. He told me more than once that Mother Earth needs more people like you." KC took a swallow of grape soda and tried not to grimace. "It takes time to acquire a taste for finer things." Ageni chuckled. "I try to make you smile. We have cried many tears. Your father was a special man and so was Charlie."

"Tell me, grandmother, what it is like to live here." KC sat back and listened as Angeni spoke about life on the reservation, good times and bad, and how she and Sam's father wept when he returned from Vietnam and decided to live in Washington. "We were proud, but we missed him." KC paid close attention, fully aware just how precious this time was with Angeni.

Her voice, aged by time and tempered by wisdom, mirrored humor and sadness in the same rich timbre and cadence that KC recognized as distinctly Lake Ponsiteau. She loved to talk about the tribe's history, how before the white man came, the Lake Ponsiteaus were free to roam over four million acres in the northwest, with no boundaries to speak of.

Angeni withdrew a rawhide pouch from her pocket and handed it to KC. "This holds corn, blessed by a friend of mine, a very spiritual man. You could call him a medicine man. If there comes a time, Kaya, when you search for something or someone, offer a few kernels as a gift to Mother Earth so Spirit will help you. Some of our people use tobacco, others use knick-knick leaves. I thought you would like corn best. We introduced it to the white man, you know." A mischievous smile lifted the corners of her mouth.

Tears stung, blurring KC's vision of a grandmother who still cared for a granddaughter who had made no effort to know her or be a part of the family. Angeni rose. "Be careful, Kaya. I sense you are searching for something or someone. Stay vigilant. I am tired now, but I feel better that you will remember your family."

"Thank you for the wonderful gift, Ya-Ya, and I give you my word I will remember."

—9—

Tony DeMarco spent the Friday after Thanksgiving catching up on paperwork at his office. A few other agents on his floor showed up, but they were gone by mid-afternoon. At five o'clock, Tony rose and stretched, noting his clean desk with satisfaction. Thirteen years with the FBI had earned him a small office, but it was private, which signified a degree of seniority. He made a pot of coffee before he tackled his next project, this one for KC. No reason to hurry home; she was still in Idaho. She had called, as promised, to thank him, again. Seeing her, even under these terrible circumstances had brought back feelings he thought were gone. *If I get involved with her again, I'll be back where I started, fighting her attitude about mixing marriage and career.*

Tony retrieved the CD from his briefcase and inserted it in the computer tower. His FBI friend, Joe Rogers, had made it from the four surveillance cameras they installed at the Church of the Sacred Heart the day before Sam Blackhawk's funeral. "Great job," Tony mouthed as images began to appear on the monitor. An image of the priest reminded him of his lie, that in addition to any surveillance coverage the CIA may have requested, the FBI needed their own. Tony cringed at the thought of his mother finding out that her son had lied to a priest. And not just any priest, but *their* priest at *their* church.

Tony started with coverage from the two outside units, which recorded the first guests to arrive. Next came a cadre of Foster Grants, CIA agents, ushering in the President and Mrs. Champion and Secretary Valerie Beckman. A limousine delivered KC, her mother, Kathryn, Sally Calder, and Santana Dawson, son of the man who died in the car with Sam. Congressman

Gray Rossiter and his wife arrived shortly after, followed by a church full of mourners.

The high definition cameras provided crystal-clear images. Despite the church being packed, the fact that everyone was seated in neat rows made identifying them easy. By the fourth run-through, Tony had the guests memorized, but searched the footage one last time. Finding nothing suspicious, he fast-forwarded to outside coverage of the street during the service. A bent old woman with a scarf covering her head, walked by on the church side of the street; she crossed herself without glancing up. Across the street, a young woman pushing a baby stroller entered camera range, at the same time a man came into view from the opposite direction. The man walked past the woman with the stroller, then paused to light a cigarette.

Instinct made Tony freeze the picture on the suit-clad figure wearing aviator sunglasses. As he lit his cigarette, he cast a momentary look at the church, at first glance an ordinary guy enjoying a walk in the sun. But, again, instinct made Tony zoom in on him. "Elliott Wolf? What the hell were you doing there?" Wolf wasn't part of presidential security, and the Tuesday before Thanksgiving seemed a strange time for an FBI agent to be out for a leisurely stroll. Tony enlarged and sharpened the image, then pressed print.

Wolf's presence told Tony he could be onto something. Wolf was one of a few remaining old guard of agents whose careers began when J. Edgar Hoover was Director. Joining the Bureau toward the end of Hoover's reign, Wolf's membership in Hoover's elite inner circle was rumored to be because his father had been killed in the line of duty. The younger Wolf had a reputation, how much of it fact or fiction, Tony had never cared enough to inquire, until now. It took a few minutes to access personnel records and scroll through the Ws. "Here you are." Tony read from the screen. "Wolf, Elliott. Born April 18, 1950, Syracuse, New York. Dropped out of the University of Syracuse after two years to join the Bureau, September 15, 1970. Six-feet, one hundred ninety pounds, blue eyes, brown hair. Note: left-handed. No record of a marriage. Father: William Elliott Wolf, Special Agent, died July 17, 1966. Mother: teacher. One sister, address unknown. Basic stuff."

The scuttlebutt about him was far more interesting, such as Hoover taking Wolf under his wing, a surrogate father of sorts. Known as a virtual potentate feared by anyone in Washington with something to hide, J. Edgar was said to have used his young protégé to intimidate or punish any politician who opposed his reappointment when a new president assumed office. Another rumor had Wolf scaring the hell out of a powerful senator who had the audacity to call for Hoover's resignation. Wolf's reputation, built escapade by escapade as Hoover's go-to guy, abruptly ended in May 1972 when Hoover died. The only item of interest about him since was his designation of *agent-at-large,* by his friend and former fellow agent, Alonzo Volking, when Volking became FBI Director in the late eighties.

Tony's gut and brain simultaneously rejected Wolf's presence being a coincidence. KC's journal documenting the facts and timeline, pointed to someone powerful who considered Sam a threat needing to be eliminated. The visual of Elliott Wolf raised the hair on the back of Tony's neck. *Who felt threatened by Sam enough to have him killed?* Intuition told Tony whoever it was had to be pretty high on D.C.'s political food chain. *KC is hell-bent on finding Sam's killer. How long will it take for whoever killed Sam to consider her as much a threat as her father?*

Tony closed up his office and exited the building into a cold, blustery wind. He walked hurriedly toward the Metro, wondering when KC would be back from Idaho. She hadn't said in her one phone call or two brief text messages. He had no idea if KC realized how much danger she was in. Tony dismissed as premature any notion of their getting involved again. Instead, he concentrated on her reason for calling him in the first place—his help. He considered keeping KC safe to be his top priority, but safe from whom? That thought produced a whirl of theories on who might be responsible for Sam's death, all of them he nixed.

Tony DeMarco didn't need or want theories. He wanted what the FBI ingrained in every agent— incontrovertible proof.

* * *

KC and her mother caught a red-eye flight from Sherman Falls, Washington, and touched down in D.C. at 10:00 a.m., Sunday. Sally Calder picked them up and drove to KC's apartment. Following her up the stairs, Sally set down KC's suitcase. "Don't worry about your mom. I'll stay at the house as long as she needs me. But, I do need your help on something. Could you call me later this week? It's important."

"I will call, thanks, Sally." KC glanced at her watch. "Agnes Richardson is receiving her doctorate today. The hooding ceremony starts at 1:00 p.m. I can just make it." KC hugged her godmother and blew Kathryn a kiss. The minute she entered her apartment, Ivan bounded out from her office demanding attention and food. KC fed him, then quickly showered and dressed. She took a cab to the university and joined the crowd filing into George Washington University's Lisner Auditorium. KC was lucky to find an available seat in back of the orchestra section. Including friends and colleagues, she had attended a dozen hooding ceremonies. Knowing what to expect, KC vowed not to get impatient with the lengthy speeches, hundreds of presentations, and slow-moving ceremonies. This was a hugely important day for Agnes.

KC's first glimpse of her came when Agnes walked up the short flight of stairs to the stage. Smiling, looking very academic in her black robe and velvet cap, she shook hands with the Dean of George Washington's law school, then turned to face the audience. Agnes waited as two law school professors, one on each side, lifted a hood over her head and draped it around her shoulders. She was now officially a juris doctor in the field of law. Proud and excited for her friend, KC rose and applauded, it suddenly dawning just how much she would miss Agnes.

After the ceremony, KC, Agnes, and Danny found each other in the huge crowd via their cell phones. KC's temporary melancholy proved no match for Agnes' exuberance in the cab ride to the Four Seasons Hotel on Pennsylvania Avenue. KC had never seen Danny in anything but jeans or his karate Gi, and was surprised at how handsome and grown up he looked in a suit and tie. The maître d' seated them in an elegant booth that offered a view of the neoclassic restaurant.

Agnes' smile said it all. "Wow, what a day. And now this? This place is awesome!"

Danny lowered his giant menu, a sly smile lighting his face. "Now I get why you made me buy this suit, Mom. Cool, I fit right in." His comment elicited chuckles from KC and Agnes. A tuxedoed waiter took their orders and poured wine for KC and Agnes. When Danny ordered a Pepsi to go with his prime rib, KC grimaced, remembering Angeni's grape soda.

Their dinners arrived, served with a flourish. After her toast, KC asked, "What now, Ms. Richardson, Attorney-at-Law. Have you given any thought to what you want to do?"

"Attorney-at-Law, that sounds so good! No, I haven't. Not a clue, any suggestions?"

"Actually, I do," KC said. "I would be happy to talk to Tyler Jackson. He's always on the lookout for good attorneys. With your emphasis on environmental law, what if he hired you to work on the Arizona case with me?"

"I would love that!" Agnes' instant reply left no doubt about her sincerity. "I would like to stay where I am at least for a while." Her glance signaled she had a reason. "Did I tell you Danny's father wants him to come live with him?"

"No, you didn't," KC said. "But I thought Neil's wife didn't want–"

"She dumped him." Danny interjected. "Dad told me he came home a couple Fridays ago, and all her things were gone." He shrugged dismissively. "Man, this is awesome prime rib."

KC and Agnes shared a grateful glance that Danny seemed over being hurt by his father. "I didn't mention it," Agnes said, "because you had enough to deal with. I like the idea of staying long enough for Danny to decide what he wants to do. I could go through the boxes of evidentiary material and organize it. That way I'd be up to speed if Tyler decides to hire me."

"Could I help, Mom?" Danny asked. "I could input the information in the computer." So visible was his excitement over the possibility of a job, KC and Agnes couldn't help but agree. Their approval elevated even higher the mood of an already happy occasion. At the end of their four-course dinner, Danny declared, "my prime rib was as delicious as food can possibly get."

KC returned to her apartment, her pleasant mood diminishing at the sight of six days of newspapers stacked on the coffee table. Before she left for Idaho, she had refused to look at a *Washington Post*, not ready to face an article about her father's supposed accident. "It's not going to get any easier, Ivan." She plopped down in her favorite chair and began searching *The Post's* various sections.

She found the article on the front page of the Metro News section. *Newly Appointed BIA Secretary Dies in Storm-Related Accident.* The subtitle, *Blackhawk's Death Mourned by U.S. American Indians,* was an unexpected surprise. In the six columns of text, the reporter did not go into the details of how he died, but instead highlighted: *Sam Blackhawk's long and distinguished BIA career and his role as a leading advocate for American Indians from every tribe.* A picture in color above the fold showed President Champion shaking her father's hand. Tears came, accompanied by a now-familiar empty feeling. Unable to shake it, KC extracted the section and put it on her desk, then called Tony to tell him she was home. He sounded relieved and happy to hear from her. "I know you'll be swamped this week, but is there a chance we could get together?" The anticipation in his voice proved to be the perfect anecdote.

On the way to work Monday morning, KC caught glimpses of Christmas everywhere.

Office and shop windows sported painted frosty holiday scenes, and Salvation Army volunteers on street corners served to remind her that Christmas was less than a month away.

Agnes followed KC into her office with a stack of rescheduled cases, also reminding her of the court date on the Dunlap case, sixty days away. "By the way, your favorite polluter's attorney called. He wants an appointment 'to discuss a potential financial resolution rather than a protracted court battle, which my client would like to avoid.'" Agnes' imitation included a dramatic roll of her eyes and her best effort at a New York attorney imitation.

KC laughed. "He's getting nervous because I've been so quiet. Scott Dunlap is going to find out soon enough that he can't buy his way out of criminal charges. Remind me to give the District Attorney a call. I'd like his opinion on a couple of issues, but not this week, I'm buried."

Agnes nodded and made a note. "I called Tyler Jackson and asked his secretary to have the boxes of evidentiary material brought down. I've got Danny lined up to start next week helping me. He is jazzed about it and I don't want to rush. It's an opportunity for us to spend time together, so I'm actually in no hurry for you to talk to Tyler about a job for me."

Agnes stepped closer. "KC, I want to thank you, again, for everything. For hiring Danny and for the wonderful evening. The food, the wine, the Four Seasons, I haven't seen Danny that excited and happy in—actually I can't remember when. I don't know how else to tell you, except just say it. You've restored my son's pride. You are awesome."

KC stared after her, overcome with gratitude, and vowing never to lose the two of them. Agnes wasn't just a secretary or a good friend; she was family and so was Danny. KC dug into the work awaiting her. She first tried Donyell Crawford's New Mexico office again and heard the same message. KC made a note for the following day to try again. Approaching her work with renewed energy, she returned a stack of calls, confirmed the schedule of new dates on continued cases, and then finally tackled the Arizona mine case.

EPA's tiered set of proposals to reduce acid mine drainage had caused a backlash. The attorneys representing the mine called the proposals political blackmail and moved to have them dismissed. The lawyers representing the area's business interests said they would destroy their city. As the Department of Justice lead attorney, KC first had to prove the mine knowingly released toxic waste on nearby land and into rivers over an extended period of time. And second, she had to convince the federal judge that the corporation that owned the mine should share in the cost of cleanup, the price tag projected to be hundreds of millions. Two hours of reading the history, the various positions, and the timeline of the case, KC found it difficult to put down; it was the equivalent of a good mystery novel.

Nevertheless, the totally unrelated idea KC had thought up on the flight home simply refused to go away. Whether the risk was worth it, she had to decide. KC retrieved the BIA September 30 statement on Lake Ponsiteau's

Camas Mine and read it again, noting Victor Ludlow's signature. Six years of no change in the tonnage extracted, which directly affected the tribe's income, made Charlie Dawson suspect the statements were being altered. It seemed the only way to prove whether or not they were, was to go through with her idea. With any luck she might find out that Victor Ludlow was the mastermind behind the IIM thefts. The bigger prize would be if she discovered who ordered her father killed.

Decision made, she phoned her godmother at BIA. "Sally, I'm leaving right now, can you wait for me?" She changed into her all-black sweat suit, running shoes, and then put the tools she needed into a duffel bag: a flashlight, knit cap, latex gloves, and a penknife she had borrowed from Tony but didn't tell him why.

She walked the six blocks to BIA headquarters at Eighteenth and C Streets, mentally trying to justify what she was about to do. But she couldn't. *This qualifies me as certifiable.*

—10—

There were only a few people inside BIA headquarters when KC arrived, most of them gathering up their things to leave. She took the stairs to the second floor and found her godmother in her office on the telephone. KC sat down to wait, a smile forming at Sally's end of the conversation. Sally Calder's job, BIA Director of General Assistance Programs, was procuring money for special education and health programs for tribes. "Don't tell me it can't be done," Sally said. "These kids are hurting. Figure out a way to make it work and get back to me by the end of this week." She slammed down the phone. "Does anybody in this country actually help the people we're supposed to help?" Full-blood Navajo, her godmother was feisty, stubborn, and decisive.

Sally hugged KC and then, true to her nature, wasted no time on small talk. "I need your lawyer help. My Ogalala Sioux friend, Lily Deerhorn, has worked here for ten years in the accounting department. We went to mass together every Sunday and usually had brunch afterwards. Sometimes we'd go to the movies. We were good friends, at least I thought so. Two Sundays ago, I called her home and her cell, both of them no longer in service! I asked about her at work on Monday. The people in accounting said Lily had been transferred, but didn't know where or why. So this Sunday after Mass, I asked Father Hidalgo if he had heard from Lily. He said no, but he wouldn't look me in the eye, KC. Lily hasn't emailed or called and I'm worried." Sally handed her a card: *Fr. Isidro Hidalgo.* "Victor Ludlow was her boss. He's the one who would have transferred her. If Lily told Father Hidalgo in confession why or where Ludlow transferred her, could you force him to divulge it?"

"Maybe," KC said. "I will talk to him, hopefully this week. But what a coincidence your bringing up Victor Ludlow. He's one of the reasons I'm here. Before we get to him, though, I have something for you." KC handed Sally a check. "From Dad's Will, he left you ten thousand dollars with a proviso that you use it to take a trip. Go to Paris, Rome, or someplace you've always wanted to go. Dad's statement was that you work too hard and care too much."

"Oh, KC, how I miss Samuel. We were going to accomplish such great things here." Sally brushed away tears. "What a loving thing for him to do." She managed a smile. "But wouldn't you know your father would get the last word."

"Now, about Victor Ludlow," KC squared her shoulders. "You need to know this, but it's going to be a shock." She told Sally how she suspected Ludlow was altering mine reports and stealing IIM funds, sending them out of the country. "Unfortunately, that's not all of it." KC summarized the conversation she overheard outside her office and then told her godmother she believed Sam's death was not an accident. "Whoever killed Dad made it look like an accident. Charlie Dawson just happened to be in the wrong place at the wrong time."

"Dear God, this is too horrible to comprehend. You think Victor is involved?"

KC nodded. "Too many clues point to him, but I need proof. He may even know who had Dad killed. I'm not going to quit until I find who did it. Will you help me?"

Sally took note of KC's all-black outfit. "You intend to break into Victor's office!"

"I have to, and I'm wasting time. I need to know where his office is, if there are surveillance cameras, and whether or not it takes a code or key to get out of the building." Sally simply closed her eyes and made the sign of the cross.

"His office is one floor up, the southwest corner of the building." Sally added that half of the building lights automatically turned off at 7:00 p.m., and the exit doors opened from the inside, no code or key needed. "The janitors start on the sixth floor and work their way down. I will pray for you. Call me when— "

"I will," KC said and gave her godmother a hug. She exited into the hallway. At the stairwell, she opened the door and listened for voices. Hearing none, she made her way up to the third floor. It was deserted; no one was working late on this Monday night. KC found the women's restroom and slipped into a stall to wait. She tried to think about the Redskins' Monday night game, think about anything other than she was risking her career and could end up in jail.

As Sally predicted, at 7:00 p.m. sharp, half of the lights in the restroom went off. "Now or never," KC whispered. She slipped Tony's penknife into her pocket and pulled on latex gloves. A peek into the hallway confirmed there were no cameras. Private offices ringed three sides of the third floor, with cubicles in the center for secretaries, clerks, and extra staff.

KC located Ludlow's office and put her ear to the door. No sound from inside. She fumbled with Tony's penknife in the lock; the thicker blade didn't work. The thinner blade slid right in. *Don't you dare break off.* The lock released with a click; KC said a silent *thank you* and entered. She relocked the door then glanced at the wall clock, 7:12 p.m. This was the suite's reception room, a secretary's desk occupying the center. The wall straight ahead had two doors, one opened to a storage room. The other door was locked. *Ludlow's private office.*

This time the penknife worked the first try. The room was pitch-black. KC locked the door behind her and shined her flashlight around the room. Photos and certificates covered the wall in back of Ludlow's desk and credenza. Two chairs faced the desk. Not a swanky office, but spacious. To her right was a seating area with a couch, two chairs, and a coffee table. I wonder who *he* entertains, she thought. Her flashlight came across a long row of steel file cabinets against the wall backing the reception room. *Alright!* According to the labels, nine western states were represented, Arizona, Utah, Wyoming, and Idaho each taking up two cabinets. Idaho was the one she was interested in. KC located the Camas Mine folders and removed the most recent one. The top report inside was the original September 30 statement Santana had shown her; the tonnage figure matched. *Of course, that would be too obvious.*

Not about to give up, KC began going through Camas Mine folders, noting the bottom figure on a page, the bottom figure on the next, and the next, until she had skimmed reports in two folders. In total, they represented the immediate six years of production, the years Ludlow was in charge. They verified the fact that the ore extracted had remained unchanged.

Impatient, KC skipped to the back of the drawer, to the two oldest Camas Mine files. The folder tabs indicated the reports covered from 1964, when the mine first came into production, to 1974, long before Ludlow took over. Using her method of noting only the total figure on the bottom of each report, KC was able to check five years of production, all five reporting annual increases from 3% to 7%. *I don't get it. Improved technology should have increased production, unless the silver is petering out. Or, Ludlow is altering the results. So now what?*

Frustrated, KC glanced at her watch: 7:48 p.m., thirty-six minutes since she entered Ludlow's office. *I can't quit yet.* KC bypassed a dozen folders and removed the one at the very back of the drawer. Her quick look-through method found nothing—until she reached the last report at the bottom of the folder. *What's this?* Feeling a bulge, KC peeked underneath the report. Taped to the folder was a cardboard envelope with a CD inside. "I knew it—I knew it!" She crossed to the desk and placed her duffel bag at her feet. A touch to the keyboard, and the screensaver appeared, sleek-looking yachts gliding through crystal blue waters.

Her heart beating faster, KC inserted the CD and stared wide-eyed as data from Camas Mine filled the screen. Each year created two to three pages, the top page of each year comprised the annual summary. KC fast-forwarded to the latest September 30 summary, the one she and Santana saw in Idaho. The ore figures should match exactly—they didn't! The tonnage on the screen was double. *He's skimming half! I knew it. Now, how do I prove it?* Scrambling for a solution, KC heard a click. *The suite door!* Her split-second response—poke the *off* button to the monitor. The screen went black.

"Just a sec, I left my briefcase in the office," it was a man's voice from the reception room. At her feet next to the duffel bag was Ludlow's leather briefcase. KC kicked her duffel bag farther under the desk, then grabbed the briefcase and put it on the chair in front of the desk. Hurrying across the room to the seating area, she crawled into the narrow space behind the couch. KC took a deep breath and froze at the sound of a key unlocking the door. *Please don't let him sit down at his desk.* "We need to talk, Victor, but I'm due at a fundraiser." *Valerie Beckman?* The ceiling light went on. "There it is in the chair," Ludlow said.

KC held stock-still as she heard the briefcase scrape the back of a chair as Ludlow retrieved it and then his footsteps retreating. The ceiling light went off. "I'll walk you to your car. We can talk on the way." She held on, refusing to exhale until she heard the suite door click shut. Feeling dizzy and clammy, KC backed out from behind the couch. Straightening up very slowly, she didn't know whether to laugh, throw up, or give thanks that her risk paid off. Victor Ludlow being involved was no surprise, but sadly, it looked like Valerie Beckman was too.

KC went back to the desk and turned the monitor on. Ejecting the Camas Mine CD, she deposited it in her duffel bag. From a box of new CDs in the credenza, she used one to replace the evidence CD underneath the bottom page. KC put the folder away and then shined her flashlight around the room to make sure she had left nothing to arouse Ludlow's suspicion. The minute she exited the building, KC checked her watch, 7:59 p.m. Forty seven heart-stopping minutes that could have landed *her* in jail, but instead were going put Victor Ludlow behind bars.

KC power-walked all the way to the Federal Triangle Metro station. When the car finally began to move and no one even glanced her way, KC's heartbeat finally slowed.

Ludlow was guilty of more than just altering ore figures. He was some-how involved with Mr. Southern accent, the second man she heard outside her office, the one who said there was only so much he could cover up. That statement meant he had political power; identifying him was critical. KC stared unseeing at lights racing by, mentally going over names and images of people who could help her. A circuitous mental route, but she arrived at the perfect person. Congressman Gray Rossiter knew everybody in the House and Senate, certainly the elite power crowd. He loved her father, Gray would help. KC's next thought: she would have to tell him the truth that his best friend was murdered.

KC called her mother's number as soon as she got home. Kathryn's answering machine came on. "Hi, Mom, hi Sally. Just calling to say hello and let you know that I had a very productive day. In fact, I accomplished way more than I expected."

At her office Tuesday morning, KC noticed her post-it on the December 3 page of her calendar. She called Donyell Crawford's number in New Mexico again, but the message hadn't changed. That's odd, she thought, and moved the post-it forward in her calendar a few days. Next, KC called Gray Rossiter's office to set up a date for lunch and then hurried to her appointment at the U.S. Attorney's office. A deposition related to the Scott Dunlap case, it surprisingly took an hour less than she had scheduled. KC left, figuring this would be her only opportunity this week to keep her promise to Sally. She called Saint Matthew Parish, and the secretary passed her through to Father Hidalgo. "Father, this is KC Garrett with the Department of Justice. Would it be possible for you to meet with me for a few minutes this morning? I would very much like to talk to you."

"Department of Justice? Why would the government wish to speak to me?"

"It's regarding Lily Deerhorn, a former member of your parish. I would just like to chat with you; however, I can subpoena you if you prefer." She disliked being heavy-handed, but if Sally was right and he knew something, she needed to find out. The priest reluctantly agreed to meet her in John Marshall Park, a ten-minute walk from St. Matthew's.

Low-hanging fog gave way to sun as KC approached the young priest. Even from a distance, Father Hidalgo appeared nervous and apprehensive. She thanked him for meeting her and suggested they sit on the bench. "I hope I did not give you a wrong impression," he said. "But, I do not wish to get in trouble with my church or with your government."

"There is no reason you should get in trouble with anyone, Father. All I want to know is if you have any information on Lily Deerhorn's whereabouts or why she left in such a hurry."

"I see." Hidalgo's anxious expression remained intact. "Would you be kind enough to tell me, under your laws, do I have the right not to answer?"

"You do unless you withhold information relevant to a murder, which I sincerely hope is not the case. Do you know why Lily left abruptly or if somebody threatened her? Did you speak with her before she left?"

"*Madre de Dios,*" he mumbled and crossed himself. "Yes, several times. Lily told me she had stumbled onto something at work and did not know what to do about it." KC asked if Lily had told him what it was. Hidalgo nodded, his expression resigned. "Lily's boss routinely gave her documents to shred but three weeks ago, she noticed that some of the papers did not look like the outdated reports and correspondence he usually gave her. These were statements with withdrawals, she said, from a master trust account. Lily was certain her boss did not mean to give them to her."

"What made her think that?" *Sally was right to be worried about her friend.*

"Because the day after he gave them to her, he kept asking if she had shredded *everything* he gave her. Lily assured him she did, but she didn't think he believed her. He began watching her, in Lily's words, 'with eyes as cold as death.' I begged her to go to the police. I offered to accompany her, but she ran out of my office. When she did not return to church for two Sundays, I looked up her address in our records and went to her apartment. Lily told me to go away, but I convinced her to let me in."

Hidalgo looked to be reliving the experience. "We talked of simple things at first, her life on the reservation, my growing up in Cuba. I finally asked about the papers, but Lily would only say that her boss was a very powerful man. She said many of her fellow employees are afraid. She called them *apples,* red on the outside, but white on the inside. They know things, but turn their head. If not they would lose their job."

KC could almost hear her father's lament about the ills of BIA. She shivered at how frightened Lily must have been. "Did you see her again?"

"Yes, at her last confession. I inquired again, but she said nothing." The priest withdrew an envelope from his black coat and slid it across the bench. "When we stepped outside the confessional, Lily handed this to me and said if something happened to her, to give these to the police." He rose. "I am new to this country and to my parish. Confession is sacred, but in my defense, Lily did not ask for absolution, and I did not administer it. In my mind, I did not break a sacred oath, but I do not know if Monsignor would see it that way. I should have spoken up. I pray that Lily is all right. If her boss has harmed her, God help his soul."

"Did Lily tell you his name?"

"*Si,* Victor Ludlow."

God help him anyway. He's going to need it.

KC walked back to her office, frightened for Lily Deerhorn. Ludlow and Mr. Southerner had threatened her father, then *somebody* killed him. Had they done the same thing to Lily?

Still thinking about Lily as she entered her suite, KC's mind was forced back to the present by the stacks of boxes of Arizona evidentiary material. Agnes was on the phone. She hung up. "Danny's on his way over, still excited about the job."

"Good," KC said. "Do you have a minute before he gets here?"

"I do. Does this mean you are *finally* going to tell me about your father?"

"Oh, Agnes, this is so ugly." Almost memorized at this point, KC began with the hallway conversation and then summarized everything up to her meeting with Hidalgo. "The CD Dad mailed from the Jefferson Hotel has one clue, *RIC,* after one withdrawal. No name, just the initials." KC handed Agnes the CD and the papers from Hidalgo. "Hopefully, these will help."

"There are a slew of websites on off-shore trust locations: the Cook Islands, Bermuda, the Isle of Man, the Caymans," Agnes said. "This is going to be fun. Big-time crooks hiding assets, and little me catching them. I taught computer systems to college geeks before I got the bug to be an attorney. If I don't like it, maybe I'll become Agnes Richardson, Super Sleuth."

Her enthusiasm was contagious.

—11—

KC followed Gray Rossiter into the Congressional dining room. "Very impressive," she said.

"Yes, it is counselor. And the bean soup is even more impressive. It's good to see you, KC. I guess the last time was at Sam's funer—" Gray stopped.

"Only two weeks ago, hard to believe, isn't it? Anyway, how are you doing?"

"Absolutely adequate under the circumstances," Gray said. "And you?"

"Good description. About the same."

Gray looked the part of a distinguished congressman and had the reputation to match. Known for being straightforward and conscientious, he was also recognized for spurning lobbyists and pork-barrel politics. "Seriously, are you okay?" Gray asked.

KC shrugged. "Yes and no. I've just been handed a huge case. I need to be rested and sharp because it's going to be a dogfight." The waiter approached. "Just order me whatever you're having." When the waiter moved on, Gray wanted to know more about the case. "It's the caliber I've waited for my entire career, a mine contamination case, maybe a Superfund site."

"Sounds challenging," Gray said as the waiter arrived with two bowls of bean soup.

"Wow, this smells good." KC tasted a spoonful and nodded appreciatively. "The business leaders want to promote tourism, so they don't want to hear the word *Superfund*. They've enlisted the governor and state legislators, and they claim EPA is overreaching its power. People never cease to amaze me, Gray. The area is contaminated from a hundred years of mining, but some don't want to hear it. Toxins are killing fish in their rivers and reservoir, the soil and water samples exceed safety levels by fifty to sixty times. For all I know, the people glow in the dark."

Gray nodded at her bowl. "Fascinating, but eat your soup. You look like you could use a good meal." He was right; the soup was delicious. They finished the last spoonfuls as the waiter arrived with their sandwiches. "So you have this huge case facing you, what else is going on?"

His question was casual and, no doubt, he expected a casual answer. But Gray and her father were lifelong friends. He deserved to know the truth. "This is going to shock you," KC said, not able to find a kind way to say it. Gray's eyebrows arched expectantly. "The truth is Dad's death was made to look like a storm-related accident, but it wasn't. He was murdered."

Gray's face, at first, mirrored shock and then pain. "I know you, KC. You wouldn't make that statement if you didn't have proof."

"I'm sorry to spring it on you like that, but yes, I have proof." KC laid out the facts, starting with Sam's investigation into the missing IIM funds and ended with the CD. "It was postmarked the day after he died. The return address was the Jefferson Hotel where Dad and Charlie went that night. A lawyer Dad met there gave him the draft of a class action lawsuit against the Department of Interior. Dad was scheduled to announce it at a news conference on Monday. Gray, that suit would be the largest lawsuit ever filed against the U.S. govern—"

KC stopped mid-sentence, seeing Gray's expression turn grim. Glancing back over her shoulder, she saw two men approaching. Gray rose and nodded curtly. "KC, I would like to introduce Senator Hayden Culpepper, and his guest, Al Fitzsimmons, CEO of Rollins Tobacco. Gentlemen, this is my guest, KC Garrett."

KC offered her hand. Senator Culpepper took it, his eyes twinkling. "The pleasure is all mine. Casey is it?" His glance at Gray was full of mischief. "Why you old dog, lunching with this beautiful young woman. Y' hear what I'm sayin'?" He chuckled.

KC jerked her hand back, her face flushed. "Have we met before?"

"We have not, my dear," Culpepper said. "I would most certainly re-member meeting a lovely thing like you."

"My name is not Casey, Senator. It is the initial K and the initial C. KC Garrett, Attorney- at-Law, Department of Justice." KC flashed a patronizing smile, her mind locking on the phrase and his accent. Her heart almost stopped when she made the connection. She rose and stared at him, eye-level. "I remember now. We came very close to meeting, Senator Culpepper. Too bad we didn't." Even to her own ears, her voice sounded threatening.

Culpepper's smile vanished. "I appreciate the correction, counselor. I do apologize." He turned and quickly steered the CEO away.

Gray sat back down. "What the hell was *that* all about?"

"Y' hear what I'm sayin'?" KC mimicked Culpepper's accent. "Unless you know someone else who uses that phrase with that accent, he's the second man I heard outside my office that night. The other one is Victor Ludlow, Chief Operations Officer at BIA, the man who suggested bribing Dad to back off his investigation." Culpepper's threat came rushing back as she repeated it to Gray. "I heard Victor Ludlow say Aubert hasn't told *her* yet about using trust fund money. I figure *her* is Secretary Beckman."

"Jules Aubert is Valerie's campaign manager," Gray said. "I've been around a long time, but I've never seen a campaign quite like that one. Now we know how they're paying for it." They both finished their sandwiches, KC struggling with the fact that a senior member of the U.S. Senate would be involved in her father's murder.

She pushed her plate away. "My guess is Aubert runs the show, Ludlow does the transferring, and Culpepper's job is to cover it up. But why would a senator risk that?"

"Culpepper was instrumental in getting Randolph Beckman elected to the House in the first place. Then after the accident, he pushed Valerie to seek her husband's congressional seat. Culpepper considers himself her mentor. If she wins the election, which it looks like she's going to, he will have unlimited access to the president. Power and money are what Culpepper's all about. Guaranteed, if there are big bucks involved, he has a hand in it. He's a corrupt, arrogant bastard, but not a killer."

"No, but I bet he knows who is." KC shuddered. "I'm going to get these guys, Gray."

"Count me in," he said. "If he had anything to do with Sam's death, I will nail Hayden Culpepper's hide to the wall and invite the entire Senate and House to watch."

* * *

Tony tapped on Captain Appling's closed door and heard him holler, "Enter." He rose behind his desk. "Agent DeMarco, what can the U.S. Park Police do for the FBI?"

"Hopefully identify somebody." Tony sat down and handed him the computer picture. "Ever seen this guy? He may have been at the river the night Sam Blackhawk died."

Appling studied the photo. "Who is he?"

"Elliott Wolf, an FBI agent."

"FBI? I heard that the driver of the Camaro was some kind of big shot, but why is the FBI interested in a storm-related accident?"

Tony wanted Appling's cooperation but hesitated to reveal too much. "I question whether the accident was actually storm-related. If Wolf was there, it wasn't. "

Appling studied the photo. "My deputy and the tow-truck driver were already at the scene when I arrived. If I can keep this picture, I'll have my deputy look at it."

"I appreciate that," Tony said. "Think he could be the tow truck driver?"

"Possibly," Appling said. "I remember it striking me as odd that he 'just happened' to be in the area. He said he responded because he saw the patrol car's flashing lights. My deputy didn't question it because of the storm. I wouldn't have either, but. . . ." Appling tapped his temple. "Why the elaborate explanation?" He handed Tony two sheets of paper. "Copies of our accident report and Sunset Towing Company's claim form. "That's his signature at the bottom."

"Can't make it out, but if Wolf was at the scene, shouldn't he be easy to ID?" Tony said.

"Ordinarily," Appling said. "But it was really cold. He wore a ski mask the entire time it took to raise the Camaro, but the minute it came out of the water, he took the mask off."

"That doesn't make sense," Tony said. "Why do that if he's trying to hide his identity?"

"I understand why he did. He needed a smoke, bad. He inhaled it down to his toes. I quit three months ago, so I pretty much watched every drag he took." Appling stood up and consulted a schedule on a bulletin board. "My deputy's on vacation for a couple weeks, someplace warm, he said. Soon as he gets back, I'll show him this picture and give you a call."

Tony put the claim form and accident report into his briefcase. "I appreciate that. In the meantime, would you mind keeping this under your hat?"

"No problem. Don't take this wrong, but I get the impression you think Elliott Wolf had something to do with the Camaro ending up in the Potomac."

"I don't know for sure, but Sam Blackhawk was my girlfriend's father. He was an intelligent, careful man. Not the type to end up in the Potomac, storm or no storm."

Appling looked puzzled. "Then maybe I should re-open the case."

Tony rose. "For now, let's leave it as a storm-related accident until we see what your deputy says. I need incontrovertible proof before I confront Wolf. If you both ID him, you would automatically be asked to reopen it, based on new evidence." Tony glanced at the calendar. "Today's December 6, I've got a few other leads to check out. How about we meet in a couple of weeks when your guy gets back?"

Appling offered his hand. "You got it. After all, justice is what we're looking for. Good luck, DeMarco."

* * *

KC dug into the Arizona case, more from necessity than from choice. Tyler Jackson had attended Sam's funeral and then apologized about the timing of assigning her a case of such magnitude. Abandoning the search for her father's killer was not an option, but KC conceded she couldn't let Tyler down either. She gave herself ten days to get familiar with the parameters and positions of the three opposing factions in the case, hopefully finishing by Friday, December 16.

Danny claimed that, "more hours mean more money." A system soon developed where he logged in the files according to the codes his mother provided. Agnes categorized them and provided KC with historical documents, relevant cases, and EPA rulings. What time she didn't spend pouring over evidentiary material, KC spent on the phone with representatives of the three groups. At the end of ten days, she told Agnes and Danny that their system had given her the facts and the confidence to meet with the claimants. "And hopefully prevent war." KC handed him his paycheck for two weeks. After thanking her for "some serious money," Danny asked her whose side she was secretly on.

"Nobody's," she told him. "My job is to find a solution acceptable to all three factions," which prompted a giggle from Agnes.

"Oh sure, a solution acceptable to a bunch of business guys hell-bent on developing tourism, the mine's team of lawyers who are going to say it's not the mine's fault, and EPA, who just wants the mess cleaned up, to hell with 'em, right?" Agnes joked.

KC burst out laughing. "Right, how hard could that be?" Agnes and Danny's help allowed KC to give Tyler Jackson a report on December 16, her self-imposed deadline.

His secretary ushered her into his office. Tyler rose and smiled. "I'll be damned, you said you would have a handle on this case in ten days, but I didn't think you could do it."

"I had help, but shame on you for doubting me." Tyler laughed and offered to grovel. "No, I prefer you just listen. There is concrete evidence of serious contamination in and around McCrary. EPA's investigator, Hoffman, says tests show twenty percent of the preschool kids have blood lead levels over the 10-deciliter level. And toxins exceed the safety levels 50 to 60 times in the soil and water samples. Tyler, the problem is there are three factions: the people who want it cleaned up, McCary's business leaders who want to promote tourism, and the attorneys for the mine who say it's not their fault. Did you know Hoffman had to hire secur—"

"Hey, take a breath, Garrett. You sound like you've been main-lining caffeine."

"Darn, you discovered my secret!" KC laughed. "Bottom line—I'm flying to Arizona the day after New Years. I don't want you to get upset if things escalate, because they may."

"A legal slugfest. . . right up your alley, Garrett. Want to talk strategy over dinner?"

"Thanks, Tyler, I can't tonight." His invitation was a reminder that she needed to level with him about Tony. But not right now because she had work to do on her own case—to research Valerie Beckman who appeared to be involved. A search of several databases gave KC a basic dossier:•*Born Valerie Rogers 5/10/62, Macon, Georgia, SS #021-66-4974• Present address; Bethesda, Maryland •Graduated Macon High School, 6/12/80• Graduated University of Georgia 5/28/85 with M.S. degree in Economics• Married Randolph Beckman 6/21/92•Assumed husband's Congressional seat 6/10/99•Appointed U.S. Secretary of Interior 11/19/2005.*

Equally curious about Jules Aubert, KC did a search on him. His background was one of privilege and private schools as a youth; a 1982 graduate of Princeton University. Both dossiers referenced articles in the *Washington Post,* so KC walked over to the public library and accessed their archives. An article dated June, 1999, *Georgia Congressman's Wife Named to Fill Vacancy,* gave the details of Congressman Randolph Beckman's and six-year-old Jason Lee Beckman's deaths. *Returning from a ski weekend in Vermont, Beckman's SUV hit a patch of black ice on a dark highway and slid head-on into an eighteen-wheeler. Father and son died at the scene.*

Because Valerie's husband was the son of *"well-known southerner"* Georgia Governor Wilford Beckman, the newspaper compared the deaths of Randolph and Jason to a Kennedy family tragedy. *I remember Mom mentioning that.* The picture of Valerie at the funeral was heart-wrenching; she had planned to go with them, but a bout of the flu changed her plans. *The Post* referenced the *Time Magazine* cover of Valerie embracing a little Foster-

Program girl, claiming the adoption ended her mourning. A happier picture in 2005 showed Valerie being sworn in as Secretary of Interior, a smiling President Jonathan Champion watching.

Are you what you appear, Valerie? KC had to admit that for a person whose political career was born of the worst circumstances, her courage had to be admired. The consensus of all that KC read seemed to be that between her popularity and her politically savvy advisor, Valerie Beckman could very well become the first woman president. KC had mixed feelings; no one would deny she was a tragic victim, but was she also an incredible opportunist? A Sunday *Washington Post* feature story on the Aubert brothers contrasted happily-married, hard-working Gregory, versus handsome, playboy Jules.

The article intimated that Jules' infidelities and contentious divorce were responsible for derailing a promising political career. But skilled in business as well as politics, Jules Aubert cashed in on both by establishing Aubert & Associates, which *The Post* claimed, "set the standard for political consulting firms."

KC checked her cell messages before leaving the library, including a dinner invitation from Tony at his place. She called Jess and Rose and asked if they would let Ivan in and feed him, and then she followed Tony's directions to a high rise building on Connecticut Avenue. Admittedly nervous, KC rang the doorbell. Tony answered the door, a glass of wine in one hand. He took her jacket and handed her the wine. "I'm really glad you came." In the few minutes it took Tony to hang up her jacket, KC downed the contents of her wine glass. He turned back to her. "Wow! You evidently had a tough week. Come and sit at the bar while I finish dinner."

Tony's apartment held wonderful aromas: Bayberry fragrance from a candle in the living room and something delicious from the kitchen. The carpets, the drapes, and the large LG flat screen TV looked brand new, the leather couch she remembered. It seemed Tony had gotten on with his life after their split, a sporty new car and a decorated apartment, tell-tale signs of a woman in his life. KC acknowledged that her memories after their split were mostly about work. All of a sudden, she felt awkward. "This is beautiful. When did you move here?"

He refilled her glass. "Couple months ago." His expression hinted there was more to it than just the move. KC wondered who she was—the woman he was thinking about as he busied himself. *We broke up two years ago. I wonder if they were married.*

Tony glanced up and smiled. "I can almost hear what you're thinking. Look, she and I went together for about six months. We gave it a try, but all I can say is it didn't work out."

KC swiveled her bar stool to face the living room, surprised at how much his statement hurt. "When you say it didn't work out, are you talking about us, or the woman who prompted all this?" She gestured at the room.

The next thing she knew, Tony was standing in front of her. "I wasn't talking about us. And s*he* did not prompt any of this. She happened a long time after you and I broke up. I meant it, Tiger, when I said I am really glad you came." He took her face in his hands. "I'm not asking or promising anything. Right now, this just feels really good, and I hope you feel the same way." He bent forward and kissed her, their kiss lingering. He kissed her cheek and then stepped back.

"It does feel wonderful, Tony, and I'm not asking or promising anything either." The awkward moment passed.

Tony refilled her wine glass. "Dinner will be ready in a sec, but I need to tell you something. A suspicion, a theory, I have no proof. But don't let this spoil our evening, okay?"

"Okay, but what is it?" The look on his face gave it away. "It's something to do with—"

"Yes, finding your dad's killer." Tony showed her a computer-generated, file-photo of a man's face. "This came from our FBI data base. His name is Elliott Wolf, long-time agent. I checked him out after he turned up on the church video tapes across the street during Sam's funeral. KC, he had no plausible reason to be there. It made me suspicious so I showed this picture to Captain Appling with the U.S. Park Police. He's going to show it to his deputy when he returns from his vacation, but there is a possibility that Wolf was driving the tow truck the night of the storm."

"That would be a huge clue, Tony. I can't wait to hear if his deputy ID's him. What a break that would be. I view it as positive and I'm not going to let it spoil our evening."

"That's good, Tiger. I just want you to be aware. And to let me know if you see him."

Tony's dinner of Chicken Marsala was delicious. KC cleaned her plate.

"Good, you like my cooking," Tony said. He emptied the bottle of pinot noir into their glasses. "Ice cream and coffee coming up." He took their plates into the kitchen.

Encouraged by Tony's news, KC relaxed, appreciating the dinner, the evening, and being together. Though Tony had brought up the case, KC's gut feeling that her telling him about burglarizing Ludlow's office would definitely ruin their evening. *Some other time.* Fatigue born of anxiety and little sleep, settled over her like a warm blanket. KC drained her wine glass. "Hurry up with that coffee, okay?"

KC woke up Saturday morning on the leather couch, dressed in her skirt and sweater. She threw the blanket aside, sat up, and squinted at the wall clock. "Eleven? I don't believe it!"

Tony left a note next to the coffee pot. *You checked out while I was dishing up dessert. Coffee is ready, just push the button. Call me on my cell, okay?*

"Bless you, Tony." She downed two cups of coffee and filled her cup again, glancing at the calendar on the side of the fridge. Saturday, December 17, an important date, but what? KC dug through her briefcase for her Day Planner. "For goodness sakes, Mom's birthday!" She called Tony's cell. "I am so sorry. The dinner and wine were fabulous. Actually, too good."

He laughed out loud. "I was dishing up ice cream, and I asked you a question. When you didn't answer, I peeked around the door. Your head was on the placemat, and you were so out, you were snoring." Tony couldn't stop laughing.

"I just remembered, today is my mother's birthday and I promised her and Sally a trip to Glenwood. I know they would love it if you joined us. So would I, Tony, so please say yes." Surprisingly, he agreed without hesitating. "Pack for one night so we can have brunch tomorrow. See you at Mom's house." She hung up before he could tease her any more. KC called Crystal Waters Casino on her cell. Her brother was on a conference call.

Santana answered. She could hear slot machines in the background. "This is the first chance I've had to call. Charlie was right. Camas Mine's tonnage is under-reported by half."

"Hang on, I'm walking to my office." The background noise disappeared. "Did you say under-reported by half? How the heck did you find that out?"

"You don't want to know."

"Yes, I do," Santana said. "And I'm sure your brother would too. Why don't you and Kathryn come for Christmas, and you can tell us. We guarantee a white Christmas, not to mention courteous pick-up and delivery from the airport."

"Thank you, Santana. I wish I could, but my workload right now is impossible."

KC showered and changed at her apartment, then stopped by her favorite Georgetown boutique and exited with a gift-wrapped hand-knit sweater. Tony was loading luggage into Kathryn's car when KC arrived. He had gotten a haircut, his black hair close-cropped. Lean and fit, with a square jaw and a small scar on the outside of his lower lip, Tony looked incredibly rugged and handsome. He glanced up and grinned. "Hey, sleepyhead, how are you?"

"Awake and glad you came," she answered as her mother and Sally came out the door. "Happy Birthday, Mom. Hi, Sally." KC hugged them. "I suppose Tony told you." Their smiles confirmed that he had. "I am never going to live that down."

"Probably not," Tony said and took the front seat beside her. KC drove, listening to the three of them visit for a good part of the drive. "I forgot what a beautiful drive this is," Tony said. Maple and birch trees carpeted the hills, their bare limbs stark against the dark green of occasional pines. They had made this drive at least once a month when they were a couple. A happier time, KC thought with a tinge of regret. Tony loved Glenwood; it was quiet and away from the city and their jobs.

Five miles west of Hillsboro, Virginia, KC turned into a drive marked by a weathered Sign: *Glenwood Estate, 1899, National Register of Historic Places.* She followed the winding drive around a thick grove of trees and pulled up in front of the house. An impressive structure, Glenwood boasted three stories of Pennsylvania blue stone, the stately front defined by four classic columns. Dormers set in the steep roof formed valleys filled with snow, creating geometric patches of stark white against the black slate roof.

"Look," KC said. Saturday's late afternoon sun slanted long rays of yellow and orange across the expanse of snow sloping downward from the house to the Shenandoah River. "Remember the crayfish?" *Why did I say that?* KC thought as she got out of the car. Kathryn and Sally alighted and went on into the house.

Tony's expression signaled he remembered all too well the July 4 family party two and a half years ago. They were fishing from the dock; a perfect day until, out of the blue, Tony asked her to marry him. The memory still hurt. The word *marriage* had come up occasionally, most often jokingly. Caught off guard, she remembered answering off-handedly that her job was so demanding, she didn't think she would ever be able to handle marriage and a family. *That was the last time I saw Tony until three weeks ago when I called asking for his help.*

"Tony, I'm sorry. Sorry for a lot of things. But I'm overwhelmed with trying to find out who killed Dad, and getting up to speed on this big case. I certainly didn't mean to—"

He stood facing the river, staring transfixed at the water. "I understand," Tony interjected. "You don't need to apologize. I realize it isn't healthy to dwell on the past." In his tone, she heard cool restraint and a warning that he didn't intend to get hurt again.

—12—

Victor Ludlow did not appreciate his Sunday being interrupted, especially the fifteenth week of NFL season. This was the Denver-Giants game, *his* Giants that he backed with a hundred bucks. He had looked forward to this game all week, but an invitation to Jules Aubert's condo had potential; important decisions came out of these meetings. The first one he attended fifteen months before had resulted in his becoming part of this group and getting the job to transfer IIM funds offshore. Illegal yes, but definitely a faster track to retirement. Safe in a Bermuda bank account, his take insured that his teenage daughters would get the Ivy League education his wife insisted on. And the money he *didn't* have to put in a college fund, he put into slush fund that his wife didn't know about. It covered moorage fees at the same marina where the power-elite moored their yachts.

Ludlow glanced around Aubert's condo with new appreciation. His penthouse reflected impeccable taste and the money to back it up. *Architectural Digest* quality. The twenty-foot wall of floor-to ceiling glass that offered a panoramic view of Rock Creek Park set the elegant tone. But the Carnelian marble fireplace, with its carving just above the glowing fire, said it all: *To live well is the best revenge.* "Amen to that," Ludlow said under his breath.

Ludlow acknowledged that if it weren't for Aubert, he wouldn't have a fifty-foot Hunter moored alongside other sailing yachts at the Annapolis Yacht Club. Nor would he have a mistress who didn't care that he was married. Money aside, being a member in one of the most powerful groups in DC, albeit covert, had significantly elevated his status. DOJ attorney Bill Berkeley, Senator Hayden Culpepper, and former BIA Secretary Carson Marsh were fellow members, each one with a role and receiving a cut. Aubert was close-mouthed about the money, saying only that he knew how to get the funds into Valerie's campaign, yet circumvent the Disclosure Act. Everyone in D.C. credited him for Valerie's remarkable lead in the polls.

The doorbell rang. "Victor, would you get that?" Aubert called out from the kitchen. Ludlow greeted Bill Berkeley and Senator Hayden Culpepper. The senator said hello but little else; he took a seat and gulped down the scotch Aubert had put on the coffee table for him. Powerful, and one of the oldest members in the Senate, Culpepper was known as a political piranha; nobody crossed him. He asked for another drink and then wanted to know if the meeting was about to get underway. "As soon as Carson arrives," Aubert replied.

The doorbell rang again. "Thanks for getting that, Victor," Aubert said. Ludlow greeted Carson Marsh, the former Assistant Secretary of BIA. The two of them had worked well together during his tenure. Ludlow wondered why he was invited; Carson had retired for health reasons.

Seeing that everyone had a drink, Aubert addressed them. "Thank you for taking valuable time from your weekend, therefore I will get right to the point. It appears that Mr. Blackhawk's accident affects us in two ways. On a positive note, it quashes potential litigation against Valerie, Hayden, and Carson. The negative is finding a temporary replacement. We need someone acceptable to Valerie, to insure that she doesn't look outside this group. That would end our use of IIM funds and seriously jeopardize her campaign. I don't need to remind you of her lead in the polls, but suffice it to say, I want to keep it that way. We need a person who can step right in and quell stories in the press about Blackhawk's death."

"Ludlow could step right in," Marsh said, glancing his way. *Maybe that's why Aubert invited me,* Ludlow thought, hope blossoming.

"No, Ludlow is needed where he is. Valerie's campaign depends on him." Aubert turned to Carson. "I spoke to Valerie yesterday. She, of course, is concerned about your health, but she agreed you are the logical choice. She will name a permanent appointee as soon as the campaign is over, but with the lawsuit shelved, your reputation remains untarnished, Carson. Your leadership would be a tremendous relief to Valerie."

"Is that the reason you asked me here?" Carson spat out the words. Ludlow almost choked at the venom in his voice. "That takes gall. You ousted me like yesterday's garbage, and now you want me to bail you out? Not bloody likely!" Carson looked livid.

"Carson, please," Aubert's voice remained pleasant. "It would only be for a few months, and I did no such thing. You and Emily made the decision because of your health. May I remind you, your cut continues to get deposited in your Bermuda account each month." Aubert was trying hard to be conciliatory.

Marsh straightened up in his chair. "And may I remind *you* that when you approached me with your idea of pilfering trust funds to finance Valerie's campaign, you didn't have a clue how to implement it. Not only did I show you *how*, I introduced you to Bill Berkeley here who set up the offshore corporations for you." Carson glanced at Berkeley for affirmation. "*That* is why I receive my cut. Consider it my retirement compensation. I do."

The instant silence felt like an impending storm. Taken aback, Aubert leveled a cool gaze on Marsh. "Perhaps I didn't fully explain. We have a crisis on our hands that could bring all of us down. I acknowledge your contributions, but I'm not asking for me. I am asking for Valerie because I want to give her this chance, Carson. Perhaps you could take Fridays off and spend your weekends in Florida, an opportunity for you and Emily to look for the condo you want." He looked at Marsh expectantly.

"Don't insult me by sugarcoating your offer." Carson slammed his glass down on the coffee table and struggled out of his chair. "I'm quite certain Valerie has no idea what you're doing. Perhaps she should because your actions could destroy her. Frankly, I want no more of your scheming. You will have to do it without my help."

Ludlow sucked in his breath as Marsh walked toward the foyer, his labored breathing audible. When he reached the door, Carson turned around. "I expected more of you, Jules. I thought you sincerely cared for Valerie. What you are is an opportunist, using her to get what you could never win." Carson gestured at the room. "You may surround yourself with priceless art and furnishings, but it doesn't change what you are."

They heard the heavy door shut, leaving behind tension thick enough to slice. Ludlow realized he was still holding his breath; he exhaled quietly. All eyes were on Aubert. He put his drink on the bar and, without a word, removed Marsh's glass and wiped the coffee table.

Bill Berkeley cleared his throat. "Does anybody else feel Carson may be a security risk?"

"Risk, hell!" Culpepper rose. "That man's sittin' on a powder keg givin' off sparks. You better do somethin', Aubert, or he'll destroy our gal. She won't get to the White House."

Aubert appeared the picture of calm. "Carson's health has obviously deteriorated to the point it is affecting his judgment. I'll call this evening after he's had a chance to calm down."

Culpepper poured himself another drink. "And if he doesn't? Just like Blackhawk and that Indian lawyer from Albuquerque, we need another backup plan. You hear what I'm sayin'?"

Blackhawk? What Indian lawyer? Culpepper's words took a few minutes to register. When they did, Ludlow jumped up and looked directly at Aubert. "You said Culpepper's talk of a 'backup plan' for Blackhawk was just his usual senatorial posturing. You assured me the storm caused Sam's car to end up in the river. What Culpepper just said doesn't sound like senatorial posturing to me. So, what does he mean by *another* backup plan?" Ludlow said.

The senator turned around in his chair and glared. "What are you, stupid?"

"He means we will deal with Carson in an appropriate fashion." Aubert said it so matter-of-fact that, for an instant, Ludlow felt relieved. Until Aubert's cold eyes betrayed the truth. Ludlow collapsed down on his chair, nausea overtaking him. "You can't mean that. There has to be another way! Carson is a proud man. What about a bigger percentage for the months he's in office?" Aubert's frown deepened, but he said nothing. "I have a good relationship with him," Ludlow said. "What if I were to talk to–"

"Assuming," Aubert interrupted, "that Carson does not melt down, Valerie is almost certain to get the nomination. Tell me, Ludlow, you surely aren't willing to risk her future on an old man's deranged state of mind." He sounded like he was reprimanding a disobedient child.

Aubert and Culpepper's insolence hit a nerve. Ludlow rose, intent on saying his piece then getting the hell out. "I agreed to transfer funds to finance Valerie's campaign. Not murder. You had somebody kill Blackhawk and some Indian lawyer? That's insane! I am a respected member of the Annapolis Yacht Club. I have two daughters. My wife is president of the PTA!"

"Sit down, Ludlow, and shut up," Aubert said. "You have no idea what's at stake." He motioned for Berkeley and Culpepper to leave.

Ludlow noted their noncommittal glances toward him as they deposited their glasses on the bar and then let themselves out. He then went on the offensive when Aubert approached. "It's obvious how far you are willing to go to put Valerie in the White House." Ludlow said. "I don't need this risk. My kids' college tuition is sitting in my Bermuda account, and my house is almost paid for. Sam Blackhawk was a good man, and so is Carson. This is unbelievable."

Aubert bent forward, his contorted face inches away. "Listen, you idiot. Our window of opportunity will slam shut with the convention. If Carson follows through with his threat, Valerie won't be president. With her *this* close, do you think for a minute I would let that old sonofabitch destroy her? She WILL be the next president!" Aubert's voice carried the threat of nuclear war.

Ludlow cowered. "Okay, okay, I won't say a word. But what if I want out?"

"For starters, your wife will meet Debbie Radcliffe."

Pain exploded behind Ludlow's temples. "How the hell do you know about—?"

"I know everything about you. Believe me, if I tell your wife about Radcliffe, you will be out on your ass and your ex-wife will have the almost-paid-for-house. Trust me on this."

Ludlow felt like puking. Aubert had him by the balls and there was nothing he could do. "What do you want from me?" he managed to whisper.

Aubert straightened up. "Do the transfers every month or I call your wife. Which is it?"

"I won't bring it up again," Ludlow said.

"Wise decision. Now get the hell out."

* * *

After Sunday brunch, KC drove everyone back to her mother's house, then got into her own car and waited while Tony embraced Kathryn and Sally. He came up to her window. "I had fun this weekend. Kinda like old times." Sunlight framed his face and, for a moment, she wished they could magically go back to those times. Tony bent forward and kissed her. Instinctively, she kissed him back. He straightened up, and she stared into honest eyes asking where he stood in her life and whether they had a future this time around.

"I would love a do-over on dinner and another wonderful evening with you," she said. Tony's smile indicated that was what he wanted to hear. KC drove away, the fragrance of his aftershave lingering, their kiss stirring old feelings. She deliberately pushed them aside; she had no time for reminiscing or for Christmas, only a week away. The thought of shopping, going through the motions of a joyous holiday when she felt anything *but* joyous, seemed hypocritical. Her mom's birthday sweater was too large; she needed to exchange it. *Darn, I should probably do that now.* KC glanced at her mother's gift box, Valerie's and Aubert's dossiers on top.

"Or not," she said. Impulsively KC passed the turnoff and headed for Silver Spring, Maryland. Jules Aubert seemed to be the central figure. Who might he entertain on a Sunday afternoon? Learning *anything* about him would be worth her time. Aubert's address turned out to be Gaston Towers, a high-rise condominium on the west side of Rock Creek Park. "Okay, I've learned he lives in fancy digs," she mused from across the street as she observed several luxury cars enter and exit underground parking. Delivery vehicles evidently used a service entrance at the back; she watched a floral van disappear around the building. Under the building's front portico, party-dressed people got out of their car. The doorman greeting them called for a valet.

She glanced at her watch, three-thirty; it would be dark in an hour. KC got out of her car and walked toward the building. Dressed in jeans, a sweater, and running shoes, she couldn't pass as a dinner guest, so she watched from across the street. A Cadillac drove up and a well-dressed, older couple got out. The doorman again signaled for a valet to park their car. Next, a sports car pulled up and four people piled out, laughing and talking. Dressed casually and each carrying a gift, all four looked to be her age and clearly in a party mood.

KC crossed the street and stood behind a pillar, out of the doorman's sight. "We're surprising Edie Sutton in 1408," one of the men said and tipped the doorman. "Her birthday."

KC returned to her car, convinced there was a reason why her mother's sweater didn't fit. The box had been opened, but the paper and ribbon were reasonably intact. She rewrapped it as best she could and walked back to the portico. She smiled as the doorman approached. "Edie Sutton, suite 1408? A bunch of us are surprising her. Today is her–"

"Birthday," the doorman added. "Take one of the elevators on the right side of the lobby." KC slipped him a five. "Give Miss Sutton my regards," he said as another car drove up.

The impressive lobby boasted several seating areas, each one defined by a furniture grouping atop a Persian carpet. There were alcoves on both sides of the lobby, each alcove with three elevators. The brass directory on the wall listed two penthouse units: Aubert, 2001, Morris, 2002. KC pressed the button for floor fourteen and noted the time, 4:02 p.m.

Exiting on the fourteenth floor, she first checked for security cameras in the hallway; they were strategically placed. "Darn it, Edie, I forgot your unit number," she said for the benefit of the camera. A walk around the floor told her there were four units. KC made her way to the opposite side of the building and slipped into the stairwell. She walked up the six flights, stopped to catch her breath, and then cautiously opened the door.

The twentieth floor hallway was much wider than floor fourteen, but thankfully also deserted. She walked past unit 2002, taking note of its oversized double doors inset in a privacy niche about three by ten feet, then made her way around the corner where she had a view of Aubert's hallway. The niche in front of his doors was midway down the hall on her left, the elevators beyond his unit on the right. She could see no place to hide except the stairwell. KC stood pondering what to do, when she heard a bell. *The elevator!* She drew back, counted to ten, and then peeked again, in time to see Victor Ludlow disappear into the inset of Aubert's unit. *Paydirt!* Unable to suppress a smile at her luck, she hurried past Aubert's unit to the stairwell and stepped inside. Hopefully, security would view her as a confused guest looking for the correct unit.

KC removed one shoe and jammed it in the door opening as the elevator bell sounded again. This time, a tall, slender man exited. He looked familiar. KC had to clamp her hand over her mouth when she recognized Bill Berkeley, DOJ attorney in international law. He walked to unit 2001 as though he had been there before. *His office is down the hall from mine. That's where Ludlow and Culpepper were coming from that night!* KC crossed herself, thanking the heavens for her impulsive hunch. Berkeley kept a low profile at DOJ; now she knew why. Five minutes later, an older gentleman arrived and went directly to Aubert's.

KC forgot about security cameras and the cold gray space. Pieces of the puzzle were slowly coming together. Aubert wasn't merely involved; he was the key figure at the center of everything. She kept watch on the hallway, her mind imagining one scenario after another until she realized how cold she was. The open stairwell door sucked in a strong current of frigid air. KC undid the gift box and pulled on her mother's sweater over her own. She folded the box and paper again and again then crushed it under her foot.

After an hour she was too tired to stand, so KC sat down with her back against the wall. Still cold, and now needing food and a bathroom, she decided to leave. The meeting could go on for hours. KC retrieved her sneaker from the opening and was tying the laces when she heard the elevator bell again. She stood up and peeked, wondering who would show up this time. It was the older gentleman who arrived last—and he was leaving. Pacing back and forth in front of the elevator, his angry expression telegraphed he was upset about *something.*

KC raced down the stairs to floor fourteen and then took the elevator to the lobby. She exited a few feet behind the man. KC held back, intent on either getting the license number of his car, or tailing the cab if he took one. *I have to know who he is!* He handed the doorman a bill and a few minutes later, a valet delivered a dark green Jaguar convertible. KC watched from inside as he put on his seat belt and adjusted the rear view mirror.

As the Jag pulled away, KC walked out the double doors and broke into a run to her car. Staying a comfortable distance behind his car, she called Tony on her cell. "Aubert had a meeting at his condo. I'm following the first man to leave. He's in a green Jag convertible." She gave Tony the license number. "How about looking up his name and address?"

"Did I ever tell you your talents are wasted at Justice?" Tony said. He asked her to repeat the license. "Why didn't you tell me what you were going to do? I would have come with you."

"An impulsive decision, but guess what? Bill Berkeley came, DOJ's top international law guy. His office is down the hall from mine. What does that tell you?"

"That's where the two men were coming from that night."

"Did I ever tell you, you're not just a pretty face, DeMarco?" He was laughing when she disconnected. Twenty minutes later, the Jag entered an exclusive Georgetown neighborhood. KC recognized his Brownstone from an old article she remembered reading in the Sunday *Post* about former Senator Ted Kennedy; his Brownstone was on the same street.

She drove by slowly as the gentleman pulled his car into the garage beside a Mercedes. When Tony called back, KC found out she had followed Carson Marsh, former Assistant Secretary of BIA, who along with Hayden Culpepper, was the second man named in the class action lawsuit.

Things are finally looking up. Now I need to find out whether Valerie is involved.

–13–

KC's good feeling lingered the following morning until a glance at her calendar revealed it was December 19 and the realization that her Christmas might have to be delayed. Just then, Agnes tapped on the door and swept in with a flourish. She deposited a binder and a stack of printouts on KC's desk. "This detective stuff is so cool," Agnes said. "Perseverance pays off!" RIC Ltd. is Royale Insurance Company Limited, headquartered in Bermuda."

"You found out, that's great! But an insurance company and not a bank?"

"A *captive* insurance company. It's complicated, but they more-or-less insure regular insurance companies by assuming a portion of the risk. Paragon Insurance here in D.C., is one of RIC's clients. Paragon covers federal employees' life and health insurance—that's us."

"But why would a captive insurance company receive IIM funds in the first place?"

"There is no *legal* reason," Agnes said. "But it was the connection between RIC and Paragon that gave me an idea. No doubt, those two companies have been doing business for years. So, KC, I want you to think like a crook just for a second." Agnes looked serious. "You're wondering where you can safely stash your stolen IIM funds, and then you remember— you're *already* doing business with a big offshore company! Knowing that, KC, what would you do?"

KC thought for moment. "I would find somebody willing in *that* company who, for a specified cut, would hide my stolen funds in a secret account, or bunch of accounts."

"Absolutely!" Agnes applauded. "Why look someplace else when you already have an established connection." Agnes'eyes were fairly dancing.

"Which leads me to my best idea ever! Think about this, KC. Crooks high on a corporate food chain don't do stuff like that themselves. They get someone lower on the chain to do the actual work, especially if they're dealing with millions of dollars. Wouldn't the services of a computer systems analyst, who just happens to be a lawyer, be attractive to that crook?"

"Agnes Richardson, what are you saying?"

"Remember me telling you that Neil, my ex, is one of the personnel bosses at the Treasury department? Part of his job is overseeing employee life and health coverage. Don't you get it, KC? Treasury has been one of RIC's biggest contracts for years. Neil *has* to be familiar with the company, maybe even knows some bigwigs. What if he helped me get a job at RIC?"

KC stared at her in amazement. "You're not serious. That is crazy, absolutely not."

Agnes grinned. "Nice try, counselor, but Bermuda is where the rat is storing the cheese. *Somebody* at RIC is on the take. *If* that person could find an expert systems analyst who doesn't give a hoot if the money is legal or not, I'm betting he would hire that person in a New York-minute. KC, if Neil can get my foot in the door, we would have access to names, account numbers, balances—everything!"

KC felt her face flush. "That's an incredible idea, but too dangerous. Besides, what would be Neil's incentive to help you?"

Agnes' smile vanished. "Danny doesn't know this, but Neil told me the *real* reason Ms. tight-body dumped him. He told her he wanted to patch things up with Danny, and would like to ask him to come live with them for a year or so. Neil said she seemed okay with it, but then Friday when he got home, she was gone and so was all her stuff."

KC's intuition screamed *no,* and she said as much, but Agnes persisted. "KC, the last four years have been the toughest in my life. I feel like I've earned a break. And, it would give Neil and Danny a chance to mend their relationship. Maybe Neil can learn to be a father."

KC grinned. "Oh, you're good, Agnes, really good."

"I am, aren't I?" Agnes chuckled. "Think about it. Neil will be so busy congratulating himself for getting rid of me that he won't have a clue he just handed us the keys to the vault."

"Okay, but I capitulate with reservation," KC said. A jubilant Agnes departed singing, leaving KC free to write her notes in preparation for her McCrary meetings. She finished two hours later, her thoughts reluctantly returning to Christmas, the first without her father.

All she could think about were the crooked deals going on behind closed doors. In the whirlwind of Capitol Christmas parties, illicit bargains were being struck and favors pledged in this season of peace and brotherly love. Her father and Charlie were pawns in one of those deals. The mere thought of Christmas without her father was overwhelming. The only solution she could think of was to send her panic to an imaginary box to deal with *tomorrow*. She refused to envision that *tomorrow* actually arriving. It had to work; she could not fathom the alternative.

Agnes tapped on her door. "Tyler Jackson is on line one. He sounds serious."

"Uh-oh." KC motioned for Agnes to come in. "What can I do for you, Tyler."

"I'm not sure. Maybe the locals are up in arms, but I just got a call. EPA is making noises about shelving the case, and I'm getting pressure not to let them."

"How can EPA do that? After all the money and work, why would they pull the plug?"

"They can put it on hold indefinitely and mothball it, which means as good as dead. I know you didn't plan to go until after New Years, but is it possible you could get down there the day after Christmas?" Tyler sounded upset, but also apologetic.

"Sure, if that's what it takes." KC replaced the receiver and glanced at Agnes. "You'll probably think I'm crazy, but I am actually glad to go."

"No, I don't," Agnes said. "Divorce and death aren't that far apart on the Richter scale–especially at Christmas. Keeping busy is good."

KC flipped through her case calendar. "How about trying to get me a flight to Phoenix on the twenty-sixth, and a flight back late on the thirtieth? Unfortunately, that means rescheduling all of my appointments." KC looked up at Agnes. "This is ridiculous, less than a week until Christmas to shop and mail gifts to Idaho. Go ahead and shoot me."

"If you buy the gifts, I'll ship them UPS for you." Agnes said.

The phone rang again. KC answered and held up her finger for Agnes to wait. Gray Rossiter asked how she was. "I am swamped, my favorite Congressman. Say, Claudia loves to shop. Do you think I could get her to do my Christmas list?"

"Ordinarily she would love nothing better, but she spent most of the night throwing up and is still sick this morning. That's why I'm calling. I'm expected to attend a reception at the White House Wednesday evening for the Canadian Prime Minister. Since she can't go, Claudia suggested I call you. Would you like to go to a fancy party at the White House?"

"Are you serious? I was just telling Agnes I don't have a spare minute, and you invite me to a party at the White House? You've got to be kidding." Agnes shot her a stern look and mouthed *don't you dare say no*. KC shrugged. "Of course, I would love to go. But I would need a dress and I'd have to go to the beauty shop. And I—"

"I'll send a cab for you, Wednesday, six-thirty. *Ciao*." The line went dead.

'I don't care what you have to do," Agnes said. "You do not turn down a chance to see the White House at Christmas. Quit worrying, somehow everything will get done."

* * *

Jules tied his bowtie and cast a final glance in the mirror at his Armani tux. "Almost ready, Gregory?" he called out to his brother.

Gregory Aubert strode into the dressing area, looking distinguished enough to *be* the Canadian Prime Minister, rather than a guest at a reception for him. He held a glass of wine in each hand. "Congratulations on your excellent wine cellar, little brother. A 1989 Bordeaux, very nice." Jules took the glass and ignored the *little brother* remark, savoring a compliment from the brother whose sterling shadow he had chased for too many years.

Jules swirled the wine in his glass to release its bouquet. "Valerie shares my enthusiasm for good wine. She should be here tonight, but she is very upset with me."

They walked into the living room. "*Beau monde,* beautiful world," Gregory said, taking in the view. "Why is she angry? I thought things were going well with her campaign."

"They are, but remember the IIM funds issue I told you about? I felt I had to tell her. Valerie works with Ludlow, who could slip and say the wrong thing. Or Valerie could figure it out. Either way, she would get rid of me. I swore to her I would replace the funds, but she almost fired me. What I will never tell her is that only $20 mil was spent on the campaign, the other $25 million went in Bermuda accounts to buy off Ludlow, Marsh, Berkeley, and Culpepper. Senator Culpepper is a pompous ass, but he's done a good job so far covering our tracks. And he helped me convince the other three to leave their account intact until they retire. By that time, Valerie will have served her two terms. I did it to protect her."

"Are you telling me, Jules, you didn't keep any of the funds for your-self?" Gregory's question was accompanied by a wry smile.

"You are perceptive, Gregory. Fifteen of the $25 million is in my Bermu-da account. Whether or not I leave it there until I retire will depend on the election and Valerie. She was angrier than I've ever seen her. Once she is in the White House, it wouldn't surprise me if she ended our relationship. Just a feeling, but I don't think Valerie will ever forgive me."

"Money is the ultimate power of destinies," Gregory said. "Valerie is an excellent candidate, but the reason she remains above the fray is the campaign you've conducted. She is obviously unaware how many millions a campaign of this caliber requires."

"Why thank you, Gregory. No, I don't think she does."

"Speaking of your fellow, Ludlow," Gregory said. "His alterations on the reports of our Camas Mine operation have yielded enough for me to outbid my competitors on a promising mine site in Montana. I hope you will come up when the sale is completed." He retrieved the wine bottle from the bar and refilled their glasses. "This is a major *coup* for Vanguard."

"It has been a long time since I've been to Vanguard headquarters. I will make it a point to come," Jules said. The phone rang; Jules was shocked to hear Valerie's voice.

"Do not read anything into this call. I have not forgiven you. But I listed you and Gregory as my guests at the President's private dinner. Shall we meet at the White House?"

"No, Valerie. Please allow us to pick you up. Excellent, we will be there shortly." Jules turned toward the view. "Perhaps all is not lost after all." They gazed out at the expanse of Rock Creek Park nestled amidst a sea of lights. "Valerie has a chance to make history," Jules said.

"Indeed, but do I recall you promised to stop the transfers?"

"I don't like lying to her. And they will stop soon enough anyway. It is those IIM funds that have made the critical difference in Valerie's campaign, but I could never convince her of that." Jules sighed. "I admit I will never understand women."

Gregory chuckled. "Any man who claims he does is either a liar or a fool."

Jules led the way to the elevators. "Last week, I learned it takes unwavering commitment to reach *any* worthwhile goal. I discovered I have it, Gregory. I will allow nothing to stop me." His brother's expression reflected admiration. How good that felt!

Gregory checked his reflection in the brass doors. "I expect to be the first guest in the Lincoln bedroom when Valerie moves into the White House."

Jules fairly beamed. "I sincerely hope that will be at the wedding, *monsieur* best man."

* * *

Valerie peeked in the kitchen; Phoebe and Marguerite were eating dinner, watching a Christmas special. She backed away and made her way to the library. *I am so grateful to have Phoebe in my life.* Marguerite had the fireplace on. Valerie sat down in her favorite chair and glanced at today's *Post* on the table beside her.

The front page article and picture covered her appearance and speech before Detroit's autoworkers, a potentially volatile rally that Jules skillfully handled. He was a paradox; one minute a brilliant strategist, the next a devious opportunist. Jules' insistence that she meet with every major European leader had resulted in the defining event that sealed her lead. After two days of meetings with the British Prime Minister, their visit ended with him speaking in front of #10 Downing Street, obliquely endorsing her candidacy. The momentum that trip created had yet to slow, but fifteen months later, it remained a mystery how Jules could commit such a colossal blunder. *I will never trust you again, Jules.*

A tap on the door and Marguerite entered with a tray, a glass of wine on it. Phoebe came in right behind her. "I counted fifteen presents for me under the. . . . Wow, you look awesome!" Marguerite tousled Phoebe's hair and told her the minute her mother left, it was bath time.

When Marguerite exited, Phoebe grimaced. "How do you say 'bath time sucks' in Spanish?"

Valerie pinched her nose. "I believe P.U. is universal." Phoebe's shirttail stuck out below her sweater, the knees of her jeans covered with grass stains. "How did your pants get so—"

"Get so what?" Phoebe's incredulous glance made Valerie smile.

"So vintage-Phoebe," Valerie said. "Will you wait with me? Jules will be here soon."

"Sure." Phoebe sprawled in the leather chair. "If you talk to the President tonight, will you ask him when we can come to Camp David?" Valerie told her that wouldn't be proper, and they would have to wait for the invitation. "Okay." Already forgotten, Phoebe jumped up and went to the wall of framed pictures. She stopped at the photo of Randy and six-year-old Jason. Valerie joined her, noting how much their images had faded. It still hurt.

"Jason would be my brother, and Randy, my Dad." Phoebe touched Randy's image. "I would've liked that." She inched back into Valerie's arms, wanting to be hugged. She had grass and leaves in her hair. Valerie asked how that happened. "Billy kicked the ball into the bushes, and I went in after it." She wriggled free and turned to face her. "Will you come see me when you get home? Even if I'm asleep, come in and say goodnight, please?"

"Of course, I will. But here's a kiss to hold you." Valerie pressed her lips to Phoebe's forehead, leaving a perfect print. "Branded forever, go look in the mirror."

Phoebe grinned at her reflection. "I like it!" She blew a kiss. "Have fun!" Valerie shivered. Her daughter's exit seemed to suck all the energy out of the room. Thankful when the doorbell rang, she scooped up her fur coat and opened the door.

Jules appeared tentative. "Good evening, Madam President."

* * *

Gray escorted KC into the State Dining Room, which looked more beautiful than she recalled, but then that was ten years ago, a reception with her parents. *Hurtful memory.* KC sent it to the imaginary box and reminded herself this was a special evening. He introduced her as they made their way around the room.

One of the Congress's leading members, Gray Rossiter knew everyone; he remembered wives' names, asked about their children and their upcoming holiday plans. KC listened as he joked about endless party fundraising. "No," he didn't want to run for president. "No," he wasn't interested in a vice-presidential bid. As they strolled, KC couldn't help checking as many place cards as she could without being obvious. They read like a list of Fortune 500 and, according to Gray, the Who's Who in the party in power.

The room was a sea of Christmas sparkle, each round table covered in green linen, with a miniature twinkling Christmas tree in the center. Burgundy and white china trimmed in gold amidst a sea of crystal goblets flashed diamond-like sparkles in the lights. KC and Gray worked their way through the crowd to the west wall and paused in front of an ornately mantled fireplace. Over it hung a thoughtful portrait of Abraham Lincoln. Carved into the mantle: *I pray Heaven to Bestow the Best of Blessings on this house and All that shall hereafter inhabit it. May none but honest and Wise Men ever rule this roof.*

KC looked up at Gray. "Think Champion is an honest and wise man?"

He stared at the painting with a pensive expression. "I do, but he's only one man. Things have changed so much. Washington used to possess a degree of civility and honor that doesn't exist anymore." A forced smile signaled that he wanted to end the subject. "You look beautiful tonight, counselor. Sam would be very proud."

Another sad thought went into the imaginary box. "He would, wouldn't he?" KC said. She smoothed her new dress, long, black, and chic, the one she had stormed Bloomingdale's to find. Feeling a little guilty for taking the time off, she nevertheless went to the beauty shop and afterward admonished herself for not going more often. Pierre's scissors gave style to her long hair, the luscious-smelling shampoo and conditioners leaving it shinier than she'd ever seen it.

"You are the prettiest woman here." Gray smiled mischievously.

KC laughed. "You'd say that to your housekeeper if you brought her."

Gray joined her laughter. "You have to understand, KC. Claudia trained me and she expects me to say that. If I don't, she gets upset, so I say it to whomever."

"Good grief. I forgot how weird men are!" That elicited a loud laugh from Gray, other guests glancing their way. "Behave yourself, Rossiter."

KC was about to tell him that she would be leaving for Arizona soon, but spotted two Marines entering the room. They took up positions on either side of the door, hands behind their backs. One marine announced: "President and Mrs. Jonathan Champion." Gray offered his arm, and he and KC moved forward. The President and First Lady walked in, a thrilling sight that made KC shiver. President Champion looked handsome in his tuxedo; he began shaking hands as soon as he was through the doorway. Mrs. Champion let go of his arm and did the same as the crowd parted and formed two informal lines.

Following behind them was a group of elegantly clad guests. "Close friends of the President plus cabinet members and a few big spenders," Gray whispered to her. KC recognized the Vice President, the Speaker of the House, and their spouses. And Valerie Beckman, who looked stunning. Two men in tuxedos were with her.

Valerie glanced their way and approached. "Congressman Rossiter, how nice to see you." She shook his hand and turned to KC. "And you're Sam Blackhawk's daughter. I have thought of you and your mother so often. It's wonderful to see you. Please give your mother my best and tell her if there is anything I can do, anything at all, to please let me know. That applies to you as well." Valerie's empathy rang sincere. She moved on, the two men following.

KC gazed after her, puzzled that the Secretary hadn't introduced the two men, and that both of them avoided looking her in the eye. She asked Gray who they were. "The younger one is Jules Aubert, her political advisor. I don't know the other man."

Just then, KC spotted President Champion striding toward them, a broad smile on his face. He took her hand. "KC, I'm so glad to see you. How is Kathryn, and how are you?"

"We are both doing well, Mr. President. Thank you so much for the State Department plane and the ceremony. They made a wonderful difference."

"I am delighted to hear that. Your father was a great man and a good friend." The President shook Gray's hand as Lila Champion joined her husband; he turned and put his arm around her. "Lila, you remember Sam Blackhawk's daughter?"

"Of course. KC, it is wonderful to see you." She looked up at her husband. "Wouldn't it be nice if KC and Kathryn came to Camp David for a weekend?"

The President responded instantly. "It would indeed." He addressed Gray, looking stern. "You and Claudia, too. That's an order, Rossiter. I am still your Commander."

Smiling, Gray saluted. "Yes sir, anytime, sir!"

Mrs. Champion told KC she would have her secretary check both calendars but wanted to do it soon. They moved on, leaving KC with good feelings for a change, none that needed depositing in the imaginary box. Gray made sure she met every political luminary: Vice President Leighton Benchley and his wife, and the Speaker of the House Donovan Bishop and his wife. Gray steered KC out of the way when Hayden and Sally Culpepper walked by. Several Hollywood stars in attendance drew almost as much attention as the President. Corporate giants and mega-millionaires mingled with senators, congressmen, and media moguls.

The food and the wines were exquisite. Gray sat on KC's left; on her right, a Canadian gentleman introduced himself as CEO of British Columbia's largest hotel chain. KC spotted Valerie two tables away between Aubert and the older gentleman. "Darn it, who is he?"

Gray peered in their direction. "They look a lot alike, don't you think?"

"Oh, for goodness sake, of course they look alike," KC said. "That's his brother, CEO of Vanguard Mines in Montreal." Several toasts and a speech by the President and the Prime Minister offered no further opportunity for conversation. At the close of the reception, Gray retrieved KC's mother's mink coat for her. She thanked him for the evening as he tucked her into a waiting cab. On the drive to her apartment, the more KC thought about Valerie Beckman and Jules Aubert, the more curious she became. *I have to find out if she is involved. How could I do that?* KC mused in the dark of the cab. Even as she said it, she had an idea.

KC's first Christmas without her father went better than anticipated, attributed in part to Tony and to breaking with tradition. Tony offered to spend Christmas Eve with his family so he could spend Christmas Day with her. She hosted a casual dinner at her apartment, no sad comparisons: Tony cooked prime rib and everyone brought a dish to share. Danny brought a set of dominoes and got them involved in a spirited game. After everyone left, Tony was at the sink hand-washing wine glasses. Impulsively, KC came up and put her arms around him. He turned around, pulled her close and kissed her, a passionate kiss that made her want to ask him to stay the night. Before she had a chance to invite him, Tony asked the time of her flight the following morning.

A bit disappointed, KC was still thinking about their kiss when she fell asleep.

-14-

Tony held KC's hand as they approached National Airport's security area. "I want to ask you something before you get on the plane. Would you like to spend New Year's Eve together? If so, I'll make reservations at The Roof Terrace. Tuxedo, a gourmet dinner, bubbly—the works."

"I would love to spend New Year's Eve with you. The Roof Terrace sounds fantastic."

"Great, a New Year's Eve to remember. Take care of yourself, okay?" Watching her go through security and blow a kiss his way from the other side, he admitted things were going great. So far anyway, but the Arizona case represented the intangible goal she had coveted since they first met at a DOJ/ FBI picnic six years ago. Tony remembered almost turning down the junior attorney from the Justice Department, but finally relented and rounded up enough of his FBI buddies for a decent baseball game: "DOJ against FBI."

The game came first and later, the picnic. After being tagged out at first base by a dark-haired lawyer named KC Garrett, Tony made sure to get seated next to her at the picnic table. He remembered walking away with her phone number and a date. But, between her DOJ job and his FBI training and assignments, their relationship didn't advance past group get-togethers for a year or more. Until a weekend in New York City, he could still recall when friends became lovers after a perfect day, a bottle of Mumm's Cordon Rouge, and a bubble bath in a giant tub for two. That led to nearly three years together. *Wonderful years*, Tony thought as he exited the airport. He walked to his car, telling himself not to get swept away. KC's career was still important, and now she had the career-defining case she had worked hard to earn.

He drove toward Rock Creek Park and Elliott Wolf's Shepherd Park condo complex. Entering the grounds, he noted faded signs that warned: *24-hour security,* but saw no one. He found the common garage. Elliott Wolf's Buick was covered in a fine layer of dust, indicating he'd been out of town for a while. A cursory search located the main telephone terminal on the front wall. Tony hooked up a wiretap on Wolf's line, acknowledging that he had breached FBI policy more times in the last three weeks than in his entire career. But the image of how Sam and his friend died dispelled his misgivings. If Sam's death was at the hands of an agent gone bad, this illegal phone tap was damn-well worth it.

On his drive home, Tony smiled at how quickly KC said yes to his invitation. Amazing that the traits that led to their breakup were the very qualities he admired about her: passionate about her career, decisive, intelligent, funny, and independent. After observing her compete in karate tournaments during their time together, he also had a healthy respect for her as an athlete.

New Year's Eve could be a new beginning, a celebration just being together, no talk about marriage or careers. Tony thought back over his recent relationship and, in the quiet darkness of his car, it came to him why it didn't work. *Fate, karma, or Providence, KC and I are meant to be together.* Buoyed by his revelation, Tony entered his apartment and, like always, first checked his messages. His supervisor's call dashed all happy thoughts.

"You've got twenty-four hours to be in Miami. Call me for details." Tony returned the call; he was in charge of a three-man FBI team, partnered with a Drug Enforcement Administration three-man team in an undercover operation to nail one of the biggest drug lords in Florida.

* * *

After four days of back-to-back meetings, KC boarded her December 30 flight to back to D.C. and took her seat in first class, a treat authorized by Tyler Jackson. The minute the Boeing 777 was air born, an attentive flight attendant delivered a spicy Bloody Mary, and wished KC a "Happy New

Year." She raised her glass in a silent toast to her trip. *I hope the progress we made holds.* When announced it was okay to use electronics, KC retrieved her laptop and began her report for Tyler. Because she discarded DOJ's standard public meeting format, KC decided an informal description of her meetings would be best.

She summarized her meeting with the attorneys and "rowdies" and then addressed the most successful meeting. *My idea to meet over dinner (thankfully) worked great. I asked everyone to make the evening as much social as business which surprised them, especially Hoffman. I asked that everyone use first names only, and when expressing their opinion, to speak with the respect they would like directed their way. I had to intervene (nicely I might add) only twice. I kept the beer and wine flowing, but no one got drunk or disorderly. In fact, as the evening progressed, the dialogue became friendlier. Amazing, but I think discussing issues over a pleasant dinner reminded everyone that they were neighbors first.*

You told me to get them to agree on something, and I did. All twenty agreed the prime rib was great, and that wine is probably better for our health than beer, though that took a couple of rounds. KC smiled; Tyler would appreciate that until he saw the bill. *I know my dinner idea wouldn't have worked in a big city, but McCrary is small. These twenty people have known each other for decades. They want to work together and agreed to meet again, which I think will translate to substantive progress. I plan to keep in touch with them to see that it does.*

It was dark by the time the cab dropped KC off at her apartment. Jesse and Rose had the lights and heater on and had placed her mail on her desk. Ivan let her know he was happy to see her, purring and rubbing against her leg. After she pet him, predictably he made a beeline to the kitchen to his spot and looked up at her with that expectant look of his.

"Dinner coming right up." She fed Ivan and then called Tony and left a message. The lengthy beep on his answering machine indicated he hadn't been home for a while. KC made a pot of coffee and started on the stack of mail. On top, she found a letter from Stacey Morgan, her roommate in law school who quit DOJ and moved to Montreal to marry a Canadian lawyer.

Stacey's letter said she was six-months pregnant and hoped KC would visit her before the baby came. I should do that, KC thought, and put her letter in the *answer* stack.

KC recognized Tony's writing on an envelope postmarked Miami. "What? I'm out of town five days and you go to Florida?" Inside, she found a handwritten note: *Have to make this quick. Didn't want to leave this on your answering machine. I'm in Miami. Major drug bust with DEA. I hope to fly back for New Year's Eve but will call if I can't make it. Love, Tony.*

That sounds dangerous, she thought. New Year's Eve dawned sunny, but cold. KC slept late, and by the time she unpacked and did her laundry, it was two o'clock, time to get in a run. Not alongside the Potomac this time, but around the nearby campus of Georgetown University.

When KC returned from her run and discovered no message from Tony saying he couldn't make it, she had a long bubble bath and took her time getting ready. She spent extra time on her makeup and hair and then put on the black dress she wore to the White House. She turned on TV to watch the action in Times Square. The telephone rang, the number showing it was Tony's cell. "Cinderella speaking, is this Prince Charming?"

"Yes, and Prince Charming is in deep trouble with Cinderella." Tony sounded distraught.

"I'm still in Miami, dammit. I am so sorry. It's been crazy. This is the first chance I've had to call. Go ahead, holler at me. I'm sure you look gorgeous. How mad are you?"

"On a scale of one to ten, about a four. On a disappointed scale, I'd say a ten."

"Me, a twenty," Tony said. "I had a great evening planned." She heard excited voices in the background. "Damn! I promise I will make this up to you." She started to tell him to be careful, but he had already hung up. Admitting she was a great deal more disappointed than she let on, KC changed out of her party clothes and fixed a salad for dinner.

Out of the blue, an image came to mind of Tony staring at the river, his expression signaling he did not intend to get hurt again. The image delivered an ominous revelation. Did they already have their one shot at being together, the one she blew by turning him down? Were they destined to go separate ways, Tony finding someone who wanted a family as much as he? *My career got in our way last time, and now finding my father's killer. Maybe Tony and I aren't meant to be after all. It's hard to think about love and catching a murderer at the same time.*

New Year's morning, she had breakfast with Sally and her mother, the three of them eating while watching the Rose Parade. When she returned home, KC put the Bowl Games on her two TVs and spent the day cleaning her apartment. Before she got ready for bed, KC packed a duffel bag with a sweater, jeans, and boots, her caution/excitement meter on high alert. Tomorrow she would follow up on one of the best clues she had.

Office time Monday was jam-packed. Tyler Jackson knew she was back and expected her written report today. She found him at his desk; he looked so happy to see her that she felt embarrassed. She handed Tyler her report. "I believe I convinced the mine's CEO and CFO that it would be in their best interest to share in cleanup costs rather than battle in court. Considering the hostility the people in McCray have toward the mine, I told them their participation would go a long way in rebuilding their image."

"No threat, no chop block?" Tyler laughed. "I'm proud of you. How did they take it?"

"They agreed to kick in *some* money. They'll make an offer. I'll reject it, and we'll go back and forth until we agree on a figure to submit to EPA. I made it clear I don't give in easily."

"I'm living proof of that." Tyler's smile was genuine.

KC summarized the issues covered in her other meetings. "All in all, a success, I think."

"So you're telling me everybody is happy?" Tyler said.

"I'm telling you nobody is happy. They are equally dissatisfied, but now want the same thing and are willing to talk. You know what that means."

"All right! Equal dissatisfaction, the sign of a good compromise. Great job!" Tyler said. "How about we celebrate over dinner?"

KC could no longer avoid the issue. "You are a good friend, Tyler, so I want to be upfront. Tony is back in my life, and I want to see what comes of it. I hope you understand." His quick reply that he was happy for her did not sound heartfelt, but she thanked him nevertheless.

Promptly at five o'clock, KC changed into the clothes she brought and took a cab to The Jefferson Hotel, the envelope from her father in her briefcase. She showed the envelope to the man behind the desk and asked if he knew who mailed it. He glanced at it. "November 19, the Monday before Thanksgiving. No, I'm sorry, I don't know."

"Do you have a schedule for that day? It's important I speak to the person who mailed it." She flipped open her wallet and flashed her ID card with the Department of Justice seal. He located a schedule and wrote three names on it. "I need their home phone numbers, too."

"I'll need permission to do that." He shuffled toward a door marked *Manager* and was back in a few minutes. "Our manager would like me to ask the nature of your inquiry."

"Routine investigation. I'm not at liberty to say."

He leaned forward. "Is this about that Indian?"

"What Indian?" KC said, trying to look calm.

"Oh dear, perhaps I spoke out of turn."

KC glanced at his name tag. "Mr. Carnegie, I am very busy. What Indian?"

"The Indian gentleman who died in his room the Saturday night before Thanksgiving. From a drug overdose, my goodness. The Jefferson does not appreciate publicity like that. Fortunately, the article in the *Post* was very small and far back in the newspaper."

"Tell your manager my department wants zero publicity." KC whipped out her notebook with the DOJ seal on the cover. "What's the Indian's name?"

"Mr. Donyell Crawford from Albuquerque, New Mexico," Mr. Carnegie said.

The attorney Dad met, the one who gave him the CD! No wonder I couldn't reach him. Carnegie handed her a list and pointed to the top name. "He should be here any minute. Perhaps he can help you." Ten minutes later, the clerk showed up, but said he didn't mail it. "I worked a short shift that night. Doug came on at 9:00 p.m. He's a law student at Howard University. Nice young man. I'm sure he can help you."

She called Doug's number as she walked toward the Metro station. He answered, saying he had just come in from the campus library. KC identified herself and asked if he worked at the desk the Monday before Thanksgiving. When he answered yes, she asked if they could meet. "I'd be happy to talk to you, but you need to know this is a dangerous neighborhood after dark."

Doug sounded young. "I can't help that," KC said. "This is important."

"I was on my way to the Florida Avenue Grill for dinner. It's near the U street Cardozo Metro. Want to meet there?" KC knew Howard University, the country's premier African-American university, alma mater to the likes of Chief Justice Thurgood Marshall and novelist Toni Morrison. KC had been in the gymnasium many times competing in karate tournaments. A fresh lead and Doug was willing to talk, she had no intention of waiting. It was dark when she exited the Metro at the U Street Cardozo station.

A hangout for students and hospital employees, Florida Avenue Grill looked crowded. She opened the thick glass door fronting the sidewalk and waited in the enclosed glass foyer. The line of customers inside the restaurant stretched back to the interior door, blocking her entrance.

The outer door opened and KC felt a presence behind her. "Out of your neighborhood, aren't you?" A deep male voice.

KC turned around. "Excuse me?" She looked up at a linebacker-size, Mafia-type in all black. "Being nosy can be unhealthy, Garrett. Whatever you're looking for, give it up."

"Who are you? Who sent you?" She tried to move, but he blocked her way.

"That's on a need-to-know basis, and you don't need to know."

"Did the guy who killed my dad send you? Or did you do it, you slime-ball."

"You're in no position to ask questions." He grabbed her face and squeezed hard. KC tried to knee him in the crotch, but he blocked with his forearm. "Bitch!" KC saw his fist coming, but could only turn her face enough that he caught her cheek, pain ripping through her neck and head.

An involuntary move, she stomped down hard, her boot heel hitting square on top of his foot, basic self-defense she had practiced a thousand times. Mafia-man yelled in pain and stumbled backwards, giving her the space she needed. KC slammed an upward vertical elbow to his chin, snapping his head back, blood spurting from his mouth. His yell was a mixture of pain and rage, deafening in the glass enclosed space.

He lunged, but KC's lightning fast, side kick to his knee hit first, her momentum tripling the force of the blow. She heard cartilage breaking and then his wounded roar. Propelled backwards, he crashed against the outside glass door and slid down to the floor. Eyes closed, he lay moaning, his head rolling from side to side. Mafia man's wallet lay on the floor between them. KC knelt down and flipped it open. Nicholas Ventresca's driver's license picture stared up at her, his address: 14007 East Brentwood Dr., Hyattsville, Maryland.

She stood up and, with her boot, slid the wallet towards him and then glanced around. The people inside waiting for a table were staring wide-eyed; they had backed as far away from the interior door as they could. Only two patrons were waiting at the outside door. The rest had fled, afraid of a brawl that could bring the cops.

KC gave Ventresca a last glance and then entered, silently repeating his name and address. Young and old were staring at her as she approached the counter. "Show's over, folks." The man behind the cash register identified himself as the manager. "What happened out there?"

"He tripped," KC said. "You should probably call an ambulance. He's blocking the entrance." She grabbed a pen and blank ticket next to the cash register and wrote Ventresca's name and address as the manager dialed 911. "Lawsuit in the making," he mumbled.

"Trust me, the business that guy's in, he does not want a lawsuit. Understand?"

When her meaning registered, the manager's demeanor instantly improved. "Understood, much appreciated. Would you like some ice for your face?"

She gingerly touched her cheek, it was red-hot and throbbing. "I would, thanks."

A young, black man stepped forward. "I'm Doug, from the Jefferson Hotel." He offered his hand. "No wonder you weren't afraid. A couple of guys got up, ready to help you, but you sent that guy flying so fast, it was already over."

KC followed Doug to his table and glanced at the paper she wrote on to make sure Mafia- man's name and address were legible. "Insurance," she said in answer to Doug's curious stare.

A waitress arrived with two water glasses and a ziplock plastic bag filled with ice. "Awesome," was all she said to KC and then greeted Doug by name. He ordered the special. KC ordered the soup of the day then gently placed the bag against her cheek.

"Thanks for meeting me," she said through gritted teeth. With her free hand, she showed him her Justice ID card. "I need to know about the night Donyell Crawford died."

Doug looked surprised. "The police took statements from all of us. I don't know much about him. I didn't check him in."

KC dug through her purse and found two Tylenol. Her head was beginning to throb. "What did you tell them?"

"That I was at the desk Saturday night around 11:45 when Mr. Crawford came out of the bar. He stopped at the desk and asked to extend his reservation to check out Tuesday. Two other Native American men came out of the bar a few minutes after him."

KC caught her breath. "Did one of them give you this?" She showed him the envelope.

"Yes, the Indian with the ponytail. He gave me twenty bucks and asked if I would make sure it got mailed. I told him I would lock it in the safe and mail it on Monday."

The waitress delivered their orders, pausing as she walked away to watch an ambulance pull up in front of the restaurant. Two white-coated figures hurried into the foyer with a stretcher. Patrons stood up at their tables to watch, blocking KC's view of Ventresca being loaded into the ambulance. It was gone in a few minutes. "You do that often?" Doug said, indicating the retreating ambulance lights.

KC's cold cheek felt numb; she removed the ice. "Only when I have to."
The soup was Boston clam chowder. KC ate small spoonfuls, gingerly
chewing the clams and potatoes. "Do you remember what time the Indian left
who gave you the envelope?" KC said.

"Around midnight," Doug said between bites of blackened swordfish.
She asked about Crawford. "I worked Sunday night from nine o'clock until
five o'clock Monday morning. I had a torte exam so when my shift ended, I
sacked out in a room for a couple of hours, but I was studying at 10:00 a.m.
when the maid knocked, totally freaked out over finding a dead guy."

"Who responded to the call, and why didn't you mention Crawford
extending his reservation to the police?"

"Detective Wayne Goodall, a real smart-ass. I tried to tell him, but he
called me 'sonny,' and pretty much blew me off."

"Wayne Goodall, I'll call him." KC wrote his name. "Tell me, did the
man who gave you the envelope seem nervous or afraid?" KC steeled herself,
dreading to hear his answer. She had no idea how she would handle the
possibility that her father suspected he was about to die.

"You're referring to the Indian with the ponytail? No, he didn't seem
scared or nervous. He just wanted to make sure the envelope got mailed. May
I ask why you are interested in him?"

KC fought back tears. "His car went into the Potomac on his way home
that night. My interest is personal and professional. I'm the Indian's
daughter."

KC took a cab home, her head feeling as if it was about to explode. She
took four Tylenol before going to bed and three more the following morning
before boarding the Metro to the Washington, D.C. Police Department.
Ventresca was an important lead; she wanted answers. She asked the clerk to
see Detective Goodall.

"*Lieutenant* Goodall," the clerk corrected her, eyeing her face. "Through
that door. He's the skinny blond guy in the corner." KC entered a large, noisy
room filled with two dozen or more desks. She weaved her way around and
between cops walking as they read and talked on cell phones. There were
men and women in uniform, some in street clothes, and most of them

drinking coffee and talking. Wayne Goodall stood up and waved from a corner desk.

KC approached and handed him her card. "KC Garrett, Department of Justice. I'm here about the Donyell Crawford case, the man who died at the Jefferson Hotel."

"Have a seat. Lemme pull the file. Drug overdose, get those every day." He tossed the file on the desk. "What's DOJ interest?" He eyed her bruised face. "Run into a door?"

Doug's right, he is a smart ass. "No, I duked it out with a hit man," KC said.

"Yeah, sure you did," Goodall replied.

"Crawford was an attorney, a family man with kids. Don't you find it strange, Goodall, that Crawford would ask the desk clerk to extend his reservation to Tuesday then overdose?"

"Nobody plans to OD. Maybe he had to have one more blow before going home and being daddy again. Hey, people do weird things. If they didn't, I wouldn't have a job. You didn't answer my question. What's this to DOJ?"

"DOJ is interested, that's all you need to know. Crawford met a man named Sam Blackhawk and second man in the Jefferson bar that night, an important meeting about a secret investigation. Before he went upstairs, Crawford gave Blackhawk a CD containing notes on the investigation and a class-action lawsuit. Blackhawk's car ended up in the Potomac that night. Park Police are calling it a storm-related accident. All three of those men are dead, Goodall. Still think Crawford just wanted one more blow?"

He stopped writing and lit a cigarette. He exhaled, enveloping both of them in smoke. "How do you know Crawford gave this Blackhawk guy a CD?"

"Because Blackhawk gave the desk clerk twenty bucks to see that it got mailed—to me."

"All three, huh? That is suspicious. Let me look into it, and I'll give you a call."

—15—

A ubert's secretary tapped on his door and announced that Senator Jackson had arrived for his appointment, and there was an "urgent call" on line two. "Tell the senator I'll be with him in a second." It took only three syllables, *Ven-tres-ca,* for Aubert to recognize trouble. Nick was calling from the hospital: "an incident with the Garrett woman." His jumbled explanation lit a fire in Aubert's belly. Ventresca had five stitches under his lower lip, and knee surgery to repair shattered cartilage scheduled tomorrow.

Incredulous, Aubert *had* to ask, "How in the world could that happen? All I hired you to do was follow Garrett to find out if she was up to something."

Silence. The man he thought was the ultimate professional was scrambling for an excuse. "This happens in the security business. She caught me off-guard. Things got out of hand."

"Well, tell me, before she caught you off guard, did you learn anything?"

"Yeah, and it's not good. Garrett asked me if I was the one who murdered her father. Of course I didn't answer. A real smartass, she got in my face and asked if I was the slime-ball who did it. I admit that pissed me off. But I will correct the situation when I get out of here."

Alarmed at the word *murder,* Aubert tried to remain calm and in control. "That's too bad. I was about to call you for another assignment. How long is your recuperation period?"

"The doctor said six weeks, but I don't think it will take that long."

"Six weeks, that's unfortunate. My problem can't wait that long. Listen, Nick, I have a senator waiting. Let me get back to you. In the meantime, take care of yourself." *She asked if he murdered her father? That's bad. Very, very bad.* He did not need another crisis. Carson Marsh was already a disaster, calling from Florida saying he and Emily had found the perfect condo. Then, twenty-four hours later calling again, this time demanding that $250K be wired direct to the title company ASAP. Aubert mentally retraced their conversation, how he tried to explain why that wouldn't be possible. And then Marsh's threat. "I'm warning you, Jules. If we lose this condo, I will call Valerie and tell her everything, including Sam Blackhawk!"

That was four days ago and not a word since. I hope to hell he hasn't already put in a call to Valerie. It was that meeting. Marsh's tantrum changed the dynamics of the group. He thinks he's in charge now. Whatever he wants, I give or he blows the whistle. I dare not deal with Garrett so soon after her father. But I can have Wolf deal with Carson.

Decision made, Aubert buzzed his secretary to usher in Senator Jackson.

*   *   *

Elliott Wolf stretched his tanned legs full out on his oversized beach towel and readjusted the umbrella to shade his head. Beside his chaise lounge was a low table with his lighter, a pack of Marlboros, and a tall glass of Stolichnaya with two lime slices. Wolf toasted the sun and the peaceful sound of waves, the antithesis of holiday bustle back home. The *Cayman Times* lay on his lap, still unread. There was something about this seven-mile stretch of cream-colored sand and the waves, the two main reasons he kept coming back to Grand Cayman. This place soothed the soul. And it made even the loftiest dream seem possible.

For years, his someday dream had been to buy a condo here when he retired. But that would only be after attaining his even bigger dream, being part of Mrs. B's security force when she became president. Dinner with her and Phoebe the night before he left, exchanging gifts, getting a hug from both of them, *was* Christmas. They cared about him. Mrs. B had admonished him for smoking. And Phoebe asked when she grew up and got married, if he would give her away. Picturing her brought a smile.

A cool hand touched his shoulder. "Mr. Wolf?" Wolf opened his eyes. "You have a telephone call, sir." The waiter handed him a note, retrieved his empty glass, and then waited expectantly. Wolf dug in his pocket and dropped a bill on his tray.

The slip of paper had no name, only a number. Fuzzy from his nap and several vodkas, Wolf sat up and took a last glance at the ocean. The sun had begun its leisurely descent to the horizon. As soon as it disappeared, a breeze would come up and the island spring to life. Reggae music, happy people dancing, their bodies glistening, smelling of coconut oil—this was nightlife in the Caymans. Observing from his favorite barstool would come later unless whoever made this call screwed up the last few days of his vacation.

Wolf walked back to his room, lit a cigarette, and called the number. It was Aubert's office. "I need to know when you're getting back," Aubert said.

"January fourth, Friday. Why?"

"A worrisome situation with serious implications for Valerie. Give me a call as soon as you return." Wolf hung up, his languid mood popped like a bubble. He shivered, whether from the air conditioner or Aubert's call, he couldn't tell.

*   *   *

The first week of January ended with Tony cursing the Bureau and every drug cartel. Helping DEA try to nail Miami's biggest bad boy, Enrique Pablo Cordoza, red-handed had cost him a fabulous evening with KC. And barely underway, the operation already ran into problems. Every year, it seemed the battle shifted in favor of the bad guys: more regulations in tangled legalese that required agents to spend more time taking classes and filling out reports than catching crooks. But what he needed right now, had nothing to do with Cardoza. He needed a favor from his lab-tech buddy in D.C. and it took five rings to rouse Joe Rogers. "Hey, man, sorry to wake you. This is Tony."

Joe yawned loud in his ear. "I know who you are. If I hang up fast, I can go back to sleep and forget you woke me up. Today's a holiday. Ever hear of a hangover?"

"I said I was sorry. I need a favor and I don't have much time. Write this down." Tony explained the tap on Wolf's phone, gave him the address and the location of Wolf's telephone box. "I need you to remove the tape, listen to it, and put in a new one. If something's going down, call me." He gave Joe the secure line number. "If I'm not here, leave your ID number. No message. I will call you."

"Sounds serious," Joe said. "By the way, how's Jared doing?"

"Driving me nuts," Tony said. "He follows me around like a puppy."

"Driving you nuts? Gee, I wonder why that makes me smile?" Joe was chuckling.

"Because you're warped and hung over. One more thing, Joe. Give the tape to KC. Ask her to put it in her safe deposit box. Looks like I won't get back for another week or two."

"Awesome lady, KC," Joe said. "Want me to keep her company until you get back?"

"She has a black belt in karate, Rogers, and KC prefers Italians. I wouldn't mess with her if I were you." Joe was still laughing when Tony hung up.

* * *

Wolf's cab pulled up in front of his Shepherd Park condominium, relieved as he always was to find nothing amiss in his front yard. For twenty years, he had taken the same three weeks of vacation, and spent it at the same hotel on Grand Cayman. He relaxed and read on the same stretch of beach and dined at his favorite half-dozen restaurants. Maybe boring to some, but to Wolf, a good holiday meant quiet, and none of the nonsense of shopping, decorating, exchanging Christmas cards. Everything in his condo looked very neat and orderly, just like he left it.

Buying a unit in the new Shepherd Park development had been a financial leap of faith thirty years ago. His and every unit in Shepherd Park had skyrocketed in value because of its proximity to Rock Creek Park. During those years, Wolf had explored every inch of the park, including the twelve-mile length of Rock Creek that ambled through it. At the golf course, he was known as the quiet guy that shot in the low eighties and jogged five miles a day.

Though he dreamed of one day owning a vacation condo on Grand Cayman, this was home. Washington possessed an edge, an excitement like no other city, not even New York. The Big Apple might have Madison Avenue, Wall Street, and the Stock Exchange, but the real power resided in D.C. When Washington's power boys said jump, Wall Street's boys asked how high. Even from a distance, observing people with money and power was addicting.

Wolf ate dinner at his favorite bistro and walked home, wondering what the New Year would bring. On his message machine was a bad omen, a reminder to call Aubert: "It's urgent."

"Welcome back to the real world," Aubert said, when Wolf reached him. "Could you meet me at Rock Creek Nature Center tomorrow at ten o'clock?" Wolf reluctantly agreed.

He arrived early the following morning and waited in his car until Aubert got out of his Beamer. "Must be something big to get you out on a morning like this," Wolf said, gesturing at trees whipping wildly in the wind.

"You're right, it is big," Aubert said. "Carson Marsh, do you know him?"

"No, should I?" Wolf's dread ignited.

"He was Assistant Secretary of BIA until three months ago. Officially, he stepped down because of a heart condition. Unofficially, I convinced him to retire. He was ineffective. And, more times than not, he managed to piss off tribe leaders which created grief for Valerie."

Wolf dodged an eye-level branch. "If he's retired, what's the problem?"

"Valerie doesn't have time right now to find a replacement for Blackhawk. I had a meeting at my place last Sunday. I asked Marsh if he would step in temporarily and he went ballistic. He's threatening to tell Valerie everything. I thought I had him under control, but in his last call, five days ago, Marsh demanded I wire $250K to a Florida title company. He and his wife bought a condo in Vero Beach, Florida. I tried reasoning with him, but I see what's coming. There'll be no end to Marsh's demands. If he doesn't get it, he'll go to Valerie. Then it's over."

"What's this got to do with me?" Wolf stopped in his tracks. "You don't seriously want me to get rid of this guy! You must think I'm your personal hit man."

Aubert turned to face him. "Dammit, Wolf, this is do-or-die for Valerie. She will be president unless Carson Marsh blows it."

Wolf fought the urge to slug him. "I'm done, Aubert. I've proven my loyalty."

"Yes, you have. And thanks to you, Valerie is all but knocking on the White House door. This is critical, Wolf. If you take care of this problem, the day you get back from Vero Beach, there will be an account in your name at the Bank of Montreal with $500K in it. My brother is on the board of the bank. I'll have him set it up, half a million dollars, all yours."

Wolf stood transfixed, picturing a Grand Cayman condo on a cream-colored beach.

"I realize what I'm asking, Wolf. You know what's at stake. I need you on my team. Marsh is a threat to everything Valerie wants to do. The man has a serious heart condition. If he died in his sleep tonight, no one would be surprised." Aubert stepped closer, intensity sharpening his features. "If his death appears to be from natural causes, I will see to it you get appointed to the Presidential security team." Aubert drew a folded paper from his jacket pocket. "Carson and his wife are staying at this hotel in Vero Beach. Take care of the problem, and the security job and money are yours. Aubert held out his hand. "What do you say?"

"Presidential security team?" Wolf was dumbstruck; how did Aubert know his dream?

"One of the team," Aubert said, "follow Valerie everywhere."

The most prestigious team in law enforcement. Aubert's offer was dazzling, a genie offering to grant his wish, albeit at a hefty price. In the blink of an eye, he would get to spend every day by Mrs. B's side; he would get to see Phoebe grow up. Time seemed to stop. Wolf's ultimate fantasy dangled in front of him like ripe fruit begging to be picked. A handshake and it was his. Wolf felt his hand come out of his pocket, felt it rise involuntarily, and match Aubert's grip. Words formed somewhere deep inside and spilled out in a confident voice he did not recognize. "Make it one million, tax free, plus the Presidential security job, and you got a deal."

Aubert didn't hesitate. "Glad to have you on board." Wolf tried to ignore the tight knot forming in his gut. Withdrawing his hand, he consciously pictured himself at President Beckman's side. The nice, fat bank account was just icing on the cake.

* * *

KC could not dismiss her idea on how to find out whether Valerie Beckman was involved. A desperate plan if she followed through with it. She would be breaking the law—again. Did the end justify the means? She hated that cliché; she had heard it too many times in court. In view of Valerie's association with four powerful men who were in it up to their necks, she looked guilty. Still, any attorney worth their salt knew it was wise to question the obvious. Tuesday evening, still wrestling with the idea as she ate dinner, KC glanced at the *Washington Post*. And there smiling up at her from above the fold was Valerie Beckman with her daughter Phoebe, both in ski attire. They were pictured on an outdoor deck, a ski run in back of them. KC skimmed the article. ***Coeur d'Alene, Idaho***. *Secretary of Interior Valerie Beckman's first visit to the Idaho Panhandle isn't all business.* Beckman's quote: *My daughter and I are enjoying perfect snow and this beautiful part of our country.* The article stated Secretary Beckman was scheduled to deliver the keynote address to the eleven-member Western Governors Conference on Wednesday, January 9. Surprisingly, the newspaper article made no mention of her presidential campaign.

"She's gone until Thursday. That has to be a sign!" KC couldn't wait to call Agnes. "Would you be up for a little caper tomorrow? But first, I want you to know it's illegal."

Agnes didn't even ask what kind of caper. "I'm in, what do you need me to do?"

KC detailed her plan and then said she would rent the van and supplies. She left the uniforms and paperwork up to Agnes.

The following morning, KC drove up in front of Valerie's house on Greenbriar Lane. Joe Rogers, in the passenger seat beside her, turned to KC. "Thanks for waiting until we get here to tell me *whose* house I'm supposed to bug. The Secretary of Interior? In the middle of the week and broad daylight? What the hell were you thinking? I'm not doing this."

"Valerie is in Idaho," KC said. "Don't you read the paper? Come on, Joe, don't wimp out on me. I have to know if Valerie is involved. Agnes and I planned this carefully, so give us some credit. We're here, and the housekeeper hired us to clean windows. While you do your thing, Agnes and I will make these babies sparkle. Come on." Hoping he would follow, KC got out, opened the side door of the van, and strapped a tool belt on over her blue coveralls.

Agnes got out and strapped on hers. "Geez, I look like Dan Ackroyd in *Ghost Busters.*"

KC rang the doorbell and glanced over her shoulder. Joe hadn't moved. A petite, Hispanic woman answered the door. "Good morning, Clear-View Window Cleaners." KC handed her the business card Agnes made on the computer. "Ten o'clock, as promised."

The maid nodded. "*Si, gracias.* Can you tell me how long it will take?"

KC glanced around like she'd done this a hundred times. "Inside and out? Three hours at the most." She motioned to Joe and Agnes to start hauling ladders into the foyer. "We'll do the inside, first. That way, if you have to leave, we won't interfere with your plans."

"*Que bueno,*" the maid said. "Market day today and *señora* comes home tomorrow."

KC saw Joe shake his head then get out of the van; he looked like a man about to be hung. "Why don't the two of you start down here while I look upstairs," KC said. She turned to the maid. "If you show me the second floor and point out any special windows, we'll be out of here in no time. By the way, my name is Alice," KC said and gestured toward the stairs.

"Marguerite," the housekeeper said. KC glanced over her shoulder at Joe and nodded toward the library. He shot back a look that could kill. "Lovely home," she commented as she followed Marguerite up the stairs.

*   *   *

Joe Rogers had done plenty of complicated assignments, jobs where the legal outcome depended on the equipment he chose and his ability to install it. But to hook up Universal Infinity bugs in a Cabinet member's house constituted professional suicide. He felt a thousand butterflies fluttering in his stomach as he followed Agnes into the library. She didn't seem the least bit nervous. He spotted the phone and electric outlets on the far wall. Eye-height above them was a framed picture of the Secretary and FBI Director, Alonzo Volking. "Oh, great." Agnes had set up the ladder and started cleaning the window behind an ornate desk.

She turned and glanced at him. "What's the matter?"

Joe nodded at the picture. "Volking, FBI, aren't you scared? I sure as hell am."

"No, not after KC told me how her father died," Agnes said. "Hey, I'm old enough to be your mother so for the moment, pretend I am. What we're after here are truth and justice. Yes, it's crazy, but what about KC? Some Mafia guy knocks her silly and she doesn't think of giving up. Maybe it takes that attitude when the crooks are this high up. What the heck, isn't it fun doing something a bit dangerous?" Her smile was infectious.

"If you say so." Joe unwrapped his tool blanket and spread it between the desk and the wall. His own invention, the blanket held wire cutters, clips, a cordless drill and a variety of bits, needle-nose pliers, a hacksaw, and a cordless soldering iron. With each tool in its place when the job was done, the blanket guaranteed he didn't leave anything behind. Joe grudgingly admitted KC had as much to lose as he. So did Tony.

Twenty minutes later, Agnes folded the ladder. "I'm finished here, will you be okay?"

Joe nodded, but didn't look up. He wanted to get KC's caper over with as quickly as he could. The Infinity model UIB was an old standby but still his favorite listening device. Installed on a dedicated telephone line, it needed no batteries or power supply. It could be activated by a silent ring from a fixed or mobile telephone anywhere in the world. To initiate surveillance, all someone had to do was dial a pre-programmed number to silently engage it. If someone was on the phone, the Infinity would transmit the conversation. If not on the phone, it picked up voices and activity in the room. The UIB had an eight-minute listening period, but if KC wanted to listen longer, she could redial the code number as many times as she wanted. The clincher, the Infinity was visually and audibly undetectable. Only a professional sweep would find it. Every so often, Joe heard Agnes' and KC's voices. A couple of times he thought he heard the maid's but KC kept her away from the library. The UIB installation complete, he rechecked everything and put his tools away, acutely aware that the only sounds in the room were his breathing and an annoyingly loud grandfather clock. He draped a towel over the tool blanket and opened the library door. Agnes was on her way down the stairs. "All done?"

"Got a couple things to do outside," Joe said, glancing around for Marguerite. He changed to an Atlantic Bell cap and then located the neighborhood phone pedestal a half-block away. It took a few minutes to locate the wires to Beckman's house and hook the Infinity into the system. When he returned to the house, KC was outside cleaning the first-floor windows.

"We're almost done with these, Joe. If you could do the second floor windows with the extension pole, Agnes and I will finish up, and we're out of here." He marveled at KC; she didn't sound the least bit nervous or afraid. *That figures, I'm nervous enough for both of us.*

Joe kept glancing at the street for police cars and then at his watch. They finished at one o'clock on the dot. Anxious to get this caper over, he took the initiative and suggested KC deal with Marguerite while he and Agnes load their tools and equipment back in the van. It took half the time to load it as it did to unload. He and Agnes back in the van, Joe sat nervously tapping his foot, watching KC and Marguerite at the front door. KC handed her the bill and Marguerite gave her cash. KC looked totally at ease as she thanked Marguerite. When she added, "have a nice day" to the diminutive housekeeper, Joe had to stifle hollering at KC to "hurry up!"

She climbed in the van and pulled out of the driveway. "Well, gang, how about *that!?"* KC flashed a grin. "Would we make awesome burglars or what?"

The word *burglar* reminded Joe of Tony's call. "I was so scared, I forgot to tell you, KC. Thanks to your boyfriend, I have another burglary to do today. I may end up in jail yet."

* * *

As soon as she arrived at her office the following morning, KC searched Thursday's *Post* for any story about a bogus window-washing team. She found none, but there was a follow-up article about Valerie Beckman delivering the keynote speech at the Western Governors Conference; it had been well received. When Agnes arrived, she brought two mugs of coffee into KC's office. "I can't stop smiling. I had so much fun. What's today's caper?"

"Give me a minute, and I'll come up with something." Both chuckling, KC and Agnes toasted with coffee mugs. "I am grateful you were there," KC said. "Joe was really scared. I feel bad roping him in like that, but now we'll find out whether or not Valerie Beckman is involved."

Agnes returned to her office, and KC entered in her journal the time and date they installed the bug in Valerie's house. At Tony's urging, she had started a 'case journal' the morning after Captain Appling delivered his devastating news. As painful as it was to read her entries, she was glad she had taken Tony's advice. Every call made, every return call, and each clue was recorded with the date she followed up on it. Also inside were dated copies of every piece of evidence gained so far; the originals were in a safe-deposit box that only she and Tony knew about. The journal was the method of organization Tony used on his FBI investigations.

The intercom buzzed. "Joe Rogers is on line two. He asked me to adopt him, and said he likes the idea of his mother being an attorney." Agnes was laughing.

KC picked up the receiver. "What about me? I'm an attorney too."

"If I keep hanging around with Tony and you and my new Mom, I will need two attorneys." On his cell phone, Joe asked if she would meet him at the Mellon Fountain in front of the National Gallery of Art in thirty minutes. "I have something for you."

Joe was waiting for her when she walked up. "Is this *something* a warrant for my arrest?" KC said, only half-kidding.

Joe grinned and handed her a CD. "Nah, I'm actually considering burglary as an alternate career. The second one yesterday was to retrieve Tony's tape from Elliott Wolf's phone and put in a new one. This recorded everything up to last night. Tony said to give it to you."

"I hope you didn't tell him about *our* burglary," KC said.

"Oh yeah, tell Tony about breaking and entering, bugging a Cabinet member's house with bureau equipment? No, somehow I forgot to mention it."

KC chuckled. "Good, he doesn't need to know. Did you listen to Wolf's tape?"

"I did, as soon as I got home. I called Tony, like he asked, but all I told him was Wolf is leaving for Florida, no details. Tony said he would call you as soon as he has a chance. If he doesn't call, here's his phone number. Tony really wants to know when Wolf is arriving and why. I wasn't sure you'd want me to tell him. Wolf is flying to Miami tonight and he used an alias on his airline and hotel reservations. That's ominous."

"Do you think Tony wants to know so he can follow Wolf?"

Joe nodded. "My guess is yes, but if you don't tell Tony, he can't do it." Joe didn't pose it as a question. "I asked him whether it bothered him to bug Wolf's phone, considering if the Bureau finds out, it would end his career. Tony said *somebody* murdered your dad and his friend and, if Wolf did it, putting him away is worth whatever effort it takes." Joe hung his head. "It made me ashamed for giving you such a hard time about your window-washing caper."

"No, Joe, I was wrong to put your career at risk and I'm sorry. But I'm like Tony. I need to know whether or not Valerie is involved. She may very well be the next President of the United States. And if she is mixed up in this, there is no price too high for me to stop her."

–16–

Tony stared out the window toward Miami, across Biscayne Bay's placid waters, at the moment reflecting the setting sun. This place wasn't a standard Bureau stakeout house. It was a rented, grand old estate in the best residential section of Key Biscayne. This tiny island was the antithesis of Miami with its hordes of white-legged northerners fighting for their space in the sun. Though expensive high-rise condos lined Key Biscayne's beaches, the vacationers that rented them were more the Rolex-wearing, Louis Vuitton-toting kind.

Interesting, Tony thought, how a Columbian ruffian like Enrique Pablo Cardoza had managed to fit in so well with residents of Key Biscayne's palatial waterfront estates. The DEA's informant maintained it was because the drug lord had made it a point to fit in, successfully exploiting his facade as a Miami businessman. He owned a mansion on a spectacular waterfront lot. The Cardoza family regularly attended the island's Catholic Church. He donated generously to local charities, and his wife was active in various clubs. If any of Cardoza's neighbors suspected the true source of his wealth, they did not speak up.

Drug money and Miami were like peanut butter and jelly. Laundered funds paid for elaborate security systems and armed guards to patrol palatial grounds throughout Dade County. Illicit cash bought powerful speedboats to zip away in the middle of the night should the need arise. In the offices of dozens of Miami's skyscrapers were law firms claiming to handle a full range of legal issues. In truth, their role was advising underground clients how to skirt the law to successfully launder drug money.

Though he was in warm, sunny Florida in January, this was not where Tony wanted to be. After KC called that night in a panic and then came roaring back into his life, he discovered his feelings for her had not changed. Her needing his help right now made this assignment all that much harder. *This operation can't be over fast enough.*

Cardoza was under indictment by Dade County. DEA had his giant bowling center, a cover for his thriving drug enterprise, under surveillance. Tony and his three-man team of FBI agents had been called in after the *Miami Herald* published a feature story on a tough-on-crime federal judge. Not long after being assigned the Cardoza case, the judge's daughter and her date were roughed up by two thugs. Though Cardoza was the prime suspect, no evidence could be found to connect him with the thugs, and they sure weren't talking. The thugs' felony escapade is what landed them in FBI territory and created Tony's assignment to join forces with DEA.

Now, both agencies were holed up in an 8,000 square foot estate full of over-the-top baroque furniture and enough surveillance equipment to communicate with Mars. Six agents and a rookie observer had the full-time job of monitoring Cardoza's house across the inlet from their command center. The judge wanted this drug lord locked up and, as head of the FBI team, Tony DeMarco couldn't quit until the fat lady sang.

He had objected to Jared Faver coming along. This operation was no place for a rookie agent, but FBI Director Volking, himself, had okayed it. Faver asked a million questions and volunteered for anything and everything. At this moment, Jared sat monitoring the surveillance equipment. So full of energy and determined to learn, he made Tony feel old. He thought about Joe Rogers' call. Joe said Wolf was coming to Florida, but he didn't say when or why.

Jared rose and faced Tony. "Joe gave you the information you've been waiting for, didn't he? And you want to go after Wolf, but you can't leave, right?"

Tony nodded. "My business with Wolf is private, nothing to do with the Bureau." He walked into the kitchen, Faver following. The room looked like a war zone. They had all agreed that a combined FBI/DEA team of six guys, plus Jared, would draw too much attention leaving the house to grocery shop, so they agreed to take turns cooking. Like most households in the exclusive neighborhood, the nearby supermarket made daily grocery deliveries. Tonight, FBI Higgins and Pruitt were cooking. Claiming to be lousy cooks, they finagled Tony into making the marinara sauce.

Jared went directly to the stove and lifted the lid of a saucepan. "Tasty! This smells super, Tony. Hell, if I were a woman, I would go out with you." Higgins and Pruitt burst out laughing. "Thanks, junior," Tony said. "These meatheads will hound me with that remark." Pruitt glanced up, his look questioning why Tony was hanging around the kitchen. "It's 6:30, Pruitt. How long until dinner? I'm starving."

"So am I," Jared chimed in.

Pruitt glanced at Higgins. "What a pity. Mr. Marinara and Junior G man are starving," he mimicked. "You're single, DeMarco, so you know how to cook. We don't." Pruitt wiped his hands on his apron. "Half-hour, now get outta here."

"C'mon, Faver, if I see much more, I won't want to eat," Tony said, Faver following him back to the command room. DEA agent Rodriguez was monitoring the recorder. Tony peered through the telescope aimed at Cardoza's house. "Isn't that nice, they're drinking champagne."

"No kidding," Jared came up and took a turn at the telescope. "You can't leave, Tony. Let me follow him and see what he's up to."

Tony nudged him, a warning not to talk in front of Rodriguez. "Forget it."

"I'll cover audio, Rodriguez," Jared offered. The DEA agent exited the room, and Jared plopped down in the chair. He looked up at Tony. "I know I'm driving you nuts. Hell, I'm driving *me* nuts. We both need a break." He gestured at the equipment. "I know this stuff, and I know the procedures. You said so yourself, Tony. Give me forty-eight hours to tail Wolf. What's the harm?" Jared's expression showed he was just warming up. "You're the team leader. If you take off, the Bureau will have your ass. And if somebody doesn't follow Wolf, you won't know what he's up to." Jared grinned. "You can't handle that, DeMarco, you know you can't."

"Screw yourself, Faver. Go set the table or something. Let me think." Mulling over his dilemma, Tony came to the conclusion that Jared was right;

he couldn't leave, and he couldn't stand not knowing. He suddenly remembered the CD that Joe promised to make and then deliver to KC. *She should have heard it by now.* Tony used the secure line to call her. "Hello, this is that jerk, Prince Charming. Are you still speaking to me?"

"I am, and I've been scared out of my wits about you," KC said. "Are you all right?"

Good sign, she's worried. Tony started to say they were in a $30 million old Key Biscayne palace, but thought better of it. "I miss you, but otherwise I'm okay. How about you?"

"I miss you too, Tony. Agnes is here. Danny's gone to get pizza. I have so much to tell you, but it can wait—except for one thing. Agnes has the craziest idea to help us." She explained Agnes' plan. "I didn't want to involve her, but she's stubborn, and we could use the help."

"Funny you should say that." Tony said, Jared's offer echoing. "Did Joe call you?"

"Yes, and I forbid you to follow Wolf." *Good. She did listen to the CD.*

"I knew you would say that. Listen, Joe already told me Wolf's coming to Miami, but not when or why. Was it on the CD?"

"I told you, I don't want you to follow him."

"Come on, you know I will find out one way or another, so you might as well tell me."

"Is that true, you can really find out?" He assured her he wasn't joking. "Then damn your Italian stubbornness." She sounded resigned. "He's on Delta flight 2741 arriving in Miami about now, 7:00 p.m. He reserved a Nissan Altima from Enterprise Rent-A-Car under the name of Nathan Spiller. He also used that name on his reservation tomorrow and Sunday night at the Ocean Guest Suites in Vero Beach. I didn't hear anything that told me why he's in Florida."

Tony scribbled as he listened. "I understand a Mafia-type roughed you up, so you took out his knee. Tell me, what are you doing for fun?"

"Don't change the subject. Tony, please don't go after him."

"I have to, KC. I have a hunch he's our killer. You want to know, don't you?" She grudgingly agreed. "Listen," Tony said. "My leather jacket is in your entry closet. In the right pocket, you'll find the key to my apartment. It's wrapped in a piece of paper that has my alarm code on it. The videos of your dad's service, the accident report, my whole file on the case is in the bottom right drawer of my desk."

"If you are trying to scare me, you're doing a good job. I thought you wanted to talk about us. Please don't do this, Tony."

"I do want to talk about us. The minute I get back, we'll go to that restaurant I booked for New Year's Eve. We'll drink champagne and talk. I promise." Tony rose and looked in the telescope. People were moving around. "Tiger, I have to go. I'm sorry." He paused, not sure whether to say it. What the hell, he thought. "I love you, KC. I never stopped loving you, and it would be a sin if we never get to be together." He hung up before she could say anything. He had to move fast.

Tony got on his laptop and found the phone number for Ocean Guest Suites in Vero Beach. "I'll take any room you've got for the weekend." The young-sounding male clerk responded by apologizing then telling Tony he had no rooms available. "January is our peak season." Tony wadded up a piece of paper near the mouthpiece. "Would two bills help find a vacancy? This just came up, or I would have called earlier."

A brief silence, then, "two-hundred bucks? Would you say it's an emergency?"

"Would that make a difference?" The clerk said it would. "Yes, it's a big emergency, and I'm leaving within the hour from Miami. Can you help me?" Tony said.

"I believe I can. Craig is my name. What's yours?"

"Ventano. Alfred Ventano. Two bills are yours, Craig. Thank you."

Tony hung up and ran through what he planned to tell Higgins and Pruitt: he would be gone no more than forty-eight hours and would check in three or four times a day. Convincing Pruitt would be easier than getting Faver off his back. Tony decided to assign him to photograph Cardoza's party guests and run ID's on all the adults. The last few days, talk around the Cardoza table had been about an upcoming *quinceañera,* some kind of party and obviously, a big one.

Both team leaders asked Rodriquez what it meant. He explained that when the daughter of a traditional Latino family turned fifteen, the family held a celebration to mark her passage from childhood. Socially, it was similar to a young girl's coming-out party, but with serious religious overtones. A *quinceañera* involved a church ceremony; the honoree wore a formal gown and was blessed by a priest who then gave the girl her first communion. Afterward, tradition called for a celebration, the size and sophistication of the event in keeping with the family's wealth and social stature. Rodriguez said with Cardoza's money, the party for his daughter would be a fancy catered banquet, plenty of champagne and drinks, a live band, and lots of presents to honor the young senorita. The preparations going on at the estate lent credibility to Rodriguez's prediction. Catering trucks had delivered tables and chairs and set them up in the backyard. Tiki torches had been installed along the length of the wooden dock. A marine-blue canopy erected at the end of the dock indicated that the Cardoza family expected some of their guests to arrive by boat.

This is a perfect time for me to get away. Tony smiled, congratulating the timing. He entered the dining room and took a seat, ready to tell them his plans. All talk stopped; Tony looked at Williams, the DEA leader. "What's going on?"

"A break in the case," Williams said. "We just got a grocery delivery we didn't order. The delivery was our informant's disguise. He said the party is a cover for a big drug transfer. It's going down Sunday night as soon as it gets dark."

"Dammit," Tony said, with a glance at Faver. The rookie looked like he'd just won the lottery. Tony ate his dinner, resigned to the fact there was no way he could leave to follow Wolf. What he was wrestling with was whether to allow Faver to go instead. Even if it were a take-no-action, observe-only mission, he couldn't risk it. Tony looked at Faver and shook his head.

Faver jumped up from the table. "Tony, could I speak to you in private?" Tony followed him to the laundry room. Faver looked ready to burst. "Dammit, Tony! You know I'm capable. So why not? Give me one good reason."

"Because Wolf may be a killer. That's reason enough," Tony said.

Faver's hands went on his hips, a defiant stance. "What do you think I'm going to do, challenge him to a gun battle? Gimme a break. I'm not stupid. I'll try to find out what he's up to, nothing else. Come on, Tony, don't make such a big deal out of this. I'm a big boy."

Tony eyed him, six-feet tall and two hundred pounds of pure determination. Tony sighed. "You are a royal pain in the ass, Faver, but I want your word. You will take no action. You are to observe, record names, descriptions, and license plates. Report where he goes and whatever you feel will give us a clue as to what he's up to. Keep your guard up, no heroics. And above all, no confrontations. Got it?"

"You have my word." Faver holstered his Smith and Wesson and began packing.

Tony handed him a briefcase. "Here's everything you need to pass yourself off as Alfred Ventano, businessman. Wolf has reservations at the Ocean Guest Suites on Ocean Drive in Vero Beach. Here's the address." Faver glanced at it and put it in his pocket. Tony handed him two one hundred dollar bills. "Give these to Craig, the desk clerk."

Faver listened, processing the information. As they walked to the garage, Tony delivered his strongest "be careful" lecture and then reluctantly surrendered the keys to the rented, black Buick Grand Am. "Keep yourself safe, Faver. Check in three or four times a day so I don't worry. And get back here soon as you can."

Jared handed over the keys to the sedan shared by their team. "Good luck with the raid, and thanks for this, Tony. Nothing to worry about. I promise I will be careful."

Tony watched the tail lights disappear, a cloud of doubt enveloping him. *He gave me his word he's only going to find out what Wolf is up to.* "He'll be okay," Tony kept saying as he sprinted back into the house. Williams met him in the hallway. "Glad we can finally get this show on the road." He asked about Faver.

"He left for a quick assignment up the coast," Tony said and agreed with Williams. "Now maybe we can wrap up this case. Did the informant get back into Cardoza's house okay?"

Williams nodded. "Ten minutes ago with a bunch of pizzas. Judging by the conversation, looks like he's clear. Everybody, including Cardoza, is excited about the party. There are a dozen people drinking champagne and eating pizza."

"Champagne and pizza? They're not Italian," Tony said. When the two of them entered the command room, Tony offered to call the judge for warrants. "Friday night, I hope he's home. How 'bout it, knock or no-knock warrants?" Tony grinned, knowing what Williams would say.

"No-knock. I want to see Cardoza's face when we crash through his front door."

"Gotcha." Tony placed the call, grateful to find the judge at home. When he came to the phone, Tony apologized for calling on a Friday night. "Your Honor, we have a reliable tip that a drug transfer is going down Sunday night at the Cardoza house. He's using a big party as cover. Is it possible to get warrants in time?"

"My wife and daughter would have my head on a plate if you don't. I'll call my secretary right now and see if she can meet us at my office in the morning. Get me the address plus any and all vehicle descriptions and license numbers. Boats, too, if you plan to include them. You need the standard drug warrants?"

"Yes sir, for cocaine, heroin, crack, and all the fruits of drug trafficking,"

"It's sad but that wording is as ingrained as my nightly prayers, Agent DeMarco. Knock or no-knock on the search and arrest warrants?"

"No-knock on both, sir. We'll have the manpower."

"Well done, DeMarco. I'll call you with a time as soon as I talk to my secretary."

Tony gave him the telephone number. "Thank you, Your Honor. If I'm not here, tell Agent Williams what time you want me there." Tony hung up and turned to Williams. "As soon as the judge calls back, would you call Dade County PD for tactical support? Ask their SWAT Team Commander if he could come tomorrow for a planning session. I don't think we should involve the Key Biscayne police department. They have enough to do."

"Roger that. Where are you going?"

Tony glanced at his watch: 8:30 p.m. "I want to review the logistics, so Sunday night we don't have any surprises." He checked his weapon then slipped on a black jacket. "I'll be back in an hour." Once outside, Tony glanced up at a sky full of stars. "Faver, I pray you don't have any surprises either.

* * *

Wolf adjusted the seat belt on the Altima and joined the heavy Friday traffic headed north out of Miami. He knew Florida's Atlantic coast well. Not long after he had joined the Bureau, his boss and mentor, J. Edgar, sent him to intimidate or collect markers from reluctant congressmen and senators. How it amused Hoover when he reported finding a politician with some other guy's wife or with a hooker, both of which made his assignment easier; Hoover had a 100% success rate in getting what he wanted.

The dashboard clock glowed 7:50 p.m. With his stop in Sunny Isles, he could still be in Vero Beach well before midnight. Wolf lit a cigarette and thought about those early days. All these years later, if someone were to ask who had the greatest influence on his life, he would still answer J. Edgar Hoover. Watching him was to watch power in motion. Hoover didn't play both sides; he played all sides. Whatever he wanted from whomever he targeted, he got it, Presidents included. One exception, Harry Truman, who was said to be the only U.S. President immune to Hoover's intimidation.

They were good years, Wolf thought, but nothing compared to being part of Mrs. B's presidential security team. That was the ultimate. His million dollars he hadn't really absorbed yet. It had taken nineteen years to pay off his mortgage. Now in one fell swoop, he could write a check for a condo on Grand Cayman, or fly first class to Europe. He could actually see the Masters in Augusta, Georgia—just the most prestigious golf tournament in the United States. Being at the Masters was something he'd only dreamed about. "And now I will."

A million dollars swept away a lot of moral misgivings.

-17-

Wolf made a brief stop at his former FBI buddy's house in Sunny Isles to pick up the supplies that he'd asked him to get. Boxed and ready were the ingredients for Plan A, and if Plan A didn't work, there was an unregistered five-shot hammerless .38 Smith and Wesson and a box of Plus P ammo. Wolf gave his buddy $500 and promised to return the gun on his way back to Miami. Silence, even by a good friend, had its price.

Wolf arrived at the Ocean Guest Suites shortly before midnight and registered as Nate Spiller. The woman checking him in, Rachel according to her name tag, asked if his Vero Beach visit was business or pleasure. "I plan to retire soon," he said. "I came down to find a condo."

"You've come to the perfect place, Mr. Spiller," she said. "Vero Beach has some wonderful developments, but I have to warn you, condos here range from expensive to obscene, depending on how close they are to the water. If I can be of assistance, just let me know."

"Well, I would appreciate directions to the Chamber of Commerce. I'd like to get a Vero Beach map and a list of developments if they have one. I want to look around on my own first."

Rachel paused, obviously thinking. "Would you at all be interested in meeting a couple who is doing the same thing? Nice people. They've been here almost two weeks, and from what they tell me, they've seen pretty much everything. If you're interested, I could check with them."

"Absolutely, and thank you. That would be a tremendous time-saver."

Despite the late hour, Wolf unpacked straightaway, putting his things in orderly stacks in the dresser. Tomorrow, Saturday, would be a good day to look around Vero Beach. And, if the couple Rachel referred to happened to be Carson Marsh and his wife, his job just got a lot easier.

Wolf slept in the following morning. He ordered breakfast at the outdoor restaurant, noting that none of the guests fit Aubert's description of Carson and Emily Marsh. The sun felt warm and the surroundings so pleasant, that he glanced over the *Wall Street Journal* as he ate. A millionaire now, he mused that he should read it more often.

Wanting to explore the area, Wolf went for a walk and eventually ended up at the beach. Coming across a rental shack next to beach, Wolf impulsively rented a chaise lounge with a straight-on view of the ocean. *This feels great. I would like to live near the* ocean. *With the million dollars, I could keep my Shepherd Park place and have a condo in the Caymans too.* How enjoyable, thinking about all the possibilities a million dollars offered. Even better was picturing himself with the presidential security job. Wolf closed his eyes, his mind skipping over the events that led him to be in Vero Beach.

His exhilaration was fleeting, swept aside by the huge price attached to his million dollars. *How the hell did I let myself get in this predicament?* Frustrated, scrambling for a plausible explanation, Wolf abandoned the beach and walked back to the hotel. He arrived with his answer: "Mrs. B." If Carson Marsh spilled what he knew, it would destroy her. The answer didn't make him feel any better, only resigned.

Rachel held up a note as Wolf entered the lobby. "I spoke to the couple I told you about, and they asked me to give you this." He slid a twenty across the counter. "Thank you, Rachel. I really appreciate this." He walked to the elevator, reading the names on the brass plaque beside the door as he waited: Neil Armstrong, Clint Black, Jane Fonda, John Glenn, President Jimmy Carter, Mary Higgins Clark, and Nicholas Sparks; each had stayed at Ocean Guest Suites. In his fourth floor suite, Wolf plopped down in a chair and read the note signed by Emily Marsh.

Inviting him to join them at the poolside restaurant for dinner, the note seemed almost prophetic. Wolf purposely distracted that thought by watching the evening news. Later, in the shower, he verbalized his decision. "Forget how or why I got into this predicament. I'm in it, so just get it over with." Saying it aloud helped.

Dressed in Dockers and a Jack Nicklaus polo shirt, Wolf put on his signature Porsche sunglasses and surveyed himself in the mirror. His reflection confirmed that he could pass for an about-to-retire architect who loved golf. Wolf strolled into the outdoor restaurant, noting almost every table was occupied, several with white-haired couples. But Carson and Emily Marsh were easy to spot. Their attire shouted money, and they kept glancing at the entrance expectantly.

Wolf headed their way. "Mr. and Mrs. Marsh? Nate Spiller."

Carson Marsh rose and shook his hand. "Delighted to meet you. This is my wife, Emily."

"Call me Nate, please." Carson Marsh did not look to be in poor health. While not robust, he was far from frail. Emily appeared to be in her sixties and definitely a golfer, her face and arms tanned and freckled, except for her white left hand. She noted his white right hand. "I don't know many lefty golfers," she said. "Where do you normally play?" He gave her the name of a club in Minneapolis and changed the subject, asking her handicap. She sailed off on what Wolf quickly found out was her favorite subject—golf.

For the next two hours he forgot his mission; he enjoyed their company and the pretense of being an architect from Minnesota. At Syracuse University, before he changed his major to Criminology, he had considered a major in architecture and taken several classes in it, enough to comfortably discuss the subject. By the end of their meal, Wolf had a date for Sunday golf at the Whisper Lakes Golf Resort with Carson and Emily Marsh.

"Nate, after golf tomorrow, we'll show you the unit we bought and tour the furnished models," Emily said. "Being an architect, you will appreciate the amenities. We are so excited."

Carson assured Wolf their experiences would save him at least two weeks of searching. "We bought at Whisper Lakes because it's one of the last gated communities on the barrier island," he said. "And, honestly, Nate, it has every amenity you could possibly think of."

Emily chimed in that they were less expensive than similar units in Palm Beach. "And, would you believe, a golf cart comes with each unit? Isn't that just to die for?"

"It most certainly is." Wolf pulled out Emily's chair for her. "What else could anyone possibly want?" He insisted on buying their dinner, and they parted with the promise to meet in the lobby at nine o'clock the following morning. Wolf returned to his room and checked the box of supplies from Milo. He had everything he needed. Like it or not, tomorrow was the day. Wolf refused to dwell on the fact it would be the last Sunday of Carson Marsh's life.

*   *   *

Cardoza's estate dazzled in Sunday's late afternoon sun, to unknowing eyes appearing to be the site of an impressive party in the making. To Tony observing from across the inlet, it was an elaborate cover. "The best shindig laundered money can buy," he said, watching it unfold.

A wrought iron fence, with stone pillars spaced ten to twelve feet apart, surrounded the massive Tudor mansion and grounds. The double wrought iron gates stood open as delivery vans, SUVs, and catering trucks arrived and departed. Tony called out license numbers and descriptions to Pruitt and Higgins who entered the data on laptop computers. Two men pushing dollies loaded with cases of wine used a makeshift ramp into the back of the house. Seven young men, obviously band members, alighted from a van and began hauling instruments and sound equipment into the backyard. Two guards, both with a sport coat no doubt to hide a weapon, directed traffic and assigned parking. Each one continually wiped his brow with a handkerchief. Tony had a good side view of the two-story house and a portion of the yard in back. The broad expanse of lawn ended at the bay. He also had a partial view of the estate's six-car garage with servants' quarters above.

Tony checked his watch, 4:30 p.m., and glanced at Williams, on the phone to his boss in D.C. "Both of our teams are set. Dade County PD came through big time. They're due here at five. No! No way! I need at least a week or ten days off when this OP is over. Forget it. I don't need to deal with this right now." Williams slammed the phone down. "Damn, he's got another assignment for me the minute this one's over. That pisses me off."

"You'll need some time with your family," Tony said. Williams agreed. Over the past two weeks, Williams had mentioned that he had two sons in high school and a daughter in her first year at Rutgers. "And I have a twenty-fifth anniversary coming up. I am a fortunate man."

"Does your wife work?" Tony asked, curious if she was career-oriented like KC.

Now watching Cardoza's with binoculars, Williams answered that she didn't anymore. "She taught history at Rutgers University until the kids started middle school. She switched to teaching a couple classes each semester online which she could do from home. With three teenagers, we figured it was a good idea. What does your girlfriend do?" Williams asked.

"A Department of Justice attorney with a black belt in Kenpo karate."

Williams whistled. "Wow, I used to think Sheila was scary. You got me beat."

Initially against the joint operation, Tony had come to admire Williams, a man with a dangerous job who still managed to have a good marriage and family. *Exactly what I want,* Tony thought. He glanced at his watch, wondering how Jared Faver was doing. In his call last night, Faver had said Wolf had dinner at the hotel with a man and woman, and they made a date for Sunday golf. *I hope he checks in again before the fireworks start at Cardoza's.*

Friday night's reconnaissance convinced Tony they would need a perimeter team of two men to secure the exterior of the mansion—cover any activity or movement along the outside walls. He and Williams agreed their combined teams, except for Pruitt, would comprise the entry assault squad. A former SWAT Team leader, Pruitt, along with Captain Evans from the Dade County Police Department, would jointly command the Op SWAT Team. An auxiliary DCPD tactical support team would seize yacht crews and round up any suspects from the backyard. A marine division, consisting of ten agents and five boats, had the job of searching and seizing any product on guests' boats. Four specially trained DCPD officers would break, rake, and freeze the dozen or more rooms inside the mansion to ensure no product got flushed down sinks or toilets. Dade County had also committed a fleet of vans to haul away detained suspects and or witnesses. Counting the technicians who would take over manning the equipment at the surveillance house during the bust, the combined task force numbered forty men and women.

The informant said the church part of the *quinceañera* celebration would end around five-thirty, the family back at the mansion by six o'clock. Guests would start arriving at six-thirty, dinner would be served shortly after, and then the band would play. Plenty dark by then, the music was designed to cover the drug transfer activities. The informant said large drug orders would leave by boat, smaller ones in caterer and florist vans. He promised to signal with a lamp from the upstairs corner bedroom when the transfers started.

Tony checked his watch. "Wow, it's only five o'clock."

"I know," Williams said. "I hate waiting. We need patience, DeMarco. Right now."

* * *

Not long into their Sunday morning golf game, Emily began a sales pitch to convince Wolf he should buy a condo in Whisper Lakes Golf Resort. "It's exclusive and perfectly located on the barrier island that runs parallel with mainland Vero Beach. It takes no time at all to cross one of the causeways, Nate. You will love it." After a tour of the grounds on their way to the first hole, he had to agree with them, the development was first class. Gated, sprawled over three hundred manicured acres, it had a spectacular Jack Nicklaus course and a posh clubhouse with a five-star restaurant and grill. Viewing the health center with its virtual sea of exercise machines, Wolf had to admit that Whisper Lakes was "Nirvana," delighting his hosts, especially Emily.

I *could* get used to this, Wolf decided as he waited for Emily to putt, his attitude the result of accepting his situation, Aubert included. A million dollars opened up a world of potential. For the first time, he could see himself fitting in with people in Emily and Carson's social strata. As the match progressed, Wolf observed the way they handled themselves, how they functioned in a world that would soon be open to him. He thoroughly enjoyed the golf. Emily had devoted a lot of years and money to her game. She parred the third hole, 173 yards with three water hazards. On hole four, when her second shot landed pin-high on the elevated green, a green ringed by sandtraps, Wolf took his hat off to her and literally bowed.

Carson said his enjoyment came from the scenery and being outdoors more than the game itself. But he did lament having to use a cart because of his difficulty breathing. "Carson has congestive heart failure, the same thing his father and grandfather died from," Emily said to Wolf, glancing at her husband to make sure he couldn't hear. Carson's breathing had become more labored as the temperature and humidity increased, so much so that when they finished hole fourteen, Wolf offered to suspend the match and get Carson back to the hotel. Waving it off, he retreated to the golf cart. "I'll stay out of the sun. You two play out the match and I'll watch." Wolf gave the caddy a ten-spot to bring cold orange juice, which seemed to rally Carson.

After their match, he waited in the air conditioned office while Emily showed Wolf the models and the unit they bought. He didn't have to pretend enthusiasm; their condo had a great floor plan with a spacious deck that offered an unobstructed ocean view. On the drive back to the hotel, Emily was already planning golf games and dinner parties after Wolf bought his unit.

He slowed his walk to match Carson's as they made their way from the underground garage to the lobby. "Thank you, Nate. I'll be fine," Carson said. Wolf caught Emily's worried glance as they entered the elevator. When it arrived at their floor, Wolf held the door open for them. "I discovered this wonderful ice cream shop near the beach. I would like to host a treat after you rest, Carson. Guaranteed to perk you up," Wolf said.

Emily didn't wait for her husband to answer. "Oh, Nate, that would be lovely." He asked their favorite flavors and suggested they come to his suite around three o'clock. As they exited the elevator, Emily was still thanking him for the wonderful match. Wolf rode the elevator to the fourth floor then raced down the stairwell and hurried out of the hotel.

Plan A was about to be launched.

He entered Polar Paul's cool, sweet-smelling ice cream shop and ordered four flavors in hand-packed quarts. He asked the young girl to include four extra empty cartons and several Styrofoam bowls. "Small party," he explained. When he returned to the hotel, Wolf parked his rental car in the small, outdoor lot near the entrance. Back in his suite, he went to work dividing the ice cream and marking the cartons to make sure he served Carson the right ones. That done, he disinfected the sink and counter then put everything away--phase one of Plan A complete. A few minutes after three o'clock, Wolf welcomed Carson and Emily. Carson walked in with a regular stride and his color returned. Emily entered, enveloped in a cloud of expensive perfume. "You look great, Carson," Wolf said. "All you needed was to cool off and rest a bit." The air conditioner hummed; his suite was pleasantly cool.

Emily went straight to the sliding glass door and gazed out at the sea. "I love this corner suite. The view, isn't it divine?"

Wolf joined her. The afternoon sun splashed pinpoints of light across the calm sea. "This is a beautiful area." He glanced down at the pool. A twenty-something guy got out of the pool, dried off, and stretched out on a chaise. The same guy he saw at Polar Paul's, Wolf noted. *Probably a college student on Spring break.* Wolf went into the small kitchen and began dishing up ice cream, his back to Emily and Carson. "I hope you don't mind Styrofoam bowls."

"Not at all. Are you sure I can't help you?" Emily offered.

"Thanks, but not necessary. Being a widower, I'm used to fixing food for myself." Wolf filled Carson's bowl from the marked carton then deftly changed to a different spoon to dish up a bowl for Emily and one for himself. "I admit that ice cream is one of my weaknesses," he said as he handed Emily a bowl of pralines and cream. Next, he served Carson a bowl with two large scoops of jamoca almond fudge, his declared favorite. Wolf ate his ice cream, his gaze on Carson. There was nothing wrong with the man's appetite.

Emily steered the conversation to real estate. "I'm so pleased you like our Whisper Lakes complex. Are you going to buy a condo soon?" Wolf artfully dodged her question and changed the subject to golf. If she noticed the switch, she gave no indication. Emily Marsh loved to talk about golf as much as she loved to play.

Carson finished his ice cream first, thanked Wolf, and said it was delicious. "Glad you liked it." Wolf jumped up. "But now you have to try
Emily's favorite, pralines and cream. Am I right, Emily?" She urged her
husband to try some. Using the spoon he kept separate, Wolf dished two
good-sized scoops from the second marked carton into a clean bowl and
served it to Carson. Conversation continued, Wolf asking what courses they
played.

Carson finished every bite. "No more for me, thanks. A little nap and this
treat, and I feel quite well." He set the bowl on the coffee table. "At dinner
last night, you asked where we were from, and then we got off on golf, and I
don't believe I ever told you. Emily and I are from Washington, D.C. I
recently retired from a government position."

Wolf removed the bowls to the kitchen area. "Is that right?" Recognizing
the opening to a lengthy discussion, he glanced at his watch. "I do apologize.
This has been delightful, but would you mind if we saved that topic for our
next get-together? I'm scheduled to meet a realtor. Had I known about you
two, I wouldn't have contacted him. He's showing me a few properties."

Emily frowned. "That's too bad. Carson and I were hoping you would
join us for dinner."

"How about lunch tomorrow?" Wolf said and walked them to the door. "I
want to see your condos again. I'll meet this fellow, but I'm sure your
complex is going to be the best buy."

Carson shook Wolf's hand, his grip surprisingly strong. Emily's smile
returned. "Don't you let him talk you into buying anything. I know we are
meant to be neighbors and friends."

Wolf gave a mock salute. "Wouldn't think of it." He closed the door and
then began cleaning up. Wearing latex gloves, he held open the large plastic
garbage sack from his box of supplies, then tossed in the ice cream cartons,
all of the bowls and spoons, the empty brown bottle of Paraquat, and the
small food processor. Wolf scrubbed the sink and counters with hot soapy
water and then deposited the sponge, gloves, and paper towels into the sack.
It fit inside his largest suitcase. After making sure the stairwell was empty,
Wolf exited the hotel. He drove west on Highway 60 toward citrus country.

Thirty minutes later, he was in rural farmland. Farmers didn't have garbage pickup; they had to haul their garbage to rural dumpsites. After driving two miles past orchards lining both sides of the road, he spotted a sign: *rural disposal site, one mile.* A right turn, then a quarter-mile on the dirt road, and there they were, a dozen dumpsters, side-by-side. He picked the farthest one, took out the top two sacks and threw his sack in, then tossed the two bags back on top.

On the drive back, Wolf studied his feelings: *Uneasy and anxious? Yes.* Neither was he completely confident that he'd used enough Paraquat to do the job quickly. Carson's difficulty breathing, even sitting in the golf cart, spoke of a severe heart condition. Still, telling himself that Carson wasn't going to live much longer anyway did little to lessen Wolf's anxiety.

Back in Vero Beach, Wolf drove past the hotel, noting the absence of an ambulance parked in front. A few blocks farther on, he found a parking place across the street from Waldo's, 'a Vero Beach landmark,' according to Rachel, the hotel clerk. One glance told him why: the bar, the restaurant, even the outdoor deck, had been built with driftwood. Wolf walked through the bar and found a table outside, close enough to the water to see and hear the waves. College-age waiters and waitresses in shorts and tee shirts hustled in and out of the restaurant.

Wolf ordered a beer and waited. A newspaper story about a physician who had killed his wife with the weed killer, Paraquat, was what prompted his research into poisons. Delivered in something sweet and ice-cold, like a milkshake or bowl of ice cream, Paraquat produced the same symptoms as a myocardial infarction. With symptoms so similar to a heart attack, any busy ER doctor would assume the obvious without solid evidence to the contrary. Surely it would apply to an old man with a significant history of congestive heart failure.

If so, Carson Marsh should soon appear to be having a heart attack. As if on cue, Wolf heard a siren. It grew loud and then stopped—close by. Eerily, a few minutes later, the wind suddenly picked up and dark clouds rolled in over the deck just as the siren wailed again then faded. Wolf rose and left a bill on the table, then walked out of Waldo's, his fingers crossed. Providing he had used the right amount and the toxic liquid done its job, at this moment, Carson Marsh was being dispatched into the hereafter like a noxious weed.

Wolf hurried back to the hotel, not surprised to find the light on his phone blinking. Emily was nearly hysterical, saying she was at the hospital and asking him to come. He looked up the hospital address and steeled himself during the short drive. A nurse led him to the ER, and Emily rushed into his arms, the very reaction he had braced himself to face. Carson looked dead, as still and white as the sheet that covered him as monitors beeped and hummed their life-affirming signals. A young doctor entered quietly, studied the monitors and shined a penlight in Carson's eye. "He's stable at the moment, Mrs. Marsh. We're doing everything we can."

For the next half-hour Wolf waited with Emily, watching a steady stream of nurses and technicians come and go, checking on Carson. "It's my fault. I shouldn't have let him play golf," Emily said; she couldn't stop crying. Just as he started to tell her she shouldn't blame herself, the monitor's steady rhythmic beep halted and, a millisecond later, switched to a frightening high-pitched whine.

He felt Emily stiffen. A nurse ran and yelled, "Crash cart!" Right behind her, an orderly appeared with the cart followed by the young doctor. He jerked the sheets off, and chaos followed. All eyes of the medical team were on Carson as the doctor shocked his chest. Wolf buried Emily's face against his coat to shield her.

The doctor tried four or five more times and then stopped. He turned toward them, a look of defeat on his face. "I am so very sorry, Mrs. Marsh."

–18–

J ared Faver spent the afternoon lounging in the hotel's mezzanine, a reading area with a good view of the lobby. Halfway through his third magazine, he spotted Wolf emerge from the stairway with a large suitcase and hurry outside to his car. Jared dropped his magazine and raced down the stairs to the basement garage.

After speeding for four blocks, he spotted Wolf's car and slowed, then followed three or four car-lengths behind. A half-hour later, they had left Vero Beach's suburbs and entered into citrus country. Jared dropped farther back for the next few miles and then purposely sped past a dirt side-road when Wolf turned off the highway.

Puzzled at what Wolf was doing out in the country, Jared drove another hundred yards and nosed his car into an orchard. Through the branches of a grapefruit tree, he kept his eyes on the intersection where Wolf turned. Ten minutes later, Wolf's car reappeared, turned left onto the main highway, and headed back toward town.

Jared followed the dirt road to its destination; it was a rural dumpsite. More than curious, he intended to find out what prompted Wolf to drive forty miles roundtrip to discard *something*. He ruled out the first two bins as too obvious. That left ten bins, but which ones and search for what? He called Tony to report Wolf's odd behavior, but Tony didn't answer his cell. Hands on his hips, Jared eyed the row of bins. *Crap, there wasn't anything like this in the FBI manual.*

The sun had set and daylight fading fast, when Jared jumped out of the bin, smelling as rank as the refuse he'd been rummaging through. A miserable few hours, but he found it. A black plastic bag that looked new and shiny, and felt like it had a small appliance inside. Jared turned on the headlights and peered at the contents. The bag contained a small food processor, an empty bottle that smelled lethal, several plastic spoons and Styrofoam bowls, a pair of latex gloves, and at least four sticky ice cream cartons from Polar Paul's.

"I can't believe it, Wolf took somebody out with poison."

Jared put the bag in the trunk and, heart rate ramped up, drove back to the hotel, angry, but amazed that Wolf, who arrived only an hour before him, had already killed somebody. The only people he'd seen Wolf with were an older man and his wife; they had dinner together. It had to be one of them. Jared entered the lobby ready to race to his room, but the sight of somber-looking guests talking with each other, told him he was too late. The desk clerk stared at him, her nose wrinkled, her eyes questioning. "You wouldn't believe it if I told you," he said.

Whoever Wolf poisoned would have been taken to the hospital. Jared showered and changed, then found the Indian River Medical Center's address in the phone book. He walked into the ER, showed his FBI badge and ID, and asked to speak to the doctor in charge. The doctor was young and cooperative. Yes, an older gentleman had arrived by ambulance, suffering from acute arrhythmia. "We did everything we could, but weren't able to save him." The doctor looked tired and disappointed. "He had an extensive history of congestive heart failure, but I hate to lose *any* patient." Jared learned the man's name was Carson Marsh, and that his wife would not allow an autopsy. "Mrs. Marsh signed a waiver, but I'm sure her primary physician will order one." Jared showed him a picture of Wolf and asked if he had seen him.

The doctor nodded. "He waited with Mrs. Marsh."

Jared called the hotel. Nathan Spiller checked out forty-five minutes ago. Agitated and angry at being one step behind, Jared drove back to the hotel and checked out. He called Tony's cell again as he gassed up his car. Still no answer, so he called the secure line at the house. The DCPD female manning the phone said nobody from FBI or DEA had returned. "Would you give this message to Tony DeMarco, the FBI team leader? Tell him Jared reported and that I'm leaving my location. Surveillance is ongoing, and I'll be back by morning."

Jared then joined the traffic heading south on I-95, Tony's warning about Wolf ringing true. He'd just gotten away with murder.

* * *

Wolf was grateful to escape from Emily Marsh. He did so with a promise to keep in touch, and by giving her a bogus phone number in Minneapolis. Her parting words: "Carson and I had such wonderful plans, Nate. Now I don't know what I'll do." He slipped out of her room while she was on the phone with her children. He checked out and hurried to his room and was packing when his cell rang; it was Aubert. "How did things go?"

"Mission accomplished, what's up? I'm in a hurry."

"I stopped by Valerie's house this afternoon. Volking called while I was there. He was looking for you. Valerie was busy with Phoebe, so I talked to him. He asked if I knew where you were. I told him Florida—with family stuff. Volking sounded upset. He said you'd better not be sticking your nose in the Miami operation. I don't know what to make of it, but figured you'd want to know."

"I'll call him tomorrow." Wolf started for the door as the phone on the desk rang. It had to be Emily. He closed the door, the phone still ringing. Twenty minutes later he was on I-95 south, lighting a cigarette, and going back over the day, point by point. Emily would try to locate Nate Spiller in Minneapolis which would prove fruitless. *I was in and out of there in twenty-four hours. I should be okay.* Ten o'clock, the night's quiet darkness was a relief after the hospital. The doctor and Emily both concluded Marsh's heart simply quit. Wolf agreed and offered his condolences to Emily. The ordeal was over; he did not want to think of it again.

But Volking looking for him was troubling. An enigma, the Director was known as a by-the-book guy, but on a whim would turn his head at agents' flagrant violations. From their long history together with the Bureau, and their mutual friendship with Mrs. B, they were more like old warriors than boss and employee. Volking had remarked more than once that he didn't see what Valerie saw in Aubert. It was Volking's misgivings early-on about Aubert that prompted him to assign Wolf to her security.

A vague, unsettled feeling began to take hold. Wolf couldn't pinpoint it, but he felt okay until Aubert's call. He thought back over their short conversation, word for word. 'The Miami operation,' he repeated under his breath. Those three words brought forth the image of a hotel guest. *Twenty-something, every time I looked around, there he was. At the restaurant when I had dinner with Carson and Emily; across the street from the ice cream shop; below my room.* The image ratcheted Wolf's suspicion to full-blown. *He looked like a student on Spring break, but I never saw him with any other kids. That doesn't fly.*

Awareness of a threat activated like an automatic pilot light; a chill crossed Wolf's neck. His briefcase sat open on the passenger seat, his cell phone on top. The dashboard clock glowed 10:15 p.m. The Director was probably in bed, but this couldn't wait. Wolf auto-dialed Alonzo Volking's private line. It took four rings to rouse him. "Alonzo, Wolf here. Sorry to wake you. Do you have an agent in Vero Beach that's young, good looking, looks like a Harvard jock? Tell me I'm wrong, and I'll let you go back to sleep."

"Let me think." He was silent for a moment. "It could be Jared Faver, the rookie I okayed to observe the Miami operation. But he wouldn't be in Vero Beach. You sure it was him?"

"Pretty sure. I wondered if it was your doing."

"That's absurd. Faver is supposed to be in Miami, observing, nothing else. Agent DeMarco is his supervisor. What are you doing down there anyway?"

"Family business. I took a couple extra vacation days." Wolf glanced up at a freeway sign: West Palm Beach twenty-two miles ahead. "What's the Miami operation?"

"A joint-op with DEA to net a big drug guy," Volking said. "I'll call Miami and find out about Faver. When will you be back in the office?"

"Tuesday," Wolf said. "See you then." He severed the connection.

* * *

Jared spotted Wolf's Altima up ahead on I-95. He changed to the center lane and slowed, allowing three cars in between them. He took his first deep breath since leaving Vero Beach. *Wolf's on his way to the airport—I'll make sure before I go back to the house.* "What the hell?" Without signaling, the Altima moved to the far right lane then abruptly took the Jupiter Beach exit. Jared had to hit his brakes to make it onto the off-ramp. "Now, what's he up to?" Jared muttered. He stayed three cars behind through the outskirts of Jupiter Beach to Highway One, the highway along the coast that connected Florida's beach towns.

High season in Florida meant a crowded highway even on a Sunday night. Jared kept back far enough not to be spotted, but in downtown Jupiter Beach, he saw Wolf turn at a shanty-looking bar on the corner, its neon flashing *The Rusty Anchor*. Jared slowed, hoping the car in front of him would also turn. When it didn't, Jared drove on past, craning his neck enough to see the Altima turn into the parking lot behind the bar. He turned right at the next corner, then right again into an alley that ran parallel with Highway One.

Jared drove north toward the bar and then parked close to the building on his right. Fifteen feet from the street ahead, he had a clear view of Wolf's Altima parked in back of the Rusty Anchor. Sandwiched in between two, two-story buildings, the narrow alley offered perfect cover: a black Grand Am in a pitch black alley. Jared lowered the windows, laughter and conversation drawing closer, and then four bar-hoppers walked by on the sidewalk in front of him, totally unaware of his presence.

Jared autodialed the house's private line on his cell; Pruitt answered this time. He gave him a quick report and pressed the *end* button, suddenly seized by an uneasy feeling. Jared dropped the phone. He had just violated basic surveillance procedure. *Never get distracted.* He felt a chill, the hair on the back of his neck telling him he'd made a big mistake. He grabbed for his holstered gun. Too late. Through his open window he stared straight into a gun barrel. Blue eyes just above the barrel stared at him, eyes so pale they almost had no color.

"Sorry, Faver, nothing personal." The end of the silencer glowed red. So close, it felt like diving into a volcano.

* * *

Tony and Williams waited on their patio as darkness gathered, both of them peering at Cardoza's house through binoculars. Cardoza, his wife, daughter, and a dozen guests had arrived from the church in two stretch limos an hour ago. "This party cover is bigger than I thought," Tony said quietly. He heard Williams grunt affirmation. A few guests and a dozen servants were inside. The backyard had at least eighty or ninety guests, their voices and laughter floating across the inlet. Boats that had delivered guests were anchored side by side along the dock, their crew members aboard. Night settled over the inlet, bringing with it hoards of pesky insects. Tony gritted his teeth and ignored them. "Come on, informant," he whispered, his binoculars trained on the upstairs bedroom.

Eager to help rid Miami of one of its biggest headaches, Dade County Police had come through big time. It would be difficult to identify anyone specifically as an FBI, DEA, or DCPD agent. All were dressed in black with Kevlar vests and armed with MP5s. Team leaders were equipped with standard bone headsets.

At 9:34 p.m., the informant's signal finally came. The lamp in the upstairs corner bedroom came on, went off, and then came on again. Transfer of the drugs had begun. Tony moved his binoculars down to Cardoza's office on the first floor. He was sitting behind his desk talking to five men in a semicircle in front of him.

Each team had their specific assignment, the team leader's job to make sure they "stick to the plan" that Tony and Williams devised with the help of DCPD. "Heads up, party time," Tony said and switched on his headset. "Leader one. All teams, it's a go. Stay safe. Pruitt, your SWAT Team's gonna take out the guards first? Copy."

"Copy that." Pruitt's confirmation sounded in his ear.

Festive sounds of a party filled the neighborhood surrounding the inlet, serving as cover as forty team members encircled the house and the dock. A few minutes later, Tony heard salsa music and laughter replaced by the shouts and screams of panicked party goers. The main assault team, Tony, Williams, Higgins, and Rodriguez from DCPD, used the chaos and confusion for cover to reach the front porch of the mansion. Outside the front door, Tony heard excited shouts inside Cardoza's office; they would be ready for them.

MP5 poised, Tony nodded at Rodriguez and Higgins to kick in the door. Their heavy boots struck it, splintering the frame and sending the door and glass shards flying across the grand foyer. Their team's next step, sensory overload: all four men charged in, hollering, making lots of noise, and throwing slap charges that sounded like explosions. Tony tossed a slap charge into Cardoza's office, BOOM, then Williams threw in a second one. Shots from inside the office sprayed wildly, the reaction the slap shots were designed to create.

"Cardoza!" Tony shouted. "Give it up! If you don't, you die!" With his shoulder against the wall next to the door, Tony fired at an angle into the office, instantly followed by Williams from the other side of the door. "It's all over, Cardoza. Tell your men to slide out their guns. DO IT NOW!" Tony yelled.

Silence from inside the office, and then the sound of metal sliding across hardwood floors. Tony exchanged a glance with Williams: *they've got more than six weapons in there.* Williams shouted, "CARDOZA! Send your guys out, one at a time, hands in the air, or they come out in body bags." Four DCPD tactical support guys entered the foyer and stood, ready to assist. Rapid Spanish from inside, and then one man appeared in the doorway, hands in the air.

Rodriguez and Higgins frisked him, removed a Glock from his coat pocket then turned him over to the support team. Four more men filed out of the office, one at a time, the tactical support team cuffing each one and then escorting all five of them to the prisoner transport van.

Cardoza walked out last. Tony flipped open his coat and removed a weapon from his shoulder holster. "Smith and Wesson 4506 semi-automatic, where'd you get a police issue?"

Cardoza sneered. "Take it. I have many more."

Tony merely nodded. "You are under arrest for the sale and transfer of narcotics, including cocaine, heroin, and all other fruits of drug trafficking." He read him his rights under the Miranda rule, then glanced at Williams. "Anything you want to add to that?"

"Yeah." Williams smiled. "Just to let you know, Cardoza, *you* don't have the semi-automatics anymore, *we* do. Every last crate of police issue 4506s from your warehouse. On behalf of the law enforcement community, I want to thank you. They're gonna come in handy catching assholes like you."

Cardoza tried to lunge at Williams. "You sonofa—"

Tony nodded at Williams, a silent sign for him to have the satisfaction of cuffing Cardoza. Williams looked pleased as he snapped the cuffs on him and motioned for the tactical support agent to take him away.

They exchanged a high-five. "Let's get outta here, Williams," Tony said. "I believe the fat lady has sung."

-19-

KC heard a tap on her office door, and then Joe Rogers stepped inside. One glance at him and her heart almost stopped; his eyes were red and puffy. Joe collapsed into a chair in front of her desk. "Jared Faver was killed last night. Shot point-blank. Died instant—" He couldn't finish.

"Oh, no!" She came around the desk and took the chair beside him. "I am so sorry, Joe. How in the world did that happen?"

"Official version, he was on a stakeout."

KC took hold of his hand. "You don't sound like you believe that."

"Tony doesn't either. He's sure Wolf did it. The drug raid went down last night about the time Wolf landed in Miami. Tony couldn't leave. Jared somehow found out that Tony wanted to know what Wolf was up to and talked Tony into letting him follow him. Tony's devastated too."

"Both of you are, of course." KC said, trying to absorb the news.

He looked crestfallen. "I did something awful, KC. Jared called me last night. I thought he was in Miami with our team. When he said he was in Vero Beach, I freaked. All I could think of was what Volking was going to do when he found out. Jared told me he knew the reason Wolf went to Florida and wanted to know what to do." Joe broke down. "I yelled at him. I told him to get his ass back to Miami and hung up on him! I probably got him killed."

"Joe, don't say that. You're upset. You don't know if that's true. C'mon, tell me what I can do to help—anything."

He wiped his face. "Tony's accompanying Jared's body to Andrews Air Force Base this Friday. Can you come with me?" He glanced at his watch. "Dammit, I've got to get back."

"Absolutely, but why do you have to leave right this minute?" KC still held his hand. He nodded. "Volking wants to see me, and I need to pull myself together."

She walked with him to the door and hugged him. Joe's obvious pain brought back her own anguish, full force. She closed her door, the image of Jared getting shot point-blank too unspeakable to process. Tony had intended to follow Wolf himself; Joe's news could very well have been about him. Tony telling her about the key in his jacket pocket and where he left the CD and his file, that was in case he didn't make it back.

Her father was dead, Santana's father was dead. Donyell Crawford's wife and children were grieving over him. And now, Jared Faver's parents and sister were too. KC's rational mind told her wanting justice was not the same as seeking revenge, but why did she feel the deaths were her fault? She knew the answer. *Because I promised Dad I would bring his killer to justice.* But where was this elusive justice she chased? And how many more would die because of it?

*   *   *

Tony sat lost in thought, staring eastward across the inlet. It looked beautiful outside, a great day that should have been happy, the raid successful, and Jared back with news of his surveillance assignment. Except Jared wasn't coming back. Tony tried to keep his focus on the landscape. It looked serene, and it occurred to him that until this moment, he hadn't thought of it as anything other than the space between him and a bad guy's hideout. He studied it for the first time, noting trees of every shape and variety. Like a park, Tony thought, noticing the different patterns; elongated impenetrable patches of shade; slender dense strips, and dappled pom-pom shadows that changed and moved with the breeze. *Funny, I never noticed the beauty. What else did I miss that cost Jared his life?* A lone message from him lay on the desk, received by the DCPD technician who answered the command phone during the raid. Received at 10:45 last night, Jared's message said: "Tell

Tony I'm leaving my location. Surveillance is ongoing, and I'll be back by morning."

"I never should have let you follow him," Tony muttered under his breath. He put his head down on the desk. It felt cool and dry, not sticky like it would be later in the day. He hadn't been to bed or eaten, but he didn't feel sleepy or hungry. The only feeling he could identify was a heavy feeling inside, sorrow like he felt for Sam, a hollow spot he knew would never be filled.

The aroma of coffee penetrated his fog. Tony lifted his head. Pruitt stood in the doorway of the command room with two mugs. He set one down. "Maybe this will help. You okay?"

"No, but thanks for asking." Tony took a sip and nodded his appreciation. "I'm waiting for Volking to return my call. His secretary said he had somebody in his office."

Pruitt lowered himself onto a chair, his big hands wrapped around the cup. "Williams is still asleep. When did you get back?"

Tony glanced at his watch. "Around four-thirty this morning."

"Did you find my note about Higgins and me arresting the woman in Cardoza's house?"

Tony leafed through the messages. "Cardoza's cousin?"

Pruitt nodded "Gutsy lady, she had her own key and went in right under our crime tape. The sergeant said you and Williams were still checking guys in, so we hauled her downtown." He put down his coffee. "I don't know what to make of it, but I think you need to know this before Volking calls. He called last night wanting to know if Jared was here. I couldn't lie."

"Pruitt, I would never want or expect you to lie."

"I appreciate that." Pruitt pulled a piece of paper from his pocket and unfolded it. "It was kind of weird, so I wrote it down so I'd get it right. When I said Jared wasn't here, Volking said, 'would I be correct in assuming he's in Vero Beach?' It caught me so off guard. I didn't know how to answer, except the truth that I had no idea where Faver was, but I thought you did." Pruitt looked Tony in the eye. "Did you clear it with Volking to send Faver to Vero Beach?"

"No, I did not," Tony answered thoughtfully.

"If you didn't tell him, then how did he know?"

Tony met his questioning gaze. "Good question, Pruitt, very good question." Tony's head reeled with the implications.

"I'd better tell you the rest before he calls. Two minutes after Volking hung up, Jared called, looking for you. He was on his cell. It kept cutting in and out and I didn't get much of what he said. It cleared up enough for me to ask him where he was. He said, 'I don't think Tony would want me to say.' Then I lost him. That was when I spotted the woman at Cardoza's."

The phone rang; they both glanced at it. Tony cleared his throat and answered. "Agent DeMarco." He nodded at Pruitt. "Yes, sir. Yes, I was aware Agent Faver was in Vero Beach. I sent him." Tony crossed his fingers and held them up for Pruitt to see. "The reason? I received word that an associate of Cardoza's was there. I couldn't spare Pruitt or Higgins, so I sent Faver with instructions to observe only. Nothing more."

"What was the associate's name?" Volking said. Tony raised his crossed fingers again and gave the first Hispanic name he could think of. A pause followed.

"Hmm, I see. You understand, this will be turned over to Internal Affairs."

"Yes, sir, and I will make a full report. Williams and I need a few days to close down the operation. I plan on accompanying Jared's body back to Washington on Friday. You will have my report when I get off the plane. Will that be satisfactory?" Tony held his breath.

Volking seemed not to have heard the question. "Sad, losing Faver. Such a fine, young agent." His voice sounded somber. "Very sad indeed."

Tony exhaled slowly. "More than you know, sir." He replaced the receiver and glanced over at Pruitt. "I didn't tell him because something doesn't add up. Maybe it sounds crazy, Pruitt, but right now I don't trust anybody at headquarters, not even Volking. I know Williams could wrap up everything by himself, but I would appreciate it if you would help him. I need to find out what happened to Jared. That means going to Vero Beach."

Pruitt leaned forward. "It won't go any farther, but would you tell me what's going on?"

"Trust me, Pruitt, you don't want to know." Tony gestured at Jared's message. "I don't want to involve you in this. It is too dangerous." Looking puzzled, Pruitt asked if he was in trouble or involved in something illegal. The question felt like a punch in the gut.

"No trouble and nothing illegal. You know me better than that." It dawned on Tony that Pruitt knew nothing about Sam's murder, or that he suspected Elliott Wolf. His friend was operating on trust. "I can see why you might think that, but the answer is an unequivocal no," Tony said. "I am the same square, overachiever you've known for a dozen years, okay?"

Relief flooded Pruitt's face. He rose. "Well, I can see that whatever it is, it's tearing you up. If you need my help, all you have to do is ask." Tony shook Pruitt's hand and thanked him.

After a shower and a quick breakfast, Tony took off for Vero Beach.

* * *

Friday's forecast predicted another cold front working its way up the mid-Atlantic. KC had dressed in warm clothes this morning. At five o'clock, she put on Tony's leather jacket and was about to leave when Agnes buzzed. "Lieutenant Wayne Goodall, want to take the call?"

"Okay, but then I have to meet Joe." KC picked up the receiver. "KC Garrett."

"Glad I caught you, Garrett. I found a witness. An elevator repairman was working on the service elevator at The Jefferson Hotel the night Crawford overdosed."

"I keep telling you he didn't overdose, Goodall. He was murdered."

"You may be right. The repairman said he was in the basement when some big guy, Mafia-type, showed up out of nowhere and tried to use the service elevator. The light was dim down there, and the witness was at the terminal box in back of a post. The guy looked like a hit man, so the repairman said he didn't move. When the elevator wouldn't work, the guy took off."

"Why didn't the repairman report it? Didn't he know about Crawford?"

"No, he finished the job and was long gone by the time they found Crawford's body. But he is cooperative; he offered to help our artist come up with a likeness."

"You said Mafia-looking? Hang on a minute." KC got out her notebook. "I suggest you check your NCIC computer for a Nicholas Ventresca, address: 14007 East Brentwood, Hyattsville, Maryland. I'm willing to bet he's your guy."

"You sure hang around with a strange crowd, Garrett. I'll check and get back to you."

KC hurried along Pennsylvania Avenue toward the FBI building. Turning up the collar of Tony's jacket, she caught the scent of his after-shave. *It's been one tragedy after another since I called him that night.* She experienced a fresh round of guilt as she spotted Joe looking sad, a cigarette in his hand. Blue eyes, short blonde hair, all-American looks, and ordinarily a jokester and techno freak, but not today. "I've never seen you smoke," KC said as she approached.

"The Bureau discourages booze on coffee breaks." His smile only semi-succeeded.

She fell in beside him, and they walked to his car. "Any news from Tony?"

"Not a word. I called Pruitt yesterday. He said Tony was in Vero Beach. That's all I know." Except to thank her for coming, and ask if she was warm enough, Joe said nothing during the drive to Andrews Air Force Base. His sorrow was palpable, tears just under the surface.

They joined a contingent of FBI brass and personnel on the tarmac. The wind had picked up, the American flag blowing straight out. The expected storm wasn't far away.

"Here they come," Joe said as the State Department jet touched down and taxied toward the crowd. The plane rolled to a halt and shut down its engines, a murmur going through the crowd when the cargo door opened. Three crewmen helped Tony lift the casket onto a scissors lift then retreated back into the plane. Tony rode the lift down, his eyes glancing over the crowd. Spotting her, he nodded. Even from this distance, the anguish on his face showed for all to see.

"That's Director Volking with Jared's parents and sister," Joe whispered, gesturing at four people standing away from the others. Broad, and no taller than Mrs. Faver, Alonzo Volking looked liked a bear in his heavy coat and hat.

The scissors lift came to a stop. Three waiting agents stepped forward to help Tony place the casket on a cart. Volking escorted Jared's family over to Tony; he shook Mr. Faver's hand and embraced Mrs. Faver and her daughter. They spoke briefly, and then all five turned to watch the casket being loaded into the hearse. Tony and Volking walked the Favers to their waiting car and stood by as both vehicles drove away. KC asked Joe if they should wait for Tony.

"I'll find out." Joe sprinted toward Tony and Volking. At the first raindrop, the crowd scattered as he jogged back. "Volking wants to debrief him. Tony said he'll see us at the funeral tomorrow." Joe looked as disappointed as she felt. They drove back in silence.

The following morning, KC took a cab to the First Methodist Church in Alexandria. She slipped inside and sat toward the back. The FBI had turned out in full force, Tony and Joe acting as pallbearers along with four other agents. Director Volking gave a moving eulogy, saying Jared embodied the spirit of the FBI, and he died honorably in the service of his country. KC watched Tony and Joe as Volking spoke. Their anguished expressions matched Jared's parents and sister. One of the few comments Joe had made yesterday as they waited for the plane was that he and Tony had been ordered to seek grief counseling.

The three of them walked out of the church together. "You're both without wheels. Where do you want me to drive you?" Joe said as he unlocked his car.

"How about my place," KC answered. "I'll fix dinner for us."

Joe declined, saying he had promised the Favers he would spend the evening with them. "Do you want me to drop you off at your place, Tony?"

"Thanks, Joe, but KC and I have some catching up to do."

*   *   *

Aubert hurried up the front walk, dodging a few icy spots on the concrete. He rang the doorbell, then rang it again, anxious to get out of the weather. The predicted storm had arrived. A cold wind assaulted with gusty blasts, pummeling huge camellia bushes in front of Volking's stately Colonial. Aubert wondered what waited for him inside; an unexpected summons from the FBI Director wasn't a good thing.

Volking motioned him to a chair. "Would you like a drink?" Aubert blinked at the sight of Elliott Wolf sitting there with a highball in his hand. "No, thanks. What's this about, Alonzo?"

"I asked both of you here because this is off the record. Valerie called, very upset, to tell me Carson Marsh died. It came as a real shock, she said, because the last time she saw him, he looked fine. His wife told Valerie that they played golf, he had a nap, and then boom—he was gone. When she told me he died in Vero Beach, well frankly, Wolf, I became suspicious."

"I recognize the name, but who is he?" Wolf answered.

"Used to be the head of BIA," Aubert interjected. "I knew he had a bad heart, but that is a shock. Maybe I'll have that drink after all."

Volking nodded. "Carson once told me that you two were in some kind of business."

"Real estate," Aubert replied evenly.

Volking buzzed for the maid and asked for a bottle of Chivas, some glasses, and ice. "Wolf, you called Sunday night from Vero Beach. What were you doing there?"

"Family stuff. My sister and I took my niece there to visit our mother." He spoke unhurriedly with no hint of nervousness. The questioning stopped when the maid arrived. Volking poured two drinks and handed one to Aubert.

"This business you were in with Marsh, do you benefit in any way from his death?"

Aubert sensed it was time to go on the offensive. "Absolutely not, Alonzo, and I resent the implication. Our real estate deal was penny ante."

"I want the both of you to look at this from my viewpoint. A man in business with you, Jules, suddenly drops dead in Vero Beach, where Wolf just happens to be. And, Wolf, Jared Faver, the kid you thought was following you, gets shot point-blank. Don't screw with me, either one of you. I want the truth. His stare was cold and calculated. Did either of you have anything to do with Jared's or Carson's deaths?"

Aubert spoke first. "Certainly not, I was as shocked as Valerie when I heard about Carson. And I have no idea who Jared Faver is. This is the first I've even heard the name."

Wolf shook his head. "I didn't know either one of them, Chief. As far as the kid is concerned, you've been in the field. Being paranoid is part of the job. I thought he was following me, because everywhere I went, he showed up. Actually, my niece is the one who noticed him. Come to think of it, she was probably who he was looking at. She's beautiful." Wolf shrugged as though apologizing for jumping to conclusions. Aubert relaxed a bit; Wolf was the model of a cool professional. To show he wasn't nervous, Wolf refilled his glass, his hand steady as a rock.

Aubert accepted Volking's offer of a refill. Whether they had dispelled his suspicion, or he simply gave up, the Director converted to polite conversation and thanked them for coming.

*   *   *

Wolf took his leave, acknowledging they had just dodged a bullet. The only reason Volking backed off was because he didn't have proof, but it was obvious he didn't buy their stories. Wolf waited in his car until Aubert exited a few minutes later and signaled for him to follow. Aubert's BMW pulled into the Christ Church parking lot two miles from Volking's house. A Friday evening, the lot was full. Wolf parked close by then got into Aubert's car.

"Great job in there, Wolf. You were cool under fire."

"Don't think for a minute Volking was fooled," Wolf said. "If this happens again, I'll be toast. And I'm telling you right now, if I go down, I'm taking you with me."

"Don't worry, it won't happen again." Aubert's hand rested on a manila envelope in his lap. "You came through for Valerie. Now it's my turn. There's $10K in cash in this envelope plus a Proof of Deposit slip for $950,000.00 at the Bank of Montreal. The rest of your million, $50K in cash, is in a safe deposit box in your name at the same bank."

Wolf removed the Proof of Deposit slip. On it was his name, an account number, and $950,000,00. *More zeroes than I've ever seen.* Awestruck, he felt his misgivings slip away.

"I'm a man of my word," Aubert said. "You saved Valerie's career. The $10K is a bonus, but I'm hoping you wouldn't mind keeping an eye on Garrett, just to know what she's up to."

Wolf could feel several square stacks of bills inside the envelope. "I can do that."

"But not tonight. Valerie and I are hosting a get-together at her place. I told her I was meeting with Volking over a security matter and that you might be there. Valerie wants you to come, not as security, but as our friend. Phoebe said to tell you, you have to come."

"What kind of a get-together?" Wolf wanted to know.

"A dinner party. Vice-President Benchley and his wife are coming, a couple senators and their wives, about a dozen guests in all. Valerie said to tell you she won't take no for an answer." Aubert's invitation sounded genuine and friendly. "You might as well get used to it, Wolf. You will soon be included in everything. What do you say?"

This guy is legit. All Wolf could think to ask was whether he should wear a tux. "A suit is fine, but eventually you're going to need one. Come early. Phoebe said she wants to tell you all about her ski trip."

"Thanks, Aubert. Tell Phoebe and Mrs. B I'll be there."

"I will. I'm glad you're on board, Wolf. We make a great team."

* * *

KC's weekend with Tony seemed an oasis of calm amidst the chaos that engulfed her life. Her battered psyche took a vacation from sorrow and frustration for the first time since her father's death. She and Tony went for a long run; they cooked dinner together and drank wine. They made love, KC thrilling to Tony's touch just like before.

Lying on the floor in front of the fire, he told her about his trip to Vero Beach and how painful it had been trying to find out what happened to Jared. "Wolf had everybody fooled. Everyone at the hotel thought Nate Spiller was a nice, retired guy looking to buy a condo." Tony rolled onto his side and stared into the flames. "I was with the Jupiter Beach police when they unsealed Jared's car. Something large and fairly heavy had been removed from the trunk. I'm guessing it was whatever Jared found at the dump. It's my fault he's dead. I never should have let him go." Tony's acute sorrow was something KC had never seen.

"I know how you feel." She stroked his face. "If I had made Dad go to the police with me that morning after breakfast, he would still be alive. Takoda and I talked about this very thing, Tony. He believes there is a Divine plan for each one of us. We go about our lives making choices, good ones and poor ones. People enter and leave our lives, each person playing a part. But Takoda believes no matter what they do or don't do, it doesn't alter the outcome. Our destiny plays out according to our Divine plan."

"I would very much like to believe that," Tony said thoughtfully.

"Me, too." KC watched as this rational, confident man wrestled with guilt, just as she had done. Tony looked so sad that KC tried to lighten the mood. "I haven't had a chance to tell you, but you should know I am multitalented when it comes to careers." She told him about breaking into Ludlow's office and coming away with proof that he was altering ore figures. Tony listened, clearly shocked, but impressed she could pull it off. When she told him about their window- washing caper and Joe being so scared that Agnes offered to adopt him, Tony had a good laugh.

"You amaze me," he said. "The woman I used to know would have never jeopardized her all-important career. What brought about the change in attitude?"

"Justice. For my dad and Charlie. I hate breaking the very laws I swore to uphold, but do you remember telling me that the judicial system is slanted in favor of the bad guys? It's true! That's really tough to accept if what you're after is justice."

"That makes two of us," he said, obviously thinking about Jared.

"Tony, I'm sorry that I ever got you involved. You should have said no."

"Well, I'm not." Tony fired back. "Maybe the reason I didn't was because I'm meant to play a big part in KC Garrett's Divine plan—and her in mine. I hope so anyway."

~20~

Victor Ludlow finished his $3 million monthly transfer to Bermuda and immediately put the papers in his office safe; he couldn't afford another slip up like with Lily Deerhorn. He needed food and coffee and sleep; he hadn't slept well since the contentious meeting at Aubert's. Even thinking about the meeting made him anxious. The extra money no longer seemed relevant. The more he made, the more his wife spent. Now she wanted a pool and cabana. Ludlow's sunny vision of an early retirement had a dark cloud over it.

BIA's cafeteria was quiet; the lunch shift had yet to arrive. Ludlow went through the food line and took his tray to the farthest table in the corner. The soup and sandwich combo helped, the coffee bringing a measure of clarity. He had tried to forget what came to light at the meeting, but could not. No longer was this deal with Aubert merely about computer transfers and altering ore figures. Culpepper all but admitted Sam Blackhawk's death, and some Indian attorney's too, was their doing. *Aubert has gone too far. I didn't sign up for murder.*

Sally Calder's image intruded into his thoughts; she was headed his way. A friend of Sam Blackhawk, he had no desire to get into a conversation with her. She sat down at another table, but turned toward him. "Isn't that terrible about Carson? Are you going to the funeral?"

"Funeral? Was that what you said?"

"Oh, I am sorry! I just assumed you knew. Carson died of a heart attack."

Ludlow looked at her blankly. "Carson died? Are you sure? Where did it happen?"

"Sunday, someplace in Florida," Sally said. "He and Emily were down there to buy a condo. I didn't mean to blurt it out like that, Victor. I know you two were close."

He recovered enough to reply. "Yes, we were. I must have missed it on the news."

Ludlow thanked her for telling him then hurried back to his office. He called Aubert and Associates but Jules was on his way out the door to a meeting. "I'll let him know you called," the secretary said. Ludlow collapsed in his chair, his mind reeling. *Carson dying from a heart attack? That's too convenient. Aubert did it, I know. But how?* He popped an antacid pill and stared at the telephone, willing it to ring. Aubert's call came ten minutes later. He sounded fine, as though their argument had never taken place.

"I just heard about Carson," Ludlow said. "What a shock. What happened?"

"A heart attack is all I know. A real shame."

Yeah, right. "Who are you going to get to take his place? At the meeting, you said it had to be somebody from the group."

"Taken care of," Aubert said curtly.

"That doesn't answer my question," Ludlow fired back, infuriated at Aubert's arrogance. Ludlow heard him tell someone to go on inside; he would be right with him.

"Listen to me, Ludlow. I'm running this show and I've got my hands full. Just do your job and keep your mouth shut. Philip Jeffers will fill in temporarily, that's all you need to know." Ludlow heard a click; Aubert disconnected. *That was a threat!* Hands trembling, Ludlow flipped back through his calendar to the page noting the meeting: December 2, 3:00 p.m. Aubert's. *The Sunday Denver-Giants game.* Ludlow counted backwards from today's date Monday, January 14. "Six weeks almost to the day that Carson threatened to tell Valerie everything."

I need to talk to Jeffers quick before Aubert calls him. Ludlow almost ran to Jeffers' suite, waved off his secretary, and strode into his office. "I just heard about Carson, and you filling in temporarily. When the hell did all that happen?"

"Six o'clock this morning," Jeffers said. "Out of the blue, Jules Aubert wakes me up and tells me Carson died of a heart attack. Then he tells me Secretary Beckman authorized him to speak on her behalf and asked if I would fill in. I said sure. That's it. You know as much as I do."

Ludlow mumbled a thank you and walked back to his office, frantically trying to sort out the implications. Jeffers was a good guy, but he was someone Aubert could manipulate and keep in the dark. *Aubert just needed a name to give to the newspaper.* Ludlow turned to his computer and accessed the *Washington Post's* obituary page: *Carson Marsh, seventy-three, died at 8:17 p.m., Sunday, January 13, Vero Beach, Florida. Funeral arrangements pending.*

"Carson died last night, less than twelve hours ago, and Aubert already called Jeffers? He couldn't know *that* soon unless he arranged it!" Even as the words left his mouth, Ludlow realized he was next. He had enraged Aubert at the same meeting and now again on the phone. Clammy and nauseous, Ludlow loosened his tie and buzzed his secretary. "I'm going home. I think I'm coming down with the flu. I'll let you know when I will be in."

He headed for the one place he could be alone and think; his yacht in the Annapolis marina. Knowing Aubert, he was already looking for someone to transfer the funds for him. Ludlow climbed aboard, the main salon's quiet orderly space instantly calming. His pride and joy, the sleek fifty foot Hunter was seaworthy, spacious, and comfortable.

He enjoyed every time he'd taken it out. It suddenly occurred that the Hunter could take him anywhere. He could disappear! The mere thought felt like a reprieve from Aubert and the whole mess. Ludlow stared out at nearby yachts rocking gently in the breeze. It was a bold idea.

"But can I pull it off?" Answers filtered in, slowly at first then forming faster how he could escape. *I'll seek immunity for supplying evidence on Aubert. I've got more than enough to send him away for good. The minute I turn over the evidence, I'll motor out of here in the middle of the night. Just disappear. Once Aubert is in prison, I could come back—maybe. Yes, I love*

my daughters. But right now I don't have a choice. I have to disappear. As
soon as I can.

* * *

When KC arrived at the office Monday morning, she found someone else
behind Agnes' desk. "Hi, who are you? And where is Agnes?" "Phyllis, and a
friend of Agnes," the woman replied. Agnes had asked her to fill in today, but
didn't say where she was going or why. KC was curious, but didn't have time
to dwell on it; her day was spent in trial or taking depositions. She returned
to her office at six o'clock and started in on her stack of dictation. Halfway
through a motion, there was a tap on her door. It couldn't be Phyllis; she left
at five.

KC watched the door open and then stared at Agnes, her transformation
nothing short of amazing. "Agnes Richardson, attorney-at-law, at your
service," she said and then bowed. She looked ten years younger, her plain
brown hair stylishly cut and highlighted with streaks. Agnes' professionally
applied makeup looked gorgeous, as did the chic business suit, a polar
opposite from the casual clothes she usually wore.

"Agnes, I don't believe it!" KC could not stop smiling as she came
around her desk for a closer look. "I was here all day. Where the heck did
you spend yours?"

"Bloomingdales, Saks, Estee Lauder's Salon, courtesy of my ex-
husband. A combined graduation present and thank you for my encouraging
Danny to move in with him." She could not contain her excitement. "And I
got the job, KC. I'm going to work for RIC! Neil got me a telephone
interview, and I convinced them that they needed me."

"That's unbelievable, Agnes!" The implications were dazzling, a spy in
the offshore company that received the stolen trust funds. "You're sure you
want to do this?" KC said.

"You bet. The fact that our little window-washing caper was the most fun
I've had in years is pathetic. If there is danger involved, so be it. I'm ready

for adventure. And while she can't possibly compare to me, my friend Phyllis will fill in for me. You'll like her."

"Nobody will ever compare to you," KC said. "How much time do we have?"

"One week," Agnes said. "So let's get with it."

Their week consisted of ten-hour days every day, ending Saturday afternoon at 4:00 p.m. when they declared "mission accomplished." Twenty-four hours later, KC drove Agnes to National Airport to catch her flight to Newark. "How do I look?" she asked.

"Gorgeous and professional," KC answered. "I'm disappointed there isn't a direct flight this time of night. You're staying at the Hyatt in Newark? Be careful, okay?" KC said.

Agnes nodded. "I am so excited, KC. I have never done anything like this. I look back on my life, and all I remember is an eight-to-five job. Right out of college, I started teaching, and the only time I took off was my six weeks of pregnancy leave. Finally, when I burned out doing that and decided I wanted to be a lawyer, I met *you!*" Agnes giggled, which started KC laughing. "Now, I'm on my way to a place I've never been, to do something I've never done. I love it! Agnes Richardson, super sleuth. But you're the one I worry about, KC. Please be careful."

KC waited until Agnes cleared security, then took the elevator to level three of the parking garage. *Agnes really wants to do this, but so did Jared Faver. Tony gave in to him, and now I'm doing the same thing.* The thought that Danny could lose his mother made KC want to turn around and drag Agnes off the plane. Exiting the elevator, she paused, trying to remember where she parked the Honda. Level three was mammoth, the size of a football field, its expanse interrupted only by massive cement pillars. Every parking space looked filled, yet she didn't see a single person. Creepy, she thought, walking toward her Honda. The echo of her boot heels striking concrete, eerie and chilling.

As KC retrieved her car keys from her purse, a movement in the distance caught her eye. A man stepped out from behind a pillar then quickly stepped back. She instinctively ducked behind the closest car and crouched. *I hope he did that because he forgot something in his car.* But uncertain and a sixth sense warning her not to step into the open, KC tiptoed to the nearest pillar and peeked around. Eight or nine rows ahead, the man emerged from behind the pillar and walked to the center. He stopped square under an incandescent light, hands on his hips, looking around. *Nick Ventresca!* "Oh, damn. Oh, damn."

KC drew back and looked toward the elevators, gauging which distance was shorter. The Honda was closer; she peeked around the pillar. *He has a gun!* She didn't wait to find out what kind of gun; he was closing the gap between them. She dropped down and crab-walked forward, keeping three cars between them until she was a row past him. KC went down on her knees and peered underneath the two cars and van that separated them.

All she could see were Ventresca's feet. She froze and watched as he turned around in awkward increments and then stopped, his feet pointing toward the elevators. KC straightened up enough to see him limp forward. She was mystified at still not seeing one person or any cars arriving or departing. *Ten o'clock. Where the heck is everybody?*

She crept forward, stopping only to pick up an orange traffic cone that lay abandoned against a cement pillar, not sure why she picked it up. Finally reaching her car, KC unlocked the driver's door as quietly as she could then inserted her key in the ignition. She peeked over the Honda's roof just in time to see Ventresca on his way back, limping a few steps and then pausing to check each row. *He's getting close!* Suddenly aware she was still gripping the traffic cone, KC backed up for clearance and then sailed it through the air in her best NFL imitation.

Ventresca whirled and fired at the cone. No sound, he had a silencer. She started the Honda and zoomed out backwards, tires screeching to an abrupt halt. KC stomped on the accelerator and aimed her car toward the down ramp. The rear window exploded as the Honda ripped through the wooden arm across the ramp. Careening down the spiral drive, she slowed only when a car nosed in front of her on the ground floor.

Ventresca couldn't follow, but she nevertheless took a circuitous route home. Each turn and bump rained grass shards down from the rear window frame. Amazed that she didn't feel the cold or particularly afraid; she actually felt giddy. Ventresca either had a personal vendetta for her taking out his knee, or Jules Aubert had put out a contract on her. Both scenarios made her chuckle. *It has to be the adrenaline.* Even KC's reliable remedy of a bubble bath and hot chocolate failed to calm her; she hardly slept.

It wasn't until KC dropped off the Honda at a body shop the following morning that she spotted the bullet hole in the dashboard and the two in the trunk. *I'm lucky he didn't hit the gas tank*! She learned that getting shot at and driving through barriers was expensive. After the surprised manager said he would check with her insurance company to see if bullet holes were covered, KC took the Metro to her office.

Her leftover adrenaline seemed to fuel a flurry of creative ideas about the case. One that she decided to follow was to call Emily Marsh. Hopefully, Carson's wife could shed some light on what happened in Vero Beach. After Mrs. Marsh agreed to talk to her, KC decided that idea alone was worth a sleepless night. *Now I know why they say adrenaline is addicting.* An interview with a grieving widow would take diplomacy, KC kept reminding herself on her drive to Georgetown. Mrs. Marsh answered the door of her townhouse, a martini in hand and definitely inebriated. She ushered KC into a large step-down family room, with deep green carpeting, elaborate wainscoting, and cushy oversized club chairs. Emily went straight to the bar and refilled her glass. "I hate drinking alone, Ms. Garrett."

"A martini sounds good." Emily's expression told KC she had said the right thing.

Emily put their drinks on the coffee table. "I am curious. As I recall, you said that you had information I should know," she said, eyeing KC over her glass.

KC sipped her drink, not quite sure how to proceed. Emily Marsh certainly didn't need more heartache. "I don't want to upset you, Mrs. Marsh, but what I have to say might do that."

"Please, call me Emily. If you have information that I should know, I want to hear it, so just tell me."

"Thank you, Emily. All I ask is that you keep our conversation confidential. Do you remember a man in Vero Beach by the name of Spiller?"

"Yes, Nate Spiller. He was looking for a condo when Carson and I were there."

Here goes, thought KC. "What I thought you should know is Spiller isn't his real name, and he wasn't in Vero Beach to buy a condo like he told you. He came to find your husband."

Emily blinked back tears. "You know, I suspected something after every number in Minnesota I tried was either wrong or disconnected. But I never dreamed…"

Now came the most difficult part; telling Emily that Nate Spiller may have caused her husband's death. KC waited, gauging Emily's reaction. With each of KC's words, she leaned closer, her demeanor changing from languid to interested, to alert. Emily set down her empty glass. "This sounds like it's going to hurt. Let's make a pot of coffee. Martinis dull the senses which is why I've been drinking them like water since Carson died."

They moved to the kitchen and spent the next two hours drinking coffee while Emily talked about their trip. Surprisingly, talking seemed to help. She explained how the hotel clerk arranged their initial meeting which led to the three of them playing a round of golf. "Nate was so attentive to Carson during the match when he didn't feel well. Later, he even invited us to his suite for ice cream. Carson and I. . . oh my God, the ice cream!" Emily's hands flew to her face. "Less than an hour after we left Nate's suite, Carson's chest pains started. Nate poisoned him!"

"Oh, Emily, I am so sorry." KC held her hand until she regained her composure. Emily asked Nate's real name. "I can't say just yet, but I give you my word, I will. Also my word that I won't quit until Nate Spiller is brought to justice." KC glanced at her watch. "My goodness, it's three o'clock. I have to get back to work."

Emily followed her outside. "I am very grateful you called, KC. The truth hurts, but it hurt worse to think my pushing Carson to play golf that day caused his heart attack. I'll ask our doctor about the autopsy."

"Be careful," KC said. "If what I told you gets out, you could be in danger. Call when you get the autopsy results, and take care of yourself, okay?"

Emily's sad smile said she understood. "No more martinis. I'll get myself together."

* * *

When KC returned to her office, she had at least six messages from Arizona affirming the truce was holding. She called Tony's cell and told him about her meeting with Emily Marsh. "After their golf game, Wolf invited them to his suite for ice cream. One hour later, Carson went into heart failure."

"That sonofabitch poisoned him! It makes sense now. Wolf dumped the evidence in a garbage bin, and somehow Jared found it. That's why he showed up at the hotel smelling like he did. Jared was bringing me the evidence, but Wolf got to him before he could." There was a long pause. "I have to get this guy, Tiger. It's personal." KC considered telling him about her encounter with Ventresca but thought better of it. Jared's death and this revelation had already shaken him to the core. She didn't want to add to it.

The following morning, her new secretary tapped on KC's door, and entered looking flustered. "There's a man on line two. He won't give his name. I told him you wouldn't talk to him, but he insists. What should I do?" Phyllis had some big shoes to fill.

"I'll take it," KC said. The man sounded out of breath or scared. "Miss Garrett, you don't know me, but I know you. I need to talk about immunity. Can you help me?"

"I'm not sure, immunity from what? Are you talking about a felony?"

"I wish I were." His sigh was audible.

"I gather you are talking about a serious crime. If that's the case, freedom from prosecution depends on the strength of your information about the crime and your evidence."

"Have you ever granted immunity?"

"Yes, several times, but it's not that simple. It would help if you told me the crime."

His one-word answer: *murder.* "I strongly suggest we meet and discuss it," KC said.

"Not at your office. And you would have to come alone." KC concentrated on his every word, his accent vaguely familiar. *How does he know who I am? Could he be involved with Aubert?* She agreed to meet his conditions, hoping it would encourage him. It didn't. "I have to think about it. I'll get back to you." The line went dead.

She buzzed Phyllis. "I'm glad you asked what to do about that call. It could be important. The man said he would call again." Phyllis promised to put him through if he did.

Tony called. "I've got steaks for grilling, salad fixings, and French bread. You hungry?"

"Are you kidding? All I've had today is a martini and four cups of coffee. I'm starving."

He picked her up and drove to her apartment. Ivan flew past them up the steps and then waited, looking up at the doorknob as KC entered the alarm code on the system Tony installed after the burglary. The cat headed straight for the kitchen and took up his position by his empty bowl. "In my next life, I want to be Ivan." Tony filled his bowl with kibble. "If I got treated as good as this guy, I would purr too."

Tony sounded better, perhaps encouraged at the clue from Mrs. Marsh. He casually asked her about the Honda. So far, she hadn't actually lied. She told him her car was being repaired, but failed to mention it was for bullet holes and a shot-out back window. KC poured two glasses of wine and, as they jockeyed around each other in the kitchen preparing dinner, she confessed. Tony reacted the way she feared, incensed that she didn't tell him, and frustrated at heroics that he said were going to get her killed.

She poured more wine, listened attentively, and said 'okay' three times. "Please, Tony, grill the steaks, or I'm going to faint from hunger." He complied, his frustration seeming to diminish. Over dinner, KC told him about her mystery caller. "He wants immunity for his knowledge about a murder. I agreed to meet him because I think he may be involved with Aubert. That's why he called me and not some other lawyer."

They sat on the floor on opposite sides of the coffee table, Tony framed by the firelight. "This is nice, Tony," she said, indicating the dinner and the fire.

He nodded and raised his glass. "To future good times. And, speaking of that, Williams, the DEA leader of our Florida operation, and his wife want us to come to dinner. I think you will like them. She taught at Rutgers University until their kids became teenagers. Now, she teaches online classes from home so she can ride herd on them."

"I know where this is leading, Mr. FBI. There is no gender restriction for riding herd on teenagers. A special agent would make a great wrangler." Tony's laugh was music to her ears. KC told him she hoped mystery man would call back tomorrow and would agree to meet her.

"Well if he does, you should tape the meeting. And no more solo heroics, Tiger. I'm going to be close by." After dinner, he called Joe Rogers. "I know it seems that the only time I call is for a favor. This is one of those times. I need a favor." Tony held the receiver away from his ear, grinning at Joe's comeback. He then told Joe about KC's mystery man. "Would you fix her up with a body wire? Pick up something to eat, and I'll have a cold beer waiting."

Joe arrived an hour later with a calzone, a suitcase full of equipment, and his briefcase. Tony gave him a beer while KC dished up his food. "I don't know what I will do with my spare time when this case is over," Joe said between bites. "Why do you want to tape mystery man?"

"I think he may be involved with Aubert."

"Good enough. We can do audio only or audio and visual. What do you think?"

"Audio only," Tony spoke up. "Less to worry about, and I plan to be close by anyway."

"Okay, you can have your choice of receivers. We have available, at our special introductory price, one hundred to two hundred megawatt output board level transmitters—crystal controlled. Hold your arms out, KC." Joe started hooking her up. "When talking about surveillance equipment, the smaller it is the better. This one has milled aluminum housing which allows it to be ultra thin, so it's easy to conceal. You get to pick the transmitter."

"He calls me at work, so I'll be in office clothes," KC said.

"Gotcha, no baseball cap or a fake pack of cigarettes. I've got it." He pulled out a glass case. "This will work great. The T-60 eyeglass case transmitter, two hundred megawatt output." Joe seemed more like himself, joking, talking technology and equipment. "It's easy to operate." He showed her how to turn it on and off and tested the transmitter. When they finished, he repacked his duffel bag. "What do you hear from Beckman's house?"

"Nothing. I don't have the access number, so I haven't done anything."

"Oh yeah, I forgot. Could have been because I was scared out of my freakin' mind over our window-washing caper." He wrote the number on a pad. "Just dial it like any call, and it activates the Infinity. By the way, have you heard from my surrogate mother?"

"No, but if you've got a minute, I'll check." KC had a dozen or more messages, one strange one from a *rotcodsiruj*. Joe and Tony were standing behind her.

Joe chuckled. "Juris doctor spelled backwards. Pretty smart, Mom. Looks like she encrypted the message." He retrieved a card from his briefcase. "Each letter has a numerical value, but in varied sequences. Watch this." Joe printed Agnes' message about island food and suffering from jet lag, then showed KC how to decode it. It read: *Let me know if you can decipher this. Tight security here, cameras, guards, the works. Will start learning the system soon. I dig this secret agent stuff. Snail mail address, Cottage #23, Surf Side Beach Club, Warwick, Bermuda, zip WA72. I'm being careful. You do the same.*

"Amen to that," Tony and Joe said in unison.

–21–

The following day, KC took the body wire equipment to work in case mystery man kept his promise. She couldn't help noticing the area code of incoming calls, the one ringing at the moment from Arizona. It was the lead attorney for the mine. "Ms. Garrett, we have a problem."

"I so dislike that phrase. What is it?"

"In short, complicity by the DMEA. I have two staff members going through old boxes, and the more they go through, the more evidence we uncover."

"What kind of evidence?" Familiarizing herself with the case, she had come across the DMEA, Defense Minerals Exploration Administration. Created by the government during World War II, its role was to speed up finding deposits of lead and zinc critical for the war effort. But relevant to this case, before and during the early part of the war, the DMEA had joint-ventured exploration with several mining companies, the mine near McCrary being one of them. "So, what have you got?" she wanted to know.

"Bottom line, the government not only found and extracted ore, but willingly participated in discharging waste into rivers and streams around McCrary."

KC recognized a legal fishing expedition when she heard one. "Let's be straight, okay? Are you looking to reduce your client's cleanup percentage or weasel out all together?"

He chuckled. "That's your version of 'straight'? You know as well as I do that this suit is political, the government covering another screw-up."

Phyllis appeared in the doorway. "Mystery man, line two."

"Counselor, I have an urgent call. I'll get back to you," KC answered line two, hoping she sounded calm and professional, not at all like she felt.

"I called yesterday about immunity, do you remember?"

"Yes, I remember." KC crossed her fingers. "What did you decide?"

Silence, then a sigh. "I guess it would be a good idea to meet."

"I think that's wise. Tell me when and where."

"Today, four o'clock, Bartholdi Park, the Third Street side of the Reflecting Pond near Pennsylvania Avenue."

"Short notice, but I'll make time. How will I know you?"

"You don't have to. I know you." The way he said it made KC shiver.

She hung up and called Tony. "I'm meeting mystery man today at four o'clock, Bartholdi Park. Can you get away?" She gave him the location.

"You bet I'll be there. I will have the R-90 in my pocket and use the earpiece receiver. If anything goes wrong, say *copy now*. You won't see me, but I'll be close by."

KC and the Arizona attorney played phone-tag until mid-afternoon. "Our client has no intention of weaseling out, as you put it, Ms.Garrett. I'm working with the owners right now. We intend to present a sizeable proposal for your consideration very soon." *Sure you are,* she thought. She thanked him and glanced at her watch, 3:40 p.m.; she had to be at Bartholdi Park at 4:00 p.m. KC strapped on the body wire under her blouse, then redressed and threw on a heavy jacket and exited into blustery weather.

The cold wind and threatening skies made her think of sunny Arizona— and the case that took her there. For years, she had put such stock in achieving a *big* case that would '*make a difference.*' Now, after getting to know some of the people in McCrary, that clichéd phrase had a different meaning. It wasn't about achieving a lofty, abstract goal; it was about people. It was about helping McCrary's doctor, the worried mother, the residents fearful of their future, and the children affected by toxins. *Exactly what Dad wanted to do for his people.* "My people, too," she added under her breath as she reached Bartholdi Park.

KC spotted her potential mystery man seated on a bench, but walked on past in case she was wrong. His footsteps sounded behind her. "Take the path to your right." KC followed his directions to a lone park bench. *Oh great, he picked an isolated spot. I'm glad Tony's close by.* "Thank you for coming on such short notice. And alone," he added.

"You're welcome, but I'm freezing. If you have something and decide to pursue immunity, how about next time we meet someplace warm." She caught the flicker of a smile.

"Rest assured I have something. Do you know who I am, Ms. Garrett?"

"No. And I am curious how you know me." *But I do recognize your accent. You're the Mr. Boston accent I heard outside my office that night!* "Why don't you tell me your name?"

"If it's all the same to you, I would like a few answers before I reveal anything about myself." He looked scared. "What I need to know is, if someone has knowledge of a crime and presents evidence, legally can that person be granted immunity for a crime he committed?"

"Yes, depending on the evidence. I'm assuming you're the one who wants immunity or you wouldn't be here. You said murder. Did you witness it?"

"No! I learned about it afterwards." He looked ready to bolt.

"Sorry, I had to ask. I would need the name of the person responsible for the murder and whatever information you have about him—or her. In other words: the when, where, and why that ties the perpetrator to the crime. Also information about the victim, of course. Having knowledge of a crime, but learning about it after the fact, we call *evidence aliunde*—evidence from another source. Say, for instance, the perpetrator let it slip where or when it happened, or maybe it was made to look like an accident." Mystery man flinched at that. "Evidence aliunde isn't as strong as physical evidence or an eyewitness account, but under certain circumstances, it can hold up in court."

The sun slipped below the tall bushes surrounding them, the fading light creating instant shadows. He asked if she would grant immunity solely on the basis of evidence aliunde. "Immunity from what?" KC asked as she withdrew the T-60 glass case receiver from her pocket. His two-word answer: "stealing money," KC hoped Tony was hearing this. "Stealing from an individual or a company? It makes a difference."

"The government," mystery man said.

"Okay, from the government. How much?" she said.

"Millions." He kept looking around and fidgeting with his gloves. "I am afraid."

"Afraid of what? I think I can help you. I just need evidence that I can corroborate and you've got a deal. I do need to know your name."

"Victor," he said and rose. "I am dealing with extremely powerful people. I need to be absolutely sure before I do this." He turned to go.

KC jumped up. "Victor, wait. Murder won't stay a secret for long. If it comes to light before we strike a deal, I can't help you. Give me the details, and I'll get started."

"I'm sorry. I need time to think." He hurried away and disappeared into the shadows.

KC spoke into the glass case. "Mystery man now has a name. Victor Ludlow."

*   *   *

From his spot across the street, Wolf watched Garrett enter Bartholdi Park. Why Aubert wanted her followed, he wasn't sure, but $10K in untraceable cash was good pay for merely keeping track of her. Unfortunate that it required him to lie to Volking and say it was "security for Secretary Beckman." Wolf pondered for the hundredth time how a political slick like Jules Aubert managed to get a dedicated veteran FBI agent into this mess. *Loyalty to Mrs. B, which isn't a lie.* But he did have to admit that the million bucks helped seal the deal.

Wolf jogged across Constitution Avenue, against a red light, amid a cacophony of horns. He caught sight of a man get up from a bench and follow Garrett into the park. *Now, what's she up to?* He took a shortcut through the trees and took up position as close as he dared. Garrett and the man sat down on a bench. His black curly hair and tan beret gave him a Slavic appearance.

Wolf made his way back to the street. Garrett meeting the guy, whoever he was screamed trouble. He joined a small crowd waiting at the bus stop, a safe place to watch the path. Ten minutes later the Slavic-looking man hurried out of the park and hailed a cab. Assuming Garrett must have taken a different exit, Wolf dashed back across Constitution Avenue. He glanced over his shoulder, the sight of Garrett and FBI agent Tony DeMarco exiting the park together shattering all sense of his inner safety.

Wolf sprinted to his car and called Aubert. "I need to talk to you ASAP."

"I'm just leaving the White House," Aubert said. Call back in fifteen minutes."

Wolf waited in his car, the vision of his dream job and million dollars evaporating like smoke in the wind. DeMarco captained the Florida operation that Volking authorized Faver to observe. *Instead, DeMarco had Faver tail me.* The puzzle pieces fit with frightening clarity. Faver figured out how Marsh died and was on his way to Miami to deliver the evidence to DeMarco. *He was on his cell when I walked up to his window. He'd already told DeMarco!*

The threads of Aubert's high-flying plan were unraveling, and his ticket out of this mess was sitting in the Bank of Montreal. *I better get my money while I can.*

* * *

Aubert nodded at the guard as he exited the East Wing then walked to his car. He took a final glance at the White House, ablaze in lights. There was no greater goal, no bigger prize than this, and he was *so* close. This ought to be a glorious moment, except something or someone had tough guy Elliott Wolf scared to death. Fifteen minutes on the dot, Wolf called back. "Who do you know about six-feet tall, mid-fifties, dark curly hair, and wears a beret?"

"Victor Ludlow, why?" Aubert's dread now had a face.

"Who is this guy, anyway?" Wolf sounded shaken.

"The money man at BIA. He transfers the IIM funds for me. Why are you asking? "

"Because he just met with Garrett in Bartholdi Park. They walked into the park together, but Garrett came out with Tony DeMarco, one of our agents. He was head of the Florida operation. I bet Jared Faver, the kid Volking grilled us about, found out how Carson died and told DeMarco. He and Garrett were doing some serious talking."

Wolf's words landed like blows, taking his breath away. Aubert swerved his car to the curb. "This is bad, really, really bad, Wolf. This can't happen now. I just left the President. He's meeting with Valerie at Camp David in early February. He's going to announce his endorsement. There has to be a way out of this."

"If you know of one, I'd love to hear it."

"I need time to think." Aubert dropped his Blackberry, his image vanishing of standing beside Valerie in the Rose Garden as a priest pronounces them husband and wife. Rattled, he couldn't remember when Valerie was due back from her campaign trip. But, he vividly remembered the evening when he told her about using IIM funds. *Valerie kept the papers I showed her. I wrote on those papers. I have to get them back!* Aubert joined the heavy traffic heading for Bethesda, his only purpose to retrieve evidence that could send him to prison.

He parked his BMW across the street. Valerie's house was dark except for the kitchen lights at the back. Phoebe and Marguerite were probably having dinner and watching television. He used his keys to open the pedestrian gate and front door and quickly entered the alarm code. Pausing to listen, the only sound the kitchen television. And the house smelled of popcorn.

Aubert slipped into the library and eased the door shut before turning on the light. "I never should have left those papers," he said under his breath. He retrieved the key to the filing drawer and located the file. The two sheets of paper were still stapled together, but Aubert's relief was short-lived. There were no hand-written figures in red. *Dammit, she put the originals in her safe!* Aubert straightened up, wondering what to do, when the door opened, Phoebe's frightened look nearly stopping his heart. "Phoebe, you startled me!"

"Well, you scared me more. What are you doing?" She approached the desk.

Aubert put the papers down. "I just stopped by to pick up some papers for a meeting."

"You sure go to a lot of meetings. We made popcorn. You want some before you go?"

"Can't right now, but how is your mother? Did you talk to her today?"

"Last night." Phoebe plopped down in a chair. "She bought me a *real* Navajo dream catcher. I can hardly wait." Her expression mirrored blissful anticipation.

"Wonderful." He kept his hands on top of the desk. "On second thought, that popcorn smells good. I think I will have some."

"Okay, I'll go get it." Phoebe jumped up and skipped out of the room.

He had two minutes, no more. Aubert crammed the copies back into the file and slid the drawer shut. He tried relocking the drawer but he was trembling. The phone rang, so close and loud, he dropped the keys. As he bent down to retrieve them, Phoebe opened the door. "Jules, Mama wants to talk to you. Did you find your papers?" Unnerved, he tried to think of a credible answer, but couldn't. "Are you okay, Jules? You look funny."

"No, Phoebe, I'm fine, just fine. I thought you were going to get me some popcorn."

"We ate it all, but I'll make some more while you talk to Mama."

Aubert waited until Phoebe closed the door and then dropped into the chair, no longer able to stand. "Get yourself together," he said and took a deep breath to calm his heartbeat. He picked up the phone. "Valerie, great timing! How are you?"

"I'm okay. Phoebe said you were in the library."

"Yes, I dropped by to see how she and Marguerite were doing and thought I would check my answering service. Phoebe and I are going to have popcorn."

"Really, *that* would be a first." *Sarcasm noted*, he wanted to say.

"There's a first time for everything, darling. Phoebe said you are bringing her a *real* dream catcher. You should see how excited she is."

"I know and I am so ready to come home," Valerie said, sarcasm missing from her voice this time. She abruptly asked to speak to Phoebe without saying goodbye.

What's that all about? He pressed the kitchen intercom. "Phoebe, your mother wants to talk to you." *And I need to talk to my brother. Right now!* While Phoebe and her mother talked, Aubert used his cell to call Montreal. "Gregory, I'm glad I caught you. I don't have much time, but I just found out Victor Ludlow met with a Department of Justice lawyer about an hour ago. On some isolated bench in Bartholdi Park, so what does that tell you?"

"That sounds ominous, Jules. What do you make of it?"

"At our last meeting, Victor told me he wanted out. I'm thinking he's seeking immunity and plans to turn me in. I need advice, Gregory. I'm a bit rattled. I don't know what to do."

Silence for several minutes, and then Gregory spoke. "The evening, before we left for the White House reception, do you remember telling me that it takes unwavering commitment to reach any worthwhile goal? You said you have it. My advice, Jules, is to act on that. "

"I remember now. I said I would allow *nothing* to stop me." Jules drew a deep breath. "Thank you for reminding me, Gregory. I absolutely cannot allow that to happen."

* * *

KC and Tony returned to her apartment, disappointed about Victor Ludlow. She accessed her emails and found one from Agnes that said she now had secure Internet at her cottage so no more encrypted messages. She had spent a weekend exploring the island. Agnes wrote: I love the beach and the shops in Hamilton. I'm having fun, but I remember why I'm here. This detective stuff is so cool. Nothing definitive yet but I'm learning the mainframe. That's the key."

Tony walked in with two coffees. "Let's listen in on Beckman's house."

KC took the coffee. "Okay, but according to today's *Post,* Valerie isn't back yet from her campaign trip." KC dialed the code, and they listened. All was silent for a few minutes followed by a click. A light switch flipped on, and then the sound of a drawer being opened and papers rustling. "I never should have left those papers," a male voice.

It had to be Jules Aubert; KC felt like cheering. Valerie was out of town, and he was in her library—doing what? Next, they heard Phoebe enter and Aubert tell her he was looking for some papers. Tony gave a thumb up; Joe's bug worked so well, Aubert could be sitting across the desk from them. His brief conversation with Valerie did not sound like it went well. As soon as he hung up, Aubert called his brother in Montreal. KC and Tony listened, shocked that Jules already knew about her meeting with Ludlow. Jules sounded confused until Gregory asked him if he remembered something he'd said. "Yes, I remember. I said I would allow *nothing* to stop me. Thank you, Gregory for reminding me. I absolutely cannot allow that to happen." They heard the light switch click off and then the door close.

KC turned off the recorder. "There's no mistaking what Aubert means. Agreed?"

Tony rose. "Absolutely, and I bet he's going to call Wolf at his condo. I'd better get over there and put in a new tape, in case the one in there is full." He grabbed his jacket. "You've got things to do and I don't have a change of clothes. I'll call you tomorrow." KC slipped into his arms, not wanting Tony to leave—not wanting him to go anywhere near Wolf.

Elliott Wolf had already shown in spades that he was capable of murder.

Another restless night caused her to be late getting to the office the following morning. Before her first cup of coffee, KC called her godmother at BIA to ask about Ludlow; Sally said she had seen him in the cafeteria. That's good, KC thought. Phyllis buzzed that she had a call.

It was Lieutenant Goodall. "Good news, Garrett. A repairman fixing an elevator at the Jefferson Hotel identified Ventresca. The bad news is he's skipped. I talked to his landlady. Ventresca hasn't been around for a couple of weeks."

"Interesting word, *skip*," KC said. "Ventresca would have a hard time doing that."

She heard Goodall exhale and pictured him in a cloud of cigarette smoke. "Is that right? And you would know this how?" He sounded amused.

"I took out his knee. Ventresca can barely walk let alone skip. Trust me, he's in town."

"Doesn't matter anyway, Garrett, I don't have the manpower to stake out his place."

KC felt like shaking him. "Well, how about this? You check for other Ventrescas in the area. Italians usually have big families. Maybe Nick is hiding out with one of his relatives."

He chuckled. "I would've thought of that—eventually." Goodall said it facetiously.

Phyllis waved from the doorway. "Mystery man on hold."

He's no longer a mystery, KC thought. "Call you back." She hung up on Goodall.

"I do want immunity, Ms. Garrett. Could you meet me at the American Indian Museum, Monday at 5:30? I'll have the evidence together by then."

KC agreed and then was surprised when Victor Ludlow thanked her. He sounded relieved, or maybe just hopeful. She was writing the date and time on her calendar when Tyler Jackson tapped on her open door and entered. "Sorry to bust in unannounced. I hope you're in a good mood because I'm here to make my problem your problem. And you're scary." He grinned.

Therein lay her attraction to Tyler. Hidden beneath that casual, glib demeanor was one of the sharpest legal minds she had ever encountered. Handsome, funny, and charmingly polite, Tyler could find humor in any situation, even his numerous ex-wives. At one point, he told her he was considering hosting an ex-wives' reunion. "We have high school and college reunions, why not an ex-wife reunion? Good food, lots of wine, and I guarantee it would be entertaining. And, Ms. Black Belt, you can be my bodyguard." Tyler was hard not to like.

"Our EPA guy, Hoffman, called," Tyler said. "Some McCrary citizens are ready to draw down on two back-hoe operators that he authorized to dig a couple of new test areas. I guess they interpreted it as EPA going behind their back. Hoffman halted the tests, but everybody wants you to come and sort it out." KC frowned and started to protest. "Phyllis is on the Internet as we speak. A couple of days is all. Calm things down, KC, or this will end up in court, and you know what that means. If we don't do something– make that, if *you* don't do something, taxpayers will get stuck with the cost. Would it help if I got down on my knees and begged?" Tyler dropped to one knee.

KC burst out laughing. "Oh, Tyler, get up."

"Works every time. Thanks, KC. This case has dragged on so long, we're on our third president, and the first lead attorney is drawing social security. I know this wasn't how you planned to spend your weekend. I owe you."

Phyllis handed KC her reservation. Her flight to Phoenix left in four hours, the return flight on Monday at 8:00 a.m. She could still meet Ludlow. Tyler was right. This case needed attention. Hopefully, she could bring these people together again.

*   *   *

Wolf left the FBI building at six o'clock and took up position outside the Bureau of Indian Affairs. A few minutes later, Ludlow emerged and walked four blocks to the lot where he kept his Jaguar. Parking there cost mega bucks, but Aubert had told him Ludlow lived the good life: a pricey house in Langley and a fifty-foot Hunter moored in Annapolis.

Wolf waited behind a big Lincoln SUV as the attendant delivered Ludlow's car. He walked around it looking for dings and scratches and, evidently not finding any, tipped the attendant and got in. When the attendant turned to another customer, Wolf rushed forward and jumped in the Jag's passenger seat. "Drive, Ludlow. We need to talk."

Ludlow turned onto the street and crept along in the right lane. "Who are you?"

"All you need to know is Aubert sent me." Ludlow looked like he was about to lose it. Wolf spied a car pulling out of a lot. "Turn in there."

Ludlow pulled in and parked, his hands shaking so badly he couldn't turn off the motor. Wolf reached over and turned the key.

"Chill out. If he'd sent me to kill you, you would already be dead. What did you tell Garrett last night in the park?"

Ludlow gasped. "Nothing! I wouldn't. . . .I didn't tell her anything."

"Bullshit. You want immunity. WHY?" Ludlow hunkered against his door. "Answer me," Wolf warned, "or I'll blow you away right here and mess up your fancy Jag."

"Yes, yes, I called her." Ludlow started blubbering. "I knew this guy, Carson. Everybody thinks he died of a heart attack, but he didn't. He pissed off Aubert, so he had him killed."

Wolf had his answer; Ludlow was a time bomb. "Aubert may be power hungry, but he didn't have Marsh killed. I would know."

"How? How would *you* know?"

"You really want me to answer that?" Wolf said. Ludlow shook his head. "You don't need immunity. You're important to the group. If Aubert's plan holds, we'll all be rich. I plan to retire unless you screw everything up. That would be a huge mistake, Ludlow. Don't do it."

Wolf got out and waited as Ludlow drove away, the thought occurring with disquieting awareness how easy it had become to say whatever was needed, with no regard for the truth. Wolf called Aubert on his way back to his car. "I just had a chat with Ludlow."

"Cut to the chase, Wolf. I can't handle much more."

"He did talk to Garrett about immunity," Wolf said. "Mrs. B doesn't have a snowball's chance in hell with Ludlow running scared. He's a loose cannon."

"Then that's it, Wolf," Aubert said. "It's over for Valerie and all of us. You said you wouldn't touch him."

"Forget what I said. This one's on the house."

—22—

K C was amazed at how quickly people and positions changed; pledges to sue instead of talk because "government fellows are digging around the school." She learned EPA had requested the tests to determine whether the level of contaminants had increased, decreased, or remained the same. Once she learned the results: *no significant change*, KC wasted no time. She met with members of the school board; she called on McCrary's hospital administrator, and she met with chamber of commerce members.

KC gathered members from each group who were willing to meet. From the hospital, a prominent physician claimed the instance of cancer and leukemia in McCrary children was significantly higher than the national average. A school board mother remarked how afraid she was for her children's health. She told KC. "Tell us what we can do, and we'll do it." The fourteen-member group's consensus: "Get going on cleanup; assure EPA that we're serious, and we have the same goal."

KC's job: get EPA to accept their compromise, and get serious start-up money from the mine. In other words, "get all factions to show good faith." At their final meeting, KC thanked the group. "What you want is reasonable. I see how committed you are to serious progress, and I will do everything I can to make that happen. I want this done as much as all of you."

She deplaned in D.C. with a sense of accomplishment, thanks to a group of common sense people. Tony was waiting outside the security area. Dressed in a navy blue suit, white shirt, and nondescript tie, he looked like Mr. FBI. He opened his arms, and she slipped into his embrace. "I'm so glad you're back." He held her hand as they walked to the luggage carousel. "You said your trip was worthwhile."

"It was a good trip. Last night you said you had some news. I hope it's good news."

Tony squeezed her hand. "It isn't, and I know how you're going to react. Ludlow's yacht blew up Saturday while he was working on it. A propane leak, according to marine patrol. He's in intensive care. That's all I know."

"No! I can't believe it! Yes, I can. Victor Ludlow told me he was afraid, that he was dealing with powerful people. It had to be Aubert and Wolf. Dammit, Tony! Why didn't I charge him for altering ore figures. If I had, Victor Ludlow would be in jail, but safe."

"So far you've reacted exactly like I thought you would. In the words of the Bureau's shrink that Joe and I are seeing, blaming yourself is counterproductive."

He draped his arm over her shoulder as they exited onto the third floor, the same floor where Ventresca shot up her car. Leading the way, Tony stopped at a car that looked very much like her Honda, only nicer. "The body shop left a message that your car was ready, so I picked it up and had it detailed. The manager was amazed your insurance still covers bullet holes. Know what that means?" Tony grinned. "C'mon, Tiger, smile. It means we are meant for each other!"

* * *

Valerie returned from her campaign tour anticipating family time. When she came downstairs the following morning, she found Phoebe in the kitchen eating cereal. Valerie poured herself a cup of coffee and sat down across from her daughter.

"Jules told me about you two having popcorn. Did you have fun?"

"No, and we did *not* have popcorn," Phoebe said, full of ten-year-old indignation. "Jules asked me to bring him some popcorn, so I made it just for him. But when I took it to the library, Jules was already gone. I guess he found the papers he was looking for."

"What papers, Phoebe?" Valerie asked.

"I don't know, for a meeting, he said." Phoebe shrugged. "That's why he came by."

"Is that what Jules told you?"

Phoebe was certain that's exactly what Jules told her. When Valerie extracted that he let himself in and was in the library going through a file at her desk when Phoebe walked in on him, she experienced a rush of emotions, none of them positive. The issue with Jules would have to wait, however. Her first day back would be hectic. There were times, today one of them, when Valerie Beckman longed to be a wife and mother, seeing her husband, Randy, off to his job as Secretary of Interior. It was Randy's dream, his goal from the minute he won his first election in Georgia. She shook off the sad thought and did as her grief psychologist had advised—replace the sad thought with a positive one. *I am grateful to have Phoebe in my life.*

Valerie arrived at the office braced for the day. Her chief aide brought her up to date on appointments then gave her a stack of messages. "You'll like the top one. I promised to get back to her as soon as you decide on a date." From President Champion's appointment secretary, the message was an invitation to spend a weekend with the first family at Camp David, Phoebe and Jules included. The President's secretary offered two weekends in February.

Valerie called Jules' private line at his office and got his voice mail. When he didn't answer his cell phone or pager, she called Aubert and Associates, not sure whether to be angry or alarmed. Jules' embarrassed receptionist apologized to Valerie, saying she was surprised Jules didn't let her know he was leaving town "in spite of the circumstances." Valerie immediately asked what circumstances?

"His father had a heart attack. Jules left for Montreal last night."

Mystified, Valerie accessed her private voice mail. Jules' message at 9:00 p.m. last night was about the time she arrived home. He said not to worry, that Richardson would manage her appearance schedule until he returned. Jules ended with, "I love you, Valerie. By the way, since I will be in and out of L'Touissant, rather than play phone tag, I will email or text you a report each day. Take care of yourself, darling."

Valerie replayed it to see if his message sounded as ridiculous the second time. It did, and again she detected no fear or concern in his voice about his father. His 'I love you, Valerie,' and then his 'take care of yourself, darling' had an almost singsong quality, both of them laughable. Deeply disturbed, Valerie forced aside all thoughts of Jules and dealt with her day. She asked her aide to arrange her schedule to accommodate the President's invitation. "Please relay I can't guarantee Jules will be able to join us, but Phoebe and I are very much looking forward to it."

Exhausted after a day of meetings and phone calls, Valerie spent the evening with Phoebe and then, at eight-thirty, tucked her daughter into bed. She slipped into her robe and went to the library in desperate need of quiet and time to sort out her tangle of misgivings about the only man beside Randy Beckman to win her heart. That was now in serious jeopardy, for it was in this room that Jules admitted stealing from the Indians and passionately defended his actions. So self-assured was he that the end justified the means. He'd even intimated that, without his guidance and the IIM funds, she wouldn't be the front-runner, or perhaps even a serious candidate. Valerie moved to her desk, unlocked the drawer, and retrieved the file from the back. The photocopies had been ripped apart then hurriedly jammed back in the file, probably when Phoebe burst in on him. "Oh, Jules, where are you, and what have you done?"

*   *   *

Jules Aubert settled into the soft leather seat as the Air France flight lifted off Montreal's Dorval runway and climbed into the night sky. Three intense days at L'Touissant with his brother had left him afraid and uncertain. When he confessed to Gregory about Carson and Victor, his brother immediately called a contact for a fake passport. It was delivered the following morning, Gregory giving it to Jules along with confirmation of his flight to Paris. "Jules, you have no choice but to leave the country, if only for a while. I will cover for you with Valerie. Our story is that Father had a heart attack."

Now aboard an Airbus A-380 bound for France, Jules questioned following his brother's advice so readily. But then that was what he had always
done; Gregory was the *good* son. Whether running away would prove wise or
premature depended on Wolf, and Jules had no word from him. He couldn't
stop wondering if Wolf got scared and had also left the country. Or if Victor
Ludlow had already spilled his guts to KC Garrett for immunity. If either of
those scenarios were true, not only was his dream of residing with Valerie in
the White House gone, Jules Aubert could never return to the U.S.

Absorbing the implications drove Jules deeper into depression. Valerie
was innocent, the potential consequences of his abandoning her at this point
in her campaign, too immeasurable to even think about. He blinked back
tears at the thought of her preparing for her Camp David meeting without
him. At stake, the President's endorsement and, very possibly, the outcome of
the election. *My God, what have I done?* Jules had fight to keep from
breaking down as he watched the lights of Montreal disappear into the night.

At Orly Airport outside of Paris, Jules tried to appear calm as the customs agent looked over René Garzon's passport, the one Gregory had made
for him. Jules' heartbeat did not slow until the agent handed the stamped
passport to him with a curt nod. A commuter flight five hundred kilometers
south delivered Jules Aubert to Montpellier, and then parading as René
Garzon, he checked into Château Roussilion, the five-star hotel he knew
well.

Aubert took a stroll, the crisp January air sweeping away some of his
fatigue. He passed a small bistro, the sight of two lovers inside drinking wine
a reminder of just how much he may have lost. He returned to the hotel and
went straight to the bar, two straight-up martinis only intensifying his
melancholy. Two years ago, before the madness of her campaign enveloped
them, he and Valerie had planned a stay at Château Roussilion then spend
another week of quiet and rest at the family villa. *Too bad we didn't get to do
that.* Aubert ordered a third martini and took in his surroundings. *Valerie
would have loved the old-world elegance of this hotel.*

Originally built as the residence for a member of Napoleon's court, in
1845 the heirs had converted it into a hotel. Gothic in design, constructed of

stone, it had undergone expansive changes over the years but never lost its grandeur. The castle-like structure towered above ancient trees scattered over acres of manicured gardens dotted with classic statuary. The park-like grounds surrounding the hotel gave its guests the experience of a different era, and helped isolate the hotel from the traffic and noise of Montpellier.

Aubert stumbled to his room and flung himself on the bed, the telephone's ring intruding like a hammer-blow to his head. He considered not answering, but it was his brother. Gregory was the only person who knew his location. "Jules, you must call Valerie immediately. She just phoned again. She is very upset. Be sure to use the Vanguard cell phone, and then call me back." Gregory hung up with no goodbye. His brother telling him what to do was annoying, but then again, Gregory had given him a Vanguard cell phone that disguised the location of his call. Vanguard engineers and project managers were issued the phone to call headquarters from around the globe. According to the phone, all calls originated from Montreal, their actual location known only to Vanguard.

Aubert tested the phone by calling Aubert and Associates. "Richardson, I lost my cell. This is my new number. About calling me at L' Touissant, unless it is a dire emergency, I do not wish to disturb anyone here. I rather prefer to check in with you at my convenience."

Richardson chuckled. "Do not wish to disturb...I rather prefer... is that the way they talk in Montreal?" Aubert hung up, shaken by his slip. It was 6:07 p.m. in Montpellier; 12:07 p.m., lunch time in Montreal and Washington D.C. He dialed Valerie's private office line, hoping he would get her voicemail. Two rings. "This is Valerie Beckman."

"Valerie! How good to hear your voice. How are you, darling?"

"Going out of my mind, Jules. Didn't you get my message about Victor?"

"No, I'm sorry. What about him?"

Valerie sounded almost hysterical. "His boat blew up, a propane leak, his wife said. Victor is in intensive care. Jules, he may not make it! I don't understand. First Sam Blackhawk, then Carson, and now Victor. What is happening?"

"That is horrible!" Aubert listened to Valerie's account of the explosion. She apologized for not inquiring about his father and asked if he was with him at the hospital. "No, at the moment I'm at L'Touissant, Gregory's estate in Montreal. I miss you." *That last part is the truth.* "I'm sorry things are so difficult."

"These deaths have totally derailed me, Jules. And, I don't appreciate your brother being terse with me when I call." She now sounded angry. "When are you coming back, Jules?"

"The minute my father is out of danger. I spend a great deal of time with him. The doctor thinks my presence has had a beneficial effect."

"Well, of course," she said, a tinge of sarcasm in her voice. "By the way, how is the weather in Montreal?" Taken aback by the switch in subject, Jules tried to think how to answer.

I should have asked Gregory. "I've been inside, so I haven't noticed. How is it there?"

"Gray skies, cold, and raining. Not nice at all."

"Let me check." He walked to the window. It was clear; he could see the stars. "It is raining here as well, darling, very nasty. You sound upset, Valerie. I am sorry, but be assured your campaign will progress just as I planned."

There was an awkward silence. "Do you really believe that, Jules? But you have to admit, life sometimes hands us very unpleasant surprises."

"It certainly does, Valerie, but I hope you feel better. I will talk to you soon." Jules hung up, not sure exactly what she meant, but hoping she hadn't figured out his charade.

He next called Wolf's condo: "Where the hell are you, Wolf? Call me!"

—23—

KC took the Metro home Monday evening, disconsolate that for every step she took forward, the bad guys took four. She returned Mrs. Marsh's call, hoping the autopsy report would tie Wolf, alias Nate Spiller, to Carson's death. It did not. "I don't understand, Emily, did your doctor ask the coroner to check for poison?"

"Yes, both of them said that unless they know exactly *what* poison to check for, it is impossible to identify. I know Nate poisoned Carson, but it looks like he'll get away with it."

"Don't give up, Emily. I will get him." KC hung up, her pronouncement sounding hollow to her own ears. She took her dinner, a peanut butter sandwich and glass of milk, into her office. Ivan jumped up and stretched out on the desk. KC dialed the entry number to the Infinity bug in Valerie's house. Joe said this equipment offered the same options a federal agent would have on a stakeout: to listen, record, and trace incoming and outgoing calls. KC ate her sandwich and skimmed through the Infinity operations manual. "Okay, Ivan, if I hit rewind, the tape is supposed to stop on the last call. Here goes." The tape rewound and stopped at 7:30 p.m.

KC listened to Valerie place a call. Gregory answered. "I'm sorry, Valerie. Jules is not here at the moment, but I will be happy to have him return your call." A brief conversation followed with Valerie inquiring about his father's condition. Gregory's answer was brief; it was obvious he wanted to get her off the phone. "What is going on?" Valerie groused the minute she hung up. Her exasperated voice came through incredibly clear. KC pressed the rewind button a second time and the tape rewound to 6:45 p.m., a call from her aide that lasted ten minutes.

The following morning, KC awakened, ready to go on the offensive with Goodall. She phoned him. "You said you would call me back, Lieutenant. Did you mean this year?"

"What's with the attitude? No coffee? I did find more Ventrescas, but only one, a Salvatore Ventresca, has possibilities. His address is pretty close to Nick's."

"Let me check it out," KC said. "I need to get out of this office and you don't have the manpower." He refused, insisting that he would get to it but couldn't say when. "Come on, Goodall, for all we know Salvatore could be Nick's eighty-year-old grandfather. Besides, you wouldn't even have a case if it weren't for me." Goodall relented, but ordered her to not get out of her car. She left the office, thankful to be outside, if only for a short while.

Thirty minutes of driving and she located the address on a tree-lined street in Hyattsville, Maryland. Older, single-story houses lined both sides of the street, each one with a single car attached garage. Salvatore Ventresca's even-numbered address had to be midway down the block on the right. KC slowed when she spotted a car in the driveway. If the black Corvette belonged to Salvatore Ventresca, he definitely was not eighty years old.

She drove past the house, the numbers next to the front door confirming she had the right address. No one in the neighborhood parked their car in the garage. Every house had a car in the driveway and another parked at the curb. Except Salvatore's house. *Why would Salvatore leave an expensive car like that out front?* Covered with dust, the car needed washing. Was that the reason? Or could it be that Nick Ventresca's car was in the garage because its description and license number were on his arrest warrant?

"That's it!" KC's every instinct told her Nick was in the house.

She drove east four blocks and pulled into a strip mall parking lot. Goodall wouldn't come without visual confirmation. Driving by the house too many times would tip them off, but Nick and Salvatore would eventually get hungry. Since they dared not go out to eat, Salvatore would need something from the grocery store or pick up dinner from one of the takeout restaurants in the center. About three hours to dinnertime, she had time to research poisons at the library. With any luck, she might be able to give the coroner the name of a poison to test for; it was better than waiting.

KC drove back on Ventresca's street, expecting to see the dirty Corvette in the driveway. Instead, Nick Ventresca was out front washing the car, for all the world to see. "Oh damn, oh damn." Afraid to turn around, KC flipped her sun visor to the side. A furtive glance revealed he wasn't Nick. Salvatore Ventresca looked like a younger Nick. *He's got to be his brother.*

KC took a different street back to the shopping center and left a message on Goodall's voicemail that Nick Ventresca was at his brother's house. She gave him her cell number. "Call me ASAP." After fifteen minutes and no return call, KC phoned the precinct. "This is KC Garrett, Department of Justice. I have located a fugitive, and I need to speak to Lieutenant Goodall. You have two choices: either page him, or give me his pager number."

"Why didn't you give me your pager number in the first place?" she said in her message. He called back immediately. "Pay dirt, Goodall, Salvatore Ventresca is a younger version of his brother. He's washing his Corvette in front of the house which means Nick is inside. We need a warrant." She gave him the address. "How soon can you get here?"

"I'm not sure about the warrant. You know how slow the wheels of justice turn."

"Then grease them, dammit. Nick is in there. If you aren't arresting a mass murderer, you'd better get over here with a warrant, or I'll get one and make sure every cop in your precinct knows who got it." To her incredible relief, Goodall didn't hang up on her.

"Just chill, I'll get it. Leaving now. I'm twenty minutes out, driving an unmarked, white Buick. Where are you?" She told him the name of the grocery store and the cross streets of the shopping center. "Roger that," he said. "What are you driving?"

"Just get here, Goodall. I'll find you." KC parked in a diagonal space facing the street. Twenty-two agonizing minutes passed before Goodall's white Buick pulled into the lot. She flashed her headlights, and he drove up next to her, his car facing away from the street. He lowered his window and lit a cigarette. "Is Nick's brother still washing his car?"

"He was ten minutes ago. You have the warrant?"

"It'll be here any minute." Goodall directed his exhale out the open window. "Be patient. I moved mountains to get it." KC let that pass. He smoked one cigarette after another over the next fifteen minutes, until she told him he was asphyxiating her and closed her window. KC observed the street through a Marlboro haze and the rear window of Goodall's Buick.

At 4:15 sharp, a shiny black Corvette turned into the parking lot. "There he is!" KC started the Honda. Two car lengths into the lot, Salvatore Ventresca spotted them and spun his car around. Tires squealing, rubber smoking, he took off on the street away from his house.

KC gunned the Honda to the entrance and, catching a break in the traffic, jammed down on the accelerator and careened across the oncoming lane, and left toward Salvatore's house. Right now he was calling Nick, telling him to run. Once Nick stepped outdoors, she didn't need a warrant. Slowing only slightly, KC sped through three intersections. Four houses away from Salvatore's house, she got a rush of adrenaline when she saw the garage door start to raise. Reaching the driveway, KC yanked the steering wheel hard-left and hit her brakes. The Honda skidded to a wobbly stop in front of the garage, Ventresca's legs visible from the thigh down.

She jumped out and sprinted to the side of the garage, her shoulder against the wall. The garage door squeaked upward, laboring until it hit the top with a thud. KC peeked around the corner at Ventresca, fifteen feet to her left. His side was toward her, and he had a gun. He was staring at the Honda. "I recognize your car, Garrett? You are dead!"

KC pulled back as flashing lights and a siren roared up from the right. Goodall's Buick slid to a halt at the curb, five feet past the Honda. Too late to back up, Goodall was staring straight at Ventresca's gun, now aimed at his open window.

"NO!" KC screamed and lunged at Ventresca, her shoulders ramming into his ribcage, deflecting his shots at Goodall. His right arm whipped around at her, thirty-six inches of solid muscle landing full force, knocking her off her feet. KC rolled into a crouch as Ventresca turned back toward the Buick. *He's going to kill Goodall.* She charged hard, ramming his knees. He lurched forward but didn't go down. Stunned, it felt like she had tackled a brick wall. Yelling and cursing, Ventresca twisted around and rained blows down on her neck and shoulders.

Hunched, trying to avoid his blows, KC caught a glimpse of Goodall rolling out of the Buick, gun drawn, and then disappearing behind her car. "Drop your weapon!" he yelled. Ventresca answered with two shots at Goodall, her Honda the unintended victim. KC shielded her face from flying glass as Ventresca limped toward her. He stopped in front of her, his back to the street. She was staring straight at his injured leg encased in thick black rubber and supported by heavy metal stays—the orthopedic brick wall she had tackled.

"I owe you Garr—" KC looked up into the barrel of a Beretta, no silencer this time. Goodall's yell was followed by a shot. Ventresca flinched, his hand releasing the Beretta. It hit the ground in front of KC a second before he collapsed onto the grass.

"You hit?" Goodall yelled. "No," she shouted in his direction, her eyes on Ventresca.

Two patrol cars roared up and immediately silenced their sirens. Four patrolmen piled out, guns drawn until Goodall signaled to put them away. One patrolman rushed to Ventresca and knelt beside him. "He's alive, but I need something to stop the bleeding." The cop was looking right at her. KC ripped off her cardigan and tossed it to him, glass fragments following. He gave it a quick shake then pressed the sweater against Ventresca's wound. The cop touched his neck. "He's got a pulse." A crowd had gathered, cars stopping on the street, people gawking.

KC started trembling, unable to stop. This was not the justice she sought for Ventresca killing Donyell Crawford. Nick was supposed to be arrested and stand trial, not be lying on the ground, her sweater stemming his blood. She felt a hand on her shoulder. "Don't question yourself. He'll make it. I aimed away from the heart." She turned to look at him. For all his cockiness, Goodall looked and sounded genuinely concerned. More people had arrived from across the street and on each side of Ventresca's house.

A television van screeched to a halt at the curb, a cameraman panning the crowd as he and a reporter jumped out. When he spotted KC and Goodall, he aimed the camera straight at them. She turned away. A loud siren wound down as an ambulance pulled up, the crowd parting to let two paramedics race to Ventresca. Two cops moved the crowd back and then began to string yellow tape around the area. Her shot-up Honda was now part of the crime scene.

A second television van pulled up. Traffic on the street had come to a halt, drivers staring out their window, until a patrolman motioned them to move on. Goodall used his handkerchief to retrieve KC's purse and briefcase from the front seat of her car. He motioned for her to follow to a patrol car at the curb and opened the back door. "Where'd you learn to tackle like that?"

"Monday night football," she answered automatically.

"You saved my life," he said.

"You saved mine too."

"It's a miracle one of his shots didn't hit you or me, or the gas tank on your car. I guess it wasn't our day to die. We'll need a statement. I'll call you when it's time." He rose and lit a cigarette, then told the deputy to take "Ms. Garrett to the hospital."

As soon as they were out of the neighborhood, KC spoke to the deputy, "No hospital. Please take me home." He replied that he had to follow orders.

"Deputy, it might help you to know that I have a black belt in karate. I do not want to go to the hospital. I want to go home. You do understand that, don't you?"

"Yes, ma'am, I hear you loud and clear."

*   *   *

KC was barely inside her apartment when the phone started ringing, her mother and Sally the first call. They had watched the evening news, and Kathryn could not believe, "a woman as intelligent as you would tackle a man with a pistol!" KC put her phone on speaker and listened to the two of them as she used tweezers to remove glass fragments from her hands and arms and then apply antiseptic. Finally able to get off the phone, she quickly showered, grabbed a beer, and then collapsed in her big chair in front of the TV. The reporter who asked for her statement at the scene was interviewing two animated bystanders, both of them trying to describe in detail her tackle of the shooter. He had to politely end their description then signed off with "more on this breaking story at eleven." The studio anchor announced that one suspect was still at large and "the victim of the shooting is in critical condition."

"I wouldn't call him a victim," KC said as she rose. The phone rang again; Tony was on his way and wanted to know what to bring. "Bandages, liquor, dinner? Forget it. I'm bringing all three." Following his call, she answered a string of calls from Grandmother Garrett, Tyler Jackson, Gray Rossiter, Joe Rogers, and Danny Richardson. She was too tired to ask Danny how things were going with his father. Even her brother called from Idaho. Their mother had phoned him, saying "you won't believe what your sister has done now." A morning talk show host called wanting her to give his viewers, "the story behind the story." KC declined and took her phone off the hook.

While she waited for Tony, KC decided to use her time to access Valerie's phone tap. Hearing no sounds in the library, she rewound the tape and pushed the search button. The machine auto-stopped on an incoming call at 7:43 a.m. from Aubert saying his father's condition remained the same. Valerie asked if he would please fly down for her Camp David visit. Aubert responded that he couldn't promise anything without the doctors' okay.

"It would only be for two days, Jules." Valerie sounded hurt. "I don't mean to be insensitive, but couldn't Gregory cover for three days? This meeting with the President is crucial." Aubert rang off with a promise to confer with the doctor and Gregory and call her. KC turned off the machine, silently agreeing with Valerie. *She's right. Why couldn't he come for a couple of days?* "He's lying. I'd like to know the real reason," KC said under her breath.

Tony arrived with Philly cheese steak sandwiches, a bottle of cabernet, and a bottle of aspirin in case she didn't have enough. "Philly cheese steak sandwiches are the supreme NFL treat, so this is appropriate." His attempt at humor did not match his visibly shaken demeanor. A worried Tony had arrived prepared to spend the night. KC did not object; she slept pressed close against him, comforted by his presence and warmth.

He was gone when she woke up, a note on the kitchen table instructing her to call him. He had the coffee pot set to go. All she had to do was push the button. "Bless you," she said and waited at the kitchen table. Her journal lay open to her last notation on January 29, a call from Aubert during which Valerie asked him about the weather in Montreal. "What a strange question. Why would she care about the weather in Montreal?"

KC called her office and learned from Phyllis that, "Per Tyler Jackson, you are not to come in today." Appreciating the time, KC made several calls to Arizona, thankful to hear positive news. The mine had kicked in the $500K that she "strongly urged to get things started." After learning that, EPA's Hoffman ordered cleanup to begin at the school. Several committee members congratulated her for "finally making some progress on this mess."

KC finished breakfast and, reluctantly, hung her phone back up; it instantly rang. No name appeared, and it was a number she didn't recognize. She answered tentatively, ready to disconnect. "Ms. Garret, this is Valerie Beckman. I apologize for calling so early, but—"

The Secretary was crying. KC nearly dropped her coffee, fervently hoping she hadn't found the bug. "It's okay, not too early for me, Mrs. Beckman."

"Would you mind if we use first names? This is so difficult."

"Not at all. Is something wrong?" KC asked.

"Yes, very wrong. And serious enough that I need an attorney. You immediately came to mind. I cannot explain why, KC, but you did. The truth is I need someone I can trust."

Trust? I bugged your house! "I'll be glad to help if I can. Would you like to meet?"

"Yes, but I don't have a spare minute today. I apologize again, but could you meet me at my office tomorrow morning at seven?"

"Yes, I can. Seven tomorrow morning at your office." KC worked from home the rest of the day, periodically checking in with Phyllis. She said that word of "KC's Wonder Woman Escapade" had made the rounds at DOJ, especially the Environmental Crime Division. Flowers had arrived from Tyler Jackson with a card that read: "Way to go, Ms. Crime Stopper!" And several ECD attorneys had dropped by to wish her well, some to razz her.

KC hung up and called Santana Dawson in Idaho. He had already heard about Ventresca from her brother. She assured Santana she was okay. "Do you remember the name Victor Ludlow, the guy who altered Camas Mine's figures? His yacht blew up Saturday, supposedly from a propane leak. I just know Aubert had something to do with it." KC then told him about the call from Valerie Beckman. "This could be the break we need."

–24–

Seven o'clock sharp the following morning, a subdued Secretary Beckman ushered KC into her spacious office, her demeanor the polar opposite of the dynamic woman who nominated her father. From a table in front of a tall window, she poured two coffees from a footed, sterling silver carafe. "This was a wedding gift that never got used at home, so I brought it here. For some reason, the coffee tastes better." There was a hint of sadness in her voice. KC glanced around the tastefully decorated suite. Framed certificates, awards, and photos of her with Washington's political heavyweights adorned the walls. On the credenza were pictures of a young girl at different ages.

Valerie set their coffees on the desk. She looked like she had been crying. "I am so upset. I don't know what to do. The enormity of this situation, not to mention how utterly stupid I feel for not reacting sooner, it is. . . how can I put it? It has undone me."

"I can see that," KC said, anticipating that Valerie was about to confess *something.*

"I've asked myself a dozen times if I didn't see things for what they really were because I didn't want to? The answer is no, but it doesn't matter. I see them now. I'd like you to see these." Valerie handed her two sheets of paper. Curiosity aroused, KC studied them, one at a time. Both sheets contained columns of numbers, one with $45 followed by six zeroes, written in red ink at the bottom. "KC, over the last fifteen months, $45 million dollars was stolen from Individual Indian Money trust accounts and spent on my campaign. It may be more now."

What Dad was investigating! "Stolen by whom?" KC tried to sound calm.

"Someone inside did the actual transferring, but Jules Aubert, my campaign manager. He claims he borrowed it and will pay it back. I was a fool to believe him."

"When did he give you these, and why?"

"Mid-November, along with an impassioned speech about the end justifying the means. Jules told me without these funds, I wouldn't stand a chance. KC, he knows what I want to accomplish as President, but I make no excuses. I should have reacted the minute he told me."

"Why didn't you?" KC asked in as sympathetic a voice as she could manage.

"Jules had already stolen the $45 million. I think he purposely waited until we were so far into the campaign, in effect he neutralized any opportunity I would have to expose him. Jules is clever. He put me in the untenable position of either appearing naïve or complicit."

"What exactly do you want me to do, Valerie?"

"Before we get to that, I want you to know, I will pay back every cent he took. It is unconscionable that Jules stole from the very people I want to help. He must be held accountable regardless of what happens to me or my campaign. So you see my need for a good lawyer. KC, I assure you, I agreed to run for all the right reasons." Valerie looked ready to cry. "I didn't sleep at all last night, but I came to the only decision I could make."

"You want me to bring charges against Jules?"

"Absolutely. I authorize you to investigate me, my campaign, whatever you feel is necessary. I will cooperate one-hundred percent." Valerie leaned forward, her eyes beseeching. "Now, for what I want. But you have to promise you will think this through." Valerie paused, "As far-fetched as it sounds, if there is a prayer or a shred of a chance to save my candidacy, I want you to help me accomplish the impossible."

Valerie's plea touched off a host of KC's emotions: pain, indignation, pity, anger, frustration, even compassion. She sat silently searching Valerie's eyes, the set of her jaw, her hands, and her posture, for any hint of duplicity or guilt. Lawbreakers routinely lied under oath, their attorneys skirting the truth like skilled downhill skiers dodging snow-laden pine trees. KC prided herself for being able to spot lies and liars, and her every intuition told her Valerie was telling the truth. She was an intelligent woman, deceived by a man she loved and trusted. "I'm curious why you chose to call me."

"This will sound strange, but it is God's truth. When I arrived at my decision, it was your father who first came to mind. I could literally see him. Call me crazy, but I felt as though Sam Blackhawk was telling me to call you, that you would help me."

With that, what little reluctance KC had melted away. She knew better than to give a guarantee, but she answered, "Yes," and the decision felt right. "I will do everything possible to help you, Valerie. Your sworn statement and these papers constitute probable cause to request Aubert to be extradited—if you know where he is. But extradition can be a lengthy process."

"That's the problem, extradition from where?" Valerie said. "Jules would have me believe he's in Montreal, but I know he isn't. His brother is evasive every time I've called. And Jules lied about the weather in Montreal. I asked him about it because of Gregory and this whole façade about their father. After we hung up, I checked Montreal's weather on the Internet."

"That was smart. It proves he lied," KC said. "It makes me wonder about this façade, as you call it. Strange, isn't it that Jules disappeared about the time Ludlow's yacht blew up?"

Valerie's reflective expression changed to recognition and then shock. "Dear God, no!" I've had this feeling that something was terribly wrong, but couldn't identify it. First, your father dies, and then Carson, and now Victor! It is too monstrous to fathom. Could Jules be that evil?" Valerie's face drained of color as the implication registered. "I don't know what to think."

"There's only one way to learn the truth," KC answered. "Find him."

Valerie nodded, her color slowly returning. "Jules couldn't do it himself. He would hire someone like he did to make the transfers. If he *is* responsible for these horrific crimes, I think I might know where he would hide." She rose and withdrew a large Atlas from a bookshelf. "Two years ago, we made plans to visit his family villa in France. We even booked reservations, but ended up cancelling. That was about the time my campaign came to life. The villa is close to a big city, but I don't remember the name. Let me find France."

Valerie flipped through the Atlas. "What's this?" She removed a folded sheet of paper that book-marked France. "For goodness sake, it's our old itinerary." Tears sprung. "That's where he is, I just know it. Now I understand why Gregory was so evasive. He's covering for his brother."

The intercom buzzed. Valerie answered and thanked the caller. "I'm sorry, KC, I'm due at the White House for a Cabinet meeting. I'm not sure I can pull myself together enough to go."

On an impulse, KC went around the desk, coaxed Valerie from the chair, and hugged her. "You are not in this all by yourself anymore. I will do everything I can to help you."

"Thank you, KC, you are an angel."

Valerie's itinerary in her hand, KC exited the building. In her mind, Valerie's reaction to the revelation about Aubert proved, beyond a doubt, that she had no part in his plans. *If Valerie's right and he escaped to France, I could petition for extradition on embezzlement charges and then file murder charges when I get him back. If I get him back.* The sad part, it would take forever and a ton of work. Deep in thought as she walked to the corner, KC waited for the light to change, traffic whizzing by in both directions interrupting her view of a man across the street.

Just as the light turned green, he turned and hurried down the side street, but not before she recognized him. *Elliott Wolf. He now knows I met with Valerie which means Aubert will soon know.* KC walked to her office, puzzled why Aubert would back his client, the leading presidential candidate, into a corner? *Valerie's right, to prevent her from incriminating him.* KC's logical attorney mind told her there had to be more to it. The answer didn't take long. *I know why. Aubert stole a lot more money than he confessed to Valerie.*

Ideas swirling, KC discounted them all, admitting it would take a miracle to salvage Valerie's campaign. How sad that Valerie possessed the emotional strength to rise from unimaginable personal tragedy to triumph in the toughest political arena in the country—the hallmarks of a true leader—only to be undone by the likes of Jules Aubert. KC looked skyward. *You are right, Dad. I will help her.*

Back at her office, she phoned Santana at Crystal Waters Casino. "My meeting with Valerie Beckman is the break we've been waiting for." She told him what she learned. "She wants to nail Aubert regardless of how it will affect her campaign. He's claiming to be in Montreal. His phone shows that area code, but she thinks Jules is actually in France."

"Out of reach of the law," Santana sounded disheartened. "Be honest with me, KC. What are the chances of getting him back to face charges?"

"Truthfully, not good. It could take years. And with his money, who knows?"

"Did your dad ever talk to you about Justice, the Indian way?"

"I'm sure he wanted to, but no," KC said, sending the sad thought to the imaginary box.

"Justice, the Indian way absolutely works," Santana said. "But it can take a long time, and I'm not willing to wait. I want to bring Aubert back to face charges for what he's done."

"Santana, as an attorney, I am duty-bound to tell you that is absolutely ill-advised."

"Really? As ill-advised as you tackling an armed guy, twice your size, to save a cop?"

She had no answer for that. "Okay, what can I do?" Santana asked her to pick him up at National Airport on Friday and share what information she had to help find Aubert. Supplying him information could legally be interpreted as condoning Santana breaking the law, but KC could not deny that she wanted to see Aubert in court. She would make him pay for what he did.

That evening, she used the information from Valerie's old itinerary to search on the Internet. Their plans were to fly to Paris, then take a commuter flight to the city of Montpellier near the Mediterranean. On the itinerary, Aubert had written the names of three hotels, two of them crossed out. A checkmark by *Chateau Roussillon* helped KC locate the five-star hotel on the Internet. Valerie's happening onto their old itinerary was a godsend. That it surfaced just in time to help Santana—did that qualify it as being part of Justice, the Indian way? KC mused.

Tony interrupted her thoughts, calling to ask to come over and fix dinner. "I can't tonight, Tony. Santana is arriving tomorrow, a stopover on his way to France. My dinner's in the oven, and I have to clean my apartment."

"Why is Santana on his way to France?" Tony sounded annoyed.

"Because Valerie Beckman believes that's where Aubert went. Santana isn't willing to wait for extradition. He wants to bring him back. And, yes, I absolutely advised him not to do it."

"Okay, so he's coming tomorrow. Why can't I see you tonight?"

"Because I've already broken laws that I swore to uphold. And by giving information to Santana, I am, in effect, breaking the law again. I don't want you involved. You have already risked your career. I'm firm on this, but how about dinner Saturday?" Tony agreed, but he sounded none too happy about Santana spending the night.

The following afternoon, KC left her office early and met Santana's flight. "It's good to see you. You look wonderful," he said and held her hand as they walked through the airport. He laughed when they reached her bullet-riddled car. "Believe it or not, this is the second time it got shot up. The body shop manager said my insurance won't cover bullet holes a third time."

Over a pasta primavera at Guiseppe's Little Italy, KC told Santana her good news. "I have a lead on where Aubert could be, a city called Montpellier, about five hundred kilometers south of Paris. And if we're lucky, he might be staying at a hotel called *Chateau Roussillon.* I don't know for sure, but it's a start. If Aubert isn't there and he's using an alias, it will be like looking for—"

"A needle in a haystack, I know. But trust me, I will find him." Santana smiled at her. "Too bad Aubert's villa isn't close to Paris. That would be fun, wouldn't it?"

"Wow, I would love to see Paris about now." Her words came out with more feeling than she intended. KC quickly added there was no way she could get away. *I hope he didn't read anything into that. I need to tell him the truth about Tony and me.* KC drove to her apartment, not exactly sure under the circumstances, what that truth would turn out to be.

KC left her car parked in front of the garage and joked that she hoped somebody would steal it. Santana took a closer look. "I count seven bullet holes. I'm hanging out with a gangster, albeit a beautiful one." He didn't try to mask his appreciative gaze.

KC chose to ignore his comment and led the way up the stairs. "Thank you for dinner. Excellent wine and wonderful food. I didn't realize you knew so much about wine."

Santana chuckled. "One of white man's better gifts."

"Touche." *I love the quiet way he talks, gentle on the ear like Angeni and Takoda.* "By the way, have you seen my grandmother? It's been so crazy I haven't had time to call her."

"I see Angeni every Thursday. She has lunch with Takoda, then plays bingo with her friends." KC turned on the living room lights. "Rustic, very nice," he said, gesturing at the diagonal cedar and rock fireplace. "Next time you visit the reservation, I'll cook dinner for us. I'd like you to see the house I built."

"Takoda said it is amazing." She hung up her jacket. "We have a lot to talk about. Would you like to build a fire while I make coffee?" KC went to the kitchen. Ivan was curled up asleep in his basket under the table. She ground beans and prepared coffee, wondering as she waited for the pot to fill, what it was about Santana that she found so intriguing. He was sitting in the big chair when she brought their coffee. She sat on the floor in front of the fire and glanced at him.

He was staring at her with a slight smile. "What?" she said.

"I was thinking about a conversation I had with Dad before he left. I told him that I remembered you as a pushy kid who took me on at basketball and kicked my butt. Now look at you, beautiful and a lawyer, with a black belt in karate. It occurs to me that you could still kick my butt. I'm wondering why I now find that attractive when it bugged the hell out of me when we were kids. Are you and Tony–?"

"At the moment we are kind of up in the air." She felt a rush of guilt for the immediacy of her answer. "How about you? No wife and little Dawsons?"

His eyes didn't waver. "I came close, but getting the casino off the ground got in the way. By the time the casino got going, Andrea was married and had two little boys."

"Regrets?" KC couldn't believe this turn in their conversation.

"Yes, at times." He sounded reflective. "Andrea is divorced now, but I believe things turn out the way they are designed to."

The same thing Takoda says. There was that look again. KC jumped up. "I'll get us more coffee." *What the heck am I doing?* She returned with their coffee refills. "I plan to take you to the airport. What time does your flight leave?"

"Seven o'clock tomorrow morning. That's too early. I'll take a cab."

"No way. I'm taking you. I think it would be a good idea if you call me from Paris. Who knows, I might find out some new information about Aubert while you are in the air."

Santana agreed and added wood to the fire. "I had hoped we could have a quiet evening and share some stories about our fathers, but right now, I need your help."

For the next hour, they went over ideas and information on how to find Aubert. She gave him a copy of the dossier she compiled on Aubert and a photo of him from *The Post.* He appreciated getting the Internet information and the maps she obtained on Montpellier and *Chateau Roussillon.* They were both yawning when they finished. "Before I get a pillow and blankets for the couch, I am curious about this Justice, the Indian way. I know it's late, but would you mind telling me?" KC said.

"I could try to explain, but an example is easier. About three years ago, a member of our tribe got in trouble for poaching game on his neighbors' properties. He did it over and over, even though he had his own land where he could hunt. His neighbors asked him to stop, but he ignored them, even after he accidentally wounded a neighbor's dog and spent a couple days in jail. This guy refused to listen to anybody. Then about eighteen months ago, he was hunting again on his neighbor's property. Somehow, he tripped over a stump, and his shotgun discharged. The blast ripped through his boot and did tremendous damage to his foot. The doctors did everything they could to save it, but ended up having to amputate his foot. Now, he's not able to hunt at all, and it was because of his own doing. *That* is Justice, the Indian way. Somehow it always fits the crime."

Santana rose and offered his hand to pull KC up from the floor. She came up, her face inches from his. Santana pulled her to him, his hand sliding up her back to her neck, tangling in her hair. "Are friends allowed to kiss?"

Santana's kiss answered all her questions about his look and remarks. Red lights went off in her head, but she ignored them and kissed him back, wanting more. KC's arms went around his neck and she pressed against him, his lips and body inviting.

KC wavered, the red lights winning. "I'm sorry, I can't do this...."

Santana's lips lingered against her cheek. "I'm sorry too, but I understand." He released her. "No matter what happens, Kaya Calder Blackhawk, I will remember this."

‑25‑

D espite knowing little French except *bonjour* and *bonsoir,* Santana managed to find a hotel in Montpellier and a restaurant where he had an excellent dinner. Rumors about the French being unfriendly did not hold true; they were helpful and even intrigued by a genuine *indigène Américain.* After two glasses of French burgundy with his meal, Santana went to bed, his last thought before sleep, the kiss he shared with KC.

The following morning, he checked out the two hotels KC said were crossed off the old itinerary Valerie Beckman found. From what he'd heard about Aubert, neither hotel would satisfy a man like him. Santana hailed a cab, silently hoping Aubert was at Château Rousillon. If so, Aubert would be facing murder charges soon. *KC would like that.* The cab driver deftly navigated Montpellier's traffic-clogged streets onto the hotel's private two-lane road that wound through park-like grounds.

Santana alighted from the cab, a bit surprised at the number of cars, limousines, and taxis arriving and departing. Considering Château Rousillon's serene, old-world setting, the chaos didn't seem to fit. But once inside, it took only a brief glance to decide the hotel was a perfect fit for Aubert's high-flying lifestyle. Santana overheard snatches of German, French, and Spanish conversations as he strolled around the grand salon, but no sign of Aubert.

Choosing a seating area that offered a view, Santana pretended to read *Midi Libre,* Montpellier's newspaper. If Aubert were here, at eleven o'clock in the morning, he could be any number of places in the hotel. Seeing several guests exit through double doors at the back of the grand salon, Santana decided to follow. He expected to enter an elegant formal dining room, but instead found a modern-looking solarium/restaurant. In striking contrast to the hotel's old world interior, the powers that be must have decided to surrender elegance for function.

February's cold, blustery wind aside, a bright sun flooded the interior, as though defying the elements. An ornate fountain, encircled by leafy ferns, added a garden atmosphere. The restaurant was filled with well-dressed patrons drinking cáfe and having breakfast. Santana followed the receptionist past two tables with chess games underway.

This is a great spot. If Jules Aubert is staying at the Château, he is bound to show up here eventually. Santana ordered the breakfast crêpes the waiter recommended, and opened his *Guide to France.* Sunglasses allowed surveying the guests without being obvious. For the next hour, Santana glanced at his book as he ate and then took as much time as he could to finish the carafe of coffee. He checked his watch, 12:30 p.m., still no sign of Aubert. Santana paid his tab and returned to the lobby, taking his time walking around the grand salon. He casually glanced over the guests seated in the half-dozen conversation areas. Not spotting Aubert, Santana bought a *Midi Libre* and returned to the solarium. Over lunch, he continued comparing every man who entered against Aubert's photo in his travel book.

Bingo, at 1:30 p.m., Jules Aubert strolled in with a *Midi Libre* tucked under one arm. Thinner than his picture, he was dressed in a Fila jogging suit, collar-up, and sunglasses atop his head. Taking a seat on the opposite side of the fountain, Aubert closed his eyes and turned his face up to the sun. "Enjoy yourself while you can," Santana said under his breath. He retrieved the throwaway camera from his pocket and furtively snapped a picture. The epitome of a wealthy Frenchman on holiday, Aubert looked as if he didn't have a care in the world. Santana had to remind himself that Aubert was on the run because he was a thief and a killer.

Over the next ninety minutes, Aubert consumed three glasses of wine, a sandwich, and appeared to read every section of the newspaper. Santana paid his bill and managed to get three more pictures before Aubert signed his tab and walked into the hotel. Santana followed in time to see him disappear down a first-floor hallway. After ten minutes, he discovered Aubert had gone into the hotel spa. A monogrammed glass door allowed a view inside; there was no one at the desk and no sign of Aubert. Santana strode in, grabbed a towel, draped it around his neck, and hoped he looked like a guest checking out the facilities. Aubert wasn't in the weight room or the swimming pool. Nor was he in the Jacuzzi.

Puzzled, Santana returned to the spa foyer and held back to allow a mother and daughter approach the desk ahead of him. The mother tapped the bell and a male attendant in his twenties emerged from a room marked *office*. Pretending to wait in line, Santana stood a respectful distance behind and caught the word *massage*. The attendant asked the women to sign in and then, telling Santana he would return momentarily, he directed the women to follow him.

As the three walked down the hall together, their backs to him, Santana stepped forward and turned the appointment book around. The signature immediately above the two women's was *René Garzon, suite 201*. Quickly turning the book back, Santana tossed his towel in a bin and exited the spa. KC's detective work had paid off in spades; he had Aubert in his sights.

Finding suite 201 was easy: the first set of ornate double doors on the second floor near the curved staircase. All the suites along the hall had the same double doors. Old world opulence, he thought. Another old world sign, the Chateau did not issue electronic cards to open doors; they used heavy, ancient-looking iron keys. Spying a maid's cart at the end of the hall gave Santana an idea. He paused in front of the suite to listen; the maid was vacuuming inside. A quick search of the top shelf produced nothing, but he found what he was looking for on the second shelf. Stuffed between stacks of towels was a basket with at least a dozen keys guests had left behind when they checked out. His search produced just what he wanted: the key to suite 210. *Perfect. I hope I can pull this off.*

Santana hurried downstairs and stopped to observe. Behind the registration counter, a distinguished older man was busy with a couple, but the attractive, young woman was free. Santana walked up to her and smiled. "I hope you can help me." He handed her the key. "I was given this key by mistake. I'm assuming the number was transposed." She checked her computer. "And you are?" Anticipating the question, he replied. "René

Garzon, suite 201." She looked at him with a questioning smile. "I know,"
Santana nodded, feigning embarrassment. "I get this every time I come to
France. French father, American Indian mother. She very much wanted me to
have an Indian first name . . . obviously my father won."

"I see," she said and chuckled. "I apologize for the error, Monsieur
Garzon," she said in perfect English, then wished him good day. Santana
walked away with the key to suite 201, silently congratulating himself for his
performance. Ten minutes later, he was inside Aubert's suite and checking
the time, 3:45 p.m. He had a safe window of about fifteen minutes before
Aubert returned from his massage.

The suite looked like a movie set, with ten-foot windows draped in
velvet, antique furniture, and elaborate gilded mirrors. The maid had been
there; the bed was made. Santana searched through Aubert's clothes in the
armoire but found nothing in his jacket pockets. A dresser held shorts, socks,
pajamas, and sweaters, all neatly stacked. A large suitcase stood on-end next
to the armoire, nothing inside, but a zippered pocket felt bulky.

Evidently lunch and a massage did not require Aubert to carry his wallet
because inside were several credit cards and an international driver's license.
The license listed an address: Route de l' D138 Joncelets, FR. "That has to be
the family villa." Santana whispered. Also inside Aubert's wallet were a
generous supply of Euro bills, and a printed paper folded several times. It
was a purchase agreement for a new Mercedes from a Montpellier
dealership. *He must not be planning to go home anytime soon.*

Santana put everything back in place and let himself out, silently thanking KC for her detective work. He'd found Aubert, but exactly when, where,
and how he would grab him, he would need to figure out. His mission now:
"Keep the target in range," a term from his three-year stint in the army. The
image of his father and Sam delivered fresh resolve. "You will pay for what
you did."

* * *

KC spent the next two days at work going over the proposed schedule in McCrary. More equipment had arrived with cleanup progressing at the school. Her contacts sounded hopeful. Santana's message from Montpellier offered more good news. He said thanks to her detective work, he'd found Aubert, aka René Garzon, who was still at Chateau Roussilon. "To look at him, KC, you'd think he doesn't have a care in the world. He's bought a new Mercedes, so what does that tell you? I have the address of his villa. When he leaves, I'll be right behind him. Trust me, one way or another, I *will* bring him back."

Valerie Beckman's call that Victor Ludlow had died of his injuries offset Santana's good news. It also brought KC a rush of regret for not formally charging Ludlow before she left for Arizona. Ready to go home, she opened her office door and nearly collided with Tony. He had been running; he was breathing hard, holding a CD, and clearly panicked. "Thank God I caught you! Joe made this CD from Wolf's phone tap. You're not going to believe it, but Aubert already knows Ludlow died. He told Wolf they would both be home free if 'that Garrett woman disappeared.'" Tony's face was ashen. "Tiger, I can't protect you 24/7. I'm begging you to leave town, hide at your grandparents or go to Idaho where your brother can help protect you."

His plea, a poignant reminder of her father, hit home. Had he complied, Sam Blackhawk would be happy at work as the new Assistant Secretary of BIA right now. That image and Tony's anguish were enough to convince her. "You're right, Tony, but not Idaho. To Bermuda. It's less obvious, and maybe I can help Agnes." Tony's embrace erased any doubts about their relationship. He released her only after she promised to stay in constant touch.

KC called Agnes' cottage in Bermuda. No answer. The connection on her cell was so broken, KC asked her to get to a landline and call the office ASAP. While she waited, KC wrapped up as much work as she could. Agnes' call came thirty minutes later. "Tony just confirmed that I am now on Wolf's hit list. I need a place to hide."

"I'm not surprised, KC. It's time to get outta Dodge. If I'm still at work, the key will be under the purple flower pot by the front door. Can hardly wait to see you!"

KC kept her eye out for Wolf on her way home. She called Rose and Jesse; they were happy to take care of Ivan. She phoned Tyler Jackson and requested two weeks off for a family emergency; he stopped short of pressing for details. She hated to lie to her mother, but she told her she was going out of town on business. Her last call, she left a message on Valerie's personal cell. "Valerie, this is KC. The next time Jules calls you, it is absolutely critical that he thinks you believe he is in Montreal. I promise to explain soon, but right now, I'm leaving town, maybe a week, maybe two. But you have my cell number. Call me."

KC closed down her apartment, but before she walked out the door, she picked up Ivan and hugged him. "Oh, Ivan, I hate leaving you. Stay close to home, kitty, and you be here when I get back." She put him down and exited quickly; she couldn't look back.

Assuming that Wolf was following, KC took a cab to the train station and mixed in with the crowd lined up to buy a ticket to New York. During the ride, she walked the length of the train. If Wolf had boarded, he was staying hidden. Fifteen minutes out of New York City, she went into the restroom and changed. KC arrived at Grand Central Station, dressed in jeans, boots, a jeans jacket, and wearing a baseball cap and owlish glasses.

She saw no sign of Wolf when she boarded a commuter train to Boston. Checking into the Hilton near Logan airport, she paid cash for one night and went straight to her room. KC locked the door and automatically headed for a bubble bath. Submerging herself in warm soapy water up to her chin, she thought about Wolf. It wouldn't take him long to realize she was gone, and he had the FBI's resources to find her. *He will come after me. It's just a matter of time.*

All the cards were on the table now. Strange that being aware she was Wolf's target, she felt more resolute than fearful. Santana's message said Aubert looked as though he didn't have a care in the world. Was he *that* sure he could have her-his final obstacle- removed? *How arrogant he must be.* She pictured him ordering her death with no more thought than ordering an entrée off the chateau's menu. He had certainly been successful so far, even turning a long-time FBI agent into a cold-blooded killer. But she had been forewarned. "If you think I'll be an easy target, Elliott Wolf, think again."

* * *

Wednesday morning's flight from Boston skirted the eastern end of Bermuda, flying in an arc around St. Georges Island. A spectacular sight from the air, the chain of islands resembled a giant fishhook, each island fringed with white sand beaches. The plane banked left, offering KC a view of the red and white tower of St. David's lighthouse, the island's stately guardian of Clearwater Bay. She felt the landing gear lower for the plane's final approach to Kindley Field.

Emerging from the terminal into bright sunshine and warm, tropical air, KC bypassed the pink and blue striped island bus for a taxi. "Surf Side Beach Club in Warwick," she said to the smiling, black man as he loaded her luggage.

"Yes, mum, Surf Side is very nice." His Bermudian greeting, a mix of British and the tropics, was as friendly as his smile. He asked if this was her first trip to the colony. "No, I was here ten years ago, but it doesn't look like it's changed very much."

He had a deep, resonant laugh. "No, mum. We like it the way it is."

"Why wouldn't you?" KC said. "You can't improve on paradise."

They drove over the Causeway connecting St. Georges and the airport to the rest of the island, past Harrington Sound, the water so clear and turquoise-tinted it didn't look real. The Easter egg-colored houses hadn't changed; pink, blue, yellow, and turquoise cottages, each capped with a smooth, white-washed roof to collect precious rainwater. Farther on, they passed fields of Easter lilies, their blossom heads bowed as though in prayer. The driver entered Warwick Parish, and a short distance later pulled into Surf Side's grounds.

She paid the driver and waited until he drove away before fetching the key from under the purple flowerpot. One step inside, the cottage gave new meaning to the word *compact,* Agnes's one-word description in an email. It had a small living room, one tiny bedroom, a tinier kitchen, and the smallest bathroom KC had ever seen. The entire cottage was no more than four hundred square feet. Agnes' laptop sat on the table, a note taped to it. *Can't wait to see you, Cuz.*

KC unpacked her lone suitcase and then showered in a stall barely large enough to turn around. She called Tony on her cell as soon as she dressed. "I'm in Bermuda, how are you?"

"Going crazy." Tony said. "Did you see Wolf? Are you okay?"

"I'm fine, and no sign of Wolf. I need to ask a favor, Tony. I really hate leaving Ivan for so long. Would you mind staying at my place?"

"No problem. I was going to mention that anyway because I stopped by your place to get my jacket. Good thing I did. I checked your phone, and there was a message from Santana. He was on his way to Aubert's villa. I'm hoping he calls back so I can put him in touch with my Interpol buddy in Paris. Dammit, KC, here we go again with business talk. I love you, and I can't imagine my life without you in it." There was no hesitation in his voice.

"I love you, Tony. And I feel the same way." It felt right and good to say. "Promise me you'll be careful. Staying at my place, don't forget Wolf wants me dead."

–26–

Wolf recognized the Montreal area code on his cell screen. "I called you three days ago, Aubert. Where the hell have you been?"

"Montreal, now France," Aubert sounded scared. "Is it safe to come home?"

"I don't know what to tell you. Ludlow didn't make it. I'm fairly confident the cops won't find any evidence, but according to today's paper, they haven't ruled out homicide."

"You're fairly confident?" Aubert's voice oozed sarcasm.

"Don't give me any crap, Aubert. I'm here fixing your screw-ups. What I called to tell you was that Garrett had about a two-hour meeting with Mrs. B at her office last week."

"She did WHAT?" Aubert let loose a string of expletives. "If that damned Garrett woman disappeared for good, so would our problems. She is relentless."

Aubert's meaning was clear. "Forget it," Wolf said. "I'm through doing your dirty work."

"Would another $500K in your Montreal account change your mind? That would give you a total of $1.5 million." There it was, Aubert upping the ante again, bidding for his soul in that arrogant tone.

"Hmm, another $500K." Wolf sounded matter-of-fact, even to his own ears.

"Yes, tax-free and wired direct to your Montreal account. This is it, Wolf, and then you're done. We'll be home free."

Time seemed to stop, Wolf's mind spiraling. Acceptance would mean severing all ties with the Bureau and what little pride he had left over a career that had defined him for almost forty years. It would mean walking away from Mrs. B and Phoebe; that would hurt more than anything. *I've been a fool to think the presidential security job would happen. Just another Aubert pipedream, upping the ante to get what he wants. Another $500K means I would have $1.5 million, enough to buy a hideaway anywhere.* "Enough to buy a new start," he whispered.

"Wolf, are you still there? You know I'm good for the money."

"Yeah, I'm still here," Wolf said, his struggle reluctantly resolved. "Okay, you deposit $500K tax-free into my Montreal account ASAP, and you got a deal."

"I will wire it ASAP, Wolf, you have my word. And don't give up on the presidential security job. I haven't. With Garrett out of the way, this will all work out. I prom—"

Wolf disconnected, cutting Aubert off. "And pigs can fly." Loyalty to Mrs. B aside, he had already sold his soul to a devil named Jules Aubert. His next move loomed clear: get himself to Montreal and get the $50K cash from his safe-deposit box. "And, if Aubert deposits another $500K ASAP like he said, I'll wire all the money in my account to a bank on some sunny island. I can live a damn fine life with $1.5 million. And if he doesn't do it, Aubert is a dead man."

Unfortunately, before he could do that, there was Garrett. He decided to view the job as eliminating an annoyingly relentless obstruction to Elliott Wolf's retirement plans. It had been four days since he'd seen her in front of Mrs. B's office, four days he'd spent in Virginia on an assignment for Volking. Wolf acknowledged he would miss his old friend as well as the Bureau. But a new identity, more money than he could spend, and a life far away from his past would make it easier.

That evening, a contemplative Wolf ate his fill of crab at his favorite diner. He visited with Maude and left her a far larger tip than usual. He would miss her; Maude had been serving him for so many years, they joked about growing old together. Though he knew he wouldn't be back, Wolf couldn't muster the courage to tell her goodbye.

Resigned, he drove to Garrett's neighborhood and parked down the street, curious that her Honda was parked to the side of the garage instead of in front. But seeing lights going on and off in her apartment, he drove on home; this job could wait one more day. The following morning, Wolf arrived at 7:15 a.m., just in time to see Garrett's apartment door open.

But it wasn't Garrett who emerged. "What the hell?" Watching through binoculars, he watched Tony DeMarco descend the stairs and then drive away in a sports car. Thirty minutes later and still no sign of Garrett, Wolf called her office on his cell. The secretary would only say that Ms. Garrett was away and didn't know when she would be returning.

Furious at being duped, he called Bill Berkeley, the DOJ attorney with an office down the hall from Garrett's. It took persistence to get through, and Berkeley answered by reminding Wolf that he was never to call him at work. "I need to know the whereabouts of KC Garrett, this order from the guy who sends your cut to your Bermuda account every month." Berkeley started to protest. "Listen, jerk, I don't give a damn who you are. I'm five minutes away. Why don't I come over and we talk about this in person?" Silence.

"I'll see what I can do," Berkeley said. He called back ten minutes later. "Nobody will say where Garrett went or for how long. But my secretary told me that the buzz around the department is that her secretary, Agnes Richardson, quit a month ago to take a job in Bermuda."

Wolf severed the connection, Garrett's four-day absence glaringly clear. *Bermuda, where Ludlow wired the money.* Wolf wasted no time; two hours later he had a reservation on a Delta flight to Bermuda. Back at his condo packing a few clothes, Wolf swore this was the last time he would underestimate KC Garrett. "It doesn't matter. This time tomorrow she'll be dead."

*   *   *

While she waited for Agnes to return to her cottage, KC called Valerie Beckman's private cell; she answered cautiously. "KC, I'm glad this wasn't Jules. Can you hold a moment?"

KC heard Valerie ask her driver to raise the privacy shield. "I'm on my way to a meeting at the White House. You sound far away."

"I am, and I apologize for what I'm about to tell you, Valerie. I'm glad you're sitting down. Elliott Wolf and Jules are in this together. And the worst part, Elliott Wolf is responsible for Ludlow's death, also my father's, and Carson Marsh's. And now he's after me."

"Oh no, not Elliott, too. He is like family, KC. This is devastating." The seven hundred miles separating them did not mask Valerie's pain.

"I know, and I am sorry to spring this on you, but I just learned that Aubert hired Wolf to 'remove' me. But you can't let on that you know, so please be careful what you say around him."

"This is too much." KC heard her sigh. "Don't worry, I will be careful, but under the circumstances, I insist you forget about the favor I asked—the one about my campaign."

"I can't, Valerie. You being President is more important now than ever. I'm in this for the long haul. I want to help you do the impossible."

"I don't know what to say. But I want you to know, regardless of how all this turns out, I value your trust in me. And I won't forget it." Valerie sounded as grateful as her words.

KC apologized again for delivering Valerie devastating news and then couldn't believe what she did next. KC Garrett gave unsolicited advice to, perhaps, the next President of the United States: "Stay strong, Valerie. Don't give up on your dream."

KC paced in a tiny circle after her call, worried that if Valerie saw Wolf, he might detect a change in her. *Nothing more I can do about it from here.* Her jumbled thoughts made KC's two-hour wait for Agnes, seem endless. She arrived, happy and excited to see KC and right-away told her that she had a surprise. "Soon as I change." Five minutes later, Agnes emerged from the bedroom dressed in jeans and a tee-shirt and flashing a triumphant smile. "I swear, KC, you show up exactly when you are supposed to. I accomplished what I came to do!"

"Agnes! Are you telling me you found the account numbers?"

"We'll find out soon enough. But the good news is, if my electronic caper worked, the good guys *will* win." Agnes booted up the laptop. "Employees aren't allowed to have keys, but my boss was so anxious for me to get up to speed, he let me work until the janitors finished and the guards locked up. That's when I was able to figure out the main frame and search the central system for BIA accounts. But before I could do that, I had to figure out Royale's security which is tight. Their cameras sweep the hallways 24/7, and guards check briefcases coming and going."

KC stood behind her and watched as folders began to appear. "Royale's building is huge, but I was given a brief tour, so I could find the employees' lounge and the copy room, places like that. The clerk and I came across a storage room; she called it a junk room. They store old records and some computers in there. They don't lock the room, so after hours, I'd sneak in there and check out the computers. The computer gods must be smiling on us, KC, because I found one that was operational."

"That's obviously a good thing, but I'm not sure why," KC responded.

Agnes' fingers were flying over the keys. "It is, because I was able to program it and assign the computer an ID number. So now, according to Royale's mainframe, it is just one computer out of the two hundred or more terminals in the building. The number constantly changes as new computers get added and others replaced. But here's the tricky part. Last night, I sent the BIA data I found to the computer in the storage room. And, if I programmed it right, that computer forwarded the data on to this baby." Agnes inserted a CD in the tower. "Backup."

KC squeezed her shoulders. "Agnes, you are brilliant."

"Hold the kudos." She hit *Enter,* crossed her fingers, and they waited. "Look!" Data began flooding onto the screen, hundreds of dates, numbers, and balances. "Whoa, it worked!"

"Unbelievable," KC said, squinting at the screen. "Are all of those BIA accounts?"

"No, not all of them. Royale's mainframe stores accounts first by country of origin, then by region, and finally, by individual states. When I figured that out, I isolated accounts in the District of Columbia—where BIA is. What you see are Royale's U.S. accounts in D.C. The storage room computer, right now, is acting like a telegraph, automatically transferring the data it receives to this terminal."

She turned on the printer. "We'll need hard copies. What's coming through now are account numbers and balances, no names. I need to isolate the accounts we're interested in, then with the data in the second file, we can identify the individual ones we want." She described the second file as Royale's master code that linked names to account numbers. "But for us, it's our key to the kingdom." Agnes opened the second file, and names began to appear, followed by ten-digit numbers. "This is awesome," Agnes said. "As soon as I print this file, we'll cross-check names and account numbers. That'll tell us who stole, and how much they squirreled away."

KC's heart was racing as if she were running. "I can't stand it, Agnes, read some names."

"Yes, oh impatient one." Agnes scrolled down. "I see Aubert, Jules; Berkeley, William; Culpepper, Hayden; Ludlow, Victor; and Marsh, Carson, about $25 mil between them."

"How about Valerie Beckman or Elliott Wolf?" KC said.

It took a few minutes for her to search through the Bs and the Ws. "No account for Beckman. But Wolf, ooh, that's strange. Wolf *had* an account here with $950K in it, but it came in and went out the same day. According to this, it was wired to the Bank of Montreal, account number 226435." Agnes scrolled back up. "So, all together, Aubert stole about $25 million. He has $15 million in his account, the balance he divided between the four other scuzzbags."

KC looked for herself. "I just thought of something. With Victor Ludlow and Carson Marsh now out of the way, Aubert will clean out their accounts. I'm surprised he hasn't already. I hate the fact those crooks will live like kings on Indian trust money."

Agnes glanced up at her with a smirk. "Not necessarily, my skeptical friend. The computer giveth, but it can also taketh away. Say the word, and I can zip all of these funds to a holding account in the Cook Islands. Those guys won't have a clue where their money went, and we can transfer it back into the BIA trust account from wherever we go. Yes or no?"

"That's pure genius." KC's euphoria vanished as quickly as it appeared. "You do that, and we're dead. Think about *that,* my mastermind friend. I say yes, and the Indians get their money back, but you and I may not live to see it. I say no, and Aubert wins, and my promise to Dad goes up in smoke." KC watched red splotches form on Agnes' tanned cheeks. Her fingers remained poised above keys that could launch a strike against men powerful enough to kill six times and get away with it. "You're asking me to make a decision that could leave Danny without a mother. I can't do that, Agnes," KC said.

"Come on, girlfriend." Agnes' hands didn't move. "Follow your heart. Don't let fear decide this." Both her voice and expression were resolute.

KC bent down and looked her in the eye. "If we do, we run. What do you say?"

Agnes giggled. "Geez, what a high! I've never had power like this."

KC laughed at her bravado. "Okay, go for it. Take every dime those slimeballs stole. I just hope we live to tell our grandchildren about this."

"If we do, they'll think we're the coolest old ladies on the planet. It will take about forty minutes to isolate the accounts and transfer the funds. I'll print as I go. We can deal with getting Wolf's money in Montreal later. Okay, are you ready?" Agnes looked up, and in her eyes, KC saw the humor and courage she so admired in her friend.

"While you do it, I'll book our flights. The minute you transfer the last dollar—we run."

*   *   *

Wolf deplaned at Kindley Field, his only luggage a carry-on. In his other hand was a tourist book with the phone numbers of every hotel on the island. He stopped at a phone booth and quickly found out there was no Agnes Richardson staying at the hotels. Next, he looked over a list of long-term rentals he printed off the Internet. Four were in the expensive category, seven moderately priced. Wolf played the odds that Richardson picked moderate. He started phoning, using the same story that he'd just arrived and wanted to surprise his daughter for her birthday. The first three had no one by that name; the other three would not divulge the information.

Wolf tried the Surf Side Beach Club in Warwick, deciding at the last second to take the approach that he already knew she was there. A woman answered; "This is Agnes Richardson's father, and I have a favor to ask. I just arrived, and I want to surprise Agnes on her birthday. Please don't give me away, but can you tell me if she's in?"

"What a lovely thing to do." The woman sounded British. "I don't believe Agnes is home right now, but I expect she will be in later. Your daughter is a delightful lady."

"How kind you are," Wolf said and paid her a few more compliments. He learned Agnes' cottage was number twenty-three. "I was ill on her last birthday, so I want this one to be special. I appreciate your help." She assured him she would not spoil his plans. Wolf exited the terminal into the evening breeze and took the first cab in line.

* * *

An uneasy feeling gripped KC, refusing to let her heart slow. Thankfully, she was able to reserve a flight with American Airlines as she gathered up their wallets and passports. Now on her cell phone with Continental Airlines, she stuffed a wad of cash in her jeans pocket then peeked in at Agnes. "How much longer?"

"About five minutes," she said, continuing to type. "What's wrong?"

"I don't know—something." Her cell in one hand, KC searched through the clothes in her suitcase until she found the leather pouch of sacred corn from her grandmother. She stuffed it in her other pocket as Continental's agent confirmed their second reservation then reminded KC they needed to check in one hour before their flights. KC hung up. "I hope we make it on time. What I really hope is we make it, period."

KC turned off the bedroom light and walked into the living room, just as the gleam of car lights crossed the window. She lunged for the wall and flipped off the lights. "Lower the laptop cover, and get on the floor." Agnes silently complied. KC slid the dead bolt into place and stood with her back against the door as a car pulled up in front of the cottage, the motor idling.

"It doesn't look like your daughter is home. Would you like to talk to the manager?"

"Yes, take me to the office. Maybe I can get a key and wait inside." *Elliott Wolf. How did he find me this fast!"*

"Call the office, Agnes. Tell her not to give him a key!"

Agnes grabbed the phone next to her laptop as the cab backed up slowly and then turned around. "I'm calling," she said from floor. "Mrs. Wilson, Agnes Richardson. There's a man on his way over. No, Mrs. Wilson, listen! He's going to ask for a key to my cottage. I beg you, do not give him a key! And you don't know where I am." She severed the connection.

"Good job," KC whispered as she eased the curtain aside and peered toward the office. In the distance, she saw a figure enter the office as the cab waited and then the dark figure get back in the cab. Its backup lights came on, and the taxi slowly exited the grounds.

The phone rang twice, stopped, and then rang twice again. Agnes answered. "Oh, thank God! Surprise me on my birthday? No, my father died nine years ago." Silence again and then: "I have no idea who he is. Yes, I will report it to the authorities. Thank you, Mrs. Wilson." Agnes got up off the floor. "He offered her a hundred dollars to give him the key, but she told him she would lose her job. She told him I was probably out to dinner, and she heard him tell the driver Southhampton Princess Hotel."

KC's eyes had grown accustomed to the dark. "He'll be back. Are the transfers done?"

Agnes lifted the laptop cover. "They are." She checked the printer. It was still spitting out copies. "I'm glad the cabbie didn't turn off the motor. He might have heard the printer. By the time I burn a CD, the printer should be done, and we can get out of here."

"The sooner, the better," KC said. "If Wolf bought her story and checks into the hotel, he'll grab a bite to eat, which would give us maybe an hour. But if he checks in and comes right back, we have twenty minutes, tops. We'll go out the kitchen window. All we take are the laptop, the copies, and the CD. I have our passports and wallets. Leave everything else."

"No problem," Agnes said. "I can call Mrs. Wilson from home and have her ship our stuff." Burning the CD took a few minutes; Agnes finished about the time the printer shut off. She slid the CD and copies into a manila envelope. "Okay, let's get out of here."

KC opened the kitchen window at the back of the cottage and climbed out. She signaled for Agnes to wait and then crept forward to the corner. Except for chattering birds and the distant noise of a party, the night was still. She returned to the window. "Looks clear." Agnes handed KC the laptop and manila envelope and then climbed out.

KC led the way keeping in the shadows, moving east through the complex away from the entrance. They stayed close to a thicket of tall bushes that formed Surf Side's north border. Reaching the next resort, KC skirted its buildings and took a worn path through the trees. "It won't take long for Wolf to figure we're not coming back. Do you know where this path goes?"

"Toward the beach," Agnes answered. "But there's a solid hedge that runs along this side of the beach. Without a flashlight, I'm not sure we can find an opening through it."

Clouds drifted across the moon, making it impossible to see. KC banged into a rock and went down on her knees. "Ouch! Is there more than one opening?"

"Yes, one of them is close here somewhere. If we can find it, we'll be on a path that runs the length of south shore all the way to Devonshire. We'll cut inland there." Agnes helped her up. The moon peeked out from a bank of clouds. "Look up ahead; there's the opening."

The beach path was narrow; they moved at a fast clip, single file, and twenty minutes later, reached Devonshire. Pausing under a light, KC checked her watch, seven-twenty. "We don't have much time, but there's something I have to do." She dug the pouch of sacred corn out of her pocket. "I'll explain later." KC emptied the kernels into her cupped hand then turned her face skyward. She held up her hand. "Spirit, guide us on this dangerous journey, and keep us safe until our job is done." She tossed the kernels into the air and then brushed her hands. "Okay, we've got twelve minutes to get to the airport."

* * *

Wolf checked in at the Southhampton Princess and found his room then stopped in the bar for a quick sandwich and a beer. He walked the short distance back to Surf Side, and for the next forty-five minutes, hid in the shadows, his binoculars trained on the dark cottage. "Dinner wouldn't last this long." He pressed the button on his watch, 7:50. "Sonofabitch, they're making a run for it!" Wolf spun around and sprinted back toward the hotel, cursing the woman in the office and himself for not realizing she was on the phone with Agnes when he entered.

Wolf lengthened his stride and cut across the expansive lawn in front of the hotel. His duffel bag was in his room, but it only contained a few clothes. He ran up to the entrance. "Cab, please," he felt every tick of the clock as the fancy-clad doorman waved a cab forward. "Airport," he gasped. "A hundred bucks if you get me there in ten minutes."

"I'll do my best, sir." The cabbie pulled away from the hotel at a reasonable speed, then floored the old Chrysler as soon as he turned onto South Road. He passed every car they came across all the way to the airport, where he pulled up behind a line of cabs. "Eleven minutes, sir."

"Good enough." Wolf tossed a C-note over the front seat, hopped out, and ducked behind a potted palm when he saw Garrett and Richardson emerge from the dark and enter the terminal. Garrett had a computer case in one hand and an envelope in the other; neither had any luggage. *Hell, it's time I retire. I blew it.*

Wolf entered the terminal, telling himself to view this job like any Bureau assignment, but it didn't work. The truth was, as long as Garrett was alive, Mrs. B's career was done. Silently acknowledging that he had just underestimated Garrett again, Wolf felt his blood pressure spike and wished like hell he could blame anybody but himself.

He glanced around Kindley's small terminal, crowded with high-season tourists. He spotted Garrett and Richardson pausing at the Continental desk; it looked like the clerk handed Agnes a boarding pass. From there, they hurried to the American Airlines counter and stood in line. "Different airlines. Garrett knows I'm here," Wolf said under his breath. She kept looking around as she talked on her cell phone. *Probably calling DeMarco.*

As soon as Garrett and Richardson disappeared into the area security, Wolf bought a ticket to Washington, D.C. and went through security stuck behind a group of chatty tourists. By the time he entered the boarding area, Garrett and Richardson were hugging in front of the Continental Airlines gate. When Richardson disappeared into the boarding tunnel, Garrett made a beeline to a restroom. Wolf checked the monitor; Richardson's flight was to Washington, D.C.

The fact Garrett didn't also board the flight to D.C. surprised Wolf. He bought a copy of the island's newspaper and found a spot with a view of the restroom entrance. He raised and lowered the newspaper periodically. Fifteen minutes went by, and no sign of Garrett. American Airlines announced flight 1384 was open for boarding. Two more announcements and still no sign of Garrett. *What the hell?* Wolf looked around.

At the last word of the final call, Garrett burst from the restroom and sprinted like a track star toward the gate, the door closing behind her.

Wolf sat, stunned. Apparently aware that he was watching her, Garrett was playing FBI Agent Elliott Wolf like this was a damned chess game. He rose and threw down the newspaper, startling the people around him. He quickly walked away so as not to attract security.

The American Airlines board showed Garrett's flight was to Montreal. Surprised, his fury gave way to relief. He had another chance to redeem himself. He had to go to Montreal anyway to get his money. Whether she was afraid, it was part of her game, or she intended to throw him off, her reason for going to Montreal was irrelevant. KC Garrett had just played into his hands.

—27—

Santana paid his hotel bill each morning before leaving for *Chateau Roussillon* to keep track of Jules Aubert. For a man supposedly hiding out, he appeared totally unconcerned at being spotted. After three days, Santana was ready to get on with his mission. He left his hotel Wednesday at noon, his patience at an end. *If he doesn't leave soon, I'll have to nab him here.* Like a prayer answered, when he walked into the Chateau's grand salon, he saw Aubert checking out.

An hour later, Santana was four car-lengths behind the Mercedes when Aubert turned west onto Highway D138 and into a service station on the outskirts of Lodève. While Aubert put petrol in his Mercedes, Santana drove to the other side of the station and checked his map as he filled the Citroën. The map showed D138, west of Lodève, passed through a few tiny villages, Joncelets at the end, eighty kilometers away. Surprisingly, D138 was the only road to Joncelets.

Santana kept the Mercedes in view through Lodève and four more villages, each one smaller than the one before. The road became narrower and winding, the terrain so hilly and unfamiliar that when dusk gave way to darkness, Santana returned to Lodéve. Finding Joncelets in the daylight would be easier and safer. He checked into a *hoteliere* and, after two glasses of burgundy and the best *bœuf bourguignonne* he had ever tasted, Santana went to bed. Thursday morning when he paid his bill, Santana learned that Thursdays were market day in Lodève.Each week, local farmers and merchants offered their products in the town square. Santana joined the early-morning crowd as they looked over tables laden with fruits, vegetables, cheeses, and breads of every description. Sampling his way around the square, he came away with wine, bottled water, and a sack full of bread, cheese, and fruit.

The village of Lodéve was like stepping back in time, the impression enhanced as he drove west past small villages. Orchards, small vineyards, and stone-enclosed pastures now lined both sides of the narrow road. Grazing cows and horses glanced up at the sound of his car. Forty minutes later, Santana rounded a sharp curve and braked, almost missing the tiny one-word sign, *Joncelets,* at the road's edge.

Santana eased the Citroën off the abrupt drop from asphalt onto a dirt road not much wider than the car. Following it up and around a curve to the top of the hill, he passed waist-high stone fences that crooked their way around stone houses with rows of vines. Dogs lazing in the sun raised their heads, looking too sleepy to bark. So far, Santana had yet to see any citizens of Joncelets. A half-mile farther on the road, he rounded the gentle curve of a low hill and stopped.

Santana could only stare. His idea of a *villa* was a sprawling, white mansion overlooking an azure sea. Aubert's villa was the antithesis of his image, rising from the mountainside like a medieval castle. At the base of a vineyard, rows of vines radiated outward from the structure like a fan, so far into the distance that they disappeared.

Remote and almost inaccessible, it was as if a hundred years ago when the villa was built, someone knew that one day Jules Aubert would need a place to hide from the law. He was there, the back of his new Mercedes half-hidden by shrubbery.

Santana pulled the Citroën behind a thicket beside the road, then got out and stretched. Retrieving his bag of knick-knick leaves, he poured some into his hand, and then turned his face to the sun. "Spirit, guide me on this journey, and return me safely to the reservation when my job is done." Santana tossed the leaves into the air and watched his gift to Mother Earth settle onto the ground. "Great Spirit, I ask that this man receive justice for the death of my father and Sam Blackhawk. If not by white man's law, then by Justice, the Indian way."

* * *

KC sat amongst a group of happy, tanned Canadians returning home from their mid-winter vacation in Bermuda. Her flight touched down in Montreal a few minutes before midnight. With no luggage, she sailed through Customs and paused at an arrivals monitor. The next flight from Bermuda wasn't due until ten o'clock tomorrow morning. She called her friend, Stacey Foster-Morgan, from the main terminal. "Sorry, roomie, this is not how I planned to visit, but I'm in Montreal." Stacey said she wasn't surprised, that Tony had called earlier saying he was on his way. Only then did KC remember she had called him from the airport in Bermuda.

She took a cab to the Morgan's house, a very pregnant Stacey greeting her. Over a cup of cocoa, KC learned the baby was due in seven weeks. Stacey wanted to know why Tony sounded so scared when he called. "Stacey, you have my word, I will tell you the minute I can," KC said, glancing at her watch. "I have seven hours to show probable cause on three very bad guys and email everything to my secretary. And, I *have* to be at the Bank of Montreal tomorrow morning when it opens, so roust me out of your office, okay?" Stacey said the bank opened at 9:00 a.m. and promised to have coffee ready at eight o'clock. "I'm sorry about all this," KC said.

Stacey led KC to her second-floor office and jotted down her email password. A glance at the shelves of U.S. and Canada law books reminded KC just how much work she had to do. The comfy-looking recliner beckoned until she thought of Agnes, who had risked her life to do the right thing. It was 1:45 a.m. when KC called Agnes' apartment to tell her where she was.

"KC, I'm so glad to hear from you. I hated leaving you at the airport. Any trouble?"

"None. I am safe and ready to get started. I'm on Stacey's computer. I'll email you so you can email me back the data as an attachment."

"All right, girlfriend!" Agnes said. "I've divided the data into four files. Four attachments will be on their way in about ten minutes. I read through the printed copies on the flight home. We have strong probable cause. If we can finish this paperwork, I will be at the U.S. Attorney's office at eight o'clock in the morning." Agnes sounded anything but tired.

"First, I need a favor." KC gave her Valerie Beckman's private cell number. "Valerie is leaving with the President for Camp David on Friday. Before she leaves, it's important she knows that the IIM money is safe, and we'll get it transferred back to the BIA account soon. If not, Agnes, I'm afraid she might withdraw from the campaign. We can't let that happen." Agnes said she would make sure to call Valerie.

KC booted up Stacey's computer, acknowledging that even counting the Arizona case, she was about to tackle the most important job of her career.

* * *

Santana waited until dusk to make his camp in back of the villa. Hidden behind thick bushes, he enjoyed his food from Lodève and then stretched out on his makeshift bed. In a deep sleep within a few minutes, Santana, at first, incorporated the loud cry he heard into his dream. When he heard it a second time, he bolted upright, adrenaline delivering full-alert. An anguished scream; it sounded like Aubert was in extreme pain.

One of the ground-floor windows was lit. Santana followed the beam of light and peered inside. Aubert was sitting at a table, an open laptop in front of him. He didn't appear to be injured. Santana ducked when Aubert abruptly jumped up and disappeared from the room. Something was up. Santana grabbed his flashlight, found his way to the front of the house, and waited in the shadows.

A few minutes later, Aubert stormed out of the villa, carrying a suitcase and what looked like papers in his other hand. He had obviously been drinking. Aubert half-staggered to his Mercedes, which evidently, he had failed to lock. He opened the driver's door and threw down the papers onto the seat. Then, yelling expletives, he slammed the car door so hard it rocked the Mercedes. Aubert fumbled with a key fob, finally opening the trunk. He had difficulty getting the suitcase into it. When he at last succeeded, he slammed the trunk and cursed aloud all the way to the house.

On hearing the front door slam, Santana hurried to the Mercedes and crouched down beside the front door. When a light came on in the upstairs window, he eased open the car door and shined his flash-light inside. On the driver's seat was a map, on top of it some papers and a small bank book. Santana examined the bank book by flash-light, *Banque Chalus* was stamped on the front. Inside were entries dating back several years, the balance $13,000 Swiss francs.

Underneath the bank book, he found a computer-generated bank statement. *Royale Insurance Co., Ltd., Account holder: Jules Romain Aubert, #2001 Gaston Towers, 4500, Audibon Dr., Silver Spring, Maryland, U.S.A.* at the top of the page. Below the heading was series of deposits, the total near the bottom was *$15-plus million U.S.* There was one entry below the total. Santana directed his light on the last figure. It was a withdrawal, dated yesterday, and the same figure as the balance. *No wonder he screamed. Someone zeroed out his account!*

The map beneath the papers was of France, the city of Clermont-Ferrand circled in red. Next to the circle, Aubert had placed a post-it printed with: *Banque Chalus, 5, Place de Jaude, Clermont-Ferrand.* Santana glanced up at the second floor window, light and movement allowing him a few more minutes. On the seat underneath the map, he found a single paper. Santana shined his flashlight on an email from Gregory Aubert.

According to the date and time, Jules had received it within the last hour. Santana read by flashlight. *Mon frère, I am dispatching the Gulfstream tomorrow with the cash from my safe. Unfortunately though not to Montpellier as you wanted. Vanguard's jet flies to Clermont-Ferrand routinely, therefore drawing no attention to our directors. The cash is in a Vanguard briefcase, combination ZX0874. Our pilot, Henri Gerard, is picking up the briefcase tomorrow, 5:00 a.m. with instructions to deliver it to Banque Chalus on Place de Jaude. Henri will take off at 6:00 a.m., his ETA into Clermont-Ferrand, 1:30 p.m. The briefcase should be available by 2:30. Mon frère, you must know I am extremely worried about you. Call me as soon as you can!*

Santana glanced at the second-floor window—still lit. *No sleep tonight for you or me.* He returned to the Citroën and retrieved his map from the rental car company. Clermont-Ferrand was north of a large shaded area in the middle of France, marked *Massiff Central*. Montpellier was south of it. Trying to guess Aubert's plans, he realized was pure speculation, but there were only two ways to get to Clermont-Ferrand—drive or fly. If Aubert flew, it could mean he planned to return to the villa and hide out for a while. If he drove, it might be that Aubert found the villa too isolated, and Rene Garzon planned to lose himself in the city. *I don't know why I'm wasting my time. Aubert's plans don't matter. I'll be waiting for him at the Banque Chalus.*

Santana had planned for their return trip to the U.S. As he always did when he traveled abroad, Santana used his Lake Ponsiteau Nation passport. This time, however, he also carried a pair of handcuffs and a picture ID identifying him as Lt. Santana Dawson, Lake Ponsiteau Tribal Police Department. Takoda had procured both items; how and from whom, Santana preferred not to know. Aubert being led away in handcuffs made Santana smile. *It will right a lot of wrongs.*

He put his camping gear into the Citroën and kept vigil for the next three hours. Aubert left in the Mercedes just before daylight, Santana following with headlights off as far as the highway. Two hours later, when the Mercedes sped past the entrance to Montpellier's airport, Santana had his answer—Aubert, aka Rene Garzon, planned to disappear in the city.

He turned the Citroën in at the airport, and then passed the next two hours in the boarding area reading the global edition of *The New York Times*. His flight on time, Santana took his seat on the French Airbus, his resolve rock-solid that today would be Jules Aubert's last day in France. Flying over the *Massiff Centrale* reminded Santana of Idaho, the mountainous terrain appearing a blanket of white interrupted by occasional dark stands of trees, and rivers shining like silver threads from twenty thousand feet. Clermont-Ferrand looked similar in size to Montpellier, his first glimpse of it, a sprawl of red-tiled roofs, church spires, and a large manufacturing plant in the middle of town. Santana checked his watch, 2:30 p.m. *I hope Aubert makes it before the bank closes.*

A taxi delivered him to the *Banque Chalus* on *Place de Jaude* a few minutes after four. Santana sought permission from the manager to wait in the bank's lounge area "for my colleague." He took a seat facing a small television. The program, *NYSE Euronext,* evidently a financial news show, had two serious-looking commentators speaking bullet-speed French.

Hearing the bank door open, Santana turned around expecting to see Jules Aubert. Instead, it was a man and woman followed by two young boys. The woman and boys sat on the couch across from Santana; her husband took a seat at the manager's desk. As the show ended, Santana checked his watch, 4:30 p.m. *Aubert should have been here by now.*

The woman's husband walked up and acknowledged Santana with a polite nod. Abruptly, a terse announcement by the TV anchor drew Santana's and the French family's attention. The statement was followed by a flurry of flashing lights, police cars, and a long line of trucks and cars at a standstill on a snowy highway.

"My wife and I heard this on the radio on our way here," the man said in perfect English to Santana. "In case you are wondering, it is an accident near Mont Dômes." He shook his head. "Every winter this happens. Apparently, an auto went into the river. The police are saying the driver lost control—*en glace noir,* in French. Black ice in English."

A chill raced across Santana's shoulders. "Did they give a name? Or what kind of car?" Several bank customers had walked up and stood watching as the TV camera zeroed in on a crushed vehicle being raised from the water by a crane. *"Mon Dieu!"* The man's wife said and looked away. One look at the car, Santana recognized Jules Aubert's Mercedes. "They will not release the identity of the driver until the next of kin is notified," the Frenchman said. *They don't need to give a name. I know who it is.*

Santana thanked the man for his assistance and hailed a cab to the airport. It took a while to buy his ticket and get through security. When he finished, Santana found a quiet spot to wait. He couldn't help reflecting on what had happened. There was no doubt in his mind that it was Aubert's Mercedes they fished out of the river. Nor was he surprised how Jules Aubert died.

Santana had no idea where KC might be. And he disregarded the time difference between France and D.C. It was important for her to know about Aubert. Santana called her apartment and left a message: "KC, remember the poacher example I gave you about Justice, the Indian way? Well, I have another one to tell you about when I get back."

—28—

Wolf stopped his Buick behind a line of cars at the Locolle-Champlain border crossing into Quebec. A dozen or more floodlights illuminated the pre-dawn morning. At this hour, only three of the ten car lanes were open plus a separate lane for commercial vehicles. The few times he'd crossed here, the agents had been efficient but not officious. Wolf knew what papers to have ready, and his seat belt buckled. From past visits he knew to turn off the motor when the agent approached and look the agent in the eye when answering questions.

A Montreal guidebook lay open on the passenger seat to insure that his visit appeared to be pleasure, not business. The SUV in front of him had skis on top, probably New Yorkers on their way to ski Mont Tremblant. It took the agent fourteen minutes to talk to the four people inside the SUV and check their luggage. When the skiers' vehicle pulled away, Wolf drove forward, lowered the window, and turned off the motor.

A forty-something agent approached, her uniform and stride commanding respect. "Good morning, sir." September 11 had changed things; no friendly smile.

"Good morning," he replied. Wolf handed her his passport, driver's license, and car registration. She took her time looking at each one, then shined a flashlight around the interior as she asked rote questions: destination, length of stay, whether he possessed any plants, food products, or firearms. He answered politely and looked directly at her. "I have my golf clubs, which I always bring regardless of the weather. My buddies call them weapons depending on my game." He smiled. "I don't mean to joke. You have a tough job."

"The world has indeed changed." Her voice softened. "I'll check the trunk, Mr. Wolf."

"No problem." He punched the release button. "Would you like me to get out?"

"Yes sir." He followed her to the rear of the car. "That tragedy made this job a lot less fun." Her voice was casual, but not her actions. She removed several golf clubs from the bag then shined her flashlight down into it. "Frustrating game, my husband tells me." She returned the flashlight to her belt. "I'll let you put these back properly while your passport is stamped, Mr. Wolf." Aware that surveillance cameras were trained on each lane, Wolf methodically put his clubs back and then got into his car. "Enjoy your stay in Quebec, sir." She handed him back his passport and papers and waved the next car forward.

Wolf joined the traffic on the expressway, relieved at getting his FBI .38 and favorite gun, the Glock, across the border. He had hidden them in the false bottom of his golf bag. His $500K for getting rid of Garrett depended on it. The nine-hour drive had been good, giving him time to process a tangle of feelings, uncertainty and anger, and a mountain of remorse. How Aubert had managed to turn him into an assassin, Wolf conceded he would never be able to resolve. *To hell with him. When this job's over, Aubert is out of my life.*

Wolf's thoughts turned to Garrett. She was slippery and smart. And he wasn't sure about his plan to remove her; he needed to give it more thought. But his exit strategy was solid. Both guns would go in the river. He would clear the inside and outside of his Buick of fingerprints then wear gloves to drive it to a big, public, self-park lot. This would be after dark so he could remove the license plates and make sure he'd left nothing that would quickly link the Buick to him. And by the time they did connect the Buick's VIN number to Elliott Wolf, he would be out of the country. The question of what airport to use he had yet to decide.

But before any of that, he needed to wire all of his money to his account in the Caymans. The $50K in cash from the safe deposit box would be enough to get him out of Canada and cover any unforeseen contingencies.

Wolf acknowledged that it might take a day or two to find and remove Garrett, but he would use that time to wrap up his plans.

Wolf left his Buick at the downtown Le Centre Sheraton, walking distance from the Bank of Montreal. He tipped the valet a twenty to park his car in an accessible spot, then checked in, showered, and dressed. Wolf put the Glock in the holster at the back of his belt; the Smith and Wesson went into his shoulder holster. A quick breakfast in the coffee shop left Wolf fifteen minutes, plenty of time to be at the bank when it opened at 10:00 a.m.

Dealing with Garrett would have to wait. Getting his money was top priority. Wolf joined the crowd of men and women on their way to work in the city's high-rise corporate suites.

*   *   *

KC's eyes flew open, her heart hammering. *Where am I?* The room was dark except for dim light from an open door. She was in a recliner with a blanket over her. A minute ago, she was standing beside her father's casket, so many flowers all around that it was hard to breathe. In front of her was the imaginary box. Images of her father, Charlie, Ludlow, Marsh, and Jared, all the tragedies she had sent to the box were threatening to escape. It was full. It couldn't hold anymore. The box was about to overflow.

Fatigue and sorrow triumphing, KC gave in, no longer able to hold back the horrors. Her mythical *tomorrow* hit with tsunami force, releasing anguish and pain into a system with no defenses. She bolted out of the chair and through the open door, to the bathroom, barely reaching the sink before she vomited. Disoriented, KC straightened up and splashed water on her face, fighting to get her bearings. In the medicine cabinet mirror, the image of Captain Appling emerged, his hat in hand. "Mr. Blackhawk's Camaro was pulled from the river an hour ago. I am sorry for your loss." KC whirled around. There was no one there.

She stumbled through the open door back to the recliner, the dark hallway in front of her. The Potomac waiting for her, cold and black like death itself. The vision of her father and Charlie trapped and helpless inside the car, fighting for breath in cold, murky water exploded with gruesome force. She closed her eyes; she was dangling over the edge of a bottomless hole that beckoned her to let go. KC gripped the blanket and hung on, concerned only with her next breath and then the next. How long she lay there she had no idea.

When she opened her eyes, she recognized Stacey's office, her terror-driven panic slipping away as daylight flooded the room. She felt warmth flow back into her body and with it the image of her dad running beside her as she rode her new bicycle. Then the two of them racing the length of the Rossiters' pool. Her father was laughing. "You beat me, Kaya!"

She heard his voice. And there in the doorway stood her father. "Kaya, you must have faith. Destinies play out according to our Divine plan." He spoke in that deep, soft voice with the cadence she loved. "I love you, Kaya. Be strong. Allow Spirit to give you peace." His image began to fade. "Dad, Dad!" She reached for him, but the image was gone, the hallway no longer black or threatening. KC didn't move, holding onto the moment, refusing to question whether what she saw was real or part of her dream. Her father was all right. That's all she needed to know.

KC got up from the recliner cautiously and stood stock-still, acknowledging that her mythical tomorrow had arrived—and she survived it.

* * *

Tony awoke with a start and glanced at KC's pillow; it hadn't been touched. She had kissed him last night when he arrived and then returned to Stacey's office saying she had a ton of legal work to complete. He glanced at his watch, 9:00 a.m. *She can't still be working.* Tony pulled on his jeans and checked Stacey's office. Empty. He hurried downstairs. Stacey was sitting at the kitchen table, the newspaper in front of her. "Morning, Tony. KC said to tell you she emailed Agnes the Probable Cause attachments, and not to wake—"

"Where is she?"

"She took a cab to the Bank of Montreal."

"Dammit! Where is this bank?"

"Old downtown on Rue St. Jacque. What's wrong?" Stacey looked alarmed.

"She's in danger!" Tony raced back up the stairs. "Call me a cab!" he hollered over his shoulder. "Tell 'em I want the fastest trip they've ever made!" He pulled on his shirt and the bomber jacket he'd dropped on the chair. He stuffed his Smith and Wesson .4506 in his shoulder holster then raced downstairs. Stacey was at the front door with a commuter mug of coffee as a cab pulled up. She wished him good luck.

"It's going to take more than luck."

*   *   *

Wolf walked into the Bank of Montreal at 10:00 a.m. sharp and was shocked to find out it had opened an hour ago. He distinctly remembered this bank opening at 10:00 a.m. the last time he was in Montreal, but then that was two years ago. The bank looked the same: high mahogany ceiling, marble floors, and the Corinthian columns evoking a sense of grandeur. He waited in the shortest line, and three customers later, stepped to the window and presented his proof of deposit and passport. An attractive young woman greeted him in French and asked how she might help.

"I want to wire all the funds in my account to this bank." He slid a Sheraton hotel note toward her with his Cayman bank account number.

"Of course, *monsieur*," she said. "Do you see that gentleman over there?" She nodded at a man across the bank. "He is our manager and will gladly handle this transaction. One moment, *s'il vous plait*." She picked up a telephone and spoke in rapid French. Wolf turned and saw a distinguished, grey-haired gentleman approaching. "Please, *monsieur,* have a seat at my desk."

Wolf did as he asked, took a deep breath, and held it for a second, almost afraid to let go when the significance of that piece of paper and the man looking it over sunk in. This moment was his future. The manager asked to see his identification, and Wolf tried to keep his hand from shaking as he produced his passport and lifetime FBI identification card.

"Merci." The manager turned to his computer and glanced at the paper. "Aah, I see that you wish to transfer your funds to a Cayman bank," he said. Eyeing the monitor, the manager typed for a full minute, Wolf watching his pleasant expression change to puzzled. "Something is amiss, *monsieur.* Let me try again." He verified the number on Wolf's proof of deposit and typed on his computer again. This time, a frown creased the manager's brow. Wolf's throat went dry when he picked up the phone and spoke in unintelligible French.

Aubert had promised to deposit $500K for eliminating Garrett as soon as he reached his villa; that was yesterday. But even if Aubert hadn't transferred it yet, the proof of deposit showed he had $950,000.00 in his account. Wolf glanced at the safe deposit area. And if Aubert's brother did what he was supposed to do, he had another $50K in cash in a box with his name on it.

The manager hung up and slid the proof of deposit across the desk. Wolf's eyes followed the paper and then looked up into dilated eyes. "I am sorry, *monsieur,* but our records indicate that a hold has been placed on your account. I'm afraid it is frozen."

Wolf blinked, not comprehending. "What do you mean? There's $950K in my account!" He slid the proof of deposit back and leaned forward "Who put a hold on it? Tell me now!"

"Please, *monsieur,* I am doing everything I can." The manager typed furiously and then halted, alarm registering on his face. "A hold was placed on your account and the contents of your safe deposit box—just minutes ago." His voice faltered. "It was done by an attorney from the Department of Just—"

Wolf closed his eyes, disbelief engulfing him. KC Garrett went to Bermuda where Agnes Richardson was working for Royale Insurance, the depository of Aubert's BIA funds. Garrett and Richardson had names and account numbers. They tracked Aubert's $950K transfer to this bank and his account. "Garrett didn't come to Montreal because she was afraid. She came to take my money!" At Wolf's voice, the manager's hand moved toward the underside of his desk.

"I wouldn't do that unless you are ready to die." Wolf opened his jacket enough to show his .38, then rose and glanced around. There were lines in front of each teller, no one paying attention to this side of the bank. "Let's have a smile," Wolf said. "We are going to walk to the vault, and you are going to give me my money. We will do this without creating panic. You blink or make one move, and you will die along with a lot of other people. Do you understand?"

The manager nodded and then came around the desk, his hands clasped in front.

"Very good," Wolf said as they started for the rear of the bank. "Nice and easy. Nobody will get hurt unless you do something stupid. The bank has insurance. It's not worth a bunch of people dying. Let's chat as we walk." The manager mumbled in French. "Doing fine, stay cool."

Wolf leaned close as they approached the vault. "English now. Tell her I am *your* customer retrieving papers you've stored for me. Remember, you are a trigger-pull away from dying." The manager dismissed the clerk in English, and she discreetly excused herself. They passed a table with a stack of dark blue, zippered plastic bags imprinted with the bank's name in silver letters. Wolf took one and glanced after the clerk. She had retreated to a bank of filing cabinets, her back to them.

The manager unlocked the steel gate, and they entered the vault. Wolf handed him the bank bag and instructed him to put in large bills only. "Make nice conversation in case somebody walks by. You want to live to enjoy lunch." The manager mumbled more French.

A security camera moved back and forth over the space, but Wolf saw no panic button. The manager stuffed four stacks of thousand dollar bills into the bag, instantly showing how little it would hold. Wolf glanced down on the table beside him. Practically under his nose were stacks of bearer bonds, each stack a different denomination, the largest being $100K. Wolf took an inch-thick stack of those. "Put these in." The manager obliged with shaking hands. The bag could hold no more. "Zip it up, please. Okay, you've been very cooperative. I'm going to leave now, and I want you to get down on your knees and stay perfectly still for ten minutes. If you don't, I will kill you just for the hell of it, and shoot my way out of your bank. Understand?"

Without a word, the manager went down on his knees and put his forehead to the floor. Wolf took the key from him, walked out, then closed and locked the vault gate. The clerk was busy talking to another employee. Wolf walked unhurriedly to the entrance. A man entering the bank held the door open for him. Wolf thanked him and exited onto the sidewalk.

Joining the crowd on the sidewalk, Wolf walked unseeing, still stunned at Garrett's audacity. He felt disoriented, unable to remember where he left his car. A man brushed against him. His *"pardon, monsieur,"* prodding Wolf from his momentary lapse. It came to him where he left his car. Wolf continued walking, trying to decide what to do. The image of a woman up ahead invaded his consciousness. Slender, with long dark hair, dressed in jeans, tennis shoes, and a jeans jacket, she was hurrying toward a taxi at the curb. Wolf followed, on automatic pilot now. Thirty or forty feet in front of him, the infuriatingly relentless woman who just blew his future to hell. And she was about to escape.

Wolf walked faster, his mind racing over options: he could retrieve his car and drive to the border. He stood a good chance to make it across before an APB was issued on him. Or, he could hail a cab to Dorval and hop on the next plane out of Montreal. The bag under his arm held more than $950K, enough to retire in style. "That's what I should do," he said under his breath. As the last word left his mouth, the bank's alarm went off. People on the sidewalk stopped abruptly, some turning to look back, others scattering toward the curb. The alarm continued wailing, but Wolf kept his eyes on Garrett. Somebody beat her to the taxi. It took off.

Hearing the alarm, she glanced back over her shoulder, recognition registering when their eyes met. Garrett's gaze didn't show surprise. Or fear. Looking straight at him, her expression and her eyes telegraphed pure contempt and loathing. *And then again, I could kill her first.*

Wolf dismissed the first two options, his decision made at some unreachable level.

* * *

Tony's cab pulled up across the street from the bank. Even over the cab's radio, he could hear the bank's alarm. People in front of the bank were scurrying out of the way, but no sign of KC. He threw a bill over the seat, jumped out, and scanned the other side of the street. Half-a-block to the left of the bank, he spotted Wolf breaking out of the crowd and into a sprint. Tony took off running on his side of Rue St. Jacques in the same direction. He caught sight of KC's long hair and powerful stride. She was fifty feet ahead of Wolf and running full-out.

Too many people to dodge on the sidewalk, Tony cut between two parked cars and ran on the street side. He kept his eyes on Wolf and KC, the distance between them holding steady. At the red light at St. Pierre Street, he dashed across the intersection, a broken-field runner dodging two-ton tacklers with hood ornaments. Drivers vented their wrath with horns. He could no longer see KC, but a block ahead, he saw Wolf cut back to the sidewalk then disappear.

Tony poured it on, his lungs and legs on fire. The next intersection, he had to stop or get run over; four lanes of cars sped by in both directions. He tried to catch a break but no one slowed. Precious minutes passed before he sprinted to the center of Rue St. Jacque and stopped, the cars so close in front and back, their air buffeted him. More minutes passed before he made it to the far curb, racing across the Place d'Armes Square.

Straight ahead was a huge building with towering Corinthian pillars across the front—it looked like a bank. Tony raced past a bronze statue and up a dozen concrete steps. Gut instinct told him KC was inside.

Traffic had stolen precious time. He had no idea how much, but it felt like a lifetime.

–29–

K C heard the bank alarm at the same moment the cab she wanted pulled away from the curb. A glance back toward the bank, the sight of Wolf came as no surprise. *Of course he drove instead of flying. He needed a gun.* The sight of her father's killer, the monster who did all of Aubert's dirty work, sparked contempt and loathing, but a mili-second later, it activated her fight-or-flight response. KC broke into a run, weaving and dodging around startled people as she cut to the street and ran on the traffic side of parked cars. No need to look back; Wolf was there.

Adrenaline fueling her arms and legs, KC ran as fast as she could for four long blocks, every muscle burning. She couldn't outrun him, and she couldn't keep up this pace. Ahead on her right loomed a big building with Greek columns across the front. *A bank, lots of people. And guards!* She darted between two cars, flew across the sidewalk, and up a dozen concrete steps.

It took two hands to pull the massive wooden door open. KC stumbled inside and bent over, her legs trembling and heart pounding as she gulped in air. When she straightened up, it took a moment for the interior to register. There were no tellers, no lines of customers, no bank guards with guns. It was a museum! A mammoth room with a two-story high ceiling, marble and bronze statues everywhere, and over-sized paintings and gilded mirrors on the walls.

The room dwarfed the dozen or more groups of people, some of them circled around a statue, others viewing a painting, each group listening to a docent or guide. KC hurried toward the largest group clustered near the far side of the gallery, midway along the wall of the immense room. Twenty or thirty men and women stood viewing a large gilded mirror and two paintings on either side of it. An ornate wall clock completed the display. Pointing and gesturing at the objects, the guide's voice was lost in the mammoth space.

KC hurried over and slipped in front of a tall gentleman. *"S'il vous plait, monsieur?"* She glanced up at him. He smiled and made room for her. The guide, speaking French, was talking about the grand mirror. Large enough to be in Versailles' Hall of Mirrors, its reflection provided a sweeping view of the entrance and front half of the museum.

Her gaze fixed on the mirror, KC saw Wolf emerge from the foyer and bend over to catch his breath. He had something tucked under one arm. She stood motionless and watched him survey the room and then head straight toward her as though guided by radar. A regular looking guy, no one would believe he had killed five men. *And is here to kill me.* She watched Wolf circle the group. *Tony told me to wake him up so he could come with me. Critical mistake.*

The guide ended her presentation by thanking everyone. They applauded and then began to walk toward the front of the museum. KC turned to follow, but a hand gripped her arm. "Don't even think of about it," Wolf said in a pleasant voice. "You don't want a bunch of innocent people to die." Chatting with each other, members of the group left *en masse,* taking their warmth and closeness with them.

Wolf let go of her arm. KC turned to face him, noting the aviator glasses Tony said Wolf was never without. She read *Porsche* in tiny print on the edge of one lens. The beginning of a smile turned up the corners of his mouth. Wolf said nothing, waiting she supposed, to see what she was going to do. Tanned, his sandy hair peppered with gray, Wolf looked more like a high school football coach than a cold-blooded assassin.

Looking at the man who sent her father to an icy grave, KC wanted to attack him, the desire so strong it made her every nerve tingle. The .38 in his left hand pointed at her chest was the only thing stopping her. "Since you intend to kill me, the least you can do is stop hiding behind those sunglasses," KC said. "Come on, look me in the eye. Or is Elliott Wolf chicken?"

His smile broadened as he reached up with his right hand and removed his sunglasses. Pale blue eyes, nearly devoid of color, stared at her. They revealed no fear or bravado, no emotion at all. Tucked under his left arm was a large blue bank bag stuffed to the limit.

The combination of adrenaline and fatigue, or maybe the finality of the moment, struck KC as comical. She laughed. "What's in the bag, Wolf, a couple million in bearer bonds? You could have run. You've got enough money in there to go anywhere, do anything you want. But instead, you came after me. I am flattered. If I have irritated you, if I have messed up Elliott Wolf's big getaway plans, then I am immensely proud of myself."

Eyes narrowed, he tilted the gun at her sternum. "You're irritating me right now, Garrett. Enough to kill you for free, but Jules Aubert wants you dead so bad, he's paying me $500K."

"Wow, now I am really flattered! But, before you pull the trigger, you might want to hear about your employer, Aubert, et al." KC nodded up at the wall clock. "Eleven o'clock? At this very moment, simultaneous warrants are being served on Bill Berkeley and Hayden Culpepper. And right now, Aubert's condo in Gaston Towers and your condo in Shepherd Park, are crawling with FBI agents. That's thanks to your boss, Volking, who, by the way, knows everything. And your friend, Aubert? He may think he's safe in France, but about now, he is running for his life from a very angry Indian whose dad was with my father when you pushed his Camaro into the Potomac. Not only are you evil, Wolf, you are not very smart. You should have run."

Facing the foyer, KC spotted Tony over Wolf's shoulder. Gun in his hand, Tony was looking around, trying to locate her. She darted her eyes back to Wolf's face, but not quick enough. He whirled around and fired two shots. Tony yelled and jerked backwards, the shots echoing like cannon fire in the mammoth space. People started screaming, scattering in all directions, some taking refuge behind statues, others hunkering down on their knees.

Ready to fire again, Wolf raised his .38 in both hands, unwittingly loosening his grip on the heavy bank bag. It dropped at his feet, his involuntary response a downward glance.

A split-second chance, KC high-kicked his raised arms, catapulting the .38 through the air. It landed on the polished wood floor and slid out of reach.

Enraged, Wolf came at her. She spun around, enough that his fist missed her face, instead landing full-force against her shoulder. She staggered back, but managed to stay on her feet as pain ripped through her left shoulder and down her arm.

Tony shouted something then a bullet zinged over her head. She turned in time to see Wolf lunging at her. KC's auto-response, a vicious roundhouse kick landing square on his sternum; it sent him stumbling backwards. Fighting to breathe, he was pounding on his chest with his right hand. Wolf looked like a man possessed, saliva stringing from his mouth. He turned and staggered toward Tony. Wolf was trying to say something, but he couldn't speak.

Wolf raised his right hand and put his palm against his chest in a gesture of surrender, his eyes never leaving Tony's face. KC followed his gaze. Tony was struggling to stay upright. His face was chalk-white, blood covering the front of his shirt—he was going into shock.

She turned back to Wolf and saw his left hand snake under the back of his jacket—a second weapon. "GUN!" KC screamed.

Two shots rang out. Let loose in the voluminous space, the concussion from Tony's shots sounded like the building was imploding. Wolf crashed onto the floor, landing almost at KC's feet, two bullet holes in his chest.

She screamed, but didn't hear it. KC looked down at Wolf through an acrid cloud of smoke. Pale blue, sightless eyes stared up in death, in his left hand a menacing-looking Glock. Awareness hit like a shockwave. She whirled around in time to see Tony collapse to one knee and then onto the floor.

"Tonyeeee!" KC rushed to him. He was cold, unconscious, and bleeding, but alive.

* * *

The minutes following the shooting blended into a frantic mirage: speeding through red lights, siren wailing, white-clad attendants waiting at the hospital, then racing alongside Tony's gurney. By the time KC followed into

Montreal's Royal Victoria Hospital ER, Tony's gurney and the attendants were disappearing through double doors at the end of a long hallway. She stood staring after them, her heartbeat surging out of control. Had it not been for an astute nurse catching her, KC would have hit the floor.

She had no choice but to wait for the doctor. Reclining in the ER bed felt good, but what she really wanted was to find out about Tony. Was he still in surgery? Was he alive? As though she had verbalized her thoughts, the doctor walked in, his first words, "Your friend is still in surgery. He is being well cared for, and rest assured, we will keep you informed." His voice was calm and soothing. KC willed herself to relax. He positioned his stethoscope and listened to her heart. "That's better. Now, you can tell me what happened. Where are you hurt?"

Reasonable question. He wants to know what happened. She wanted to tell him, but it seemed too difficult. Any plausible answer she gave would sound ludicrous and take forever to explain. KC simply pointed to her shoulder and hoped the doctor understood. The next thing she knew, she was being wheelchaired to the radiology department. A series of x-rays revealed her shoulder was "separated, but not broken." After an injection for pain, the ER doctor pulled her shoulder back into place and insisted she rest.

When KC woke up, she learned Tony was still in surgery. She was directed to a waiting room where a dozen other people were waiting for news, all of them looking as nervous and worried as she felt. KC took a seat in an empty alcove, and for the next few hours, flipped through the pages of a stack of magazines. Occasionally a doctor would enter and ask, "who is waiting for . . ." and give a name.

KC was the only one left in the room when a doctor in green scrubs entered. A surgery mask dangling below his chin told her he was Tony's surgeon. She rose, her heartbeat doubling. His face signaled nothing other than fatigue. He asked her friend's "full name" as though about to deliver bad news. *Oh, God.* "Anthony Edward DeMarco—Tony. Is he. . . ?" His quiet response, "he is stable," reignited panic ready to overtake her. This nightmare had begun with her call to Tony for help. Was it going to end here with his death?

"Would it be possible for me to see him?" KC managed to ask.

"I'm afraid not. He is heavily sedated and being closely monitored. Perhaps in a few hours when he wakes up."

When he wakes up, that sounds good. KC checked her watch as soon as he left: 8:30 p.m. "When he wakes up, when he wakes up," she kept repeating as she paced a circle around a row of chairs in the center of the room. KC lost all track of time. Hearing a male voice, she opened her eyes and blinked, slowly realizing where she was—on a couch in the patient waiting room.

"If you would like, I will take you to see Mr. DeMarco now," said a uniformed attendant who could have been Joe Rogers' twin.

"Oh yes, please." KC followed him through quiet, empty halls. When they reached the door to Tony's room, she said a little prayer and tiptoed in, not sure what to expect. He wasn't alone; a doctor was examining him. He turned and nodded at KC. "I take it you are the KC with the separated shoulder? And the lady that Mr. DeMarco keeps asking about?" She could only nod and smile, grateful tears welling. "His vital signs are remarkably good considering his injuries," the doctor said. The ER physician informed me of your injury. I'm assuming the pain shot he gave you has worn off. Do you need pain medication?" KC readily agreed.

The doctor finished his exam and the minute the door closed, she covered Tony's face with kisses. Straightening up, KC got her first close look since she had kissed him goodnight at Stacey's. He looked pale and drugged. "Glad you're here," Tony mumbled, trying to focus on her. "What day is it?"

"Saturday. Super Bowl is tomorrow." She hoped to elicit a reaction, but it didn't register.

"Your arm. . . it doesn't look right." His voice was hoarse and raspy. Before she could tell him, Tony's expression signaled that he suddenly remembered what happened at the museum. "What about Elliott, is he—"

"He's dead, Tony." She told him about Wolf going for a second gun. "He was such an evil man and he hurt so many people, Wolf truly got what he deserved. He went down with the Glock in his hand. One more second and you would have—" KC couldn't finish.

Tony looked at her. "What a waste" was all he said.

A nurse delivered Tony's meds and a pain pill for KC and offered to have a bed wheeled into the room. When it arrived, a grateful, exhausted KC kissed Tony goodnight and then, fully dressed, crawled into the extra bed, the pain medication sending her into a deep sleep.

The following morning, she was up, face washed, and sitting in a chair by Tony's bed when he woke up. "You been here all night?" As she was about to answer, the bedside telephone rang, startling the both of them. "Who knows I'm here?" Tony mumbled. KC handed him the phone. "Hello? Yes, sir, I recognize your voice." Tony looked at KC and mouthed "Volking." "Yes, they're taking good care of me. No, you don't need to send up anybody. KC is with me." She studied Tony's expressions as he listened to his boss, detecting sadness, reflection, a fleeting worried frown, and then relief. "I appreciate that, sir. I think about another week. Yes, I will bring her with me. Yes, sir, soon as I get back."

KC hung up the phone for him. "That was short and sweet. Was he nice?"

"Yeah. Actually, very nice. The Montreal police notified him yesterday about Wolf. They told him Wolf died from two shots fired by. . . . me." Tony closed his eyes as though reliving the moment. "Funny, Volking said he suspected that Wolf and Aubert were involved in something that wasn't good, but didn't have proof, so he dropped it. Your name was in the report, so he wants to talk to both of us. I'm a little fuzzy, but I think he said whatever it was that Wolf and Aubert were up to he wants kept under wraps. Wolf and Volking go way back. I can tell he's upset. He wants to know the truth about both of them, but especially Wolf."

"How about I take the journal you had me keep when we meet with him?"

"Good idea." Tony managed a grin. "Did you tell me today is Super Bowl Sunday?"

"I did. Hospital food instead of pizza and beer, but who cares? You are okay!" The doctor's morning visit answered their questions: Tony would remain in the hospital one week, and he estimated Tony's recuperation would take two months. "I strongly advise not to rush it."

When a nurse came to help Tony with his morning walk around the third floor, KC called Agnes. "How's Tony, how are you, and when are you coming home?" she wanted to know.

KC chuckled. "Doing great-considering. Fine-except for a sore shoulder. And one week."

"All good, all good, that's wonderful." Agnes sounded relieved. "KC, you'll want to go online to *The Post's* story on Jules. It's in the obituary section, but it's more like a tribute."

As Agnes talked, KC accessed *The Post* on her friend Stacey's laptop, the first line of the story: *Jules Aubert's tragic death while on family business in France stuns political community.* The article chronicled *Aubert's remarkable life and career and his rise to become one of the top power brokers in the Nation's capital.* KC read the article word-for-word, looking for any mention of a personal relationship with Valerie. The reporter's only remark about Secretary Beckman was crediting her impressive lead in the polls to Aubert's political savvy. The article ended with a quote from Gregory Aubert, saying that he planned to attend the memorial service for his brother in D.C., but the memorial would take place after the funeral service in Montreal.

The article's reference to Gregory, and the fact Volking wanted to keep everything under wraps until the three of them could talk, confirmed an idea KC had been mulling over. "I think I know how to help Valerie. You will think I'm crazy, Agnes."

KC heard a delighted chuckle. "As crazy as our window-washing caper? I believe in Valerie, so count me in, whatever it is. Now that my Bermuda adventure is over, working your desk until you get back seems pretty tame. What can I do?"

"More detective work," KC said. "But first, I need to know the amount of IIM money we transferred out of RIC into the holding account. Second, see if you can find out how much is in Valerie's campaign account now. One more thing, Ms. Super Sleuth. Try to find out when Gregory Aubert is arriving for the memorial and where he's staying. If the FBI is still searching Jules' condo, he'll definitely want to stay in a hotel."

Agnes' call came two days later on Tuesday evening. "It took some digging, but I've got two of the answers. About the money, we emptied five accounts: Aubert's, Ludlow's, Marsh's, Culpepper's, and Berkeley's. In round numbers, we transferred about $24.6 million. Remember, we have a hold on Wolf's $1.5 mil in the Bank of Montreal. I spoke with Richardson at Aubert & Associates. Valerie's campaign account has $12.7 million in it right now. So, all together, we have $38.8 million, give or take. That's $6.5 million short of the $45 mil that Jules stole, right?"

"Hang on a minute." KC scribbled the numbers. "Round numbers, that's right. If my crazy plan works, we'll soon be able to return the full $45 million to the IIM account."

"KC Garrett, what kind of trouble are you gonna get into now," Agnes wanted to know.

"All I can say is, I'm glad you are now an attorney. I may need one."

Agnes told her Jules Aubert's memorial was scheduled for 11:00 a.m., Friday, February 18 at The Cathedral of St. Matthew. "That beautiful Catholic church four blocks from the White House," Agnes said. "I haven't been able to confirm where Gregory is staying, but I assume he'll stay at the Four Seasons where all the bigwigs stay. I'm trying to confirm that, so don't concern yourself. You've got enough on your plate. I just hope you and Tony will be back by then."

"Trust me, Agnes, we *will* be back. Valerie is an intelligent, honest person, and a leader. Aubert isn't the reason that she is so far ahead in the polls—she is. We just have to make sure she gets her chance."

* * *

Volking's directive to keep everything under wraps prompted KC and Tony to tell only Agnes and Joe Rogers that they were returning on Thursday, February 17, the day before Jules Aubert's memorial. Waiting for them outside security, Joe and Agnes delivered Tony and KC to her apartment.

Ivan greeted them, meowing and purring intermittently, demanding attention and delighting Tony. KC helped Agnes and Joe settle Tony into her apartment, then showered and dressed in her professional clothes. With not a minute to spare, she sat down with Agnes, the two of them reviewing their plan. If everything went as scheduled, KC would have thirty or forty minutes, tops, to accomplish the impossible.

"There is no Plan B, Agnes, so wish me luck."

Agnes walked with her downstairs as the taxi pulled up. "Five o'clock, you're on schedule." She handed KC her briefcase. "You don't need luck, KC. You can do this."

Admittedly nervous, KC entered The Four Seasons and made her way to The Lounge at Bourbon Steak, hopefully appearing to be waiting for a client. She ordered a glass of cabernet and took note of the time, 5:40 p.m. Despite the potential consequences of a plan that could destroy her career, KC felt more determined than fearful. Her goal to help Valerie get a fair chance at the presidency was as big as goals get.

She had a good view of the entrance to the cocktail lounge, an elite, inviting atmosphere where Four Seasons guests could meet friends and business colleagues. How Agnes not only found out Gregory Aubert was staying at the Four Seasons, but had dinner reservations at the hotel's famous Bourbon Steak restaurant, Agnes said she would only divulge if their plan was successful. One potential hitch: would Gregory go directly to the dining room for his 7:00 p.m. reservation or have a cocktail first in the lounge? KC was betting on the latter.

She noted the grey-haired man that entered at 5:50 p.m. He went straight to the bar, the bartender greeting him by name. Next, a woman and man came in, animatedly talking about their wonderful spa experience. During the next twenty minutes, a dozen or more well-dressed people came in, some taking a tall chair at the bar, others congregating around a table.

It will be a miracle if I don't get disbarred for this. In the middle of that thought, KC saw a lone man in a dark suit enter and glance around. *That's him!* Misgivings discarded, she put the sheaf of notes in her briefcase as

Gregory Aubert approached the bar and ordered. He waited for his drink and then retreated to a corner table at the opposite end of the lounge.

KC rose quickly and walked over to his table. "Gregory, how nice to see you again."

His expression mirrored annoyance. "I'm sorry, you are mistaken. We have not met."

She set down her wine and pulled out the chair across from him. "No mistake. I've been waiting for you." He started to rise, but KC pushed the table against his chest. "I suggest you listen. I'm here because of your brother." Gregory's expression changed from annoyed to surprised. "KC Garrett, Department of Justice, Environmental Crime Division."

"Environmental Crime Division? What could you possibly know about my brother?"

KC leaned closer and looked him in the eye. "I know Jules wasn't in France on family business like reported on TV. He was hiding at your Joncelets villa until Elliott Wolf got rid of Victor Ludlow. I know that your brother told Valerie Beckman he *borrowed* $45 million IIM funds and used it to finance her campaign—a lie. I know that when he checked his Bermuda account, he found out every cent he stole was gone. I know because I'm the one who took the money." KC watched as her statements registered. The blood drained from his face. Gregory looked as though he'd seen a ghost.

"Where did . . . how could you possibly—what is it you want?" he said.

"You really want to know?" Gregory nodded hesitantly. "First, this conversation never took place. You have never met or heard of me. And you will never, under any circumstances, mention my name to anyone. Never, do you understand?" He nodded again, both hands gripping his glass. "Not good enough. I want your word."

"All right, I give you my word. What the hell do you want?"

"Ten million dollars," KC answered evenly. "And Valerie Beckman to get her chance to be President. She had no part in Jules stealing the IIM funds. He confessed to her after the fact, so she couldn't do anything about it. Your brother stole $45 million, but he didn't spend all of it on Valerie's campaign. He and his cohorts stashed $25 million of it in their offshore accounts."

"That is preposterous. You have no proof, and I see no reason why I should—"

"I have proof enough to put *you* behind bars, so I advise you to listen carefully. The $10 million you're going to give me —let's call it a *donation*—along with the $25 million from Bermuda, is going to help undo the damage your brother did to Valerie's campaign. Part of it will reimburse the Lake Ponsiteau Tribe for the 50% reductions in ore extracted from Camas Mine. You remember the adjustments you paid Victor Ludlow to make? Don't test me."

KC folded her hands on the table and stared at him, letting her words sink in. Eyes downcast, arrogant expression absent; he looked shocked, at a loss for what to say. KC touched his hand. "One more thing. In case you're about to tell me you don't have $10 million or some other excuse, you should know that DOJ's Environmental Crime Division has jurisdiction over all mines in the U. S. and our territories. If your donation is not forthcoming or you do *anything* to thwart or delay receipt of the funds, I will personally see to it that we discover something wrong at every U.S. Vanguard mine. I want you to picture shutdowns, penalties, inspections, delays—endless delays. In other words, Gregory, I will rain down hell on Vanguard Mines."

KC halted her tirade, her eyes on Gregory's face. Her threat was working, but she wasn't through. "What Jules did to Valerie, and you did to the Indians, is contemptible. If you don't do this, I will make sure you're charged with aiding and abetting a murderer, and anything else I can possibly dig up."

KC took a deep breath to calm down. "That's pretty much all I have to say."

She sat back, crossed her arms, and waited for Gregory's answer. His $10 million meant that Valerie's campaign would not be tainted by Jules' crime. A "no" would open Pandora's Box and destroy any chance she had. KC forced that thought aside. It was unthinkable.

Five minutes of silence was KC's limit. "It's decision time, Gregory. Your turn to talk."

"There is no point," he said, his voice flat. "How do I get the $10 million to you?"

KC steeled herself against reacting. "A check for the entire amount right now. Leave the payee blank. You have one week—until noon next Friday—to gather the funds to cover the check. I need your word on that, Gregory. If not I will— "

"You have my word." He looked and sounded resigned as he withdrew a checkbook from the breast pocket of his suit. Heart hammering, KC watched Gregory fill out the check as instructed. He handed it to her, finally looking her in the eye. "For one so young, I find your *mèpris* formidable. It served you well."

KC ignored the comment, certain that it was an insult. She kept her emotions under control until she was inside the cab. She then called her apartment. Agnes answered. "Wahooo! Tell Tony, mission accomplished. I have Gregory's $10 million dollar check!" She held the phone away from her ear as Agnes and Tony shouted their congratulations. "I can't wait to tell Valerie she's got a green light. Nothing in her way!"

KC started to hang up. "One more thing, Agnes. I'm curious. Could you find out what the French word *mèpris* means?"

Agnes greeted KC at the door. "*Mèpris* means contempt. Why did you want to know?"

"Because it just got us $10 million dollars!"

—30—

K C glanced over at Tony, dozing on the chaise, the July 24th edition of *The Washington Post* spread across his shirt. Above the fold, and taking up the major portion of the front page, was a color photo of Valerie Beckman and Gray Rossiter, their raised hands clasped in triumph. The bold headline underneath: ***Beckman Sweeps Party's Nomination, Gray Rossiter, VP Choice*** said it all. KC reached over and retrieved the newspaper.

Valerie's dazzling smile, a visual confirmation of "goal attained," elicited a contented sigh from KC. She admired Valerie, an amazing woman strong enough to become a member of the President's Cabinet, yet compassionate enough to see at a glance the despair in a tiny child's eyes, then open her heart and home. To the average reader, the photograph of Valerie and Gray represented victory for two famous individuals. But to KC it represented much more. Good triumphing over evil and justice finally achieved. More importantly, the photo symbolized a milestone in America—the likelihood of the first woman president. Valerie had the strength and vision that would make her an excellent president. And with her choice of Gray Rossiter for Vice-President, she doubled her own wealth of experience. She picked the perfect running mate.

KC had her own opinion how everything turned out like it did. In some mysterious way Sam Blackhawk had played a part in all of it. To her attorney mind, the evidence was obvious. Valerie's first call to her about needing an attorney, she admitted first envisioning her father and then she felt as though, "Sam Blackhawk was telling me to call you." It could be said that it was her father who brought Tony back into her life; he was the first person she turned to for help. And her father appearing in the dark hallway at Stacey's telling her to have faith and that "Destinies play out according to our Divine plan." Agnes taking the job in Bermuda, then retrieving the stolen money—it all made sense. Valerie choosing Gray as her VP was Sam Blackhawk's final gift. KC silently acknowledged that people would think she was crazy, but it didn't matter. She had no doubt that was how it all happened.

In the article beneath the picture, the reporter wrote: *Secretary Beckman's victory was perhaps bittersweet in view of the tragic death of her campaign manager in France earlier this year. Founder of Aubert and Associates, Jules Aubert was credited for Beckman's meteoric rise in the polls.* "And almost her downfall," KC said under her breath. Paying Wolf and Ventresca to murder anyone that he considered a threat, it was apparent that at some point, Aubert had lost or abandoned his moral compass. Her father and Charlie Dawson, Ludlow, Marsh, and Jared were all victims of his scheming. Nicholas Ventresca had survived, but was in prison for the first-degree murder of New Mexico attorney Donyell Crawford, also a victim of Aubert's scheming. Nick's brother, Salvatore, was sentenced to three years for harboring and aiding a fugitive.

How ironic, KC thought, that just a week ago she had come across an article in *The Post* on Bill Berkeley and Hayden Culpepper, both of them facing criminal charges. Berkeley was fighting disbarment and *The Post* reported that a Senate bipartisan subcommittee was calling for Hayden Culpepper's expulsion from the Senate as allowed under Article I, Section 5 of the U.S. Constitution for "the senator's gross misuse of his office."

That is justice. KC put down the paper, wanting very much for Valerie's victory to put to rest her months of turmoil and sleepless nights. It was over, but not quite. Though the meeting with Volking had brought closure for her and Tony over Wolf and Aubert, it unfortunately led to a mountain of work: DOJ and FBI reports, hearings, and paperwork dealing with the aftermath of Aubert's and Wolf's actions. KC estimated it would take the rest of the year to resolve the legal issues they created.

KC was happy to finally celebrate a victory in her DOJ case against Scott Dunlap. The jury convicted Dunlap on one count of perjury and seven counts of reckless endangerment to the environment. She found Dunlap's sentence of eighteen months in a minimum security facility disappointing, but $15 million in fines and Dunlap Plastics landing on the watch list of EPA and a host of other vigilant environmental groups, helped make up for it.

A key accomplishment, getting Gregory Aubert to come up with $10 million, made it possible for Agnes to transfer back to BIA the $45 million in IIM funds that his brother stole. Had those funds not been returned, Valerie Beckman would have been held responsible, and her political career in ruins.

So much had happened in the last eight months, battered by an unrelenting stream of events that created fear, uncertainty, panic, and sorrow. She had survived it all, but the totality left an indelible imprint about what was important, family, friends—people. And love; her career would no longer be all-consuming. *Tony will appreciate that.* Since calling him the night of that terrible storm, Tony, through all that happened, showed love and support. His physical and mental scars had healed and he was back at work, but both of them agreed it was going to take time to process all that they experienced.

Thankfully, KC acknowledged there were good things that happened as well, like reconnecting with her brother, Takoda, and Grandmother Angeni. Another was Sally Calder, her godmother, locating Lily Deerhorn on an Indian reservation in North Dakota. Sally paid her friend's flight back to D.C and helped her find an apartment. Now, Lily was working in BIA's General Assistance Programs Department, Sally calling her, "my indispensible right hand."

A wonderful call had come from Santana Dawson, on the Lake Ponsiteau Reservation and his job managing Crystal Waters Casino. His first words were, "See, KC, I told you that Justice the Indian way works." His good news was that he had renewed his relationship with Andrea, the divorced woman with two little boys. They had been dating the last three months, his comment: "things are going well—actually really well." Santana asked if Tony had recovered and how they were doing. It felt wonderful to report that

Tony was fine, and that she and Tony were also doing well. The call ended with the promise that she and Tony would visit soon.

Emily Marsh surprised KC with a call from Vero Beach, Florida. She decided to go ahead with the purchase of the condo. "KC, I am golfing my way out of depression." She had a nice group of friends and her children loved how close she lived to Disney World. It was KC's perfect opportunity to bring closure for Emily. She revealed Nate Spiller's true identity and told Emily that Elliott Wolf paid the ultimate price for his crimes. Emily said it closed a sad chapter in her life and thanked KC. The calls and good news went a long way to help heal KC's grief.

Tony stirred and opened his eyes, July's weather evidently waking him. "Wow, it's hot, and I'm thirsty. Let's go inside. He sat up and stretched. "This feels so good, us being here again. Do you know how much I love you, Tiger?"

KC spread her arms wide. "This much?" Tony nodded. "Well, I love you, too," KC said, and sent a grateful prayer heavenward.

They drove back to the city, agreeing that they needed to come to a decision about where to live; move to his new high-rise or stay in her apartment. Ivan was waiting for them at the top of the stairs when they pulled up. "Look how happy he looks," Tony said. "I'm glad I like it here. Just think, if we moved to my place, Ivan wouldn't have the courtyard to roam in. Or those huge trees that he loves to climb. Ivan would have to be an indoor cat. He would hate that! I vote we stay here. Ivan is a great cat. I couldn't do that to him."

Ivan bounded down the stairs to greet them. KC scooped him up, unable to stop smiling.

The big move, the term KC and Tony chose to call it, took two weeks. When it was over, Tony's king size bed, a dresser, and his large flatscreen TV, had been hauled up the outside stairs. The rest of his furniture and KC's bed went to storage. Tony immediately bought furniture for the deck outside the bedroom, even a chair for Ivan.

A pleasant, early August evening, they had just finished having dinner on the deck when the phone rang. "It's Valerie," Tony said and handed the phone to KC. Valerie had just returned from the Atlanta convention, and despite the hoopla surrounding her return, she was calling to invite them to a dinner party, "for my closest friends and confidants. I don't have Agnes' phone number. Would you call and invite her for me? Gray and his wife are coming, and I would very much like for your mother to come too."

KC immediately called Agnes and extended Valerie's invitation. "I'm worried that Valerie's housekeeper will recognize us."

"Are you kidding? In Ghostbuster uniforms, baseball caps, you with a ponytail, and neither one of us even wearing lipstick? Not a chance." Agnes said it with absolute surety.

Regardless, the following Saturday evening, KC arrived at Valerie's wearing a chic, new cocktail dress, in makeup, and her long hair down. Tony looked handsome in a new Ralph Lauren suit. A dressed-to-the-nines Agnes arrived and immediately hugged KC. "Relax, girlfriend, even I don't recognize you!" Gray and Claudia Rossiter came with Kathryn, Valerie greeting all of them with a smile that matched her victory photo. KC's worry about Marguerite turned out to be unfounded; it was a catered party.

Before dinner began, Valerie introduced Phoebe to everyone. Not long after KC and Tony returned, Valerie had confided that she told Phoebe that Elliott was killed "in the line of duty." She said Phoebe reacted with many tears, her grief remaining undiminished until they visited his gravesite, with flowers, and Phoebe got to say goodbye to her friend, Elliott.

There was still a hint of sadness about her when they were introduced. Knowing Phoebe loved soccer, KC asked her what position she played, which initiated a good conversation. "Are you looking forward to living in the White House, if you mother is elected?" KC asked.

Phoebe's expressive eyes matched her answer. "I hope Mama wins! I'll get to fly on Air Force One and spend weekends at Camp David. Want me to ask her if you can come with us?"

KC smiled. "I would absolutely love it." Marguerite appeared in the doorway and beckoned Phoebe, KC noting with relief, there was no flicker of recognition.

Valerie announced dinner, the elegant crystal and china reminding KC of the White House dinner. Seated at the head of the table, Valerie raised her glass. "This is a special evening for me and for Gray. Words alone cannot express the depth of my affection and appreciation, but I toast each one of you for your loyalty and friendship." Everyone raised a glass in unspoken recognition of their bond. An attentive butler stood nearby ready to refill their glasses. "I would love to hear your toasts. Would you mind going first, KC?"

KC thought for a minute then raised her glass. "Here's to accomplishing the impossible."

Tony was next. "I toast KC, Agnes, and Valerie, you make an awesome team."

"Here's to planning and pluck. And *mèpris!*" Agnes winked at KC."

Kathryn toasted with, "To the first woman president. I say it's about time!"

Claudia Rossiter toasted, "To Valerie and my husband, another awesome team."

Gray was last. He raised his glass to Valerie. "To the next President of the United States. May you serve this country with the courage and honor you've shown throughout your career. I know you will, Valerie." Everyone applauded and congratulated each other's toast.

Their four-course dinner was festive and delicious. After dessert, Valerie apologized to her guests for "stealing KC and Gray for a few minutes," then asked them to join her in the library. KC followed into the room and immediately spied the phone on Valerie's desk. *The Infinity bug! Oh great, now what!* "Tonight is so wonderful. I will keep this short," Valerie said.

She turned to Gray. "You were Sam's life-long friend. I'm glad you know what Jules did and the risk KC and Agnes took on my behalf. They saved my career and my life. I'm saying this now because, God willing, I intend to win this election with your help. I just want you to know how much I appreciate you agreeing to be my running mate."

Gray's slight smile was accompanied by raised eyebrows, his expression inquisitive. "I was honored, of course, but you could have chosen from a dozen others candidates. Why me?"

Valerie smiled. "Well, that's one reason, you're questioning me. I don't want a figurehead VP. I want someone to work with me. I chose you because of your leadership and years of experience. But most of all your integrity. You don't cave under pressure. That's why."

KC spoke up. "Valerie, I just have to say, you couldn't have made a better choice." She turned to Gray. "It's the perfect time. You've served eight terms in Congress. If Dad were here, you know he would say the same thing. I am so grateful and happy how everything worked out, but I'm sure you two want to talk." KC was smiling as she rose to leave.

"No, KC, wait," Valerie said. "I want to talk to you, too. When you were in Bermuda and things looked the absolute darkest for me, you told me not to give up on my dream. Well, my dream is to be president. If it comes true, I will need a special counsel that I can trust with my life. I want you to be that counsel, KC. Without you, I wouldn't even have this opportunity."

Valerie paused, searching for the right words. "When your father and I talked about his leadership of BIA, he told me he wanted to right a terrible wrong to his people. It is a tragedy that Sam didn't get the chance, but I want to accomplish that for him. If I win this election, I give you my word that I will propose an equitable settlement for all tribes for BIA's years of abysmal accounting and mismanagement. My hope is that you and Gray will champion that with me."

Valerie sincerely wanting to bring about the very goal her father sought stunned KC. How could she possibly turn her down? "What a wonderful tribute, Valerie." KC brushed away a tear. A glance at Gray told her Valerie's pledge had touched him too.

Valerie reached for KC's hand. "Remember me telling you about my dream, that I felt your father told me to call you? It sounds crazy—but here we are. And come November, if Gray and I win, and you are on my team, KC, I will take on the challenges of the presidency with a great deal more confidence."

Special counsel to the President of the United States? The mere thought took her breath away. KC plopped down in her chair. "Gray, all your years in

Congress, being VP isn't that huge a step for you. But special counsel? That's enormous. I'm not sure I'm qualified to—"

"Nonsense! You certainly *are* qualified," Gray said. "A special counsel is appointed by the President, and reports *only* to the President. You investigate what she asks you to investigate. You take care of the President's problems. You are her eyes and ears. You cover her back. Tell me, KC, how different is that than what you've just accomplished—what you've been doing for the last six months? If you hadn't succeeded, we wouldn't be here." Gray was grinning at her; he knew she didn't have a comeback. "Gotcha, counselor!"

Valerie was smiling too. KC could feel herself giving in. Gray wasn't going to let her say no. KC sighed. "I believe Tony and I have a future, so I would like to talk this over with him. Assuming he has no objections, I accept." The sight of Valerie and Gray high-fiving like two teenagers made KC laugh. "But before this goes any farther, there is something I would want. I was going to do it at DOJ anyway."

KC glanced from Valerie to Gray. "In my quest—for lack of a better word—-to seek justice for my father, I found out just how much I didn't know about him, his spiritual side, how he honored Indian tradition and beliefs. It made me want to honor Dad and his legacy—by using my given name. I want to be known professionally as Kaya Calder Blackhawk. So, Valerie, how would you feel about having an American Indian special counsel?"

Gray's instant applause gave his answer.

"Oh, KC, what a wonderful idea, and so appropriate. I love it," Valerie said.

KC hugged each one of them and then hurried to rejoin Tony. "Are you okay Tiger? What happened in there?"

"Well, potentially an incredible opportunity that I'm sure is going to involve you too. I'll tell you as soon as we get home, but, Tony, we have a big problem! When we went in the library, I remembered the bug Joe put on Valerie's phone. You've got to remove it as soon as she and Gray come back in here. Valerie can *never* know about that. Please!"

Tony grinned. "No problem, but you do realize it's going to cost you, big time."

KC couldn't help but laugh. "Not a surprise, DeMarco, but I was hoping we could discuss the cost over dinner. You remember Prince Charming and Cinderella, New Year's Eve at the Roof Terrace, some bubbly and the works?"

"I most certainly do. And also that I promised I would make it up to you. So, I talked to the head guy, Gerard, the maître d' at the Roof Terrace. Thanks to him, we have a special table reserved for Saturday evening. Got my tux rented. Gerard's taking care of the champagne. Now, all I need is Cinderella. What do you say?" Tony's grin and the gleam in his eye almost shouted that he had something up his sleeve.

KC had an inkling what that something might be. "Cinderella says that she finally has her priorities straight, Prince Charming. And I can hardly wait."